THE
NORTH
WIND
DESCENDS

A LORD HANI MYSTERY

N.L. HOLMES

WayBack Press
P.O.Box 16066
Tampa, FL

The North Wind Descends
Copyright © 2020 by N. L. Holmes

The Lord Hani Mysteries™ 2020

Quotes from *"The Instructions of Any", "Love Poems"*, and *"The Instructions of Amenemope"* from *Ancient Egyptian Literature* by Miriam Lichtheim, University of California Press (1976).

Cover art and map© by Streetlight Graphics.
Author photo© by Kipp Baker.

Dedicated to my husband, Ippokratis.

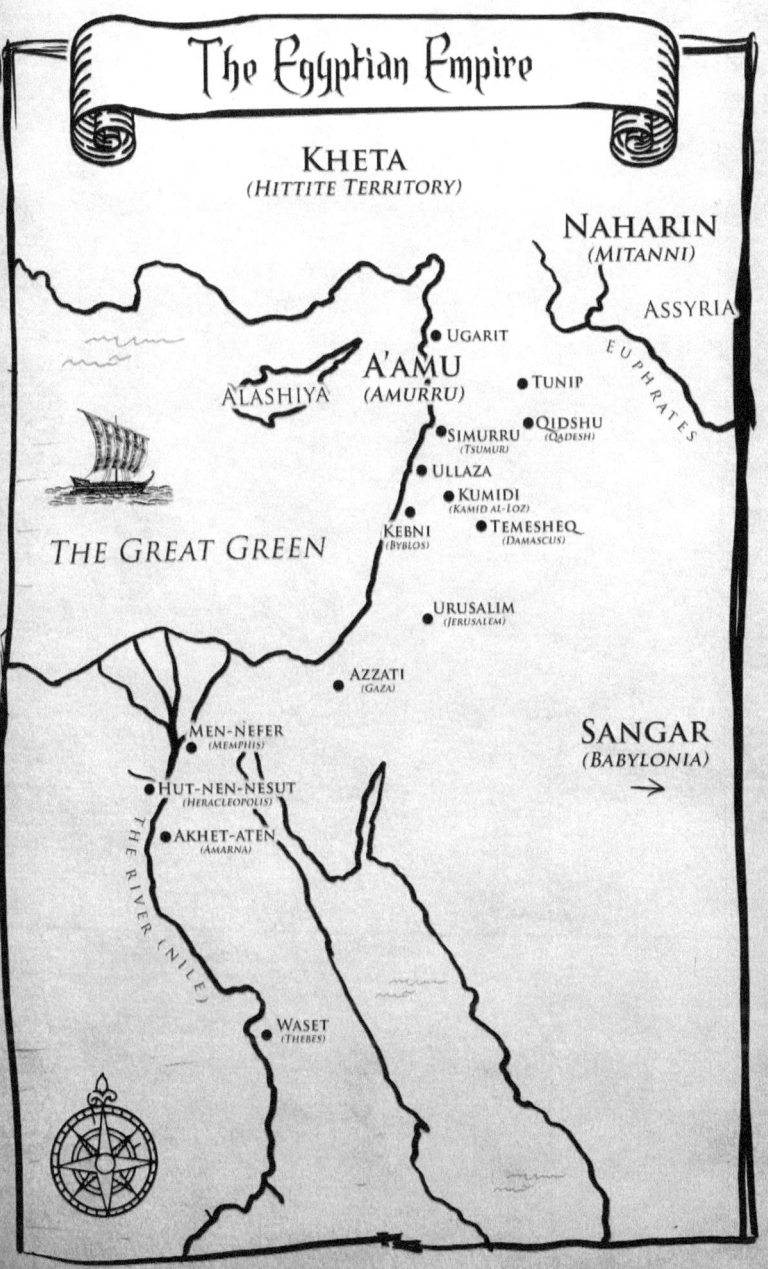

The Egyptian Empire

KHETA
(HITTITE TERRITORY)

NAHARIN
(MITANNI)

ASSYRIA

UGARIT

A'AMU
(AMURRU)

ALASHIYA

TUNIP

EUPHRATES

SIMURRU
(TSUMUR)

QIDSHU
(QADESH)

ULLAZA

KUMIDI
(KAMID AL-LOZ)

KEBNI
(BYBLOS)

TEMESHEQ
(DAMASCUS)

THE GREAT GREEN

URUSALIM
(JERUSALEM)

AZZATI
(GAZA)

SANGAR
(BABYLONIA)

MEN-NEFER
(MEMPHIS)

HUT-NEN-NESUT
(HERACLEOPOLIS)

AKHET-ATEN
(AMARNA)

THE RIVER (NILE)

WASET
(THEBES)

HISTORICAL NOTES

Our story takes place in the fifteenth and sixteenth years of Akh-en-aten's reign (by the reckoning of this account, his tenth alone on the throne), so about 1340 BCE. Those who deny him a coregency with his father would put the date five years later. We are entering one of the murkiest moments in Egyptian history, where the very identities of the monarchs are held in question. This is because the later successors of the "Heretic King" completely obliterated from the record him and his immediate successors. Scholars debate whether Ankh-khepru-ra Smenkh-ka-ra held a coregency with Akhenaten or ruled alone. Indeed, we don't even know who he was—Akh-en-aten's brother? His son? His wife, under a masculine name? A Hittite prince? The novelist has to make some choices, and they're not always the most likely in the historical sense. It does seem to be true that he occupied the Teni-menu palace in Thebes, but as usual, we can't be sure.

Egypt's territory in Western Asia was divided into Djahy (Retjenu), corresponding roughly to Roman Palestina;

Amurru, today's coastal Lebanon and Syria; and Kharu, more or less today's inland Syria. Both were divided into a multitude of small kingdoms whose kings were equated with the mayors of a city by their conquerors. In addition, several regional commissioners—generally Egyptians— administered the territory, collecting taxes, commanding native troops, and in return, defending their vassals. This system is revealed to us by the Amarna letters, a series of diplomatic correspondences between Egypt and her vassals, as well as other Great Kingdoms (empires), during the time of Akhenaten and his father.

Many of the events in our story are historical. Hani did receive the title "Master of the King's Stable." The common graves of child workers were found in the quarries that served the building of Akhet-aten. The wobbly loyalty of Biryawaza of Temesheq and Aitakkama of Qidshu, the defection of "Amanappa" (Amen-nefer) and a number of Egyptian soldiers to the *hapiru*, and the plan to send a military force to the north to clean things up are all attested. Shum-addi really was accused of robbing the Babylonians, who were then humiliated (or in our case, thought to be murdered) by the commissioner Amen-nefer. The Babylonians really invaded Urusalim. Amen-nefer's other misdeeds are fictional.

Lord Ptah-mes's involvement in the north is not recorded, but there was a high commissioner named "Maya," and I have conflated the two characters. The Egyptians did indeed annex Mankhate for a regional capital. Likewise, the real Pa-aten-em-heb may or may not be the Atenist name of Har-em-heb, later a powerful general and even king. It is known that he fought in the north in his youth.

An overall note about the spellings of Egyptian names, which many readers will notice turn up in a variety of forms in different authors. The Egyptian writing system, like Arabic and Hebrew today, had no real vowels—for instance, Kemet, the name of the country, would have been literally KMT—so the vocalization of any given word is, with few exceptions, arbitrary. For example, *Neferet* and *Nefert* are the same word in variant reconstructions. I have tried to give something approximating the original (as far as we know it) without venturing too far from familiar forms in many cases (e.g., *Aten* and *Amen* rather than *Itn* and *Imun*).

Finally, it should be noted that much of the Near East was heavily forested in antiquity.

CHARACTERS

(Persons marked with an * are purely fictitious)

HANI'S FAMILY

A'a*: the doorkeeper of Hani's family.

Amen-em-hut, Nub-nefer's brother, Third Prophet of Amen.

Amen-em-ope known as **Pa-kiki*** (The Monkey), Hani and Nub-nefer's younger son.

Amen-hotep known as **Hani,** a diplomat.

Amen-hotep known as **Aha***, Hani and Nub-nefer's elder son. Later takes the name **Hesy-en-aten**.

Amen-hotep known as **Anuia**, Amen-em-hut's wife, a chantress of Amen.

Amen-hotep called **Tepy***, Maya and Sat-hut-haru's eldest son.

Amen-mes known as **Maya***, Hani's dwarf secretary and son-in-law, married to Sat-hut-haru.

Baket-iset*, Hani's eldest daughter.

Bener-ib*, Neferet's partner and fellow *sunet*.

In-hapy*, Maya's mother, a royal goldsmith.

Iuty*, a gardener of Hani's family.

Khawy*, an orphaned student taken in by the household.

Khentet-ka*, Aha's wife.

Meryet-amen*, Mery-ra's lady friend.

Mery-ra, Hani's father.

Mut-nodjmet*: Pipi's daughter, the wife of Pa-kiki.

Pa-ra-em-heb known as **Pipi***, Hani's brother.

Neferet*, Hani and Nub-nefer's youngest daughter, a physician to the royal women.

Nub-nefer*, Hani's wife, a chantress of Amen.

Qenyt-ta-sherit*: Yellow-eye the Younger, Hani's pet heron.

Sat-hut-haru*, Hani and Nub-nefer's second daughter, married to Maya.

OTHER CHARACTERS

Abdi-hepa: king of Urusalim.

Ah-mes-ankh*: commander of the garrison at Mankhate.

Aitakkama: king of Qidshu.

Ankh-khepru-ra Smenkh-ka-ra: Akh-en-aten's brother (?) and coregent.

Amaya*: wife of Zalaya, a slave.

Amen-nefer (Amanappa): commissioner at Kumidi.

Apeny: Ptah-mes's late wife, a fervent partisan of Amen-Ra.

Ay: the king's uncle and father-in-law, a powerful courtier.

Bab-ilum: Babylon, "the gate of the gods."

Bayadi*: a slave of Amen-nefer.

Bin-addi*: a slave of Amen-nefer

Biryawaza: king of Upi, with his capital at Temesheq (Damascus).

Burna-buriash: Kassite king of Babylonia (Sangar).

Djefat-nebty*: female physician of the royal women, with whom Neferet was apprenticed.

Esagil-kin-apli*: commandant of the Babylonian forces at Urusalim.

Hattusha-ziti: emissary of Shupiluliuma, king of Kheta (Hatti).

Huy: Ptah-mes's younger son.

In-her-khau*: one of Hani's staff.

Isesi-ankh*: an infantry officer.

Kalbaya*: Amen-nefer's valet.

Meryet-aten: Akh-en-aten's eldest daughter and wife of Smenkh-ka-ra.

Mut-em-wia: Ptah-mes's eldest daughter.

Nabu-ahhe-idin*: a Babylonian military scribe.

Neb-amen*: a soldier stationed at Kumidi.

Neb-ma'at-ra Amen-hotep (III): Akh-en-aten's father and predecessor.

Nefer-khepru-ra Wa-en-ra Akh-en-aten: the king of Kemet (originally Amen-hotep IV).

Nefert-iti Nefer-nefru-aten: Akh-en-aten's Great Queen.

Pa-aten-em-heb: an infantry officer, formerly known as Har-em-heb.

Ptah-mes (known as Maya): Hani's friend and immediate superior, who has been broken in rank and sent to Djahy.

Ra-nefer (Reanappa): an otherwise unknown official mentioned in the Amarna letters, so I have made him the vizier of the Lower Kingdom. The real name of Aper-el's successor is unknown.

Shindi-shugab and **Akhu-tsabu**: Babylonian emissaries.

Shulum-marduk: Babylonian emissary.

Shum-addi: a leader of the *hapiru*.

Tut-ankh-aten: Akhenaten's son (?) and heir.

Wah-ib-ra*: archivist of the army garrison at Hut-nen-nesut.

Zalaya*: a slave of Amen-nefer.

GLOSSARY OF PLACES, TERMS, AND GODS

Abana River: the river that runs through Damascus, today called the Rabada.

akh: the perfected soul after death has reunited all its parts.

Akhet-aten: the Horizon of the Aten, the new capital built by Akh-en-aten between Waset and Men-nefer.

Amen-Ra: Amen, the traditional creator god of Waset, later joined with the all-powerful sun god, Ra, to become the chief divinity of Egypt's pantheon.

Ammit: "the devourer", a monster who annihilated the souls of those who didn't weigh out against the feather of Ma'at.

Aten: originally just the visible disk of the sun, the Aten became a kind of spiritual being, approached only through the king, that supplanted all the other gods in Akhenaten's religious reforms.

Azzati: overall administrative capital of Egypt's vassals in the north. Today's Gaza.

Bes: a dwarfish part-lion god, protector of women and children.

Book of Going Forth by Day: a text collecting prayers and spells for successfully negotiating the judgment after death. In the New Kingdom, a copy was buried with the deceased.

deben: a unit of weight equaling 91 grams.

Djahy: generic name for the southern part of the Levant, corresponding more or less with Roman Palestina. Also called Retjenu.

Duat: the underworld.

Field of Reeds: site of the beautiful afterlife that the good would enjoy.

Golden Fly: a necklace with pendants shaped like large flies, which served as a medal for bravery on the battlefield.

Great House (Per-a'o): the palace, more broadly referring to the government and specifically to the king, hence our term "pharaoh." (Cf. our use of "the White House.")

hapir (pl. *hapiru*): member of a loose confederation of nomads, social outcasts, and runaway slaves who preyed on caravans and even attacked cities. They were a serious problem in the hinterland and eventually helped to destabilize the Bronze Age kingdoms.

Haru (Horus): a sun god, specifically the youthful morning sun. Normally the king was thought to be an incarnation of Haru while alive and of Osir when dead.

heb-sed: The Festival of the Bull's Tail, a royal jubilee held after thirty years of reign and thereafter at more frequent intervals. It was thought to rejuvenate the king's powers.

House of Royal Ornaments: the king's harem in Hut-nen-nesut, where his lesser wives and concubines resided.

Hut-nen-nesut: Heracleopolis, a city at the juncture of the Nile and a canal cut to connect the river with Lake Pa-yom (today's Fayyum Oasis).

Isfet: Chaos, the primal state, opposite of all that is true, good, ordered, and just.

iteru: a unit of distance equaling approximately a mile.

Kemet: meaning the Black Land, from the rich alluvial soil brought by the annual flood. This was what the Egyptians called their own country (**Mizri** to most of their neighbors).

Kharu: the northern part of the Levant, mostly today's Syria.

Kheta: Hatti, the land of the Hittites, in central Anatolia, which is today's Turkey.

Kumidi: one of the administrative capitals of Egypt among its northern vassals. Today's Kamid al-Loz.

Kush: Nubia, a kingdom held by Egypt in what is now Sudan.

Lake of Fire: a place of torment in the afterlife.

Lover of Silence: Meret-seger, goddess of the west bank of the Nile where the dead were buried.

ma'at: the concept of justice, truth, and right order; with a capital M, the goddess who personifies these.

Men-nefer: Memphis, the pre-Amarna capital of the Northern Kingdom (Lower Egypt).

moringa: a tree that bears beans pressed to make oil.

Mut: consort of the god Amen-Ra. Her name means simply "mother."

Naharin: Egypt's name for Mitanni, an inland Syrian kingdom that had formerly been a powerful rival of Egypt and later an ally. Called Hanigalbat by the Hittites.

Neshite: the language of the Hittites.

Osir (Osiris): benevolent king of the underworld. The dead were thought to become one with him and are thus spoken of as an Osir.

Pa-yom: a lake in Lower Egypt used as a flood-control reservoir. It is now silted up and forms the Fayyum Oasis.

Qeden (Qatna): a formerly powerful kingdom on the Orontes River near Qidshu. Today's Tell el-Mishrifeh.

Qidshu: the Egyptian name for Qadesh, a city on the Orontes River. Today's Tell al-Nabi Mando.

River (**Great River**): the Nile.

Sangar: what the Egyptians called Babylonia (**Karduniash** to most of their neighbors).

Sekhmet: the lioness-headed goddess of plague and healing, as well as of the dangerous effects of the sun.

Serqet: a scorpion goddess who protected against poisonous bites and other harm.

shebyu **collar**: a necklace of lens-shaped gold beads; part of the gold of honor bestowed on someone who had earned the king's favor, which signaled his elevation in rank.

shen **ring**: The hieroglyph for *eternity*, a coil of rope with a knot. The names of kings were written in an elongated form we call today a cartouche.

Shuppiluliuma: king of Hatti, who had expanded it into a powerful empire with holdings down into Syria.

Simurru (Tsumur): a coastal city, the capital of Amurru, formerly an Egyptian vassal.

sunet (m. *sunu*): a female physician of the scientific sort, as opposed to a priest or magical healer.

Sutesh (Seth): the god of chaos, always trying to undermine right order.

Siduna (Sidon): a coastal city in what is now Lebanon.

Temesheq: capital of the Syrian kingdom of Upi. Today's Damascus.

Two Lands: another name for Egypt. It had originally been two distinct kingdoms, which were then united.

Urusalim: a Canaanite city in Djahy. Today's Jerusalem.

Waset: the "city of the scepter" (*was*). Thebes, pre-Amarna capital of the Upper Kingdom.

Wawat: Lower Nubia, between Kush and Egypt, the site of many gold mines in the desert.

Way of Haru and **the Royal Way** (Way of the Sea): north-south roads through Egypt's vassal states, well maintained for troop movement and provided with relay stations, water, and provisions.

Weighing of the Heart: the judgment of the soul after death, when a person's heart was laid in the pan of a balance against the feather of Ma'at.

Wepet-renpet: New Year's Day ("the opening of the year"). The exact date varied according to the date of the fall flood.

CHAPTER 1

H ANI STOOD IN THE RECEPTION room of the vizier of
the Lower Kingdom and wiped the sweat off his face
with his arm. The dim, high-ceilinged hall was blessedly
cool after the withering heat of the courtyard.

At his side, his secretary, Maya, said uneasily, "What do
you suppose the vizier wants to see you for, my lord?"

"I have no idea, my friend. I've had precious little
contact with Lord Ra-nefer since he took office except to
send written reports. I think I've sort of slipped through
the cracks of his notice, since I've been working locally."
Hani thought gratefully of his former direct superior, Lord
Ptah-mes, who had managed to get him off the rolls of
foreign postings. Alas, Ptah-mes himself, in disfavor with
the king, was now stationed abroad at Azzati in Djahy.

"Maybe he wants to give you the gold of honor, eh, my
lord?" Maya said sarcastically. Hani was no more in favor
than his superior. His favor with the king had plunged after
he'd only too successfully uncovered the mastermind of a
series of tomb robberies two years before.

"More likely, he needs me to take the blame for some botch-up." Hani grinned.

Their conversation was interrupted by the appearance of Lord Ra-nefer's secretary at the vizier's door. He tipped his head and said loftily, "The vizier of the Lower Kingdom will see you now."

Hani took a deep breath and strode forward through the shadowy reception room and into an office luminous with the buffered glow from its high windows. The vizier sat on a fine chair on a dais. He was a rotund figure with a long kilt knotted across the chest and a thick neck full of gold that doubled his chins up. There was a sheen of sweat on his face.

Hani folded in a formal bow, hands on his knees, and when he rose, Lord Ra-nefer said in a high-pitched, weary voice, "The famous Hani. I thought I'd never meet you."

"I'm honored by the summons, my lord." Hani was unsettled. *Famous?* This hyperbole augured nothing good. He'd tried hard to stay below the notice of the court.

"Well, Ptah-mes isn't around to intercede for you, so we'll be seeing more of one another, I daresay—at least, until a new high commissioner of foreign affairs in the north is named." Ra-nefer crossed his arms, which rested on the mound of his belly, and leaned back in his chair, while Hani waited, curious about why the vizier had called for him.

Ra-nefer eyed Hani up and down with a considering expression on his jowly face. That face was a strange color, as if a pallid green had been laid over the copper of his Theban complexion.

Does he know about my resistance to orders? Is he wondering if he can trust me? Hani asked himself.

After the two men had sized each other up for a heartbeat, the vizier resumed. "Two reasons why you're here, my friend. One is, I have a commission for you in Djahy, or maybe Kharu—I forget which it is, but Ptah-mes will fill you in on the details. See him in Azzati. And the other..."

An ominous ripple of apprehension crawled up Hani's spine.

"Our Sun God Nefer-khepru-ra Wa-en-ra—life, prosperity, and health be his—wants to recognize you. You're to be named Master of the King's Stable and receive the gold of honor."

It was as if the floor had dropped out from under Hani. Of all the events in the world he'd never expected to happen, this was surely the most improbable. *May the Hidden One protect me. Is this a sarcastic joke?* He'd been a thorn in the king's flesh for years—criticizing the foreign policy of the Two Lands, uncovering a shady bit of political intrigue that Nefer-khepru-ra would probably have preferred to keep hidden... and now he was to be honored?

Suspicion smoldered like a banked fire in Hani's middle, but he said only, "The king's favor is the breath of life in my nostrils, my lord. I fear I am unworthy."

"Well, if by that you mean you know nothing about horses, that's not an obstacle," Ra-nefer said dryly, as if Hani's protestations were an imposition. "The association with the cavalry is purely honorific. But some pompous title will give you more clout when you deal with our vassals in

25

Kharu. Or was it Djahy?" He suppressed a belch and patted himself on the chest with a fist. "Damned cucumbers."

Hani groped for words and finally managed, "I'm speechless, my lord."

Ra-nefer emitted a burble that might have been amusement, although his put-upon expression never brightened. "Don't be too speechless. We're counting on your eloquence in Djahy."

Or is it Kharu? Hani thought with the kind of giddy interior laughter of a man who has had his world overturned. "And when is this honor to be bestowed, if I may make so bold, my lord?"

"Two weeks. That gives you time to get your people down here. Any questions, Hani? If not, that's all." Ra-nefer rose, none too tall even on his feet. He hitched at the knot of his long kilt as if afraid it might all come sliding down, although Hani suspected the man's belly should hold it comfortably. Quite a difference from his late predecessor, the lean, hawk-faced Aper-el.

Hani bowed, glad the prostration hid his expression. He should have been wildly honored, but this was all too strange, and he couldn't help but wonder what lay behind his new designation. By the time he rose, the vizier had disappeared through his inner door, and Hani was left to totter, like a man in shock, back out to the reception hall.

Maya popped up from his seat on the floor as soon as Hani had crossed the doorsill. The little secretary was bright-eyed with curiosity. Whatever posting Hani had received would affect him as well—and now he had a wife and two children, whom he would miss. And Hani would miss them, too, because they were his grandchildren.

"What's the word, my lord?"

"Two things, son. One, we're going to be missioned out to Kharu again—or Djahy. We're to stop by Azzati, and Lord Ptah-mes will give us the details."

"Ah," said Maya cheerfully. "It will be nice to see him again. It's been what—two years?"

"Yes," Hani said as the two men breached the outer doorway and found themselves in the sun-bleached court. "I wonder how he's doing in disgrace and exile." *It would take more than being broken in rank to crush a proud man like Ptah-mes.* What Hani really wondered was how Ptah-mes was doing after the loss of his wife, who had almost certainly been murdered.

Because Hani had refused to exchange his family home in Waset, some five days to the south, for lodging in the new capital, Ptah-mes had graciously invited Hani and Maya to stay at his house when they were in Akhet-aten. So they directed their mismatched footsteps down the broad, glaring processional street lined with lion-bodied images of the king.

Hani, sunk in thought, remembered suddenly that he'd never completed his recital of the meeting. "The second thing Ra-nefer said was that I was to receive the gold of honor and the title Master of the King's Stable." He couldn't repress a bark of skeptical laughter.

Maya stopped and gaped at his father-in-law. "My lord! Congratulations! At last, they're recognizing all you've done for the Two Lands." But then his delight faded into a cocked eyebrow of suspicion. "After the tomb robbery investigation, I'm a little surprised, though. This isn't a cruel joke, is it?"

"I've asked myself the same thing, Maya. I guess we have to treat it as a serious offer. Perhaps the king has heard of how successfully I took care of Pipi's horses." Hani had to smile at the recollection of his brief stint as a groom after his irrepressible brother had bought a pair of horses that turned out to have been stolen from the royal stud farm.

Maya snorted, and the two of them strode along through the dust and the blare of cicadas, Hani revolving all the possibilities of what this unexpected royal favor might signify. At the southern edge of the city, the houses thinned out until only the mansions of the rich rose in white-walled splendor along the riverbank.

As they entered Lord Ptah-mes's gate, Maya said, "What sort of man is the new vizier of the Lower Kingdom, my lord?"

"I don't have a grasp on him yet," Hani admitted. "He seemed like a harmless fellow, a little befuddled, but I don't yet know how benevolent he is toward us—he was the one who rescinded Ptah-mes's commission, although perhaps he was under pressure from the Great House. In appearance, he's the opposite of Lord Aper-el."

Maya made a thoughtful *hmmm.*

Lord Ptah-mes's servants came to the door to welcome Hani, who greeted them pleasantly. They knew him and his secretary well, since their master had made it clear that Hani should feel at home even in his own absence.

"Will my lord require anything to eat?" the majordomo inquired politely, while the other servants—disciplined and smooth, as one would expect—stood behind him, attending to his every wish.

Hani and Maya exchanged an eager look. "Thank you,

my friend," Hani said to the majordomo, realizing all at once how hungry he was. "That would be splendid." He beamed at the servant, who backed formally from the room and set off toward the kitchens.

◈

Two weeks later, Hani found himself back in the capital among a crowd of his family, friends, and colleagues. Several men were being honored simultaneously, so the processional road before the Window of Appearances was thronged with a festive crowd of well-wishers. Hani's wife, Nub-nefer, was at his side and all but one of their children, Baket-iset, who had been bedridden for seventeen years, ever since a terrible accident had left her paralyzed. Aha, Hani's firstborn, was there, proud of his father for once. Pa-kiki and his wife and child were present, along with Maya and Sat-hut-haru, Hani's second girl. And the irrepressible youngest, Neferet, with her friend and fellow doctor Bener-ib trailing her, was jumping up and down with excitement despite her eighteen years.

Hani's brother Pipi, who lived in Akhet-aten, was at his side, beaming, and Mery-ra, their father, smiling ear to ear, stood just behind him with his pupil, young Khawy. The family of Nub-nefer's brother, the rebel priest of Amen-Ra, had even come. Hani saw in the crowd many of his friends and also Maya's mother, the goldsmith In-hapy, almost invisible among the taller bodies around her. So many beloved faces. *All these good people are here to wish me well. They're probably happier than I am about this.* For the first time, Hani was conscious of what an honor this recognition was rather than afraid of what hidden meaning it might be intended to convey. He resolved to suppress his suspicions and enjoy the moment.

He gazed out over the clustered throng bedecked in their finest festival clothes and most expensive wigs, flowers around their necks and in their hair. Nub-nefer, hanging on his arm, looked up at him, her face glowing with pride. She had no love for the king, who had suppressed the cult of Amen-Ra and put his priests, including members of her family, out of work. But she believed in Hani's worth. *Where would I have been all these years without her?*

Hani's nose sparked with tenderness. He leaned over and kissed her forehead through the wreath of flowers that adorned it. "The greatest honor of all is to be seen with you, my dove," he whispered.

She beamed up at him, as beautiful in Hani's eyes as she'd been the day they were married thirty-three years before.

All at once, the silvery notes of trumpets rang out. The crowd rippled like a field of wind-tossed wheat as everyone bent in a full court bow before the king, Nefer-khepru-ra Wa-en-ra, and his queen and coregent, Nefert-iti Nefer-nefru-aten, who had appeared in the window above the road. Slender columns with fluttering banners flanked them, so that the royal couple was framed like a pair of gods in a shrine. They were a dazzling apparition in their blue crowns. Clad in gauzy white linen and adorned with elaborate jewelry, almost every inch of the royal pair coruscated in the blinding midday sun—together, the living avatar of the Aten, the Sun Disk.

A herald proclaimed the names of those to be honored that day, each one greeted by the cheers of his supporters.

The first man was raised onto the shoulders of his friends, and as he stretched out his arms in ritual supplication, the royal couple showered him with sacks of grain and cuts of meat and gold necklaces and armlets—as if the very bounty of the heavens had been upended upon him. His friends scrambled for the gifts and hung the gold *shebyu* collars of honor around his neck, everyone laughing, aahing, and crying out at once.

And then came Hani's turn to be hoisted, rocking and uneasy, upon the shoulders of his father and brother and sons. His heart was pounding with the precariousness of the seat—he was not a light man—but he let go of Mery-ra's and Pipi's heads long enough to stretch out his hands to the royal couple above him. Over the bright, richly embroidered cushion that padded the sill of the window, the king leaned forward, his pointed face a benevolent and impassive mask, and gold and food began to rain down upon Hani, striking him like weighty hail, a not altogether pleasant sensation. He heard the excited cries of the family below him as they scrambled for the falling gifts, but he could hardly distinguish one bent back from another. As the men started to lower him to the ground, Hani caught the queen's eye. It was narrowed in an evaluating look, neither malevolent nor kindly.

What's she thinking? Hani wondered with a chill.

When his feet had reached solid ground once more, and the children had tied the last of the gold collars with lens-shaped beads around his neck, Hani—flushed and still off-balance—laughed and embraced his wife. "Am I prettier with these things framing my chin?" he asked mischievously. He felt rather exhilarated in spite of himself.

She was radiant, but a little tartness marked her tone as she said, "You deserved them, my love. You've deserved them for years. Anyone else would have honored you long before now, again and again."

Hani wondered once more what this honor really meant. Perhaps it was only as Ra-nefer had said—that the elevated status gave him more influence abroad. Still, the question passed through his mind: *Is the king trying to buy me?*

But this was a day of celebration. His family gathered about him, Hani made his way toward the embarcadero, where a ferry would take them back to Waset. "Who's coming and who's staying?" he called out.

"We're coming back with you," Neferet cried joyfully, hugging him hard. "Lady Djefat-nebty gave us some time off because the occasion was so-o-o special!" Djefat-nebty was the royal *sunet* with whom Neferet and her friend were studying.

An apologetic look on his face, Aha said, "I'd like to join you, Father, but I have things to do here." He clapped his father on the shoulder in an awkward gesture of pride. Aha, more than any other member of the family, would be impressed by such superficial ceremonies. He was an enthusiastic follower of the king and his reforms—much to the chagrin of his parents.

"Thank you for coming, son." Hani embraced him. "Give our love to Khentet-ka and the children."

Having bade goodbye to Aha and all their friends who now resided in the City of the Horizon, the rest of the family trooped down to the ferry they had retained. The servants, who stood grinning on the shore, sent up an enthusiastic cheer.

"Congratulations, my lord," A'a, the old gatekeeper, cried. The others echoed him as Hani and his party clumped up the gangplank, their arms full of gold jewelry and haunches of meat and sacks of grain, their steps resounding on the boards.

⁂

Maya was as proud as if he himself had received the gold of honor. He tried the words out for size in his mind. *I am the secretary of the Master of the King's Stable.* By all the gods, this would add spice to his Tales. *The Traveler, secretary to the Master of the King's Stable... was sent on a delicate mission. Saved the king's life. Single-handedly carried twenty little princes from a burning building. Fought his way back to the capital in time with an urgent message.*

There were definitely possibilities here. He found he was almost eager to head north again, despite the fact that it meant months away from his family. He was thirty-two, but he still had a young man's thirst for adventures. Especially now that he had discovered how successfully they fueled his storytelling and how much Sat-hut-haru and the children loved to hear about extravagant exploits.

At his side, his wife gave a great sigh of contentment. "Wasn't that marvelous? Papa deserves it. We've always wondered why he never got any recognition."

Because he gets up the king's nose at every opportunity, Maya answered silently. "Because he's honest and incorruptible, my love. He hasn't clawed his way up the ladder by pushing other people down."

"I wish we'd brought the children. Pa-kiki and Uncle Pipi did, and Aunt Anuia. Little Tepy would have been thrilled to see his gamfather standing before the king."

"He's only seven, my dove. I'm not sure but all that waiting in the sun wouldn't have made him cranky."

"Maybe you're right..." Her voice trailed off. It was clear she didn't think he was right.

Maya replied in irritation, "Of course I'm right."

He looked away from Sat-hut-haru and concentrated on the glorious River in front of him, gilded by the long rays of the afternoon sun, its waters like swirling malachite. He could only just see over the gunwales, and that peeved him too. On the distant bank, trees swayed, and now and again a village appeared and receded into the distance, a jumble of dun cubes looking as if they'd grown right from the dun soil. Farmers bent over their fields, setting up the sluice gates in their canals, readying for the Inundation, which would come upon them soon—that life-bringing flood of fresh, rich alluvium that gave Kemet, the Black Land, its name.

When Maya turned back to his wife, she had gone.

❖

The family had been on the ferry for three days. Most of the excitement had died down, most of the necessary conversations concluded. Hani had packed up the gold jewelry and the cuts of meat wrapped in vinegar-soaked rags and the sacks of grain the first evening, and the servants took turns sitting on them.

Hani and Nub-nefer were standing silently, arm in arm, gazing out over the River, thinking their own thoughts, when Neferet burst between them. "Papa! You make us so proud." She stretched up to kiss him with her usual exuberance.

"You've said that several times, little duckling. I appreciate it. It makes me proud to think I make you proud." He winked at her, and Nub-nefer suppressed a smile.

"I'm glad the king recognized you now, because he... well..." Neferet dropped her eyes and got that shifty look of hers. She jabbed a sealing thumb against her lips. "I shouldn't say."

"Whatever it is, you've been itching to say it since the ceremony, I'll bet," Hani said fondly. "But, Neferet, my dear, you mustn't spread stories you hear at court."

"I don't. I would never tell anybody but you and Mama. Bener-ib already knows, because she heard it at the same time I did. And this could be important." She looked about her furtively then whispered near his ear, "The king is sick."

A shiver of foreboding raised the hair on Hani's neck. "People do get sick from time to time, my duckling. Even gods on earth." Hani realized his voice was more acerbic than he had intended, and he softened it. "Please don't tell me anything you've learned at a patient's bedside."

"The king's not my patient. I heard Lord Pentju telling Djefat-nebty." Neferet looked at her mother as if for support. "That's completely different, isn't it?"

Nub-nefer locked glances with Hani behind Neferet's head. Hani could have sworn he saw an ember of eagerness in her kohl-edged eyes.

"He's young yet. It's probably nothing serious." He tried to remember whether Nefer-khepru-ra had shown any signs of illness when he'd leaned out over Hani to bestow the gold upon him, but Hani had been so blinded by the sun and so preoccupied with not falling off people's shoulders that he hadn't been at his most observant.

Neferet continued, undeterred, her voice dropping still lower. "The Osir Neb-ma'at-ra died of a bad heart. And his son has one too." She pounded a fist on her chest in a rhythm, first slow, then frantic, then slow again. Then she stared smugly at her father.

Hani felt less sorrow over this news than he would have for nearly anyone else. But a man's life was no small thing, even such a man's. *And when he dies... what then? Can Nefert-iti hold things together alone? No, there'll be a civil war. Will Lord Ay make a move? Will the Crocodiles be ready to jump into the breach with their Hittite?* He heaved a sigh. *Mut, mother of us all, guide the Two Lands.*

Nub-nefer was staring avidly at Hani. No doubt, she was praying for Nefer-khepru-ra to die so that the priests of Amen-Ra, whom Hani thought of as the Crocodiles, could carry out their plan to return the kingdom to worship of the Hidden One.

Hani said to Neferet in an urgent undertone, "Tell no one this, my little duckling. It's none of your business. And there are probably people who'd be happy to claim you'd cast a spell on him."

"May the demons of the Duat twist my tongue around my neck and make me swallow my teeth if I ever say a word, Papa. May the Lover of Silence pull out my hairs one by one—"

"She'll have to find them first," Hani said, scrubbing his daughter's closely shaven scalp with his knuckles. But although his tone was playful, his heart had frozen within him. He wanted to rejoice, but the thought of the chaos that would follow Nefer-khepru-ra's death made him fearful.

From somewhere across the deck, a girlish voice called out, "Neferet? Where are you?"

"Bener-ib is looking for you," Nub-nefer said, practically sweeping her daughter away.

She exchanged gazes with Hani, and he saw the same cold flame burning in her eye that had so frequently lit her brother's. Hani didn't want to call it fanaticism, but it was certainly fervor. Neferet scampered away and disappeared into the crowd of cousins and nephews.

"Well, my dove. Perhaps our prayers will be answered before long," he said to his wife with an uneasy smile. "I hope we don't regret what we've asked for."

"Oh, Hani," Nub-nefer whispered, "this is the first good news I've heard in—how many, ten years? Fifteen, if you count the coregency?" She clutched the front of Hani's shirt.

"We knew he'd die sometime, my love. 'Do not say I am young to be taken, for you do not know your death,'" Hani quoted apprehensively. He was ashamed of how little the idea of the king's demise moved him. The man was the father of children, after all. If something happened to him, they would be plunged into grief, and the royal family had already been in mourning for two of their small daughters, victims of the plague. *But the consequences... what will follow?*

"If only Lady Apeny had lived to see this day. She worked so fearlessly to restore the King of the Gods."

Nub-nefer looked up at him with shining eyes. "Oh, Hani, Amen-em-hut can come out of hiding!"

Hani murmured into the top of her wig, "Nefer-khepru-ra isn't dead yet. It may be a long time. He's only—what? Thirty-two? His father was nearly fifty." He stroked her back, as if to pacify some over-excited animal.

Nub-nefer drew back from him with an ill-suppressed grin of eagerness. "At least now there's hope, Hani. We can hope once more that the Hidden One will emerge into the light in our lifetime."

"Cooking up sedition again, are you, my children?" Mery-ra inserted himself between them, a crafty smile on his broad face.

"Just dreaming, Father," Hani said lightly, not wanting to spread Neferet's news any farther.

"Although it seems to me that being seditious pays pretty well. You've just acquired enough joints of meat and sacks of grain to live off of for quite some time, my boy." Mery-ra chuckled, and his ample belly bounced. "Who would have thought we'd ever see you honored after all you've done to antagonize the powers that be?"

"He deserves it," said Nub-nefer stoutly. "Honoring Hani is the first sign of good judgment our king has shown."

"Life, prosperity, and health to him," Mery-ra added, lifting a pious eye to the heavens.

Hani had to laugh. Such sarcasm was dangerous, but it seemed unlikely that anyone among his family and friends would turn them in. For the most part, the people who continued to live in Waset were those less than enchanted by the present regime. "How is Khawy working out?"

"He's an admirable boy. Tragedy has made him mature

above his age, and I'm very pleased with his progress. Not to mention his artwork. He's already caught up to me with his illustrations for the *Book of Going Forth by Day*. Guess I'd better hustle to retake the lead." Mery-ra clapped his son on the back. "He's very grateful to you for taking him in."

Nub-nefer said longingly, "He's a nice boy. I just wish Neferet..."

Hani had a sudden thought. Not quite able to conceal the anxiety under his light tone, he said, "Wait, does my being Master of the King's Stable make Lord Ay my superior? He's Master of the Royal Horses."

Mery-ra crowed, "So here's the hook inside your poisoned gift, son! You have to report to Ay! That charming and sinister old fox—somehow he manages to serve as the king's henchman without surrendering his own ambitions."

"I did him a favor once. Maybe he likes me."

"Or maybe he remembers how close you came to exposing him in the tomb robberies," Mery-ra said slyly.

Nub-nefer looked uneasy. "I thought you told me the title was purely honorific, Hani—that you had no duties related to the stables."

"That's what I was led to believe."

"What's everybody talking about?" Pipi appeared at Mery-ra's shoulder. His plump, amiable face was wreathed in curiosity.

Mery-ra made room for his younger son, who admittedly took up a fair amount of space. Pipi was broad and squat, like all the men of his family, but to that breadth he'd added quite a sedentary spread.

"We were discussing Hani's new duties, son."

Pipi punched Hani on the arm. "Oh, brother, I'm so proud of you. This sheds luster on the whole family! Imagine—I'm the brother of a man with the *shebyu* collar!" He laughed happily, exposing the gap between his front teeth.

Hani cuffed him playfully on the head. He hoped Pipi wasn't envious, in his wistful way, of this honor, which he was unlikely ever to achieve. Hani's brother had only lazily pursued his scribal career over the years, preferring to dream of some windfall. Middle age found him low in the ranks still, although only in the last few years had Hani ever heard him express any regrets.

"If we weren't on a boat, I'd take you down for that, you snide beast," Hani said.

"But I'm not being snide, I swear," Pipi cried, his little brown eyes open wide in innocence. "I only meant—"

"I'm sure Hani plans to share out all this food," Mery-ra interrupted. "With none of the children still at home, even he will never consume this much." He patted Hani on the belly, which was admittedly substantial. "And it would be a shame to have to salt all this meat when it would be so much better fresh. Not so, Nub-nefer?"

She smiled knowingly at her father-in-law. "I'm sure he will share. But ask him."

"Speaking of my belly," Hani said, "it tells me it's time to eat. The servants packed lunch for us at the last stop. Who's ready?"

Together, the four of them made their way over the tilting deck to the big basket the kitchen girls had filled with flatbread and dates and chickpea salad. It was already surrounded by a crowd of children, who were noisily picking over the goodies like a flock of magpies.

"I hope you thought to pack pickled turnips," said Mery-ra, trying to see over his great-grandchildren's heads.

"I'm sure there are some in there somewhere," Nub-nefer reassured him. "Unless these voracious little animals have devoured them all." She turned to her husband. "How long will you be able to stay at home before you leave, my love?"

"Oh," said Hani, reaching for a piece of bread, "probably a few days at most. It's a long way to Azzati. Let's see, ten days to Men-nefer, and from there, I would guess another ten to Azzati if we sail. That's two weeks just for travel. We'll need to conclude our business in the north before their winter rains start, so it's important to get going."

"Where exactly are you going this time?" asked Pipi.

"Djahy. Or maybe Kharu. The vizier didn't seem to be clear about it."

"Nice as it's been to have you in Waset, I have to say, son, the Two Lands need you in the field. How many emissaries speak as many languages as you do?" Mery-ra said.

"And how many are Masters of the King's Stable? You never know when some vassal's horse will need grooming." Hani shot his father a mischievous grin.

To Hani's surprise, Nub-nefer said, "It's not a bad thing. It gives us a little extra to tuck away for Baket-iset."

Hani replied more seriously, "You're quite right, my dove. If anything should happen to us, whichever brother takes her in will have a tidy silo of grain to help him out." He looked around. "Where has Maya gone?"

"Can't be far, unless he knows how to swim." Mery-ra craned his neck to look around. "There's Sat-hut-haru with Mut-nodjmet, but I don't see our favorite dwarf."

Hani pursed his lips in reflection. "This must be the first time since they were married that Maya has left her alone, except when he's on a mission." *I hope they haven't fallen out.* He put an arm around Nub-nefer's shoulders. "Would you like me to be that solicitous, my dear?"

She sniffed. "There's a point past which solicitude becomes control. I prefer you the way you are, Hani."

Hani wondered if there weren't buried in her words some oblique reference to the secret visits she paid her brother, Amen-em-hut, with Hani's tacit blessing. Amen-em-hut was in hiding while he stirred up people against the king. *There's the real cooker-up of sedition.*

The lengthening shadows made it clear that their day of sailing was drawing to a close. Soon they would pull ashore to spend the hours of darkness in sleep and to replenish their stock of food. In two days, they would be home.

Only to turn around and leave again. Hani sighed. His years off the mission roster had been pleasant. There had been plenty to keep him busy in the king's service at home, and he'd been able to enjoy the company of his family far more frequently than usual. But it seemed that, without Ptah-mes to cover for him, he was back in the field. He wrapped his wife closer, and they stood leaning against one another, watching the banks of the River slide past and the rays of the sun growing longer and longer until it was a burning disk of copper in the western sky.

CHAPTER 2

Hani's sojourn in Waset was brief, and apart from making the necessary preparations for travel, he resolutely did nothing. It was far sweeter to spend those last few days with his family. He and Neferet were describing for Baket-iset the ceremony of honor.

"First," Neferet said enthusiastically, "we had to hoick Papa up on our shoulders. And he is h-e-e-a-vy!"

"It was the men who did that," Hani corrected affectionately.

But Neferet said with a touch of stubbornness, "I was there, too, Papa. You just couldn't see me because I was in the back." She mimed heaving something weighty to her shoulders. "And then the king leaned out over his balcony and started throwing things down to Papa"—she made strewing gestures—"legs of lamb and big, heavy gold necklaces and sacks of grain. It was like we were being bombarded with rocks! A ham hit me right on the arm, and it hurt."

"Fortunately, you're a doctor and could set any broken

bones." Mery-ra had entered, and he drew up a stool to where they all sat clustered at Baket-iset's couch. She was drinking in her sister's recital with pride and delight, and her grandfather leaned over and patted her withered arm. "You were there with us in spirit, my girl."

"Oh, I was, Grandfather. I was thinking about you all every minute, picturing what must be happening. I had the servants make thank-offerings to the Hidden One."

Hani's nose twinged with an anguish of tenderness. His eldest daughter was perhaps the most beautiful of his children and certainly had the most luminous spirit. Despite the blighting of her young life, she was always serene and cheerful. He could imagine how bitter he would have been in her place, and it made him admire her all the more. Baket-iset possessed, besides, an uncanny ability to read people—a truly divine gift, as if in recompense for the terrible sacrifice she'd had to make.

"Let me ask you something, my swan," he said in a quiet voice, not quite sure he wanted any of the servants to overhear. "It seems so improbable that the king would honor me. I've been so much of a stone in his sandal for so long that I wonder if it's sincere—if he's really recognizing my service or, I don't know, warning me or trying to buy my loyalty. Perhaps my suspicions are totally unjust..."

"Papa, can't he do all of those at the same time? This must be partly in show for the people around him—all such ceremonies are." She gazed at him with her big wise eyes. "Everybody knows how deserving you are of recognition, so he had to do it or look terribly petty."

Mery-ra chuckled. "How many years have you spent at court, my girl, that you understand these things so well?"

"And certainly someone like Aha, much as it pains me to say it, would be completely bought by the gold of honor," Hani mused. "I suspect you're right, little swan. Nefer-khepru-ra most certainly wants me to understand that he has total power to make or break me."

"He's a ba-a-ad man." Neferet left no doubts about her opinion.

But a flicker of fear made Hani lay a finger on her lips. "Please don't speak those words aloud, little duckling. You work at the palace. If anyone realized how you felt about the Lord of the Two Lands, it would be the end of your career—and maybe your life. Besides, I'm sure he has redeeming features. He has excellent taste. He seems to love his children."

Neferet was not one to abandon her position easily. "*His* children, maybe, but what about everyone else's children? What I couldn't tell you about what I've seen at the quarries! But I won't, I swear."

The hair rose on Hani's arms. "What were you doing at a quarry?"

Neferet needed no urging. "A lot of people were getting sick in the workmen's village, and Lady Djefat-nebty took us up there to treat the wives and children. One of them died—the cutest little boy; it was terribly sad—and Bener-ib and I went down to the burial place just so someone would be there to mourn him. But nobody embalmed him, Papa. They just opened a big pit full of bones and laid him in there with the others."

Hani exchanged a look of alarm with his father.

"I could see the bones were all small. I asked someone who all those little bones belonged to, and he said they were the workmen who had died quarrying stone for the new capital. They were children, Papa! They had set little children to work in the quarries in their rush to put up that awful city! And they died like flies, so many they had to push them all together into a pit." Neferet's little brown eyes had grown shriveled with the effort to fight back tears.

A wave of nausea washed over Hani. He saw similar horror on the faces of his father and Baket. The people of the Two Lands loved and protected their children. This was a demonic thing.

"I'm sorry you had to see such a sight, my duckling. Sutesh never gives up. There is evil in the world."

"And it's sitting on our throne," Mery-ra growled under his breath.

"But maybe not for long!" blurted Neferet.

Hani rose abruptly before Neferet spilled all the other court confidences she carried. "Father, let's you and me go out into the garden and have a pot of beer."

The two men hurried from the salon onto the porch. Anxiety gnawed at Hani's gut. He had to convince his daughter not to speak of such matters. Goodhearted and intelligent though she was, she did like to be the center of attention.

As they crunched down the graveled path of Hani's beloved garden, through the pungent greenery of late summer, Mery-ra asked, "What she's talking about? Is she planning to poison his castor oil?"

"Nothing, Father. You know Neferet."

"I know she never met a secret she didn't want to spill. Everybody in the capital probably knows about my hemorrhoids."

They settled themselves in chairs under the grapevine that shaded the pavilion and gazed out at the pool, where ducks floated and occasionally upended in a dive. In the shadows of the trees, Qenyt the Younger, Hani's pet heron, made her watchful rounds, lifting each leg with exquisite care. Hani observed her with affection. Young Khawy had given him the egg as payment for his writing lessons. She'd turned out to be tamer than her predecessor, Qenyt, and in two years, Hani had become extremely fond of her silent presence. He picked up a fallen grape from the ground and held it out to her. She came eagerly but turned away in disappointment, being a lover of frogs and fish. Her pale-golden eye was reproachful.

"You can't even give your favors away, I see." Mery-ra grinned. He settled himself more comfortably into the low-backed chair and stretched out his legs. "Unlike Nefer-khepru-ra. People seem eager enough for his favor."

"Not me."

The serving girl arrived with a pot of beer and its stand. She set it up between them and arranged the straws. "Would my lord like anything else? Some dates? A little cheese?"

"What would you say to some of that good cheese Nub-nefer has had the cook make? It's yet another thing I'll miss up in Kharu. Or Djahy."

Mery-ra seconded the idea with enthusiasm, and before long, the girl had returned with a plate of cheese chunks and a little folding table. She disappeared discreetly. The men sat in silence, savoring the tangy cheese and washing it down with drafts of beer.

At last Mery-ra said, "What exactly are you going to be doing up there this time, son?"

"I don't know. The vizier had nothing to say on that score. He said only to check in with Ptah-mes in Azzati and that he would give me my directives."

Mery-ra considered that. "So you have no idea how long you'll be gone."

"None."

A squawk from the pond attracted Hani's attention. A drake was trying to draw the eye of a female duck, but every time he approached her, she would change direction and cruise away, insulting him under her breath. Finally, she hopped out of the pool altogether and waddled off on her bandy orange legs, the persistent male following. Hani and his father watched the pair of ducks in amusement. Hani observed the drake's posturing and tail-wagging, how the bird strutted around in front of the drab she-duck, who remained magnificently unimpressed.

"Look at that vain fellow!" Hani laughed. "Showing off his manly iridescent green head and curly tail feather."

Mery-ra gave a considering tip of the head. "They're not so different from us, son. Think about all the pleats and furbelows and bunches that men are wearing these days. Not to mention earrings and gold armlets and wigs that could feed a poor family for a year."

"True." Hani thought of his eldest son, who had embraced the elaborate new fashions with zeal. "It's mostly the young, though. Humans tend to sober up with age."

Mery-ra reached over and punched his son on the arm. "Like you and me, eh? Not an earring between us."

"Being unfashionable seems to be part of our patrimony, Father. Pipi's no better. We're disgraceful."

"I'll bet your friend Lord Ptah-mes was vain in his

youth. Look at what a dandy he still is," Mery-ra said with a chuckle.

Hani pursed his lips. "I'm not so sure. I think he's too proud to be vain."

"Oh? Are the two mutually exclusive?" Mery-ra asked with a lift of the eyebrows.

"The vain people I know are all signally lacking in self-confidence." Hani thought of Aha. "No, I think Ptah-mes sees sartorial elegance as a duty—to his family, perhaps. To his class."

Mery-ra eyed his son, considering. "That's very observant, my boy. I do believe you're right."

"He knows exactly who he is." *Although he doesn't like himself very much.*

"How's he doing up there at the ends of the world?" Mery-ra asked.

"I suppose I'll find out soon. I miss his sardonic humor. I'm dealing directly with the vizier until they install a new high commissioner, and Ra-nefer struck me as a pretty colorless fellow."

Mery-ra chuckled. "I could make a comment about the caliber of men Our Sun God tends to appoint to high office, but I won't."

Hani gave a snort of laughter. "Well done, Father. Somehow, you managed to do it without doing it. I wish our Neferet would learn such discretion."

"Whew." Mery-ra shook his head. "That was some story about the children in the quarry. Perhaps this happened under Neb-ma'at-ra, too, and we just weren't aware of it. Perhaps it always happens."

Hani made a noncommittal noise. He found himself

49

thinking longingly of the premature demise Neferet seemed to predict for the king, but then he repented. *Hani, you're a ba-a-d person.*

✦

The day of their departure was upon them, and with perfect symbolism, it was Wepet-renpet, New Year's Day. Maya would miss the celebrations with his family, but he found himself surprisingly eager for the journey. It had been several years since he'd visited the beautiful land of Djahy—*or Kharu*, he added with a silent chuckle. Maya joined Lord Hani at his gate, and the two men strode down to the quay with their mismatched strides, servants following with their baggage.

Maya breathed deeply of the baking air, rich with the earthy, slightly putrid smell of the River in flood. "It will be good to be abroad again, won't it, my lord?"

"It will, I suppose," Hani said, "although I must say I've rather enjoyed being back in Waset for the last few years." He grinned down at Maya. "You can't claim it's been boring."

Maya laughed, effervescent with the prospect of more adventures. "Never, in your company."

At the water's edge, they scouted out the military boat that was to convey their party up the River to a saltwater port. Their entourage—secretaries, translators, servants, and various specialists—were already aboard. Maya saw In-her-khau, his sometime nemesis, and slitted his eyes disdainfully as, in Hani's wake, he approached the man.

Hani waved from the shore, and he and Maya clumped together up the resounding boards of the gangplank. A contingent of soldiers waiting on board was to accompany them as an escort. Maya adjusted the writing case over his shoulder and stepped on board with panache. *I am the secretary of the Master of the King's Stable.* He'd treated himself to a nice expensive new wig in honor of his fresh borrowed glory.

The military vessel was sleek and low, with a broad sail—but on their northbound journey, that would be no use to them. Instead, the sailors knelt along the edge of the boat and extended their paddles into the water. Only thus could they outrun the surging current of the Inundation and maintain control of the boat. Lord Hani was busy greeting his staff, and Maya wandered off a bit. As he was gazing out over the River, he felt the jerk that told him the craft had been caught up in the stream, and away they flew. The white cubes of Waset slipped past along with the majestic pylons of the temples of Amen-Ra, soon to be swallowed up in the haze from the River. Hani had told him it was a good twelve days from Waset to the coast of the Great Green, but they would change to a seagoing ship at Peru-nefer, just north of Men-nefer.

Ah, it's good to have the wind on my face again! Maya fingered the gold amulet of Bes that hung from his neck. His mother had given it to him—her own handiwork—just before his last trip north, and it had saved his life. Who could say what dangers he would face this time?

⬥

They put in to the port of Azzati and traveled the short distance to the city proper with a caravan bringing supplies to the outpost. Accompanied by their troop of soldiers, they could travel no faster than a man could walk, and they found themselves surrounded by a landscape that was both bleak and verdant. The bare yellow brush-dotted rock of the place had been farmed into green fields and trees wherever water could be brought from cisterns or wadis that would soon run deep with rainwater. By the time they reached the low-slung town center of Azzati, Hani and his companions were pallid with dust and itchy from sweat.

The unwalled Egyptian outpost was a jumble of unimpressive native-style houses and a splendid public building or residence in the style of Kemet, blindingly whitewashed. Here and there, palms tossed in the hot wind. Hani's last trip to Azzati had been in the term of Lord Yanakh-amu. After Yanakh-amu's death, the post of high commissioner of Djahy had stood vacant until Ptah-mes had been sent in his place. For Ptah-mes, it had been intended as a place of exile, but Hani suspected the administration of the northern vassal kingdoms had at least been improved as a result of his coming.

"Here we are, my friend," he said to Maya, who—thanks to his diminutive size—had been able to share his litter. "It won't be long until we find out what we're doing here."

Maya looked eager—and then looked as if he were trying *not* to look eager. "That will be nice, my lord. Did the vizier purposely leave you in the dark, do you think, or did he not even know why you were being sent?"

"I wish I could say. However, our friend Ptah-mes will soon enlighten us."

They dismounted at the gate of the commissioner's residence—a proper Egyptian gate—and presented themselves to the porter. "Hani son of Mery-ra, joining the commissioner's staff as emissary," Hani said, pushing back his wig and mopping his forehead.

"Lord Maya is expecting you, my lord. One moment, please."

The man turned to go back inside the residence, but Hani, confused, called after him. "Maya, did you say? The commissioner isn't Lord Ptah-mes?"

"His name is Maya, my lord."

Hani and his secretary Maya exchanged a nonplussed look. *Has Ptah-mes been dismissed between the time I received my orders from Ra-nefer and now?*

"How long has this Maya been commissioner, my good man?" Hani persisted.

"Not long, my lord. Did you want to see him?"

"Of course, of course." Hani was left staring at the man's back as he clopped back to the doorway of the house. *How strange...*

Maya burst out, "What's this, Lord Hani? Didn't the vizier know there was a new commissioner? I thought Ra-nefer appointed him."

"He did. I hope nothing has happened to our friend since we left Waset."

Hani entered the building at the porter's heels, fighting off a sense of trepidation. Maya trooped in after him. They found themselves in the modest reception hall, with painted walls and high ceilings, which was refreshingly cool after the heat outside. Hani knew it well.

"One moment, my lord." The servant disappeared through the interior door, leaving Hani and Maya staring at each other in the half-light from the clerestory.

What has happened? What does this mean for our mission?

The servant reappeared, and with a bow, he said, "The commissioner will receive you."

Hani pushed open the heavy door and entered the commissioner's office. The latter, standing on his dais, had his back to the light. His face was in shadow, but his slim silhouette was altogether familiar. It was unmistakably Ptah-mes.

Hani's jaw dropped in surprise, and he cried out, "*You're* Maya, my lord?"

"Ah, Hani. It's been too long since I've seen you," Ptah-mes said. Hani made a deep obeisance, and when he rose, he found the commissioner standing over him, smiling. Ptah-mes extended his hand, and the two men clasped forearms with real affection. "Yes, I'm Maya. The 'pt' in 'Ptah' is apparently too difficult for the locals to pronounce, so they call me Atakh-maya. Since Maya was my childhood nickname, I've decided to become him while up here. His life was happier than mine."

Hani found it difficult to imagine that Ptah-mes was ever a child, let alone a child with a nickname. He shook his head and chuckled. "Well, that relieves me. I wasn't sure who I was going to encounter. I thought perhaps you'd been transferred and this Maya fellow had replaced you."

"No, no." Ptah-mes gestured Hani to a stool, and he took his own chair once more. "Much to his chagrin, I'm sure, the king seems to need my services. I am, in fact, still carrying out the same duties as before—but at a lower grade and lower pay."

Hani bit back a snort of disgust. *What sort of ruler would treat his talented servant so shamelessly?* He managed to say without inflection, "I wondered why no successor had been appointed as high commissioner. At least the vassals will have a competent intercessor."

"Although incompetence is a sort of hallowed tradition in the north. Have you met any of the regional commissioners?"

Hani shook his head.

"No doubt you remember Hotep." Ptah-mes laced together his fingers and rested his hands in his lap.

Hani rolled his eyes. Indeed, he did remember. A few years before, the lazy, unsoldierly commissioner of Ullaza had withdrawn all the garrison's troops to furnish himself with an escort, leaving the king of Kebni at the mercy of his enemies.

"He's still around. There's also a fellow called Amennefer at Kumidi, just northwest of Temesheq—when he deigns to be there."

"That name tells me something…" Hani said.

"You may have seen him at Waset or in the capital. He has one eye—hard to miss. Not a bad soldier but a wretch of a man, with a savage temper. His relationship with the natives could hardly be worse."

Hani gave a disgusted *psh* sound. "Just the sort you want to represent your kingdom abroad."

Ptah-mes sighed, a slight sarcastic smile on his lips.

Hani had to admit Ptah-mes looked well. *Age refines him, where it coarsens most of us.*

The commissioner seemed free of a certain tension that had marked him for years—the strain on his conscience. But there was a cold, dark, dangerous light in Ptah-mes's black eyes. The light lines that stretched from the wings of his nose to the corners of his mouth had deepened and etched his handsome face with a look of profound cynicism. This man was thoroughly disenchanted with life. Hani wondered what it must be like for such a cultured person to live in this bleak, rustic outpost. Certainly, he showed none of the signs of a functionary gone to seed that one saw altogether too frequently in foreign missions—wigs abandoned, shirts of dubious cleanliness, manners forgotten. Many of them seemed to fall to drinking. But Ptah-mes was not a man to relax his personal discipline a tittle. *He'll always represent us at our best.*

"The vizier gave me an assignment and said you could fill me in on it, my lord," Hani said.

"Yes. Actually, there is more than one assignment. But the obvious one is this: the king has finally decided that the restlessness of the vassals has gone too far. There have been defections to Kheta. Constant warfare among the small kingdoms themselves."

"Which Our Sun God has always encouraged. He's said it keeps them weaker."

"Indeed." Ptah-mes sniffed. "Only now, the received wisdom has it that that weakness is an open invitation to our Hittite friends. They've completely taken over the western half of Naharin, you know, with Prince Shuttarna as a puppet ruler in the east. But the real power is Shuppiluliuma's eldest son, Piyasshili, who is a sort of viceroy for his father at Karkemisa. That's not far from our borders."

Hani raised his eyebrows uneasily. "No indeed."

"The loss of Qidshu in particular would be catastrophic for strategic reasons, especially now." Ptah-mes lowered his eyes, but a thin, caustic smile made his feelings on the matter perfectly clear to Hani. "Nefer-khepru-ra's going to send troops up here at last. There will be war."

A thrill of relief mixed with reluctance raised the hairs on Hani's neck. Part of him wanted to cry, "Finally!" But he'd been in the army. War meant men would die. "If only old Rib-addi had lived to see it," he said, hoping things hadn't been permitted to slide to the point at which a war would be unwinnable.

"I needn't add that this is in large part a sop to the army, which has grown quite disenchanted with our foreign policy of neglect. They're chafing for war, and so they'll have one."

"I'm not shocked at all to hear that, my lord."

"And here's where you come in," Ptah-mes continued, leaning forward, his forearms across his knees. "Someone must be sure there will be provisions and water for our army on the march. It's a very long way to Kharu, and the generals want no surprises. Thirst is an enemy that superior forces can't overcome."

"I see, my lord. Am I to negotiate with the local kings, then? Assure they'll support us and not stab us in the back?"

Ptah-mes leaned back. "You understand me perfectly, my friend. I'll send emissaries to Hazzuru and Urusalim. Akhshaf isn't too far away either. But I need you to go inland, to Temesheq. Make sure the king there understands what we're asking of him and that he will comply. And no matter what he says, there's no guarantee of that. His neighbors are constantly accusing him of aggression and disloyalty, for whatever that's worth. He, in turn, will presumably notify the kinglets who are beholden to him."

He looked faintly sly. "I may be able to get Hotep out and someone capable in as commissioner of Ullaza."

Hani grinned. "If you could do nothing but that during your tenure, my lord, you would be worth your weight in gold."

Ptah-mes laughed and got to his feet, which Hani imitated. The commissioner's expression sobered. "There's something else, Hani. We've been receiving wild-eyed reports from some of our vassals inland that the *hapiru* are back in action, and they seem to be in the hire of Kheta."

"Aziru's people? I don't doubt that they are."

"These are different ones. Equally social outcasts and brigands, but they have no connection that I can see with our friend the king of A'amu. It's partly to counter them that Nefer-khepru-ra is sending troops. The *hapiru* have become very dangerous. They're coming close to taking cities."

"What can I do about them, my lord?" Hani asked.

"Talk to the kings up there. See if you can figure out what the city of Qidshu, for one, is up to. The town is absolutely critical to any movement of our troops inland through the pass from the coast. Their king seems to be wavering, although it's hard to sift truth from fiction when the kinglets let a constant barrage of complaints loose against one of theirs. We need a man on the ground."

Hani tipped his head in modest submission. "I'll do my best, my lord."

Ptah-mes's cool voice warmed. "Hani, my friend, my sources tell me that the king has recognized you with the gold of honor. I'm sorry I wasn't there to celebrate with you."

A hot flush of embarrassment lit Hani's cheeks. *This should be something I'm proud of, but instead, I feel I need to apologize.* "I confess to a certain amount of suspicion, my lord. There must be some ulterior motive."

"I don't know. It seems normal to recognize a lifetime of important service."

Which the king has pointedly denied you, Hani thought, pained. "I can't see myself ever wearing the *shebyu*. I feel like it's somehow dishonest."

"There's always some royal self-interest, of course. Fortunately, I received mine from the hand of the Osir Neb-ma'at-ra. It makes it less of an issue of conscience to wear them. Although it's amazing how the conscience can be rocked to sleep." He gave Hani a thin quirked smile.

Hani heaved a sigh. *He still can't forgive himself his collaboration.*

After a moment of uncomfortable silence, Ptah-mes sighed and clapped Hani on the shoulder. "Do you and your men have accommodations? I recommend you stay at the residence. I can't vouch for the quality of the natives' hospitality. And there's still plague around up here."

"At home, too, alas. I'll walk warily and trust myself to the benevolence of the gods." Hani fixed the commissioner with an amicable eye. "I accept your offer with gratitude."

Ptah-mes gave him a shy twitch at the corner of his mouth, and with a bow, Hani took his leave.

As soon as the door had closed behind Hani, Maya popped up from the floor. "Do we have our orders, Lord Hani?" he asked eagerly.

"Both the public ones and the private ones. Oh, and, Maya, my boy—the commissioner Maya is none other than our friend, Lord Ptah-mes. That was his childhood nickname."

Maya's eyes popped. He looked around in stunned pride. "He's a Maya too?"

"I think it's a common enough sobriquet for people whose name ends in *mes*." Hani clapped his secretary on the back. "But clearly, gentlemen of the best taste are inclined toward it." He grinned down at Maya, who laughed delightedly and stuck out his chest in satisfaction.

"Wait till I tell Sat-hut-haru about this."

Chuckling, Hani led the way into the street. He would round up his staff and see about rooms for them all. Then they could bathe and set themselves in order. He had a lot of journeys ahead of him, and he suspected that he should get about them expeditiously, before laziness overtook him. Once, he'd taken such trips for granted—shuttling back and forth from one little kingdom to another, undergoing the weariness and inconvenience of travel—without a second thought. Now he found the prospect distasteful. Perhaps the four years he'd worked from home had spoiled him, or perhaps he was just growing older. *I'm fifty now,* he reminded himself. *No longer a youth all eager for adventure, like Maya.*

The commissioner's majordomo met Hani's party in the courtyard. "I can take you to your rooms, my lord," he said with a bow. He looked like a Djahyite but was dressed in the Egyptian fashion and spoke the language flawlessly.

"Thank you, my man. I think we're all ready for a bath and a little sweet oil on our hides."

The servant led the way from one building to another within the walled enclosure. Hani could see that instead of being a single edifice, as he'd always thought, the residence was really a compound of many buildings. He'd never penetrated so far. Most of the structures were probably administrative offices and military barracks, but the tallest was distinctly house-like. It was a far cry from the splendor of Ptah-mes's ancestral villa in Waset, or even his "modest place" in Akhet-aten, but it had that certain dignity that even remote outposts of the Two Lands maintained—and Azzati was what might be called the capital of administration in the north.

The majordomo showed Hani and Maya to contiguous rooms and ushered the rest of the staff into a suite down the corridor from them. "I hope you find everything to your satisfaction, my lord. Dinner will be served at sundown. And Lord Maya invites you personally to dine with him, Lord Hani, if you choose."

"I'd be delighted. We're old friends." He saw the other Maya's eager face fall, so he flashed him a helpless shrug that said, *What can we do?*

That night, Ptah-mes managed to serve a superb dinner that might have taken place in some aristocratic salon in Waset. Hani wondered if he'd brought his own cook from home. After the last bone had been picked and the last sweet cake drowned in the exquisite wine of Kebni, the two men retreated to the bare little garden of the residence and seated themselves at ease in the perfumed twilight of late summer. The crickets had begun to pulse in the bushes.

"How do you like the new vizier, Lord Ra-nefer?" Ptah-mes asked.

It had grown too dark for Hani to see Ptah-mes's face well, so he wasn't sure if the question was sincere or sarcastic. "I'm having trouble making up my mind, my lord. I certainly have nothing against him yet, as I've only met him once. He seemed a little... vague. He's relatively new in office, and I'm sure it's not easy to become informed about everything at once."

"You're being charitable, Hani. The man's an idiot who is concerned for nothing but his own health. I only hope he has a good staff, or the Lower Kingdom will be in shambles in no time." There was a hard edge to the commissioner's voice. He'd never suffered fools gladly.

"I'll do my best to work with him," Hani said mildly.

"In words, agree, but in action, be prepared to correct his mistakes. That's what I do. He's happy enough to accept the credit when your deeds are successful." Ptah-mes was silent for a moment. Then he said in a lighter tone, "I'm sending a young military officer with you to Qidshu. He's slated to lead the invasion force, so he'll have a better idea about exactly what the army will need on their march. And his men can serve as an escort. I don't think you should encounter any trouble, but one never knows."

"Thank you, my lord. How soon do you foresee us leaving?"

"Whenever we can fit you out. I don't know what supplies you brought from home, but we can certainly provide for your staff whatever is needed."

Hani expressed his gratitude warmly. At last, Ptah-mes rose, and Hani followed.

"I suppose we should get to bed, since tomorrow is likely to be busy." Ptah-mes extended a hand to Hani, who clasped it with real affection. "It's good to see you again, my friend."

"Indeed. You seem well, my lord, if not happy. I hope the posting agrees with you."

"Well enough. I'm accustomed to solitude. Perhaps it's less painful in a setting where there are no sights to... to remind me." His voice wavered, and Hani understood that he was thinking of his wife, the Osir Apeny.

"Thank you for your hospitality yet again, Lord Ptah-mes. I'm substantially indebted to you."

Ptah-mes brushed off that acknowledgment with a gracious nod. "And I to you."

CHAPTER 3

To Hani's surprise, the commanding officer of the invasion force was Pa-aten-em-heb. The young man's face brightened at the sight of Hani, and he plowed through the crowd of soldiers toward the scribe, his arms extended. "Lord Hani! What a pleasure! Are we to be working together up here?"

The two men embraced. Hani eyed Pa-aten-em-heb up and down. He was the very picture of martial good looks in his scale corselet and pointy-aproned military kilt.

"We are, we are," Hani said. "You and I are going to visit the kings of Djahy and Kharu and secure their help for our forces. You'll know better than I what sort of provisions to demand."

"Water above all," said Pa-aten-em-heb without hesitation. "We have reservoirs along the route on the Royal Way and the Way of Haru, but once we strike off inland, it's risky. Some little village well isn't going to satisfy the whole army."

"Be prepared to argue with the same eloquence before

our local mayors." Hani's smile faded. "To be honest, I have more doubts about some of our commissioners than I do about the vassals."

"I know none of them," Pa-aten-em-heb admitted.

"There's a Hotep in Ullaza. He's as corrupt as they come. In Kumidi, it's Amen-nefer, and I've heard no good about him either."

The officer looked up at Hani, a cold light of recognition flickering in his eyes. "Amen-nefer? The one-eyed man?"

"I believe so, yes. I haven't met him yet." Hani sensed a history behind this reaction. "Do you know him?"

"There can't be two of them. It must be him." Pa-aten-em-heb was breathing heavily, his lips pressed thin with the effort not to speak. Hani waited in silence until the young officer blurted, "I'll rip out his throat with my teeth if you leave me alone with him, Lord Hani. I'd better warn you."

Iy! Hani thought, surprised. *He hates the man's very name. I wonder what's behind this?* Laying a hand on the officer's arm, he said, "Do you need to tell me something, my friend?"

Pa-aten-em-heb seemed to debate with himself, then he said in a low voice, "Is there a private place we can go, my lord?"

Hani led him into the darkened reception hall. It was as hushed as a temple, with the same powdery smell of enclosure and incense. An oblique ray of light, dancing with motes, filtered down from the clerestory just enough to make it possible to walk without stumbling.

In a kindly voice, Hani said, "What is it, my boy?"

Pa-aten-em-heb spoke so low Hani could barely hear him, and the officer's words trembled with rage. "I almost hesitate to tell you this, since you're the father of daughters, my lord. That misbegotten son of a jackal once courted my sister. This was seven years ago or more. She repulsed him, and in retaliation, he raped and battered her. He slashed her face so savagely that she'll never recover. She, who was so beautiful before, is now too appalling to look at. He took away her every hope of happiness." He closed his eyes as if to blot out the memory of that terrible crime. "The shock and humiliation led to my father's death. Amen-nefer is evil in the flesh."

Hani's hair stood up on the back of his neck. "May the Hidden One protect us. I've never heard such a story. Surely, you took him to law—how is it the man isn't breaking rocks in some quarry in the desert? Yet here he is, a commissioner." Bitterness overwhelmed him like a choking wave. "What kind of world is this where the evil are rewarded?" *But there will be a reckoning at the Weighing of the Heart.*

Pa-aten-em-heb shook his head slowly. His mouth was a hard slash, and his eyes, in the semidarkness, were like pools of night. "It's a world ruled by a heretic, Lord Hani. A world that has lost the favor of the gods. It must come to an end."

"Do you think you can do this job, son? Do your... your convictions come between you and your duty? We may have to defend this terrible man."

"I serve the Two Lands, my lord. Whatever I feel toward the king and his minions, I'll carry out my commands. Until..."

Until the day comes when the Crocodiles crawl out of the water. Hani, too, awaited that hour.

He clapped Pa-aten-em-heb on the shoulder, and the two men made their way out onto the porch. Hani's eyes were dazzled by the sunlight, but his heart was in shadow.

He said finally, changing the subject, "So you're head of the entire invasion force? You must have been promoted since I saw you last."

Pa-aten-em-heb forced a smile. "I have been, Lord Hani. No more standard-bearer of the Pacifier of the Aten company. I'm a regiment commander now. I understand you've been honored as well."

"Yes," Hani said reluctantly and dropped his eyes. "I feel a little guilty accepting honors at the king's hand while... you know." They were both opposed to the royal reforms.

"I didn't refuse a promotion at his hands either," Pa-aten-em-heb assured him. "It's important to have solid men in high places."

Hani nodded and said more loudly, "Good for you, my boy. That speaks well for our chances of success." He clapped the officer on the back in honest delight. "I don't suppose my son has come with you..."

"Why, yes, he has. How remiss of me not to mention it. Pa-kiki's here. I'm sure you'll want to see each other."

"Indeed. I guess he's all excited to be sent abroad on a campaign. I wonder if he knows he'll be expected to wander the battlefield after the slaughter and tally up the severed hands of the enemy."

"Or penises." Pa-aten-em-heb laughed. "I was only a lad when I started following my father out on such forays. It was pretty grisly the first few times."

"Were you a military scribe, then?" Hani asked in surprise.

"Yes, I was. Eventually, I had the chance to pass into the ranks, and so I did. Pa-kiki is talking about doing the same some day, but it's a little harder if you don't have relatives in the army."

"In fact, both I and my father were military scribes. But then, you know my father already."

Pa-aten-em-heb turned to Hani, his eyebrows raised and a warm grin of solidarity on his face. *I've clearly given the secret password*, Hani thought. He eyed the young officer. Pa-aten-em-heb was a solidly built, good-looking young man with a chiseled face that reminded Hani a bit of Ptah-mes but broader, with heavier features. His earlier grimness had disappeared into delight.

"I do, of course, but I didn't realize you had served in the military too. I look forward to working with you, my lord—getting to know you better."

"And I you, my boy."

The two men clasped forearms, and Pa-aten-em-heb made his way with brisk steps toward the garrison building. Hani smiled fondly after him. Then he remembered that at the time of their first meeting, the officer's wife had been undergoing a difficult pregnancy. *I should have asked if she had the baby safely.*

⁂

That evening, as Maya and Lord Hani discussed their mission and, side by side in Hani's room, packed the last of their things, a knock at the door interrupted them.

"I'll get it, my lord." Maya bounded over to the door and swung it open.

His brother-in-law stood in the doorway. "Maya!"

"Pa-kiki!" Maya cried at the same time.

"Is Father here?"

"Of course, my boy. Come in." Maya stepped back and let the young scribe enter. Pa-kiki was nearly ten years his junior, and while Maya had no love for Lord Hani's firstborn, he held young Pa-kiki in brotherly affection.

From within the room, Hani cried out happily, "Son!" He lumbered to the open door, and the two men embraced while Maya looked on benevolently.

"I can't believe we're going on a mission together, Father!" There was an earnest enthusiasm about the youth that made Maya want to protect him, although Hani was certainly adequate to that task. Maya thought of his father-in-law as a rock of security, as solid as he appeared to be—broad, heavy, and firmly rooted. A man felt safe in every sense under the protection of the diplomat.

Hani beamed, his little brown eyes crinkling. "I don't think this happens very often. I certainly never worked with Father once I was grown and independently employed. It's a wonderful gift of the gods, eh, son? Thanks be to Montu."

"We're just here on a sort of reconnaissance now—to check out the route and be sure there are enough supplies. But in a year or so, we should be coming back with a full regiment, ready to whip the minions of those vile Hittites into line."

Hani threw back his head and laughed. "I hope you're just as enthusiastic on the way back. That first battle can be disillusioning."

"I'm ready, Papa—er, Father."

Two days after that, Hani and Maya, too, were ready—their supplies packed, the staff gathered, the donkeys loaded for the short trip to the port—when Lord Ptah-mes summoned Hani back to the commissioner's residence. Curious, Hani waited until his superior opened the door to the office.

With a dry smile, Ptah-mes bade Hani enter. "I'm sorry to jerk you back at the last minute, my friend," he said, walking into the interior of the room where his chair sat on its dais. "But we have some visitors with information that may be useful to you."

"Ah?"

Ptah-mes drew aside his skirts and took a seat, crossing his legs. "An emissary of the king of Urusalim, who has an interesting report. And another from Qeden, to the north. I think you'll find what they have to say useful." He called out to his doorkeeper to admit the men, and before long, the two diplomats entered. They were dressed in the colorful fashion of Djahy, with long, patterned, tight-sleeved tunics, wrapped around with fringed shawls.

They must be dying in this heat, Hani said to himself.

They both made a deep obeisance to Ptah-mes, who said, "Tell Lord Hani what you told me about what's happening. He's here to set things right in the king's name."

One of the emissaries stepped forward. He was in his late fifties or even a bit older, with grizzled hair and beard that gave him a calm, venerable appearance that was belied by his bright, angry black eyes. He spoke in Egyptian. "I am the emissary of King Abdi-hepa of Urusalim, my lord. He wants you to know that the Egyptian troops to the north of us are far from loyal to Our Sun God—life, prosperity, and health be to him. They have been fraternizing with the *hapiru* and have even been identified among their troops when our cities have been raided."

Hani let out a whistle and cast a glance at Ptah-mes. *In the heart of our vassal territory.* "Where do you think they're coming from, my lord?" he asked the Djahyite neutrally.

"Somewhere on the banks of the Yardon River. It's very sparsely settled out there, and they can hide their encampments with ease in the thickets."

"And how do you know that there were Egyptians among them?"

"We have informers, loyal soldiers from your garrison, who reported their fellows," the man said. "And I've seen them myself. They had the physical appearance of your people, and they were dressed in their military uniforms. It was very confusing to the troops on our side, you may imagine."

Hani turned to his superior, curious. "Did the soldiers report this to you, Lord Ptah-mes?"

Ptah-mes, never taking his eyes from the emissary, shook his head slowly.

"Is there anything else I should know?" Hani asked the Djahyite.

"No, my lord. Only I beg you, send us more troops. The *hapiru* become bolder and bolder, and their numbers continue to grow. The more they appear to be winning, the more temptation it is for our soldiers and yours to go over to their side."

Hani nodded and thanked the man, then the other

emissary stepped forward with a bow. "I am the spokesman of Akizzi, king of Qeden, my lord." The Qedenite was a small, spare person who must have been fortyish, no more. One eyelid fluttered nervously as he spoke. "Our king wants you to know that King Aitakkama of Qidshu is up to no good. Aitakkama unashamedly abets the *hapiru* in their attacks on our cities and gives them sanctuary when we go after them."

Ptah-mes caught Hani's eye and lifted an eyebrow.

"My lord knows the importance of the pass from the coast inland that Qidshu guards," the Qedenite added a bit desperately.

"I do," Hani agreed. This was disturbing news indeed, with an invasion force poised to attack. Pa-aten-em-heb and his men would approach by ship to Kebni or some other port and march inland to the strongholds of the *hapiru* through precisely that pass. It wouldn't be hard for brigands to hold them back by hiding in the forested mountains that flanked it.

As if he had read Hani's mind, Ptah-mes said, "These gentlemen are aware of the impending war, Hani." He turned to the two Djahyites. "And I believe they are fully committed to support us."

"Absolutely, Lord Commissioner. Our army is yours to command, and we will open our granaries to you," said the older of the two, bowing with a flourish.

"Likewise Qeden, my lord," said the other man. "We can provide you with scouts who know the area near the inland border."

"Very well," said Ptah-mes. "Your testimony is valuable

and will be remembered. Unless you have questions, Hani, that will be all for these venerable emissaries."

Hani, his heart in a turmoil of suspicion, indicated that he'd heard all he needed to, and the two men took their leave, backing from Ptah-mes's presence in a low bow.

Ptah-mes turned to Hani. "It sounds as if the rumors of Qidshu's defection are true."

"I thought Shuttatarna, the old king, was loyal to us. The Hittites actually captured him and his family at some point, did they not?" Hani was still trying to make sense of the situation.

"They did," Ptah-mes said. "And after he died in captivity, they turned his son back over to rule Qidshu, as a gesture of their benevolent intentions."

"And he continued as a loyal vassal of ours..."

"Until he didn't. Technically, he still belongs to us, not to Kheta Land, but if he's abetting the *hapiru*—"

"Who seem to be supported by the Hittites," Hani interposed with a significant look at his superior.

Ptah-mes tipped his head in assent. "Then we may question his loyalty, may we not? Perhaps it's time for a regime change in Qidshu. You might remind Aitakkama of that possibility when you see him."

"I'll do that, my lord." Hani grinned. The two men clasped forearms, and Hani took his leave.

"Don't hesitate to write if anything develops," Ptah-mes called after him.

Hani found Maya—the other Maya—waiting in the reception hall, a scrap of papyrus on his knees, upon which he was writing busily. He bounded to his feet at Hani's approach, a barely contained expression of wide-eyed curiosity on his face.

"Some very interesting information for our journey," Hani said as they set off for the courtyard where their caravan was formed up. "Firsthand testimony that Qidshu's up to no good."

"The wretches," Maya said with savage satisfaction. "Just as we suspected, eh, my lord?"

"Let's just say I think Pa-aten-em-heb will have something to sink his teeth into when he comes with the army."

That officer was standing in the shade of a covered oxcart, his arms crossed, gazing patiently out over the milling people and animals that awaited Hani's return. Pa-aten-em-heb waved as the two scribes approached.

"We can leave anytime, if your men are ready," Hani called.

Pa-aten-em-heb disappeared around the corner of the wagon, and Hani could hear him bellowing out orders. He rejoined Hani and Maya as they were mounting their litter. "Anything I should know about?" he asked pleasantly.

"Indeed," Hani said with a significant lift of the eyebrow. "I'll tell you when we're on board the ship."

The officer made a little bow of his head, and a moment later, he drove past them in his chariot, swallowing the litter in a cloud of pale dust.

Maya chuckled. "You should have seen us in Lord Ptah-mes's chariot, my lord—that day we went to the police barracks, looking for you. It was quite an experience! There's nobody like Lord Ptah-mes for freezing a person in their tracks with one haughty look."

"I can well imagine it," Hani said, amused. "You recounted it very effectively for the family afterward. Your tales are becoming quite polished, Maya. I think you may have a second career waiting for you: village storyteller!"

Maya's smile grew fixed. *He's trying to figure out if I'm serious or not*, Hani thought with affection.

"Do you think it's inappropriate, Lord Hani?" the little man asked anxiously. "I had planned to write all our adventures down and thought I could test the effect on people. I don't want to embarrass you in any way. If you think it's unbecoming for a scribe..."

"Never, son. I admire your way with words. And Neferet's pantomime added to the effect, I have to say. She does our friend Ptah-mes quite well—and Mahu." *The bastard.* Mahu was the head of the royal police, with whom Hani had tangled with some frequency.

"No doubt," Maya said tartly. "That girl's not happy unless she's the center of attention."

Hani shook his head with a knowing smile. Maya was another one who didn't care to be overshadowed. But the thought of Neferet reminded Hani of the news she'd revealed to them about the king's health. Yet again, Hani's throat constricted with foreboding. Dark times were surely ahead for the Two Lands.

Once they were at sea, the heat abated, and at times, the wind blew almost chilly. But the freshness was welcome. Hani drew in a huge breath, savoring the inimitable salty, slightly fishy smell of the waves. It cleared the nose with a satisfying tingle. What a mysterious thing all that water was—clear and aquamarine as untinted glass, growing darker and darker as it sank from the light but never still. It was as if it were alive, with its swirling mesh of foam like hair. He watched the gulls dipping and swooping and floating in the air just off the gunwales of the ship, their yellow eyes fixed on him, hopeful for a treat. Sometimes he held out a piece of bread to them, and one would snatch it greedily from his hand before its fellows attacked and tried to wrest it from him. *Like Kemet and Kheta trying to snap up each other's vassals,* he thought in rueful amusement.

At his side, Pa-aten-em-heb and Maya stood. The officer, forearms resting on the wicker gunwales, was also watching the birds, but Maya, his arms crossed, had his back to them and was gazing pensively across the deck crowded with scribes and soldiers. A serious expression sat heavily upon his face. *No doubt, he's composing the most dramatic way to describe the voyage.*

"Let me bring you up to date with what I learned before we left," Hani said to the young officer. "The *hapiru* have showed up almost as far south as Urusalim. The king's emissary said they were encamped along the Yardon River. Do you know the area at all?"

"I don't, my lord—only the coast. That's why it seemed important that I make this little reconnaissance."

"In addition, Qidshu seems to be abetting the *hapiru* in attacking vassal cities. And worse still, Egyptian soldiers have been seen among the *hapiru*."

Pa-aten-em-heb stared at Hani in disbelief. "How do these people know they were Egyptian soldiers?"

"They were dressed in their uniforms."

The officer lowered his eyes, and Hani could see the

muscles of his jaw clench. "Then one of the garrisons must have gone over. I wonder why."

"I wonder whose," Hani said quietly. The two men locked eyes.

"Lord Hani, I think we're approaching the port," Maya called out excitedly at Hani's other elbow.

Hani, Maya, and the officer crossed to the landward side of the ship, where a multitude of the staff was hanging on the gunwales, staring and pointing. On the coast, misty with distance, stood the white cubes of a city. It was Beruta, their destination, the closest point of disembarkation for Temesheq, some fifty *iteru*s inland.

"I've always been surprised so few of these cities up here are walled," said Maya. "They seem to attack each other all the time."

Pa-aten-em-eb smiled grimly. "We won't let them build walls—that's why. If they could keep each other out, they could keep us out too."

Maya raised his eyebrows as if considering this reality.

"I'd like to move on to Temesheq as soon as we're able to reprovision," Hani said to Pa-aten-em-heb.

A niggle of anxiety gnawed at Hani. Things were more complicated up here than they'd seemed, the lines between the loyal and the self-serving more porous. He wasn't sure the *hapiru*, a stateless collection of outcasts and outlaws, would be impressed with his *shebyu* collars.

The shoreline grew closer and sharper, forming into a ledge of white stone and dark-green trees. Several large jagged rocks thrust up from the harbor—monstrous fangs. The city itself clustered densely at the edge of the sea like crystals of salt, with a palace farther up the slope and the towers of several temples. On his last trip down the coast of Fenkhu, Hani had tried to tempt an assassination by mounting a solitary expedition to the marshes from Beruta—but he and Maya hadn't ever actually reached them.

The recollection reawakened in him a childlike desire to see the marsh birds. "You know, Maya, we never got out to the River Natanu to see the birds."

Maya rolled his eyes, no doubt remembering how close they'd come to death.

"You like birds?" asked Pa-aten-em-heb.

"I do." A hot wave of embarrassment flushed Hani's cheeks. He suspected that people always found this love of the avian race amusing.

"You should come see the birds on the lake at Pa-yom. There are flamingos. It's quite a sight when they all take off at once."

"Next time I'm in Hut-nen-nesut, I'll be sure to get out there," Hani assured him with genuine eagerness. He turned back to the shore, which was drawing rapidly closer. "Maya, let's get our things ready. We'll be disembarking soon." He pulled back from the gunwales and led the way to the little curtained pavilion that was serving as a cabin for them, while the young officer set off in turn to organize his men.

"What are we doing here again, my lord?" Maya asked as they strapped down their wicker baskets and gathered the leather pouches that would keep documents dry.

Hani gave a snort. "I think our mission is evolving after what those two emissaries said the other day. We need to find out what Aitakkama of Qidshu is up to. And whose troops have defected to the *hapiru*. And when we find the turncoat, we'll probably have to take him prisoner."

✦

It was several days' journey through rough country before they reached Temesheq. The heat had increased with every step away from the coast, and except for the fields irrigated by the Abana River, it had the look of a high, arid place. One could still see the hazy purple mountains not far to the west. As they clopped through the narrow streets, Hani spotted a kite circling far overhead, its forked tail graceful, its pinions strong.

They were met at the palace by the king himself, Biryawaza, who prostrated himself before the emissary of the Great King of the Two Lands, murmuring protestations of his loyalty. Experience had made Hani a little skeptical of such elaborate displays.

Biryawaza was a tall, florid man, probably Hurrian in origin, with a wild head of graying curls—balding on the crown—and a beard to match. He was perhaps Hani's age and well built although inclining to stoutness. His eyes were greenish brown, heavy lidded, and shrewd. *This man is no fool*, Hani warned himself. *He's had plenty of experience ingratiating himself with authorities while giving no more than he had to.* Hani recalled that when he'd visited Temesheq some years before in search of Aziru, Biryawaza had absented himself.

"Welcome to my kingdom, which belongs loyally to Our Sun God," the king said once he'd regained his feet. "I look forward to being of service. The favor of our king is the breath of life to my nostrils."

"Excellent," Hani replied with his most amiable smile. "We have much to discuss. I'm sure you have requests, as do I. Our cooperation is mutually beneficial."

"That goes without saying, Lord Hani." Biryawaza's eyes flickered to the *shebyu* collars piled around Hani's neck, and Hani thought, with satisfaction, that he'd done well to wear them after all.

"Can I have my servants show you to your lodgings? I hope they'll meet with your approval. We are, after all, but a small country and poor, compared to the fabulous wealth of the Two Lands."

"I'm sure they'll be fine. Our military escort will garrison with your soldiers."

Biryawaza called out to his majordomo to escort the honored visitors away. Hani glanced backward and saw him watching them with narrowed eyes and hands folded in subservience.

I just don't trust him.

But the accommodations were, in fact, quite pleasant. The room was on the north side of the palace and cool even in the midday heat, its tall windows letting in plenty of breeze. Outside, a garden lazed in the sun, with high black cypresses and silver-green palms. The downside was that Maya seemed to be quartered in the same room.

Maya stared around him with a critical twist of the mouth. "I'm trying to decide what these digs say about our host," he said, unhitching his writing case from his shoulder. "He wants to look impeccable, but there's that little jab of inconvenience."

"Well observed, my friend. Still, you must realize that Temesheq is but a small, poor country, compared to the fabulous wealth of the Two Lands." Hani gave his secretary a crooked little smile, and Maya snorted.

"I have yet to meet one of these Northerners I'd trust to give me a shave."

Hani threw back his head and laughed. "Anybody with the least smidgen of power has an agenda—and it's probably not the same as ours. However, we've already learned something, and that is there may be a little truth to some of the complaints of Biryawaza's neighbors. Our plan to have him contact all his subordinate kinglets may not be as sound as we'd hoped. I've suspected for a long time that he's a bit too close to Aziru and his brigands. Pardon—former brigands, since our friend Aziru is now the king of a legitimate country."

"Lord Ptah-mes will know what to do."

"He will indeed. Let's send him our first impressions." Hani crossed his legs and sank to the floor, and Maya plopped down beside him. The secretary set out his ink blocks, wet them, and chewed the end on a fresh reed, and Hani said, "Ready to take dictation?"

CHAPTER 4

AFTER SEVERAL WEEKS OF CONFERENCES with Biryawaza, Maya's opinion had hardened. The mayor-king of Temesheq was a smooth, opportunistic man. He was probably a good administrator of his kingdom, Upi, which was thriving, but he was full of promises to his suzerain while managing few concrete actions. In private, Lord Hani had wondered aloud if it had been a good idea to move the regional commissariat from Temesheq to Kumidi. While the latter was, admittedly, not far away, the hovering presence of an Egyptian commissioner in his own city might have encouraged the king to more sincere obedience. *And yet, so far, alas, we don't have any real proof of his disloyalty—it's more the impression we get, mixed with the complaints of his neighbors.*

Lord Hani and the king—*You're nothing but a mayor*—were sitting in a small but lavishly decorated room that was perhaps meant as a council chamber. Maya alone accompanied them, recording the conversation as accurately as possible because Hani very much suspected betrayal at some point and wanted everything on record.

"Lord Hani, I will, of course send word to my dependents that Our Sun God—life, health, and prosperity be his—wants supply depots for his army." Biryawaza flashed Hani the cold smile of a crocodile as he straightened his sleeves.

Hani smiled back blandly. "Commander Pa-aten-em-heb would like to accompany your envoy to see the locales for himself, if that's no inconvenience. He'll know better than I what the army will need."

Maya scribbled away, but he continued to shoot glances at Hani and the king.

"Of course, my lord." Despite the gracious acquiescence, Biryawaza's hardened mouth betrayed an almost invisible hitch of annoyance.

In fact, Maya found himself watching the man's body language as closely as he was listening to his words—it seemed far more honest. Biryawaza had the build of a comfortably stout middle-aged man, but his forearms were corded and powerful when they emerged from his sleeves, and the undersides of his thick fingers were yellow with calluses. *This fellow has seen more than his share of battle. I wonder whose side he was on.*

"Before we leave you, I want to mention something that has troubled your neighbors, my lord. There are rumors that you've been less than aggressive toward the *hapiru*, from whom you're expected to defend your region—"

"Nonsense." Biryawaza was already expostulating before Hani could finish. "We've reduced their numbers substantially. Who told you that?"

"And that you've even sheltered them when they were pursued by neighbors' forces," Hani finished.

But the king was having none of it. "Let whoever told you that come and say it to my face. He dares not—because he's lying." He drew back in his chair, swelling in righteous indignation, but his greenish eyes were calculating.

This is bravado, but not out of fear. He's sure it can never be proved.

"I only report what others have told me, Lord Biryawaza." Hani smiled genially—no one could remain defensive before such a smile. "It's for you to think about what might have led to such a perception and to regularize it. Of course, you want to stay in the good graces of the Sun God our master, in appearance as well as reality." Hani rose to his feet, and Biryawaza had to follow perforce.

"Of course." The mayor of Temesheq dipped his head in a respectful bow, but Maya asked himself if the complaisance were not a little overdone.

"We'll meet again at least once before my party leaves. Give some consideration to any requests you would like to make," Hani said and made as if to go.

This isn't a groveling man. He doesn't like being made to truckle. Maya laid aside his writing materials and rose from where he sat cross-legged on the floor. He waited, hands on hips, watching loftily, until Biryawaza had backed from the room—just to make it clear that he, Maya, wasn't a mere lackey.

Once the mayor's footsteps could be heard echoing far down the corridor, Maya said acidly, "Oh no, he's never done anything wrong."

Lord Hani laughed. "Pa-aten-em-heb is going to feel

out the smaller states about their readiness to assist our army, so that leaves you and me some time to investigate our friend the king. I'd like to know if it was his men who were seen fighting alongside the *hapiru*. We certainly know that he and Aziru are friendly."

"Does he have Egyptian troops?"

"A few."

"Well, then," Maya said with a sniff. "We can be sure they were his."

But Hani tilted his head thoughtfully. "Let's wait for the evidence before judging, my friend. There's more than one disloyal vassal around here."

The two men made their way from the council room onto the shady porch framed by two stone columns. A pair of Pa-aten-em-heb's soldiers stood guard on either side, no doubt grateful to be posted in the cool. Beyond the shadows, the paved courtyard was radiating with heat. Maya visored his eyes with a hand and looked around, but Biryawaza had already disappeared from sight.

Lord Hani led the way back toward their residence in the palace, his broad back casting a shadow that sheltered the secretary from the sun. Maya found himself imitating his father-in-law's rolling gait, adding a bit of his own swagger, but then he forced himself to stop—it was a little too much like a parade of ducks.

They hadn't gone far when a soldier came running up and sank breathlessly to his knee before Hani. "My lord," he panted. "An urgent message from the high commissioner, Lord Maya." He held out a packet of papyrus tied with a sealed cord, which Hani accepted.

It took Maya a moment to remember who *Lord Maya*

was, and by that time, Hani was folding up the letter. He turned to Maya and said grimly, "Ptah-mes says he's been recalled to Kemet for an audience with the king. Meanwhile, there's been a murder of a Babylonian diplomat at Kumidi, and he wants us to investigate in his absence."

"Phew," whistled Maya, partly horrified and partly exhilarated at the prospect of an investigation. "Someone killed a foreign diplomat? What's the world coming to?"

To the messenger, Hani said, "Thank you, son. I guess there's no point in sending a reply if the high commissioner has left for home." He slipped a faience ring from his finger and pressed it into the youth's hand.

The soldier rose and slapped his chest with a fist in a salute of grateful acknowledgment. As he jogged away, Hani exchanged a serious look with Maya. "Burna-buriash, the king of Sangar, is an irascible old curmudgeon. He may start a war."

Maya widened his eyes. "What's he going to say when he sees our troops coming up here to the eastern border? Will he believe we're aiming at the *hapiru*?"

"You know, my friend, I'm almost as uneasy about the fact that Ptah-mes has been summoned to an audience. He hasn't been back for two years. Why now all of a sudden?" Hani seemed pensive, his thickety brows knotted. Then he brightened and flashed Maya one of his conspiratorial grins, baring the gap between his front teeth. "This may be the adventure you wanted. Come on, son. It's away to Kumidi."

He set off at a brisk clip toward their lodgings, and Maya trotted alongside, his writing case bobbing against his shoulder. *War with Sangar? But no one could blame the*

Babylonians, really. By all the gods, who could have done such a thing? Diplomats are sacrosanct. "Could it have been some brigand who killed the man, my lord? One of the *hapiru* perhaps?"

"We'll find out, Maya." After a minute, Lord Hani added, "Here's the murder I've been expecting."

"Expecting?" Maya was nonplussed. To him, this was the most unforeseen turn of events he could have imagined.

Hani said darkly, "You've never noticed how violent deaths spring up wherever I set my feet? I'm beginning to think I'm responsible in some way."

"Oh no, my lord!" cried Maya earnestly. "It's just that you're sent to investigate them."

Hani chuckled, and Maya realized with a burn of embarrassment that his father-in-law had been teasing. They regained their corridor in the royal residence, and Hani banged on the door where his staff was holed up. The frizzy-haired lower secretary, In-her-khau, opened to them, and when he saw it was his master, he bowed low.

But Hani wasted no time in polite exchanges. "We're heading to Kumidi immediately. Pack up everything and get down to the courtyard."

"Yes, my lord." In-her-khau cast a quick glance at Maya, who stood with his arms crossed and his chin lifted. Maya took pains to seem frosty toward In-her-khau, who was his inferior at work if not by birth.

Then he and Hani stalked back to the bedchamber assigned to them. Hani began pulling clothes out of the press and stuffing them into his traveling basket. "I need a valet."

Maya secretly thought that was a terrible idea. If there

were anyone more intimate with a man than his secretary, it was his valet. "I could do that for you, my lord," he offered.

"It's all done, but thank you, friend. Now, pack yourself up, and we're off to Kumidi."

＊

It was a hard two days' journey northwest through the mountains to the town of the regional commissioner. Kumidi sat at the eastern edge of a broad, fertile valley, well up on the swelling foothills of the range Hani and his party had just crossed. The temperature seemed more pleasant than it had been the last few days, or perhaps the sight of their goal gave the travelers hope.

I'm getting too old for this, Hani told himself, wiping his face with his forearm, although many diplomats were older than he. He thought of his friend, Mane, who had to be close to sixty, still tramping back and forth to distant Wasshukanni. Or the unfortunate Babylonian emissary, whatever his age, making the two-month-long slog to Akhet-aten from Bab-ilum. *The fatal slog.*

What's this business all about? Are the hapiru *trying to stir up trouble between us and an ally?* Hani had heard that the king of Kheta Land was supposed to marry one of King Burna-buriash's daughters. He gave a snort. *He and our king will be brothers-in-law. Perhaps the king of Sangar is planning on switching his alliance to Kheta.*

"What is it, my lord?" Maya said at the sound.

"Just thinking about our murder and how damaging it may be to our relationship with Sangar. And about who might find that profitable."

"I'll bet it's the Hittites again. They seem to have a

finger in every pot." Maya looked truculent, ready to take on the men of Kheta single-handed.

"That guess is as good as any other until we have some facts." Hani sighed and twitched aside the curtain of the litter. He had to blink in the glaring sun of late afternoon, which was low enough to hit him right in the eyes and blind him momentarily.

He looked out across the valley to the tall forested mountains silhouetted on the other side. Halfway there, the glinting ribbon of a river ran, and to the south of that a bright spot that might have been a lake. Closer up, in the fertile agricultural lands, a date grove waved its fronds lazily, like a group of tousle-haired prostitutes beckoning from a street corner. Hani thought he could make out a small blur of white ahead, shimmering like water.

"I think Kumidi's come into view. Look there." Hani pointed.

Maya craned his neck out the side of the litter to see. "Not a moment too soon. I'm exhausted," he said crossly.

"Ah, but think of our colleagues and the soldiers who are walking. Our lot could certainly be worse." *In more than one sense.* Since Pa-aten-em-heb had still been off in Qeden when Hani and his party had left Temesheq precipitously, they'd brought with them only a few soldiers as an escort. If emissaries were being waylaid in the region, Hani was glad not to have become one of the victims.

The rest of the tedious afternoon passed to the clop of donkeys' hooves and the soporific swaying of their vehicle. It was evening when they finally entered Kumidi and wound through the town to the commissioner's palace.

Here at last was a fortified place with strong crenellated

walls, like a proper Egyptian fortress. Spearmen stood at attention as the little cavalcade passed through the gate. *I like that*, Hani thought. *Someone's keeping discipline.*

He'd sent a runner ahead in advance of their arrival, and now the commissioner himself came out onto the porch of his residence to greet them, in a formal but military-looking short kilt and shirt with full pleated sleeves. He was properly wigged and shaven, his eye painted—because he had only one. The other was a seared and sunken pit, scarred over as if it had been cauterized. It was hard not to stare at it.

"Welcome, my lord. The emissary of our king—life, prosperity, and health to him—is always welcome," said Amen-nefer in a brassy voice that had no doubt served him well for leading his troops into combat. He bowed with proper respect and offered his hand.

Hani smiled and took the proffered grasp, which was firm and manly. "I thank you, Lord Commissioner. Despite many years in the area, I've never had the pleasure of visiting your city. The regional capital used to be in Temesheq."

"Yes. It seemed like a good idea to remove the seat of power from Biryawaza's clutches." He gave Hani a knowing smile. "Fortunately, the mayor of Kumidi is a harmless fellow who's no threat to anyone. Rather simple, like so many of the natives."

That comment raised a little shiver of distaste along Hani's nape. For him, the "natives" were anything but simple. Ptah-mes had said Amen-nefer was on bad terms with the locals, and Hani believed it. Nothing was quite as toxic as being patronizing.

"Allow me to show you to your quarters. I assume

the soldiers will be garrisoned in the barracks," said the commissioner in a jovial voice.

"More troops will be coming. They were on an assignment when we left."

Amen-nefer tipped his head in acknowledgment. "They'll be welcome. Many of my men have been here six years. They'll be eager for news from home." He led the way with a brisk, martial gait through the palace and up the stairs to a pleasant room. "Lord Hani, I trust your accommodations are acceptable. Your secretary and the others will be quartered up and down this hall. It's our most luxurious area—I used to sleep down here myself. Just abandoned it for the Babylonians. They wanted to stay together."

Hani assured him it was perfect. "I would like to meet with you this evening, my lord, about the unfortunate recent events."

"To be sure. Join me for dinner, and we can talk at table."

Hani said firmly, "I would like my secretary to be present, if you don't object. It's important the vizier has an accurate picture of the facts as we know them."

"Very well. I'll see to it you have some servants," Amen-nefer said in a pleasant tone, and with another bow, he took his leave.

Hani stared after him as he disappeared down the hall, trying to make up his mind. The man was friendly and polite, much more sincerely respectful than King Biryawaza. He obviously ran a disciplined garrison. And he was handsome, despite the loss of his eye. Muscular in build and passably tall, he had a face that was almost a caricature of manly good looks, with a cleft chin—just a little too prognathous—and a full-lipped, deeply bowed mouth.

Am I letting myself be influenced by the story Pa-aten-em-heb told me? His behavior has certainly been impeccable. He's not the only Egyptian who looks down on the vassals as if they're some sort of savages.

"What do you think, my lord?" asked Maya once the two of them were alone. "Can you picture him mauling Pa-aten-em-heb's sister?"

"Not readily. But then, I haven't refused his courtship," Hani said with a wink. "Let's take him at face value for now. I don't know when they'll call us for dinner, so we ought to bathe and make ourselves presentable, I suppose."

A timid knock on the door interrupted him, and Hani opened it. A round-eyed young Kumidian in a simple tunic presented himself with a bow. "My Lord Hani, I've been assigned to your person. Please tell me what I can do for you," he said in fluent Egyptian.

"What's your name, son?" Hani asked him kindly. The youth seemed very nervous.

"Zalaya, my lord. Thank you for asking." He bowed again. He was a meek-looking, moon-faced lad. His cheek was disfigured by a big angry purple bruise.

Hani and Maya exchanged a glance. "What happened to your face, Zalaya?" asked Hani.

The servant—probably a slave—all but writhed in discomfort. "I, uh, fell, Lord Hani."

Hani heaved out a deep sigh. *No, he was struck. But that's the lot of slaves up here. It's not for me to reform local customs.*

"I'd like a bath and a shave and some oil to rub on afterward. And then my secretary after me. We'll both need clean clothes. He can show you our baggage."

Zalaya bowed and followed Maya out in search of their baskets and chests. Hani eyed his narrow back thoughtfully. As Hani stood in the doorway, two men came around the corner, chattering in loud, animated voices, waving their hands, and exuding frustration. They were speaking Akkadian. When they saw Hani before them, the older man stopped and almost shouted, in that language, "Are you the emissary who is here to put right the murder of our colleague?"

"I am indeed the king of the Two Lands' messenger. Whom do I have the pleasure of addressing?"

"I am Shindi-shugab, emissary of the Great King of Karduniash."

"And I, Akhu-tsabu," said the younger of the two.

"Hani son of Mery-ra at your disposal, my lords." Hani smiled benevolently.

The two Babylonians seemed to calm down a bit. Shindi-shugab said in his gravelly voice, "This situation is intolerable, Lord Hani. We had all the safe conducts international custom requires. We should have been untouchable."

"And we had a military escort," Akhu-tsabu pointed out. "We're carrying gifts for your king."

"Here, come into my room. Tell me what happened." Hani stepped back, and the two men passed inside.

Shindi-shugab was a portly man at the older end of middle age. His polished bald head contrasted with the density of a long, square-trimmed beard, and his eyes were popping with outrage. His younger companion, black haired, was small and downright fat. Red faced, he glistened with sweat in the heat. He looked as if he might cry with distress.

Hani gestured to the two men to seat themselves on the bed, and he folded his legs and sat down on the multicolored carpet before them. "All I know is that your colleague was killed. You'll help us all by telling me as many details as you can."

At that moment, Maya swung open the door and burst in, saying, "Everything is ready for your bath, my lord. Shall I tell Zalaya—oh, excuse me. Excuse me, gentlemen." He backed up and was darting out the door, but Hani called out to stop him.

"Come on in, my friend. I want you to take notes."

Maya closed the door carefully and sat down. He pulled off his writing case and dripped a bit of water from his flask onto the cake of ink. Then he folded his legs and sat behind Hani, spreading a sheet of papyrus across his knees, and looked up expectantly.

"Now, my lords, please start at the beginning and tell me all you know."

"We had been on the road for a very long time," began Shindi-shugab. "We were approaching Kumidi by way of the trade route. Our caravan, in fact, was led by traders, because they wanted to take advantage of our armed guard. They were afraid of these people you call the *hapiru*, you know. We've had more than one caravan robbed, and your king has done nothing about it." His eyes bugged again, and his face grew scarlet with indignation.

His fellow chimed in, "We were coming up the valley

from the south, not far outside the city, when a howling horde of savages fell upon us. They slew right and left and seized our pack donkeys laden with goods, despite the soldiers. It was shocking! Shocking!"

"Lord Hani, I want to reiterate: we had diplomatic credentials and a letter from King Burna-buriash, asking all local governments to permit our passage. It is simply outrageous that we should be treated thus."

"And the worst was yet to come," Akhu-tsabu cried in a quivering voice. "We sought refuge with your commissioner—who, I must say, was gracious enough—but notwithstanding that, when we went to waken our colleague Shulum-marduk the next morning, he was dead! Murdered, my lord!"

Dear gods, Hani thought, apprehension chilling him. *Right in the palace? That certainly doesn't look good for us.* "How did he die? Are you sure he was murdered?"

"He'd been beaten savagely," Shindi-shugab yelled, his voice breaking. "Beaten, right in his room." He slammed his fist into the other palm.

Hani's heart sank. "Did you hear anything, my lords? Preceding your discovery, I mean? Did this happen the evening before or in the night, do you think? Could you tell?"

Akhu-tsabu said in a tremulous voice, "We saw him at dinner. After that, nothing. We all went to our rooms, a little tipsy, and while Shindi-shugab and I were on this side of the hall, Shulum-marduk was on the other side, and there was an antechamber between his bedroom and the corridor. So I don't think we would have heard anything, certainly not so as to be wakened from sleep." He mopped his forehead with his sleeve, hands shaking. Hani was concerned lest he topple over dead himself.

Shindi-shugab growled, "How safe do you think we feel now, Lord Hani? If a murderer can sneak into the very palace of your commissioner, is anyone safe?" Before Hani could speak, Shindi-shugab's voice rose irately. "And that's not the worst of it. The insult to our king is unpardonable. First we're attacked and robbed, and then that very next night, one of us is killed. Your commissioner is not providing us with security. Has he no respect for the Great King of Karduniash?"

"We've written to our king, and assuming that no one kills our courier, Lord Burna-buriash will decide what to do," Akhu-tsabu chimed in. "He may recall us, or he may instruct us to lodge a complaint directly with your king Nibkhurirya."

"You lost all your gifts, you say?" Hani wasn't sure what comfort he could offer the Babylonians.

"Not all. And the choice seems very arbitrary in retrospect. If I were a highwayman, I would have been more thorough." Shindi-shugab shot his compatriot a suspicious look, and Akhu-tsabu nodded feverishly.

Hani realized that time had passed—through the window, the garden was bathed in the luminous darkness of twilight, and the lampless room had grown shadowed. "Gentlemen, I beg you to forgive me. We have an appointment with the commissioner very soon, and we've yet to clean off from our journey." He got to his feet, and the two Babylonians rose likewise.

"I hope you, at least, will address this outrage seriously,"

Shindi-shugab said, automatically slicking back his scalp as if in memory of the days when he had hair.

"I assure you I'll take this case very seriously and pursue it to the end," Hani said earnestly. "Stay in touch with me in the meantime, my lords. We greatly esteem your king and the friendship of your nation, and I hope this terrible event won't come between us."

Somewhat mollified, the two men bowed and departed, Shindi-shugab still muttering disgusted noises. After they'd left, a silence fell. Hani turned to Maya. "Did you get all that? Did you understand their accent? You're only used to hearing Akkadian spoken badly by men of Kemet." He forced himself to smile, but a great weight had descended upon his heart.

"I think I got it all, Lord Hani," Maya said, ranging his writing tools. He folded up the papyrus he'd been recording on. "Shouldn't we be getting ready for dinner now? I'm sure the bath water is cold."

"Actually, that sounds pretty attractive," Hani said. "Call Zalaya, will you, my friend?"

By the time the summons to dinner could be expected, Hani and Maya were all clean and fresh. Hani had put on his gold of honor and painted his eyes and looked as lordly as one could look, despite his cheerful expression. As for himself, Maya had butterflies in his stomach. He'd never been included in a state dinner before, and he had a horror of muffing the formal etiquette and revealing his working-class background.

"Just follow the people around you," Hani told him

by way of encouragement. "You don't speak their language much, so probably they'll all leave you alone." He stared at Maya, evaluating. "I think you need to take the writing case off your shoulder, though. Just carry it and put it under your stool until you need it."

"Of course, my lord." Maya slipped it off but felt a flutter of shame, as if he had been stripped naked. That writing case, the evidence of his literacy, was what tethered him to the ruling class. He pulled his gold amulet of Bes—the one really expensive thing he owned—from under his shirt and let it lie visibly on his chest.

When the call came to eat, the two men set off down the hall in the wake of the servant. To Maya's surprise, they were led not to the ground floor banquet hall but to the commissioner's apartment, which appeared to have been at one time an office with a vestibule. Amen-nefer rose to greet them. "Lord Hani! Here you are in all your splendor, and me in my everyday clothes. I hope you don't find me disrespectful, but I thought an intimate meal might serve our purposes better than a state dinner."

"Think nothing of it, Lord Commissioner. I don't stand on formalities," Hani replied genially. He and Amen-nefer seated themselves at the individual tables that had been set out, and Maya, uncomfortable, hoicked himself gracelessly onto another stool. *He must use these high things purposely to embarrass little people.*

The servants began to bring in various delicacies prepared in the fashion of the Black Land—cucumbers in sour grape juice with dill and fennel, little meat-stuffed pies flavored with cumin, like the ones Sat-hut-haru had learned to make, mashed chickpeas and garlic with pieces of bread for dipping. Nothing especially fancy, just good home-style cooking. After weeks of eating cold meals on the shore where their ship had put in at night, or the rich dishes at Biryawaza's court, the food was welcome indeed. And the beer was good.

They moved on to roast larks and small fried fish as the evening wore on. Lord Hani and Amen-nefer talked of one thing and another, while Maya listened with one ear and concentrated on his food. He saw that the others were eating everything with their fingers in an ordinary way, so he did too. Little bowls of perfumed water had been provided at each table for them to wash their hands, and servants circulated with platters of food and refills of beer.

"So you're from Waset too," Amen-nefer said. "I don't get back often. Well, there's not much reason to. I don't have family there any longer."

"Your wife is here with you, then?"

"My wife is deceased, Lord Hani." The commissioner held up a hand before Hani, his eyebrows crumpled in apology, could say something consoling. "No need for condolences. It's been many years."

"How long have you been stationed here, Lord Amen-nefer?"

Amen-nefer chuckled. "I came up here as a soldier on the usual six-year posting the year of our late king's second jubilee. Then I was appointed regional commissioner, and here I still am, nearly thirteen years later."

He seemed friendly and unguarded. Maya longed to ask him how he'd lost his eye, but instead, the secretary opted to look busy with a lark carcass while he listened.

"And you, my lord?" Amen-nefer asked Hani.

"Except for assignments abroad, I've maintained my residence in Waset, so I stay with the high commissioner when I have occasion to visit the capital. We have children in both cities."

Hani wasn't rendered indiscreet by the beer, Maya knew. Anything he told Amen-nefer was by choice. Perhaps he wanted to build a rapport with him by offering personal confidences. *Learn from him. He's a master diplomat. Didn't he write in his aphorisms, "Do not reveal your heart to a stranger?"*

Eventually, servants brought out sweet cakes and the last of the autumn's grapes. Hani said in an amiable voice, "Perhaps, my lord, the time has come to talk about the Babylonian situation. Maya, would you like to make notes so our lord king can be better informed?"

Amen-nefer heaved a sigh. "Yes. Lamentable. What an embarrassment. This group of *hapiru* is like a lizard—you think you have it by the tail, but it just breaks off in your hand, and the damned creature grows a new one."

"The robbery, yes. But who could have killed Shulum-marduk right under your roof?"

Amen-nefer stared him in the eye. "You think that can't be the *hapiru* too? There's a fellow named Shum-addi who apparently has set his sights on becoming their leader, as Abdi-ashirta once did in the north. He's full of a sort of low cunning and will stop at nothing to undercut our hegemony in Kharu. Who would profit more from a rupture between us and our Babylonian allies than he?"

Hani nodded, his eyes lowered, digesting this. Then he looked up. "You think he wants to establish a legitimate kingdom like Abdi-ashirta's son?"

"What I think is we should deport the whole lot of those outlaw scum to Wawat. Let them work in the gold mines for a while—see how they like *that* legitimate kingdom." Amen-nefer's pleasant expression had suddenly grown hard as flint, which worked a disturbing change in his handsome face.

Maya swallowed with difficulty. *Bes protect us, I hope I never get on the wrong side of this man.* People who could change in a minute like that disturbed him. He'd been raised by a calm, loving mother. His teachers at the Per-ankh had been pitiless, but they were utterly predictable. Lord Hani was as solid and honest as he looked. He could get angry—although it took a lot to push him—but that anger always came from a principled place and was often leavened with humor. In short, Maya had rarely seen such an instant look of sheer contempt. His flesh creeping, he busied himself with his writing.

"That decision belongs to Nefer-khepru-ra, of course," Hani said blandly. "As I told you, he's sending an army up here soon to clean them out of their nest, and it may well be that some of them *will* end up in the mines. But you and I need to find the robbers and murderer in this particular case and try to make it right with Burna-buriash before he sees in it an act of war."

Amen-nefer tipped his head in acquiescence, his features once more relaxed.

"The commander of the proposed army should be here soon. He accompanied us up here but had a task to perform elsewhere for a while. When he arrives, we can send out some scouting parties. In the meantime, I'd like to talk to the two surviving Babylonians again."

"All my resources are at your disposal, Lord Hani." Amen-nefer rose, and Hani and Maya followed suit. Maya hastily folded up his parchment and shoved his pen back into its case. "I'm sure you're tired from traveling."

"Yes, in fact, we are," Hani said with an amiable smile.

"I leave you, then." The commissioner bowed genially and retreated into his apartment, while Hani and Maya made their way down the corridor to their own quarters.

"What do you think, my lord?" Maya asked in an undertone.

"About the food? Wonderful."

"No, about—ahem." Maya cleared his throat discreetly. "The commissioner. He wastes no love on the *hapiru*. Did you see the look that came over him?"

Hani seemed pensive. "I wonder if they cost him his eye."

CHAPTER 5

THE NEXT DAY, HANI FINALLY received a letter from his wife. It had been sent to Azzati and, in the absence of the high commissioner, had languished there until someone thought to forward it to Temesheq. From Temesheq, it had made its way to Kumidi.

Hani unfolded the papyrus with relish. How he loved these communiqués from home—news of the children, of the house, of the birds. He saw with affection the bold script of his father. Mery-ra generally wrote for Nub-nefer, sharing what she wanted to tell her husband, and Hani could picture her sweet face and warm golden body as he read, almost as if she were present.

"My dear Hani, all the children are well. Sati and Pakiki's little ones are more adorable every moment. Tepy told Mery-ra the other day that he wanted to be an emissary like his gamfather! Neferet and her friend were here for the holidays. You can imagine how much brighter the house felt with Neferet around. Although she's always too ready to tell stories about the life of court, which concerns me.

I hope she understands the difference between harmless statements and confidences. Bener-ib is finally starting to loosen up a little. She's quite sweet with Baket-iset, which makes me feel good about her.

"The Flood was very generous this year, and the fields look beautiful. I think we'll have good crops at the farm. Baket-iset sends her love. Qenyt misses you, because I won't let her eat the *bulti* fry I put into the pool to raise for eating (*our* eating). Ta-miu had another litter of kittens, but we were able to give them both to the grandchildren. I can't imagine that she'll be having too many more at her age. Sat-hut-haru is expecting again—I'm sure she's written to tell Maya.

"Hani, some news has come out of the palace, this time not through Neferet but publicly. The king has named a coregent, his brother Smenkh-ka-ra. The new coregent seems to be making his residence in Waset. What does this mean, I wonder? Are his overtures to try to win over the Thebans or to keep an eye on us? How I wish you were here to help me understand. I hope you and Maya are well and safe. Your loving Nub-nefer."

Mery-ra had added his own postscript. "Son, what do you make of this new coregency? What's to happen to the queen? We miss you. Love, Father."

"This is very strange," Hani said, troubled. "Maya, the king has named his brother to share the throne with him."

Maya looked up, goggle-eyed. "But he has a coregent. You helped get the queen to be his coregent."

"Well, as it turned out, she was something not altogether a king. I mean, she wore the crown and did all the things kings do, but have you noticed? Her name was

104

never written in a double *shen* ring like a proper king's." Hani pursed his lips in thought, his eyebrows knotted. "I don't know what to make of this."

"I thought Prince Smenkh-ka-ra wasn't quite right in the head."

"That's what I've heard, although I've never met him." *Is the king finally giving some thought to his own mortality?* Hani wondered. *Does he think a male can serve as a less controversial regent for his son? Or does he know the queen is sick and may not survive him?*

"That's all we need—more instability at home," Maya said sourly. "Lord Ay won't be happy that his daughter is being displaced."

"No..." Hani wasn't sure what to say. "And Smenkh-ka-ra's apparently going to rule from Waset."

"What?" squawked Maya. "What's going on? Are they trying to sweet-talk us Thebans?"

"I'm sure I have no idea. Perhaps it's all a facade anyway. It's hard to imagine our king sharing his real power with anyone, especially someone who may not even be competent." Hani wasn't sure why this news should disturb him so, but it all seemed so carefully contrived that it left him with a bad taste in his mouth. "I wonder if this is meant to curb Ay's power."

Maya nodded reflectively. "I'll bet that's it, my lord. He's finally onto Ay's ambitions." He gave a dark chuckle. "Our friend Pa-aten-em-heb's status just went down."

"From what I gather, being married to Lord Ay's daughter hasn't been anything Pa-aten-em-heb has exploited anyway. He seems to have wasted no affection on his father-in-law."

"True."

Hani noticed that Maya was writing on a potsherd. "Did you not get a letter from Sat-hut-haru?" he asked without thinking.

Maya's face grew shuttered. "No, actually, I didn't, my lord," he said with studied carelessness. "No doubt, she's busy with the children."

"No doubt." Hani was surprised at his secretary's reply. Normally, anything related to his wife brought out an eager and joyful response in Maya. "Well, let's go. We have an appointment with our two Babylonians. I want to find out what kind of man the late Shulum-marduk was. Perhaps that will give us a clue as to who might have wanted him dead."

They set out down the corridor to the apartments of Shindi-shugab and his colleague, where a slave admitted them. Before long, the two diplomats entered the salon, looking somber. Akhu-tsabu's eyes were red.

"Lord Hani," Shindi-shugab said in a lugubrious voice.

"My lords, I am here to repeat my condolences and to ask you some questions that may help us find your colleague's murderer." At the back of his mouth lay the sour taste of fear. *Once diplomats start being murdered, what are any of our lives worth?* "What sort of man was Shulum-marduk? Did he have enemies?"

Shindi-shugab looked pained. "Here? Not likely. He'd only been to your land once before, a long time ago—fifteen or twenty years—and never by way of Kumidi. And now he languishes in the land of Ereshkigal, leaving a family behind..."

"Was he a friendly person? Any chance he might have rubbed some local the wrong way?"

"Well, he could be stubborn," Akhu-tsabu admitted. "But a pleasant man overall. It would take a monster of irascibility to take such offense as to bludgeon him to death." His voice broke a little. "You should have seen the corpse, my lord. It was inhumanly mistreated. His ghost is going to be very angry."

"He'll haunt his murderer for sure," Shindi-shugab agreed with a bitter smile of satisfaction.

"Then it's up to us to appease him by taking vengeance. Has he been buried yet?"

"Yes, of course. It's been more than a week, and in this heat…" The younger emissary shrugged, apologetic.

Shindi-shugab smoothed his scalp automatically. "We did our best for him, but of course, who among his family is going to make offerings for him way out here? King Burna-buriash will be livid."

"With just reason, my lord. Would you object if I visited your late colleague's room?"

The Babylonians exchanged a surprised glance touched with apprehension. They led the way across the hall and opened the door reluctantly for Hani and Maya. Hani found himself in a splendid apartment with painted walls and a handsome tapestry, an attached vestibule and bathing room, and windows onto a courtyard. It was considerably more luxurious than his own yet had no furniture except a bed frame sitting lopsided on a broken leg, some of its webbing torn through. But what made it enormously less pleasant was the heavy odor of blood that still clung to the stones. Any attempt to scrub out the gore had not completely succeeded, and dark stains disfigured the paving and walls—everywhere.

Maya made a retching noise and hid his nose with a hand. Hani forced down the rising queasiness that billowed up in him. "Dear gods," he murmured in horror. He'd rarely seen such carnage even on the battlefield. *It looks like a slaughterhouse. Did killing one man really require such a bloodletting?* "Could you tell from the wounds if the attacker used a weapon or just his fists?"

Akhu-tsabu, looking distinctly green, shook his head. "Something blunt, my lord. He wasn't, er, chopped but bashed." Tears began to tremble on his eyelashes.

"I think we've seen enough." They hustled into the corridor, and Hani dared to draw a breath once more. He felt contaminated by the mere sight of such inhuman violence. *Could it have been a demon?* But no, surely a human being had done it—a man with a body that couldn't pass through walls. "Would Shulum-marduk have locked his door, do you think?"

"Assuredly," said Shindi-shugab, loosening the neck of his tunic as if he couldn't breathe. "We were all spooked after the robbery."

"And yet he seems to have opened for his killer— there are no signs the door has been forced." Hani didn't know what to make of that detail. Was it possible the late emissary knew his killer? Could it even have been one of the colleagues standing before Hani in such seeming distress? "How long will you gentlemen be around? I may have more questions for you."

"Until King Burna-buriash recalls us or tells us to continue to Kemet. The courier left immediately after the... the murder. With luck, he could be back in a week or two." Shindi-shugab, still pale from the shock of the blood-spattered room, thrust his thumbs under his sash as if to still his trembling hands.

"Let me ask around to see if anyone heard anything that night. We'll speak soon."

The Babylonians bowed and hustled back into their quarters, looking ready to weep—or vomit—and Hani and Maya started back down the hall to their own room. Hani was sunk in thought. *Where do we start?* he asked himself hopelessly. "If only we had a witness. If we could find the murder weapon…"

Maya shook his head, still looking greenish.

Hani said, "I'd like to know what could have beaten a man so badly as to leave all that blood. I've seen some pretty terrible wounds on the battlefield. Maces or axes or even bronze rods or clubs can do a pretty thorough job of smashing. But in the commissioner's palace? Wouldn't someone have seen a man creeping through the halls with a military weapon?"

"Maybe it was one of Amen-nefer's soldiers. A guardsman perhaps."

"You may be right. If so, why would he have assassinated a Babylonian emissary?"

"Sent by someone who wanted to derail our alliance?"

Hani laughed. "We're back to the Hittites."

They reached their door and entered, Maya stepping back for Hani to precede him.

Hani jerked to a quick stop, his heart in his throat. A man was sitting on the bed. His first thought was *The assassin! I'm next!*

But the man rose and said pleasantly, with a polite bow, "Lord Hani?"

"Yes," Hani said, forcing a smile. Beside him, Maya had grown pale. "To whom do I have the pleasure of speaking?"

In passable Akkadian, heavily accented, the man replied, "Prince Hattusha-ziti, emissary of the Great King of Hatti Land."

Maya shot Hani a look of shock, his jaw sagging. But Hani had already recognized the appearance of a man of Kheta, with his turned-up short boots and calf-length woolen tunic. Hattusha-ziti was exceedingly tall and fair skinned, his face reddened with long exposure to sun and wind. His graying brown hair hung down his back, not quite obscuring the ostentatious silver disks in his ears. He had a heavy-lidded gaze, squinting a little as if into the sun, and a wry half smile.

Hani collected himself quickly. "This is unexpected, my lord prince."

"I just arrived. My apologies for not giving you any warning. Your commissioner sent me up here, thinking you were in your room." He extended his hand, and Hani felt forced to grasp it. The Hittites were not altogether enemies—rivals might be a better way of putting it—but their relationship with the Two Lands was far from cordial. And Hani regretted that fact. Still, sweat broke out on his forehead at the thought of how a secret meeting with the emissary of Shuppiluliuma might be interpreted by Hani's superiors.

"What can I do for your master?" Hani bade his guest be seated and took a seat next to him. "I have no powers to negotiate, since I'm here for a very specific purpose."

"I realize that, Lord Hani. All I ask is that you hear my message and take it to your king." His smile deepened—a frank, intelligent smile—and Hani thought appraisingly, *He's considerably more likable than most of the Egyptians missioned up here.*

"And what is your message, Lord Hattusha-ziti?" he asked in Neshite, the language of Kheta.

The Hittite threw back his head and laughed. "I've heard of your skills in our tongue. It's partly why I was instructed to speak to you—although that's not the only reason." He locked eyes with Hani.

Is he referring to the Crocodiles? The rebellious priests of Amen-Ra had made overtures to Kheta, he knew. But flattery was a classic way to soften up a negotiator, and he didn't intend to fall into that trap.

"Speak, my lord," Hani prompted, with a thin smile of his own.

"Our Sun the Great King of Hatti Land believes the chilly relationship between our two nations is a waste of potential. You may or may not be aware that he's been making overtures to your king almost from the moment of his coronation. They've been met with no particular warmth, but Shuppiluliuma understands that a new king has many things to think about. There's no reason why our lands, the greatest on earth, shouldn't be friends—equals—and trading partners. He wants to try again to open diplomatic discussions with Nibkhurirya. Peace is considerably less costly than war, my lord."

I couldn't agree more, Hani thought. "It's difficult to speak of peace while you continue to pressure our vassals to defect, Lord Hattusha-ziti."

"But, Hani, if Our Sun's intentions were really hostile, would he have sent Aitakkama back to rule his city as your vassal? We could have snapped up Qadesh right then. No, your vassals, like ours, have their own agendas. They're for whoever seems to suit their needs at the moment. We don't have to pressure anyone."

"Rumor has it that you're in league with the *hapiru* to stir up trouble on our borders," Hani persisted, knowing the man would deny it and that his words would mean nothing.

But Hattusha-ziti said candidly, "We've treated with the *hapiru,* yes. They're a problem to us as well as to you, and we'd like to make them think more friendly thoughts toward us. But our goal has assuredly not been to stir up trouble on your borders. What we want is that the border should become a place of cooperation, porosity—a gateway for trade." He smiled, and the corners of his brown eyes crinkled. "We're a nation of traders, Hani. I won't be giving away any state secrets if I tell you our homeland is poor in resources. All our expansion has been to secure those resources. But conquest is costly. We would much rather exchange goods peacefully. And together, I daresay, we could control the *hapiru* much more effectively."

"How do you feel about the alliance between the Two Lands and Sangar—Karduniash, as you would say?"

The Hittite shrugged. "Another example of friendship being more fruitful than enmity. We're allies with Karduniash as well. Why should there be competition between us over that?"

Hani tipped his head, considering. It was all perfectly reasonable, of course, although he doubted if many in the bureaucracy of Kemet would see it that way. "I think your recent dismemberment of Naharin may weigh against me trusting you."

But Hattusha-ziti said matter-of-factly, "Naharin was already moribund, torn apart by corruption and civil war. It now has the blessings of a stable and competent government. Consider us peacemakers in Naharin, Lord Hani. Its people, like us, are hungry for the fruits of peace."

Hani pondered that idea. At last he said, "I can't promise you anything, my prince. The king will make whatever decision he sees fit to make."

"Just repeat what I've said. If he shows any openness to the idea at all, we can send emissaries to negotiate." Hattusha-ziti stood up, impressively tall at Hani's side, a lanky, broad-shouldered man with an easy way about his movements.

Hani wondered if the Hittite would be so friendly if he knew that Nefer-khepru-ra was planning to invade Kharu and yank its recalcitrant kinglets back by force.

"Good night, my friend," said the prince. "I hope this may be the first of many amicable discussions between our two kingdoms." He extended a big red hand sparkling with rings, and Hani grasped it.

"I, too, Lord Hattusha-ziti," he said amiably, but he watched the other man with measuring eyes. *How did he know I was even here? Not just any old emissary but me in particular.* Hani wondered if the Crocodiles had said anything. They were espousing much the same kind of commercial alliance.

The prince left, and Hani could hear his hard-shod footsteps clattering down the corridor and into silence. Hani stood for a moment, his thoughts racing.

Maya said from behind him, "I can't believe it! Do you suppose he was the one who killed that Babylonian?"

"I doubt it. But it's certainly strange. How did he know I was here? Why meet in secrecy?" He just hoped no one back home heard about such a meeting, or his own loyalty might be questioned. The sooner he could get back to court to report to the vizier, the safer he would feel.

"Do you think he was telling the truth about Kheta's benevolent intentions?"

Hani chuckled. "Not altogether. But then, how benevolent are our intentions toward Kheta? Although I must say, neither of us really wants to swallow the other up. Personally, I think a treaty would be a very good idea."

Maya's eyes widened. "You do?"

"What's the alternative, my friend? Be locked forever in this quasi-enmity that drains us both of blood and of gold? There'll be no winner."

Maya pulled a considering face.

"The real enemy is those *hapiru*," Hani said somberly. "They're bent on disruption, even though it may be for the legitimate reason of their survival. I wonder if that Shum-addi, or whatever his name is, shouldn't be permitted to become a king. At least we'd have someone to negotiate with."

"But where would their kingdom be?"

"I haven't thought this out, you understand," Hani said, grinning. "Perhaps somewhere out there on the eastern fringes. I don't know who claims the Yardon Valley, where some of them seem to be camped now."

Maya grunted, frowning. He seemed reluctant to accept

the possibility that Kheta and the Two Lands could ever be allies.

Hani turned back into the room, rubbing his hands. "But before we do anything else, we need to find out who killed Shulum-marduk. I'd like to talk to the servants, see if they saw or heard anything that night that might give us a clue."

"Would you want me to talk to some of them, my lord? That way, we could get through them faster."

"That's a good idea, Maya. You can start with our friend Zalaya—at least we know he speaks our tongue. He may be able to suggest others who do too. I'll take on the ones who don't."

"Right you are, my lord."

Maya was already heading to the door when Hani had second thoughts about sending his son-in-law into what might become a dangerous situation. He called after Maya, "Be careful, my boy. The man we're after is inhumanly violent."

✦

Admittedly, Lord Hani's words sent a little frisson of apprehension up Maya's neck. He could imagine only too readily the kind of death the Babylonian had suffered.

But what reason had he to take care of himself? Sat-hut-haru was still angry at him—so angry that she hadn't even sent a letter with the latest dispatch. He'd tried to laugh it off, but it was gnawing at his vitals. In more than seven years of marriage, the two of them had never exchanged a cross word. Well, perhaps he'd been cross a time or two; he had an irritable nature. But Sati was such a sunny person that his momentary anger was a like a brand thrown into the River, extinguished immediately. He couldn't even think of a particular collision that had precipitated their quarrel of silence. It was a sequence of little things, he supposed. Little grievances that, left unvented, had built up.

Maya had managed to forget about this secret misery for brief periods of time, caught up in the excitement of travel and the thrill of an investigation. But it was always there, a canker eating him out. He hoped Lord Hani hadn't noticed, because how was he going to explain it to him, Sat-hut-haru's father? Hani would necessarily side with his daughter, and Maya couldn't bear the thought of losing his esteem. Hani was the father Maya had never known. Through Hani's patronage, Maya, as a promising student, had been able to attend the Per-ankh, the scribal school that gave him access to the world of something better than keeping the books for his mother's goldsmith workshop. If he and Sat-hut-haru should part, it would be the end of his dreams, the sign that he'd tried to lift himself too high. To dare to think he could work his way up to wealth and prestige. To dare to think that a beautiful girl like Sati could actually find attractive such a one as he...

He sniffed back the tears that threatened, sparking in his nose. *I should write to her. Apologize. Explain how much I love her and the children.* But part of him was miffed that she hadn't written to him and was making him feel compelled to back down first. Surely, the father of the family had some dignity to maintain. *Still...*

Ahead of him, walking around the corner and heading away, Maya saw Zalaya's narrow back. "Hold up there, Zalaya," he called.

The slave turned, and despite the heavy leather sack in his arms, he came meekly to Maya and gave an awkward bow. "My lord, how can I serve you?"

"Put that thing down a moment, my good man. I have some questions to ask you on behalf of Lord Hani, the Master of the King's Stable."

Zalaya's eyes widened uneasily, but he put down the sack with a clank and stood with his hands clasped at his waist, his shoulders slumped in a servile posture. "Yes, my lord?"

Maya noticed once more the bruises on the slave's round face. *That must have been some blow. I bet he lost teeth.* "The night the Babylonian emissary was killed—it's been more than a week now—did you happen to notice anything unusual in the corridor? Any person you didn't know hanging about? Any footsteps at an unusual hour?"

Now Zalaya looked distinctly worried. "My lord, it's my duty to notice nothing."

Irritation flashed across Maya's attitude of casual authority. He said sharply, "Yes, but you're a human being. You have eyes and ears. It's the king's emissary who is asking you this, man. His orders supersede whatever your masters here have told you."

The slave swallowed hard. His worried eyes grew more and more fearful. "I... I saw nothing, my lord."

"No soldiers, perhaps? A guardsman? No one carrying a blunt weapon?"

"Nothing, my lord." Then he added in a feeble voice, "People go up and down the halls all the time, even at night."

"So someone *did* come up here?"

"N-No. I mean... I don't know if anyone did. I don't remember." He was cringing so abjectly—as if trying to make himself even shorter than Maya—that Maya wondered if the slave were going to wet himself. Zalaya was a young man, but there was something old and broken about him.

Maya gave a snort of disgust and stepped away. "Well, if your memory should come back, let me know. This is serious business. If we don't find the murderer, there may be war with Sangar."

"Yes, my lord." Bowing profusely, the slave backed up and hoisted his sack once more. Still bowing, he scuttled away while Maya watched him in annoyance.

He knows something, may Ammit take him. But then Maya realized he'd forgotten to ask which others of the servants might speak Egyptian. He let out an irritated snort. *What do I do now?* Finally, Maya marched down the stairs and out into the courtyard, where soldiers, scribes, and slaves passed back and forth, engaged in the tasks of daily life.

He shaded his eyes and squinted into the glare of pale-yellow stone and pale-yellow earth. Even the sky had grown hazy and yellow. *Something's coming.* The words chilled him. *I hope it's only a storm...*

Maya marched over to a pair of servants squatting in the shade of the enclosure wall, sharing a gourd of water. They scrambled quickly to their feet and began an orgy of bowing, but he said tersely, "Enough. Do either of you speak Egyptian?"

They each raised a hand simultaneously, as if it were a choreographed move, and Maya thought, *These people are all so cowed. I've never seen the like.* "I am the secretary of the Master of the King's Stable, Lord Hani. He's here to investigate the assassination that took place within your walls a short time ago. He's bade me ask you some questions."

The two men exchanged a look that fell between conspiratorial and terrified. "Yes, my lord," said the older of the two, a wiry little man with a narrow face and an overwhelming nose.

"Do you serve in the commissioner's residence or elsewhere?"

Again the two slaves looked at one another, and the younger of the two said in a deep bass voice that surprised Maya, "In the residence, my lord." He was a broad-shouldered man in his thirties, but despite his redoubtable build, he had the same hunched, abject carriage as all the others.

At the end of his patience, Maya said loudly, "Stop making me pull the worms from your nose, you two. What do you do there? If you aren't forthcoming and honest, I'll see to it the commissioner hears about it."

The slaves froze. The older dropped his eyes, his hands clasped so tightly that the knuckles were white. He licked his lips. "I'm employed in the laundry, my lord."

"And I'm body servant to my lord commissioner," the big younger one added.

"Now we're getting somewhere, you two. Did you see or hear anything unusual the night of the murder?"

"Unusual? N-No, my lord. I have a day shift." The big-nosed man's teeth were practically chattering.

He's lying, or I'm six cubits tall. "And you?"

"Nothing, my lord. Nothing the night of the murder."

Maya rolled his eyes in exasperation. "Very well. You can go. But if you think of something that might be relevant—if you saw or heard anything out of the ordinary—it's your duty to tell me, so the king's justice can be done. Do you understand?"

With much bobbing and murmuring of "Yes, my lord," the two men hurried off, almost tripping over themselves in the effort to get away.

Maya watched them go with a steam of anger. This had to be the shadow side of the perfect discipline that seemed to reign in the commissioner's palace. "Now what?" He suspected he'd better leave the soldiers to Lord Hani. They might well object to being grilled by an underling—and they might well enjoy heaving a nosy dwarf over the wall somewhere.

He drifted down into the work court of the residence. A small group of men, clad only in loincloths, were beating the laundry on the edge of a cistern. It was heavy work, and Maya wondered how the little man he'd just spoken to managed it. However, slaves were generally strong, or they didn't last long. He asked himself if it was worth his while to try to talk to any of these people, but they were clearly occupied. He was hot, the humidity had become uncomfortable, and he was getting nowhere with his investigation. Maya's temper was fraying. He found himself thinking about Sat-hut-haru and how she refused to write to him, and he was so frustrated he could have slammed his writing case to the ground. Instead, he pushed back his wig brusquely and mopped his forehead.

"Ah, Maya," Lord Hani called from the service doorway of the residence. "There you are. How's it going?"

Maya looked up at him, hoping his discouragement didn't show.

Hani lumbered toward Maya with his heavy, rolling gait. He was a formidable-looking man—until one saw the friendly twinkle in his little brown eyes. "Have any luck?"

"No, my lord," Maya said with a loud exhalation through his nose. "The slaves are all terrified and tongue-tied. No one saw anything, to hear them tell it. But their very demeanor made it clear to me they know more than they're telling—they're just afraid to say it."

Hani buckled his thick eyebrows in thought. "I've had the same experience. Is this the price of perfect discipline? Our commissioner must rule with a bronze fist."

"That's what I thought. What do we do now?"

"I wonder if we shouldn't go on up to Qidshu as we planned. There's the chance that this was perpetrated by the *hapiru*, after all."

Maya was skeptical. "How would they have gotten into the palace?"

"You forget that members of our troops have fallen in with the brigands. Perhaps some of them are here. No one would think to challenge an Egyptian soldier who entered the garrison."

"That's true..."

"Anyway, it's getting late, and it looks to me as if a storm were brewing. Let's call off our interviews and enjoy our supper."

❖

No proper sunset graced the close of the evening. Instead, a creeping yellow-stained mist seemed to suck the light out of the sky, swept along by darker and darker indigo clouds from the west. The temperature dropped noticeably. And finally, just as Hani and Maya sat down to their meal together, the storm hit. Its first blast almost extinguished the lamps until Hani pulled the shutters closed. The panels rattled as if someone were trying to force their way in. Hani could hear the clatter of rain on the palm fronds in the garden below, and at the end, it became a steady hiss. From the crack of the shutters, a driblet of water leaked and made its way down the wall below, pooling on the plastered floor.

"Here come the autumn rains," Hani said, exhilarated. Rain was such a novelty to a man of Waset that Hani always found himself as excited as a child to hear it. He wondered what the birds did in a rain like this. He hoped they could find themselves some shelter and not be knocked out of the air by the raindrops. "It's easy to understand why their storm god is the main god of Djahy and Kharu."

"The River from the sky," Maya murmured.

Hani wondered if Maya knew that the phrase, admittedly felicitous, was part of the king's hymn to the Aten.

They set to their supper, tasty and substantial as always—a little whiff of home. *I wonder if the cook is as terrorized as the rest of the staff we've seen.*

"I hope Pa-aten-em-heb isn't traveling in this weather. Wasn't he supposed to be here by now?" asked Maya between mouthfuls of bread.

"You're right. But I suppose many things could have delayed him. There's the man who can talk to the soldiers." Hani eyed the table full of small dishes thoughtfully then reached out for a dried fig. He took a chewy bite out of it and, enjoying the pleasant crunch of the tiny seeds under his teeth, said around it, "We won't head to Qidshu until I've had a chance to talk to him. He may be free to rejoin us for the rest of the mission."

The two men were silent for a space of time, eating. Apparently unaware that Hani's eye was on him, Maya grew increasingly long of face until he looked downright funereal. *I wonder what's bothering him.* "Is everything all right, son? You seem down in the mouth."

Maya forced a smile. "No, no. Everything is fine. How long do you think before we get letters from home?"

"It's only been a couple of weeks. I guess if there's anything newsworthy, they'll let us know." Hani was surprised Sat-hut-haru hadn't yet told her husband that she was expecting their third child, but it wasn't his part to leak the news, much as it might cheer up the little man.

CHAPTER 5

T HEY WERE FINISHING OFF THE meal with some
perfumed local wine when a knock on the door made
Hani rise. "Let me see who that is."

He opened to find Zalaya standing apologetically
before him. "Forgive me, my lord, but this officer said you
would want to see him." He stepped back.

In the hall, standing in a puddle of the rain that dripped
from each hem and even from his thick, straight hair—from
which he'd removed the wig—stood Pa-aten-em-heb.

"Ah, here you are! We were just talking about you!"
Hani clapped the young officer on both arms and ushered
him in. "My question has been answered—you did get
caught in the storm."

Pa-aten-em-heb laughed ruefully. "I should say so. It
was a pretty miserable last few *iteru*s. But then, we'll be
returning here in the fall, too, so we'd better get used to
this." He shed his drenched cloak with an embarrassed
grin. "Sorry about the water on your floor."

"I'm sure our good Zalaya will take care of it," Hani

said, beaming at the slave, who practically twitched in his eagerness to be elsewhere. Hani saw him cast a clandestine look at Maya.

"Yes, my lord. Right away." Zalaya shot away.

Hani turned back to Pa-aten-em-heb. "You must have come straight here without even drying off."

"I did. I wanted to let you know I was here, since we were later than expected. I won't keep you—I see you're at table."

"I'd invite you to join us, but I can imagine you'd like to get into some dry clothes," Hani said kindly. "After you've eaten, if you aren't too tired, come back, and we'll hear what you've found out. Otherwise, there's always tomorrow."

The officer bade the two scribes a pleasant meal and headed off into the corridor. As he departed, Zalaya reappeared with a scrubbing cloth and a basin. He crept over to the puddle and, kneeling, silently began to sop up the water. Hani watched him for a moment. Despite his headband, the slave shook his hair out of his eyes every few moments, and Hani began to realize it was more a tic than a necessity. The man was so tense he was almost fluttering.

At last, he finished and climbed to his feet, but before he could excuse himself, Hani said in a gentle voice, "Why did you lie to my secretary this afternoon, son?"

Zalaya's black eyes flew wide, and his pale lunar face grew paler still until the dark roots of his beard were visible through the skin. He staggered back as if Hani had threatened him with a fist. "I... I saw nothing that night, I swear, my lord."

"You're still lying, aren't you? Who are you afraid of,

Zalaya? No one takes precedence over the king's emissary. Did you see the man who killed Shulum-marduk?"

"No, my lord." He gave a great jerk, and snot began to fountain from his nostrils, tears from his eyes. He swiped at his nose with the back of a trembling hand.

Hani watched him, his heart wrung with compassion for a fellow human who had been so reduced by fear. *He's young, but what kind of life does he have to look forward to? His master can do anything to him he wants.* "Do you know who did it? Do you at least suspect who it was?"

"No! No! Forgive me, my lord, but I can't tell you anything. I have a wife and children."

So that's the hold someone has over him.

"You don't look old enough to have a wife and children," Maya said harshly. "Are you lying again?"

"If you decide you want to tell us, Zalaya, let me know, and I'll see to it that you and your family are taken to safety. You've nothing to be ashamed of." Hani laid a fatherly hand on the slave's shoulder. The youth was quivering like a leaf. He nodded spasmodically, and as soon as Hani removed his hand, Zalaya bowed himself out, basin in his arms.

As the man closed the door behind him, Maya whistled. "*Iyi*, there's a man who is scared out of his skin."

"Is this how our noble commissioner treats his slaves, brutalizing them into submission?" The idea depressed Hani. *What self-respecting man of Kemet would even sink to being a slave owner?*

"Is it one of them they're all defending?" Maya asked in disgust.

✦

Later that evening, the indefatigable Pa-aten-em-heb showed up again, clean and dry, his step as springy as if he hadn't just had a grueling day's march through the rain.

"Tell me how your visits to the vassal kings went, my friend," Hani said as he ushered the young officer into the room.

Pa-aten-em-heb seated himself on the floor. "They seemed to be responsive. Even Biryawaza's men toed the line nicely, although who knows what they would have said had we not been with them. I'm optimistic that the vassals will show up for us when the time comes. This is what they've been praying for, after all."

"We've had a rather exciting week ourselves," said Hani dryly. "An embassy of Babylonians en route to Akhet-aten was robbed, and then, when they sought refuge here that night, one of their number was murdered."

The officer's eyes grew wide. "Murdered? A diplomat?"

Hani nodded. "And their king won't be happy about it."

"Where did it happen? In the city itself?"

"Right in the commissioner's residence. No one seems to have heard or seen anything."

Pa-aten-em-heb gave a low whistle. "By all that's holy! Under the nose of a magistrate of the Two Lands. That could be taken as an act of war."

"We suspect the Hittites," said Maya eagerly.

"Although I'm not sure they wouldn't have done something subtler if they were out to break our alliance with Sangar." Hani didn't want to be closed to that scenario, but it did seem less than probable to him. He realized his views had been influenced by his meeting with Hattusha-ziti and admonished himself, *Don't be credulous, my boy*. "In short, we're still investigating, and so far, the clues are nonexistent. Maya and I spoke to some of the servants, who would be the most likely to have information. But they're too terrorized to speak to us."

Pa-aten-em-heb sniffed in disgust. "I don't doubt it."

"Perhaps you could talk to some of the guards. Whoever killed the man bashed him to pieces. It must have been a military weapon."

"One of ours, do you think? Or a *hapir*? They have the most reason to want to see us attacked by Sangar along the eastern border."

Hani made a moue of uncertainty. "Or one of ours who has gone over to the *hapiru*."

"That would make a lot of sense." Pa-aten-em-heb looked up at Hani intently. "Tomorrow, I'll see what I can find out."

As the officer was moving to the door, Hani laid a hand on his shoulder and asked in an undertone, "Have you met with the commissioner?"

Pa-aten-em-heb's face grew dark. "No, my lord. I plan to avoid that honor."

"Would he recognize you, do you think?"

"I'm not sure. He saw me only one time. I was assigned here and there, mostly in Waset, while he and my family were in Hut-nen-nesut." The officer's jaw was clenched with anger.

Hani wondered what Amen-nefer, a Theban, had been doing in the City of Haru. *Did he have some office with the House of Royal Ornaments, the king's harem?*

Pa-aten-em-heb let himself out, and Hani and Maya were

left staring at one another. Finally, Hani said reflectively, "We need to find the man with the motive. Who would have an interest in killing a Babylonian diplomat?"

❖

The next morning, the commissioner hailed them in the courtyard. The rain had passed over, and a fresh, brilliant sky, like a bowl of blue frit, stretched overhead. The black cypress trees and the green fields below were sparkling, and the air had cooled down noticeably. Hani was newly aware of how high the town was, there in the foothills of forbidding mountains.

With Maya at his side, Hani was caught up in his own pleasant thoughts when Amen-nefer called, "Lord Hani!"

Hani looked up. The commissioner was striding toward them with the confident steps of a soldier. A smile brightened his too-handsome face. "My lord, you've been busy, I know, but I just wanted to ask how your investigation was going."

"Well enough," said Hani vaguely. "We don't have any formal suspects yet, but our military officer is going to talk to some of the garrison. I trust that won't be a problem."

"Not at all. It seems to me that some of those renegade countrymen of ours may have entered, disguised as soldiers. You're undoubtedly looking in the right direction." He fell into step alongside them. "How is that slave working out? He isn't especially bright—but then, what do you expect? I assigned him to you because he speaks good Egyptian."

"He's fine, my lord commissioner. Very obedient. He seems a little frightened."

Amen-nefer nodded. "Ridiculously shy for an adult.

I'm trying to give him some varied experiences to make him more confident. If he bothers you, just tell me. I'll find someone else for you."

Hani protested that Zalaya was perfectly adequate. He observed that Amen-nefer made no reference to the terrible bruise on the lad's face. Perhaps he hadn't even noticed it. The youth, after all, was just a native. The three men strode on toward the residence, Maya trailing a little.

"How did you like our storm last night?" Amen-nefer asked.

"Impressive. Glad I wasn't out in it."

"It'll probably be the last for a while. It's mostly winter when we receive our rain. Fall is just getting us in the mood." His voice dropped. "Did your foreign visitor find you?"

"He did. Thank you for directing him to my quarters."

"One of *them* wouldn't ordinarily be welcome here, but since he was a diplomat... we don't want to get a reputation, do we?"

Hani chuckled grimly.

"Well, this is where I peel off," the commissioner said as they approached the palace. "We're having a review of the troops this afternoon, if you're interested."

"That's kind of you, Lord Amen-nefer. If we're not occupied, we'll gladly take you up on your invitation. Oh, there is something we could use, and that's a stool or two. I had to seat our Babylonians on the bed." Hani smiled.

"Of course, of course, my lord. There's that worthless slave for you. He was supposed to furnish your apartment."

Hani made a deprecating noise and turned toward the residence, while the commissioner headed for the barracks.

"I'll see to it the man gets you something before the day is out," Amen-nefer called over his shoulder as he disappeared through the gate.

Hani and Maya strode on into the vestibule and turned at the stairwell rather than heading into the reception hall. Hani's crystalline mood was mildly tarnished. It always depressed him to hear someone disparage others. "Let's see what progress Pa-aten-em-heb makes with the soldiers."

"Do you want me to find Zalaya and see what he can do about stools? Who knows when Amen-nefer is going to be free," Maya said.

"That's a good idea. I wouldn't mind sitting on something other than the floor for dinner tonight."

"I'm off, then, Lord Hani. Shall we meet here before the review begins?" Maya asked brightly.

Hani nodded. "Excellent idea. I'll see you then."

As he descended the stairs, Maya saw slaves passing in and out of a corridor that opened unobtrusively under the steps. The ceiling was lower than elsewhere in the rather impressive building, and no effort had been made to decorate the walls, which were covered only in whitewash, much scuffed and peeling in places. *This must be a service area. Perhaps Zalaya is here somewhere.* He started tentatively down it, craning his head to try to see some human being. Ahead of him in the ill-lit distance, he perceived a man unbolting and entering a door. A moment later, the fellow emerged with a small table in each hand, kicked the door shut behind him, and set off in the opposite direction.

"*Yahya!* A storeroom!" Maya murmured triumphantly

to himself. He picked up his pace and drew near to the door. The servant had left it unbolted, for which Maya gave hearty thanks. He'd had experiences with the bolting system of the doors in Kharu, which were well over his head. But now he had only to push the panel and enter. The room was clearly a depository, piled high with furniture and only dimly lit from a narrow slit of a window, perhaps to protect the contents from theft.

Maya waded out into the room, squeezing between tables and climbing over chairs. Some of them seemed new, while other pieces were wobbly and damaged. "Where are the damned stools?" he grumbled, barking his shin on some kind of stand. An upside-down table slid off under his weight and fell with a clatter. *Ammit take it.* He grunted and heaved it to one side. Below it lay a wreck of a stool, two legs off, and the others hanging in splinters. Even the leather-covered frame was shattered. *It must have fallen out a window*, Maya thought with a grin, trying to imagine the scenario that could have brought a substantial stool to such ruin. He picked it up, careful not to get splinters in his hand, and heaved it to the edge of his path then wiped his hands on his hips. But suddenly, in the dim light, he saw brown streaks on his kilt.

He jerked back, staring at his hands: they were rusty looking. He sniffed them, and the odor of rancid meat rose, sickening, to his nose. "Blood!" he cried in a voice higher than normal. His heart had begun to pound. *Maybe this is just a stool that was used in the kitchen. Stay calm.* But even in the darkness, he could see that it was elaborately carved. The pierced-leather webbing of the seat was stamped with designs. A tuft of hair dangled from one of the sharp up-pointed corners. It was no kitchen stool; it was...

The murder weapon! He gasped. *It must be.*

But what do I do now? I can't carry it away with me. Everyone would think I was trying to dispose of the evidence of my crime. Maya's neck was crawling with fear. What if someone came in and found him there? What if the murderer himself came looking for the weapon?

Maya hurriedly stacked several pieces of furniture over the wrecked stool to conceal it, and panting wildly, he scrambled back over the tables and chairs to the door. After a quick, desperate look up and down the hall, he ran off back to the staircase and clattered up it, gasping, as if he were being propelled from behind.

"Mut, the mother of us all, protect us," he babbled over and over.

He clutched at his amulet as if he were hanging onto a branch that could save him from falling. A wave of nausea shook him even at the memory of that smell. He passed a slave, who stared at him in surprise as he tore past. *Did the fellow notice the blood?* At last Maya reached Hani's door.

He hammered on the panel. "Lord Hani! Lord Hani!" His voice was breaking with terror, and he felt he might begin to whimper at any moment as he remembered the Babylonians' comments about the victim's angry ghost.

After what seemed like a very long time, the door opened, and Hani, shirtless and barefoot, his close-cropped curly hair wet, stood before him, smelling of soap. No sight had ever been more comforting than his square-jowled face and broad, heavy middle sprinkled with graying hairs.

Hani's smile melted off as soon as he saw Maya's face. "What is it, son?" he cried.

Maya burst past him into the room. "Please, please, my lord. Shut the door." He knew he was almost incoherent, but he fancied the Babylonian's ghost had seen him come out of the room and was after him.

Hani poured a cup of wine from the ewer on the table and passed it to Maya, saying kindly, "You're safe, my boy. Tell me what has happened. What's that all over you?"

Maya guzzled down a swig of the wine and gasped. "I've found the murder weapon, Lord Hani." He held up his hands, maroon with dry blood.

Hani's little brown eyes widened. "Here, wash your hands, and you'd better change clothes." He pulled the damp linen towel from his shoulders and passed it to Maya, and the secretary scrubbed at his hands wildly.

"I saw a servant go into a storeroom and come out with furniture, so I thought I'd just dodge in and find you a stool. But everything was all piled up inside, old and new together. I started pushing things aside to get in. It was dark, almost too dark to see. At one point, a table slipped to the ground, and when I dragged it away, I saw a heavy carved stool that had been smashed to pieces. And it was covered with blood! Dried, of course, but I got it all over me. It had to have been the murder weapon, Lord Hani. It was *covered in blood* and all broken apart."

Far from pooh-poohing the young man's story, Hani stared at him, his eyes widening as if he had suddenly seen the light. One could deal some pretty serious injuries with a sturdy piece of furniture, and a stool would be easy enough for a strong man to lift, to swing. Bones would be broken; flesh would be rent. Blood would flow and splatter.

It must have been a horrible death, inch by terrified inch, as the victim was swallowed up in pain. Maya watched the progression of emotions on Hani's face—queasy horror chased out finally by outrage.

Through clenched teeth, Hani said, "I want to see it. Can you take me there, Maya? We'll bring a torch."

Maya's first reaction was to gape with disbelief, but his natural courage clicked back into place quickly. He swallowed hard. "Yes, my lord."

The two men bolted from the room, and Hani lifted down from its bracket one of the torches that burned day and night in the corridor. Maya led the way with a determined stride, his shadow stretched out before him in the fitful light of the torch in Hani's hand. Down the stairs they clattered, making no effort to conceal themselves.

Under the staircase, Maya pointed to the nearly invisible mouth of the service corridor. "It's down there, my lord," he said, clutching his amulet.

Hani took the lead. This hall, too, was ill lit, but there were windows at its end. Long, bright rectangles of sun, swimming with motes, cut across the floor.

"The second door on your left, my lord," Maya whispered.

The door was barred now, but Hani easily reached up and drew down the cord that would lift the interior bolt. The panel opened with a subdued screech. Hani held up the torch, and by its fitful orange light, Maya saw once again the chaotic jumble of furniture. As he'd told his father-in-law, some of it seemed to be in good condition, while other pieces were missing legs or had rips in the seats.

"Where was it?" Hani asked Maya in an undertone.

It occurred to Maya they would look less suspect if they didn't seem so furtive. After all, everyone knew they were investigating. Still, he wasn't going to be the one who attracted anybody's attention.

Maya squeezed past Hani and climbed across various furnishings in a state of ruin, where he stood peering around in the flickering torchlight, his heart pounding. "Back here. I was going in a straight line toward that slot of a window."

He kept his gaze low and clambered a few more cubits into the jumble. Suddenly he dropped into a crouch and heaved a small table out of the way. Below, Maya could glimpse the splintered legs of a stool pointing in the air.

He gagged and shot to his feet, drawing away from it. "Here," he said faintly.

Hani pressed forward. It wasn't as easy for a big man like him to squeeze through as it was for Maya. But finally, he raised his torch over the stool, and in the light, they could see the seat well. It had been smashed violently to pieces and was brown all over with dried blood that no one had made an effort to clean. That stench was unmistakable.

"Mut, the mother of us all!" Holding his breath, Hani bent and gingerly lifted the piece with one hand. A tottering leg fell off with a clatter.

"It took some violence to destroy a sturdy wooden frame like this," Maya said, trying to control the tremor in his voice. He bent his head and saw the tuft of dark hair glued to the upswung corner of the seat by a hardened mass of brown. His stomach lurched. *The damned assassin smashed his brains out.*

All at once, Hani squatted and reached out a hand. Caught among the splinters of a missing leg was a scrap of fabric. He propped the torch inside the upturned feet of a table and detached the material carefully, then he folded it in his fist and picked up the torch once more.

After perusing the stool for a while until Hani seemed to think he'd seen all he needed to—*and far more than we wanted to*—the men backed their way carefully out of the narrow space and exited the storeroom in a paroxysm of relief.

⁂

They stood in the hall, staring at one another. Then, in silence, they made their way back up the stairs to their apartment. Even once they were safely inside with the door bolted, Hani, his heart still hammering, felt he couldn't find any words.

He let out a low whistle. "That was the nastiest sight I've ever seen. I think it's undeniably the murder weapon. But just to be sure"—he held out the scrap of fabric—"wash this out, Maya, and let's see what color it was. Then we'll ask the Babylonians what color their colleague was wearing the evening he was killed."

Maya swallowed and departed, leaving Hani alone with his thoughts. *So much for someone sneaking in with a war club. The killer probably just picked up the stool that was sitting right there in Shulum-marduk's room.* A shiver ran up Hani's spine. He felt that Isfet, Chaos, was opening up right under his feet, swallowing down decency and even humanity itself, and he prayed that his family might be protected from such malice. Hani was too distracted to get much done, so he paced up and down, his thoughts roiling.

Sometime later, Maya returned with his scrap of fabric. "Only partially successful, my lord," he said in a flat voice. "There's no getting out a dried bloodstain, but here's a part of the cloth that wasn't spoiled." He pointed at the corner where the dark stains appeared not to have reached. "It seems to be red, unless that's stained too."

"No, I think you're right," Hani agreed, peering closely at the threads. "Let's go see our Babylonian friends."

They tramped immediately down the corridor to the door of the emissaries of Sangar. The Babylonians' servant let them in, and Hani saw that the two men were packing.

"Ah, Lord Hani," said Shindi-shugab in his growly voice. "As you see, we've been recalled to Bab-ilum. It will be a relief to get out of here, despite your kind attentions."

"I wish you a safe journey, my lords," Hani said with a respectful nod.

Akhu-tsabu asked hopefully, "Have you found anything?"

But Hani shook his head. "Not the killer, no. But we may have identified the murder weapon. May I ask you if you remember what your colleague was wearing the night of his murder?" *Of course, he might well have changed into his nightshirt by then. We don't know at what hour all this happened.*

Shindi-shugab grimaced, scratching his scalp thoughtfully. At last he said, "No, I'm afraid I don't. I wouldn't be of much help anyway—I'm color-blind." He laughed ruefully.

"I can tell you, my lord." Akhu-tsabu was almost bouncing up and down in his eagerness to help. "He was wearing a kind of dull red. I remember it well because I commented to him at dinner that even if he spilled wine on himself, it wouldn't show. Then he laughed and said he was glad I liked it, because his nightshirt had been on one of the donkeys that was stolen and he'd have to sleep in his clothes."

A hot flush of excitement crept up Hani's cheeks. He opened his fist and exposed the cloth scrap on his palm. "This corner—does it look familiar?"

"That's it!" cried Akhu-tsabu. "Where did you find this?"

Hani was suddenly reluctant to tell the Babylonians that he'd found it cached in a palace storeroom. The implication that someone on the commissioner's staff was guilty could do no good to international relations. He said, "It had been concealed. But Haru sheds his light on evil, no matter how it hides. And it will be avenged, my lords. You may tell your king that. The perpetrator will be found and punished. 'He who does evil, the shore rejects him; its floodwaters carry him away. The north wind descends to end his hour.' You may be sure of it."

Somberly, Shindi-shugab took Hani's hands. "I thank you, my colleague. We're deeply grateful for your help. Please continue to search. I will tell my king what a friend you've been to Karduniash."

"May our alliance grow ever stronger, Lord Shindi-shugab." Hani bowed to them both, and he and Maya took their leave.

✦

"The mail is here," Maya called from the door. The Babylonians had been gone for two days, and he and Hani had not made any more progress in identifying the killer. Their search was taking on that obstinate equilibrium that cases always reached before the truth came to light and everything seemed clear in retrospect.

Maya was hopeful that this diplomatic pouch, unlike the last one, would contain a word from Sat-hut-haru—"All is forgiven. I can't wait to see you" or "I've been proud and foolish. Let's let no shadow darken a love like ours." He'd tried out those words on his own behalf, but somehow, he couldn't make himself say them. He didn't even know what she was angry about. Perhaps nothing indeed. Women seemed to concoct grievances that were beyond the understanding of men.

Still, he was anxious as Lord Hani unpacked the pouch. There were four folded packets of papyrus inside, tied with string and stamped with clay seals. Hani took up one, and by the grin of delight that beamed from his face, Maya understood that it was from Lady Nub-nefer. His heart in his throat, he glanced at each of the remaining three—one from Lord Ptah-mes, one from the vizier, one from the king of Temesheq.

A wave of sorrow and, yes, fear washed over Maya. *Nothing from Sat-hut-haru? What does this mean?* He had to struggle to contain the tears that threatened to leak from his eyes. Maya turned away before Lord Hani could see how devastated he was.

But Hani had a keen eye. "Maya, my boy, is something

wrong? It seems like a long time since Sati wrote. Have you written to her at all?" His little brown eyes were warm with affection and concern. Maya felt he couldn't bear such compassion; it threatened to unman him completely.

"No on both counts," Maya said with feigned indifference. "But that's all right."

Hani continued to stare at him, his head tilted like a bird's, trying to understand. "*Is* it all right?"

Maya's lip trembled in spite of himself. He said in a tiny voice, "I think so." He could feel the absence of hope sucking at his soul until he feared it would drain right out. *Sati, my love, say I haven't lost you.* He hung his head and turned away, no longer able to contain his grief. *I should have known it was too good to be true.*

Hani stood watching him, his hands spread helplessly. "Talk to me, son. I'm a married man too."

"What can I say, my lord? She no longer loves me. We quarreled before I left—I don't even remember why—and after that she was sulky and would barely talk to me. And now, after months, she won't say a word. Doesn't she know I'd die for her?" Suddenly his shoulders shook with sobs of misery so profound he feared he would, in fact, die on the spot. He buried his face in his hands.

Maya felt Lord Hani's arms enfold him. His father-in-law held him in a silent embrace for a long while. "Sat-hut-haru can be stubborn, my boy. If she feels she's always the one to have to apologize after an argument, she may refuse to take the first step. It's up to you. It's always up to the strong one."

"Strong?" cried Maya bitterly. "To grovel to a woman?"

"To sacrifice even pride for someone he loves."

Maya realized in an onslaught of self-pity that he had no real idea of how to be a husband or a father. He'd never known his own father. There had been no man in his youth to model that kind of strength. He'd been his mother's little prince and had known nothing about how a woman and a man interacted except to expect to rule.

As if he'd read Maya's mind, Hani said ruefully, "Sat-hut-haru has been spoiled, I'm afraid. She expects to get her way—quietly, perhaps; she's not like Neferet. But she takes for granted that others will bow down to her."

"I do bow down. I worship her," Maya whimpered.

"Not to worship, just to apologize."

Maya dashed at his brimming eyes. "But I don't even know why she's mad, my lord. I don't even know if it's my fault. Maybe... maybe there's another man." *Oh, dismal thought. She's tired of me because I'm a dwarf.* The pain was like a spearpoint in his heart.

Hani's face was crumpled with sympathy. "Listen, Maya. I have to tell you something that is perhaps not mine to tell, but I think desperate times require desperate measures. Sati is several months pregnant."

"What?" Maya cried. His first reaction was joy, but then he realized how much worse it made everything that she hadn't even told him. "She told you but not me?"

"No, she told her mother. And what I wanted to say is that pregnant women can take on strange notions. They can be very emotional. They can act in ways they normally never would."

Maya had no answer. With a leaden heart, he began to see the enormity of his assumptions. "What can I do, then?"

"Write her. Tell her you're sorry, even if you don't know what for. Tell her you love her." Hani smiled. "I think once you start, you'll find you already know what to write."

I've been proud and foolish. Let's let no shadow darken a love like ours. Yes, he knew. "I will, Lord Hani. Right away." The thought that Mery-ra or Pa-kiki would read his words aloud to Sati horrified him, but it would just be one more sacrifice for his beloved. He threw himself down cross-legged on the floor and pulled off his writing case.

※

Ah, youth, Hani thought fondly as he saw a pacified Maya scribbling away on a scrap of papyrus. *If we could learn from our experiences, I would be a wise old bird by now.*

Satisfied that his son-in-law had been dragged back from the brink of despair, he set himself to reading the letter from Nub-nefer. As always, he didn't quite relax until he saw the words "everyone is fine." Little Tepy's front teeth were already loose. Sat-hut-haru was given to fits of weeping and wouldn't tell her mother why, but she seemed to be progressing well with her pregnancy. Mut-nodjmet was expecting again with Pa-kiki's second child. Pa-kiki and his officer were heading for the north. "Have you seen him up there?"

Not often enough, Hani answered her silently, but the boy was doing his grown-up job competently and earning the admiration of his superiors.

And then came his father's postscript: "King Smenkh-ka-ra is now ensconced in Waset with his bride, the Great King's wife Meryet-aten. Lady Nefert-iti still holds whatever position she held before, but she, too, is announced as

Great King's wife. We're swimming in Great King's wives! I'm thinking of offering our Neferet up to some prince so we can be Gods' Fathers, too, like everyone else. I would be the God's Grandfather. Has a ring to it, doesn't it? Come back soon, or I'll become so cynical you won't recognize me. Love, your reverend father. (You thought I'd forgotten, hadn't you?)"

Out of respect for Maya, Hani suppressed a laugh. His incorrigible father was yet pushing along a joke that they'd shared years ago about the proper respect owed him.

Still basking in the warm glow of pleasure that news from the family always shed upon him, Hani turned to the other letters. Lord Ptah-mes, in Akhet-aten, asked after the progress on the murder case. They'd had to break the news of the murder to the Babylonian ambassador, who nearly had an apoplexy. Ptah-mes said nothing about his meeting with the king, so Hani suspected he'd not yet had it.

The final letter was from the vizier Ra-nefer. He summoned Hani back to the capital immediately for a royal audience. Hani almost dropped the papyrus. "They're pulling us off this assignment, too, before we can conclude it? What's going on?" he cried, aggrieved.

"What's that, my lord?" Maya looked up, his face beaming. But seeing the storm cloud hovering over Hani's own, he grew anxious. "What is it, my lord? Is Sati—"

"No, no. She's grieving your absence but is otherwise well. I was exclaiming over this summons from the vizier. We're to head home immediately. Doesn't he know we're in the midst of an important case? They've already made us change direction once." His breath was steaming in his nose with disgust, and he slammed the letter to the floor. "I've half a mind to ignore it and stay to finish our investigation. When it's successful, I could just convince Ra-nefer it had been his idea all along."

"But this is from the king..."

Hani curbed his irritation. "I know, I know." He stood staring into space, pondering various acts of rebellion he might commit but knowing very well that he would have to obey. Finally, he said between his teeth, "Let's go tell the staff to pack up. We're heading home. And thank all the gods our Babylonian friends have already left so they don't witness this abandonment of their cause."

Maya scrambled to his feet and trotted off to spread the word, while Hani remained immobile, struggling with his conscience. *All the stupidities of the regime are not on you, my friend*, he finally decided, and he turned to pack his baggage.

CHAPTER 6

A s it turned out, Hani's only little act of defiance
was to return straight to Waset rather than to the
capital, so they stopped at Akhet-aten only long enough for
his staff to disembark. He would have liked to have seen
Ptah-mes—perhaps vent his frustration on someone who
would understand only too well—but he wanted to see his
family even more. Hani hoped Maya's letter to Sati had
reached her and that marital crisis had been averted.

When they arrived at his gate, weary and dirty from
their journey, and A'a had opened to them joyfully, Maya
made as if to peel off to his own home, but A'a said,
"Mistress of the house Sat-hut-haru is here, Lord Maya."

Hani and Maya exchanged a glance. It wasn't unusual
for Sati to spend time with her mother when their respective
husbands were gone, but Hani felt a little uneasy. Maya, on
the other hand, brightened with eagerness.

"Nub-nefer!" Hani called as he entered the vestibule.
Although the early winter day was mild, the sun was still
unconquerably strong, and it took him a moment to regain

his sight in the semidarkness. He kicked off his sandals and reveled in the cool smoothness of the plaster floor.

Nub-nefer appeared joyfully in the interior doorway, as slim and beautiful as a figure in a wall painting, for all her forty-nine years. "Hani, my love! You're back! Maya!" She took Hani into her arms and, her head against his chest, murmured, "We didn't know when to expect you. We got the message saying you were leaving sooner than expected."

"It was sudden, my dove, or I would have given you more warning." Hani buried his nose in her wig, breathing in her fragrance of bergamot and lilies.

Suddenly a whirlwind of excitement blew into the room. It was Neferet, pelting toward her father to throw herself in his arms. "Papa! Maya! Bener-ib and I are here for the holidays!"

"What holiday is it now, my duckling? I begin to think you never work!" But he embraced her joyously and scrubbed her short-shaved scalp with his knuckles. Over her head, he smiled at Bener-ib, who stood shyly in the doorway.

"Sokar, Papa, the end of the first season of the year."

"That's a rather somber one. I wish I could be here with you to mourn the Lord Osir, but I need to leave again for the capital almost immediately."

"I'm practicing already for the sacred mourning rites. I'm going to dance. Bener-ib will have to tear her hair, because I don't have any." Neferet pulled away and began to posture more or less like a dancer, rocking backward and clutching her head, swooping forward as if bending over a coffin, one foot in the air. Hani watched her, his heart filled with tender amusement. Neferet, for all her enthusiasm, was an appalling dancer who couldn't hear the beat of the music any more than Hani could.

"Is there still going to be a procession?" he asked his wife dubiously.

"Unofficially," she said, putting an arm around Neferet as much to curb her as out of love. "It's going to be celebrated neighborhood by neighborhood."

"Pretty sparse crowd left around here, I fear," Hani said. "They may need me to punch up the dancing a little." He, too, began to rock and wave his arms and opened his mouth in a wail of keening.

Neferet shook her head and laughed. "The howls of grief will be real if you dance like that, Papa. Better leave it to us youngsters."

Nub-nefer turned at last to Maya, who stood with a pursed mouth of disapproval, or perhaps impatience, at Hani's side. "Sat-hut-haru is in the salon, Maya. I think she... she'd be more than happy to see you."

Maya slung down his basket and rushed off to the salon, murmuring, "Excuse me, everyone," while Hani and Nub-nefer stood locked together.

She said in a low voice, "Sati was very unhappy—for a long time, I think. She said they had quarreled and that Maya was refusing to talk to her. And then when he didn't write from abroad, she was brokenhearted. She feared that their marriage was over."

Hani gave a rueful snort. "That's exactly what he said to me. She did receive his letter, didn't she?"

Nub-nefer nodded. "She was happy to the point of tears. She's having their baby in another month, you know."

Hani nodded, his heart appeased. From within, they

heard a loud burst of sobs, masculine and feminine, and he smiled down into Nub-nefer's deep-brown gaze. "Were we ever like that? Did we kiss and make up?"

"It's always sweeter afterward, my love—that's my recollection." She smiled up at him from her large kohl-painted eyes, and they were wells of tenderness.

Hani forced himself to break away. "I haven't said hello to the other girls and to Father yet. Do you think it's too soon to go in there with our pair of turtledoves?"

She laughed and took his hand in her small one, freshly hennaed and perfectly groomed. *If I didn't know better, I would swear she's not the same woman I saw butchering a hog*, Hani said to himself with a smile. His heart was full to bursting. The idea of any of his dear family coming to harm was unendurable. He thought of Ptah-mes, that paragon of self-control, and how he had fallen completely apart when his wife died. *I would too*, he thought, choking.

Within the salon, next to Baket-iset's couch, Maya and Sat-hut-haru sat, their arms around one another. Hani saw tears in both their eyes. He bent over his daughter and kissed her. "How is my little mother?"

She proudly displayed her swelling belly. "Another month, Papa. I'm so glad you're home." She turned to Maya and said coyly, "I'm so glad *you're* home, my lion."

Lion, eh? The word for lion was *mai*, so it was a rather clever nickname. The pun sounded more like Maya's wit than that of Hani's daughter.

Maya caught Hani's eye and blushed to the roots of his hair, his happiness unconcealable.

Hani winked then knelt beside Baket-iset's couch. "And

how is my favorite eldest daughter?" he asked, caressing her face.

"Splendid, Papa. I just witnessed the most beautiful thing—two people humble enough to make up."

Sati and her husband exchanged a melting look. Hani caught his wife's eye, and the two of them laughed. "It takes a real lion," Hani agreed. He looked around him, suddenly realizing a beloved face was missing. "Where's Father? At his lady friend's house?"

"He's in the garden. I'm surprised he didn't come to the gate when A'a opened to you," said Nub-nefer.

Hani left his family and drifted out onto the porch. The garden was sparse at this season, the arbor naked of its grapevine. Hani could see a flash of white clothing in the dining pavilion. "Father?" he called.

Mery-ra was seated in the one good chair, his head against the wall and his feet stretched out before him, eyes closed and mouth hanging open. He jerked upright as Hani approached.

"Sleeping, were you? Up late last night at Meryet-amen's?"

"Ah, Hani, my son! You're back!" Mery-ra hauled himself to his feet, and the two men embraced. "How are things in the north?"

Hani's delight chilled. "Riddled with conflicting orders, as usual. First we were feeling out the loyalty of Qidshu and the other mayors in preparation for an apparent punitive mission against the *hapiru*—led by none other than your friend Pa-aten-em-heb."

"Well, well. Then Pa-kiki was there?"

"He was. Happy as a heron in the marshes." Hani chuckled then continued with less amusement, "We were pulled from that assignment to investigate the murder of a Babylonian diplomat right in the commissioner's palace at Kumidi."

Mery-ra's bushy eyebrows rose in horror. "A diplomat? In the palace? Oh, that's not good at all."

"To say the least. And it was a brutal murder. He was beaten to death with a stool."

Mery-ra glanced back at the chair he'd just vacated and edged away from it as if he feared it might turn on him. "Any suspects?"

"We found the stool hidden in a palace storeroom, but we didn't have time to pursue it further than that before I was recalled. My guess is it was one of the palace staff. Perhaps he was a plant on behalf of some force hostile to our alliance with Sangar."

"And that means Kheta, eh?"

Hani grew thoughtful. His father had participated in many state secrets during his career as a military scribe, so Hani felt he dared tell him. He said in a low voice, "An emissary of Kheta came to see me in Kumidi."

Mery-ra's little brown eyes opened wide.

"He seemed to have sought me out in particular," Hani said.

"His horse must have needed grooming," Hani's father said with a naughty grin.

"According to him, the Hittites don't want to be our enemy. They want to be friends and trading partners."

Mery-ra whistled. "And why did he seek *you* out, son? Has talk of your beauty reached even that distant kingdom?"

Hani's voice dropped even lower. "Someone must have given him my name. I wonder if it was the Crocodiles."

"You mean those ex-priests of Amen who are trying to pull down the government? Oh, son, stay away from them. We all admire them, but their friendship is the kiss of death."

Hani said reflectively, "I consider myself one of them." It was the first time he'd really admitted that to himself in so many words.

Mery-ra cocked an eyebrow at his son. "What makes you think this Hittite wasn't lying? He wouldn't be likely to say to you, 'We plan to strip you of your vassals and devour you alive.'"

"My gut, Father. You always tell me to listen to my gut when judging people. My gut told me he was at least basically truthful."

Mery-ra reached out and patted his son's belly. "I hope the little man knows what he's talking about in there."

Hani laughed. "Still, it makes sense for them, doesn't it? Their king has been on a years-long campaign of conquest, but that can't go on forever. They need resources, and how else to get them but by trade with allies?"

"I can see that. But this may not be received with much enthusiasm by our government."

"Probably not. I still don't know the vizier of the Lower Kingdom well enough to predict his reaction. Ptah-mes says he's an idiot."

Mery-ra brightened. "Speaking of Ptah-mes, he's in Waset. I saw him the other day, galloping along in his chariot, heading, I think, to that palace near the Ipet-isut where our new coregent has taken up residence."

Nub-nefer emerged from behind the bushes with two

cups in her hands. "Already talking politics? Don't you think the man needs a little time to wash off and rest, Father?"

She handed each of them a cup, and Hani sniffed it. Rich and fruity as a day in late summer. "This is that wonderful stuff from Kebni, isn't it? Thank you, my dove." She put her arm around his waist, and Hani took a deep draft from his cup. "Tastes as good as it smells." He wiped his mouth with the back of a hand and offered the vessel to his wife, who drew in a ladylike sip and passed it back to him.

"Don't I get any too?" Neferet stuck her head under her father's arm and made her irresistible pleading eyes.

"Go easy, my girl." Mery-ra chuckled. "I don't want to see you lose your inhibitions any worse than you have. How did you sneak up so quietly on us, anyway?"

"Why don't we go inside so Baket-iset can be included in the conversation?" Nub-nefer suggested.

Hani and Mery-ra followed her into the salon, Neferet prancing at their heels and Bener-ib trailing after like her shadow. Inside it was pleasantly warmer after the chill of descending evening in the garden. The lit lamps made a cozy little circle of light against the darkness.

Baket-iset lay there immobile, a smile on her lips. She followed her parents and grandfather with her eyes as they approached. "How did your mission go, Papa?"

Hani and the others seated themselves by the girl's couch. "Cut off short by my summons home, I'm afraid. I don't know if anyone else is being sent up there to conclude it."

"Hani, my love, you never said in your letter why you were being recalled." Nub-nefer laid a hand on his arm.

"I'm afraid I don't know." The same queasy unease he'd felt upon receiving the command swept over him again. "The king has demanded my presence."

Nub-nefer and Mery-ra exchanged a worried look.

"Normally, I'd say that meant nothing good, but since he has fallen in love with you, perhaps he's going to honor you again," said Mery-ra with forced joviality.

"I haven't a clue. I'll have to start off for the capital in the next few days, though, so I guess I'll find out."

"Be sure to visit Aha." Nub-nefer's smile was crisp with ill-concealed anxiety. Nobody in Hani's household trusted the king's benevolence. She rose. "Why don't I see to starting dinner? You'll want to get to bed at a decent hour if you're traveling tomorrow."

"Of course, my dove." Hani kissed her hand, savoring that scent that was all hers—that scent that filled his dreams when he was abroad for long months.

She made her way, with gracefully swaying hips, to the kitchen, and Hani and his father were left staring at one another. Neferet and Bener-ib talked with quiet animation to one another in a far corner of the room. At last, Hani turned to his eldest daughter. "Baket, my swan, I need your insight. I met with a man of Kheta while I was in the north. He wants me to take Nefer-khepru-ra a message from his king, protesting peace and brotherhood. They want to open trade with us."

"Why, that's wonderful, Papa."

"Yes, but can I trust him? Can I trust them? They seem to be involved in all sorts of nefarious things up there on the border."

Baket-iset pondered for a moment. "What did the man look like, Papa?"

Hani ransacked his memory. "About my age. Tall, lean, easy in his movements. Frank looking. Good eye contact."

"He believed what he was saying, I think. That doesn't mean it was true."

"You mean his king could be using him?" Hani thought bitterly of all the times he'd been used—that his own honesty had been an unwitting cover for something shady.

"I have no idea, but it could be."

"Thank you, my swan." Did she feel Hattusha-ziti *was* being used by his ruler, or was that just a generalized possibility? *I'm asking too much of her gift. It's not me who has to take that decision anyway. I just need to make it known to the king.* He'd decided to bypass Ra-nefer.

Just then, Nub-nefer appeared in the doorway from the kitchen. "Dinner is ready. The girls are going to set up the tables."

"Shall I call Khawy?" Mery-ra asked, heaving himself to his feet.

"I've already sent word, Father. He's on his way." Nub-nefer directed the servants where to set up everything, and before long, Hani was enjoying his first home-cooked meal in months among the people he loved best.

"Tomorrow morning before I leave, I need to talk to Ptah-mes," Hani said around a mouthful of stewed leeks.

"How's he doing, son? Not too cast down by his exile?"

"No. Not at all. Just made more cynical. How he's holding up inside after Apeny's death, I couldn't say. I had the feeling that something had gone out of him for good."

Nub-nefer said, her brows buckled in compassion, "He's still grieving. It's only been two years, poor man."

"Well," said Mery-ra, whose ear was to the door of every bit of gossip in the City of the Scepter, "I can tell you there are plenty of wellborn ladies of all ages who'd like to help him forget his sorrows. He's an extremely eligible catch."

Hani heaved a sigh. "They may find themselves disappointed. He doesn't have the air of a man who will ever touch another woman."

"Poor man," Nub-nefer repeated.

The adults fell silent. The three young people kept their heads down and ate. At one point, Neferet looked up and caught her father's eye then dropped her gaze quickly.

"How are you doing with your lessons, Khawy?" Hani asked kindly, hoping to set the boy at ease.

"Lord Mery-ra could tell you better than I, my lord. But I feel I'm making progress. I know a lot of symbols by heart," the boy said modestly. Khawy, an orphan, had come to them when his uncle, the chief draftsman in the Place of Truth, had been murdered. His one dream was to become literate and to be able to follow in his uncle's footsteps.

"He's doing very well indeed. He has an artist's eye. I must show you the pictures he's done for my *Book of Going Forth*." Mery-ra beamed at him.

Hani smiled proudly at the boy. Khawy was seventeen now, a sturdy youngster with a dark shadow of beard already upon his chin. It wouldn't be long before he was circumcised and shaved off his sidelock of childhood. *We did the right thing by bringing him home and training him*, Hani thought.

After dinner, Maya—feeling restored to grace, no

doubt—entertained the family with a highly colored account of the Traveler's adventures in Djahy. Hani watched how animated the little secretary became under the admiring eyes of Sat-hut-haru and the others. Before long, Neferet, reasserting herself as the center of attention, popped up and started acting out Maya's tale with her usual exuberance. Her pantomime of the obsequious king of Temesheq was especially hilarious. Then she took on the vizier, looking befuddled, and finally Lord Ptah-mes, gazing haughtily down her nose and flicking dust off her invisible immaculate sleeve. The family was rocking with hilarity, although Hani felt a pang of guilt. He didn't consider his admired friend a man to mock, even in good nature.

It was late when the party broke up and everyone headed off to their respective bedrooms. As Hani, stretching, prepared to escort Nub-nefer up the stairs by the light of a little moringa-oil lamp, Neferet called out, "Papa, where does your friend Lord Ptah-mes live?"

"In Waset? He has an enormous villa in the southern part of the city, not far from the Ipet-isut. Why, my duckling?"

"Oh, just curious." And she disappeared into the darkness.

⁜

Hani was late arising the next day—it was delicious to lie in a proper bed with Nub-nefer at his side, snuggled into the bedclothes, and not on the deck of a boat. He could smell her animal warmth and the last threads of her fading perfume. There was something about a sleeping person—a child, a woman, perhaps even a man—that aroused his tenderness. All the facades were down, all the disagreeable tics forgotten, and nothing was left but the blamelessness of a pure *ba*. Perhaps this was how they would all be in the Field of Reeds when the parts of their soul were reunited and they became a blessed *akh*—an innocent, undefended perfection of themselves.

Eventually, Hani forced his lazy carcass to get up. He was thinking now of staying the six days of the festival rather than rushing back to the capital. The king wouldn't know how long the trip home had taken, and Hani was in no hurry for his audience. With the exception of his gold of honor ceremony, he hadn't been summoned into the royal presence since the king first took the throne alone, ten years before. He'd hoped to escape the notice of Nefer-khepru-ra for another ten years at least.

He padded groggily down to the kitchen and could see from the sun in the reed-shaded courtyard that morning was well up. Hani stretched and yawned and scratched his belly. Some stale flatbreads lay on the table, covered with a towel, and he laid one gingerly to toast on the round dome of the oven, which was already heating up for the day's baking. He could hear the cook grinding grain in the court, so Hani poured himself a cup of milk and made his way to the garden, toast in hand. To his disappointment, it was still much too chilly to sit outside, so he stood in the doorway and watched Qenyt at her hunt, stalking with slow grace and freezing until the wary frogs lost their fear and went on about their task. Then her gray head darted out with the speed of a cobra, and her dagger-sharp beak snapped them up.

"You're a ruthless girl, you are," he said and turned back toward the kitchen.

"Who, Papa? Me?" Neferet appeared from the vestibule. She was already dressed, with a shawl knotted around her shoulders, and wide-awake. Her cheeks were flushed.

"No, no, my duckling. Qenyt. Where have you been at this early hour?"

"Oh, around. It isn't that early, you know." She hugged her father and hustled away with suspicious haste.

What's that rascal up to? He'd find out soon enough, he supposed—when a troop of sick orphans descended on the house, expecting lodging, or some mange-eaten dog was smuggled in, to the horror of Ta-miu and her kittens.

※

That evening after dinner, when Nub-nefer and the girls had retreated to the garden pavilion, Hani sat alone at his ease in the salon, sipping the last of his beer. Mery-ra had dined with his lady friend and was no doubt gone for the night. But—to the extent that a big meal and a half pot of beer permitted him to do much of anything with application—the solitude gave Hani a chance to think about the appalling murder of the Babylonian emissary. It would have taken some strength to wield that heavy stool, so he couldn't imagine that the reedy Zalaya was guilty. But Maya had said the commissioner's body servant was a strapping fellow. There had to be many such stalwarts at the residence. Were they all, as Maya had wondered, protecting one of their own? The punishment would be so severe for a slave who dared to raise his hand against an eminent personage that that would certainly explain their terror. Hani needed very badly to talk this over with Ptah-mes, to see if he couldn't be sent back to Kumidi before Burna-buriash lost his patience and declared war.

He was drowsing in his low-backed chair when he heard the clearing of a throat from the door to the vestibule. "My lord," said A'a apologetically. "Lord Ptah-mes is at the door, asking for you."

"Send him in, man." Hani jumped up from his chair and hustled after the gatekeeper, not even bothering to put on his wig or shirt or sandals.

Sure enough, the commissioner of northern vassals was standing in the dark vestibule with his usual cool elegance, one fist on his hip. He saw Hani and came forward, smiling. "Ah, my friend. Forgive this nocturnal visit. I have to go back to Azzati tomorrow, and there are a few things I wanted to talk to you about before I left."

"You're always welcome, my lord. Come in and have a seat, I beg you. In fact, I need to talk to you as well. I was planning to come see you tomorrow, so this is fortuitous. I would have missed you."

Hani led the way into the salon, where a few lamps were still burning, and drew out the best chair for his guest.

Sweeping his long skirts forward, Ptah-mes seated himself with his accustomed unconscious grace. "What did you need to talk to me about, Hani?"

Hani filled in the high commissioner on the gruesome details of the murder and how his investigation had hit a dead end in the storeroom.

Ptah-mes pursed his lips thoughtfully. "This case needs to be pursued, no doubt about it."

"And there's something else, my lord." Hani dropped

his voice. "A Hittite emissary came to visit me. He seemed to know I was there. In fact, he seemed to know all about me."

"Quite. I directed him to you."

Hani raised his eyebrows in surprise.

Ptah-mes smiled thinly. "Who better than you to deal with such a man? Tell the king what happened, and let him make a decision about where to go with this. I find in it a hopeful sign." His smile broadened, and Hani realized his superior was indeed part of the Crocodiles, in sympathy if not in actuality.

Hani said in a lower voice, "What should we make of their meddling with our vassals' loyalty?"

"What loyalty?" Ptah-mes asked in an acid tone. There followed a long space of silence. "Have you had your interview with the king yet, Hani?"

"No, my lord."

The look on Ptah-mes's face was so ambiguous, so studied and neutral, that Hani began to grow uneasy. He said jestingly—although the anxiety within him was real—"Have I been decommissioned?"

"No, no," Ptah-mes assured him. "Quite the contrary." He stared Hani in the eye with his own intense black-eyed gaze, and something bitter twitched a corner of his mouth. "He's going to offer you the position of high commissioner of foreign affairs in the north."

Hani's mouth fell open. "Me, my lord? But aren't *you* de facto high commissioner?"

"I am, yes. But the king seems to think I'm distracted by my overall duties and can't concentrate on the problem of the *hapiru*."

"He's demoting you again." Rage bubbled up in Hani's breast, a liquid so cold it blistered. "You're being punished for doing a good job."

Ptah-mes tipped his head in assent, as cool and gracious as if someone had just offered him a compliment.

Hani's face burned. He smashed a fist into his other palm. "*Ma'at* has been trampled on once more. How much longer will the gods hold back our punishment?" He no longer cared if the servants heard him. Perhaps, like the slaves of the commissioner of Kumidi, they viewed it as a duty to see and hear nothing.

"Feel free to accept, Hani. When our time comes, the more good men we have in place, the better."

But Hani cried, "I can't do it, my lord. It's too dishonorable. To make me your superior? This is a mockery of us both."

Ptah-mes let out a sigh. "You're perhaps the last honorable man in the government. Most of our colleagues would be only too happy to walk over my corpse in their eagerness for advancement." He gave Hani a smile of genuine affection, devoid of sarcasm for once. "But don't harm yourself to protect me, my friend. I'm past feeling any pain at insult."

Hani let out a gust of air, as if he could sweep away the evils of the world with his breath.

"The decision is yours, of course, but certainly if you accept, you'll be a good high commissioner. It will be an honor to serve under you."

The words, so sincerely spoken, were like a spear driven into Hani's heart. "I'm... I'm stunned, Lord Ptah-mes. Why is the king suddenly honoring me again and again, when he has shown me such hostility up to now? I almost feel it's dangerous to let myself fall into the trap of gratitude toward him. Is he trying to buy me?"

Ptah-mes sighed once more. "Who knows?" After a moment of silence, he said placidly, "We must stay calm. And resist."

Hani shook his head, helpless in his confusion. "What will happen if I refuse the position?"

Ptah-mes shrugged.

The two men fell silent again, Hani struggling mightily with the vile choice before him. "I'll refuse," he finally said.

"As you wish, Hani. But I doubt that means I'll be reinstated."

"Oh, my lord, how I wish this weren't happening. It pains me to be a cause of misfortune for you like this."

"Think nothing of it, my friend." Ptah-mes cleared his throat. "There's... there's one more thing I would like to bring up before I go."

"Anything, my lord."

Ptah-mes sat in silence, his hands clasped tensely in his lap, while Hani waited for him to speak. Curiosity had begun to rise in Hani like the first curls of smoke from a newly built fire.

At last, Ptah-mes said uncomfortably, "This is a difficult subject to broach, Hani." He drew in a deep breath and straightened in his chair as if preparing for battle. "I... I would like to ask your daughter's hand in marriage."

Hani's jaw dropped. He didn't know what to say or even what to feel. This was the most unexpected, not to say absurd, proposal he'd ever heard. *Dear gods, can he be joking?* But Ptah-mes was not a man of levity. Hani gaped at his superior, hoping to read some sense into his words. Ptah-mes gazed at him gravely, a little diffidently. He was still an extremely handsome man, slim and strong looking, and in a costly wig, with his black eyebrows, his age was by no means apparent. Hani had a painful flash of memory of seeing him with his own thinning gray hair, but it seemed obscene to call that to mind.

Hani finally managed to stammer, "You don't need my permission, my lord."

"No, but I would never do it against your will. I would hate to see such a thing break apart our friendship"—Ptah-mes dropped his eyes a little shyly—"which I value. Now more than ever."

Hani waved his hands in a helpless gesture. "I'm stunned, my lord. Your status is so much above ours. I… I can't imagine what would make you even consider her. You do mean Neferet, I assume? How have you even met her?"

Ptah-mes emptied his lungs with a deep breath that spoke eloquently of how difficult the conversation was for him. "In fact, she approached me."

Once more, Hani gaped, dumbfounded. So that was why she'd asked about the whereabouts of Ptah-mes's villa. "She asked you to marry her? Please forgive her temerity, my lord. She's an impetuous girl—"

"On the contrary, Hani. She had thought this out quite reflectively, I think."

Hani reeled in shock. "Oh, my lord, whatever it looks like, I can't believe she's after your property. She cares nothing for wealth."

Ptah-mes smiled, his dark eyes remaining untouched. Hani had watched him grow more and more bitter and sarcastic since his wife's death until Hani wondered if his superior were capable of happiness anymore. He was by no stretch of the imagination able to picture the irrepressible eighteen-year-old Neferet yoked to such a man, even beyond the difference in class and age—Ptah-mes was Hani's senior by three years.

"Not at all. I'm acquainted with that sort of woman," Ptah-mes assured him.

That Hani could well believe. He tried not to sound insultingly resigned when he said, "If you're both sure of this, then I can only give it my blessing. She's said nothing to us."

"I'm afraid it will be even more difficult for her than for me, but… it will be a white marriage, my friend. Please don't see any insult aimed at your daughter, but I just can't… after Apeny, I…" Despite his self-control and casual expression, Ptah-mes's voice shook a little and trailed off. He didn't look Hani in the eye.

"I understand, my lord," said Hani. And he did, but it just confused him the more.

"That's what your daughter wanted. I swear I'm not imposing this on her." Suddenly, Hani began to see what was going on, and Ptah-mes's next words confirmed that suspicion. "I'll be gone most of the time, of course, but she won't be lonely. Her friend will live with her."

Hani's cheeks blazed as embarrassment flooded him, washed over him, threatened to drown him in its burning waves. It seemed to him that Neferet was abusing his superior shamelessly. Hani dropped awkwardly to his knees and burst out in a voice of passionate apology, "Oh, my lord, after all my family owes you, I can't believe that girl is exploiting you like this. Forgive us for treating you so disgracefully." He pressed his forehead to the floor.

But Ptah-mes drew Hani to his feet and gestured him to be seated once more. "Disgrace and I are old friends." He said it caustically, but then his voice grew pleasant again. "And anyway, Hani, it's mutually agreeable. She'll stay in Akhet-aten; I'll be in Azzati. From time to time, our paths will cross. I'll see to her every material need. She'll keep my would-be suitors at bay." He smiled, and this time it was warmer. "I'm not going to suffer. She's a charming young woman, and I admire her dedication to the sick."

Hani groaned and put a hand over his eyes as if to blot out this evidence of Neferet's conniving.

"I know it's unexpected..." Ptah-mes murmured apologetically. His face had grown serious once more, as if he feared Hani would refuse his permission.

But Hani was trying to calm down and see the bizarre union in a practical light. "As long as I don't have to call you 'son,' my lord," he said, forcing a crooked grin.

Ptah-mes gave a bark of laughter. "Please don't. You might try 'inbred scum,' as our friend Mahu calls me." He rose.

Hani threw back his head and laughed with him as he, too, got to his feet. "Never, Lord Ptah-mes. I wish you both well. You know that, don't you? This all just caught me by surprise."

"I understand, my friend. This has been an evening of surprises for you, no doubt. I'm sorry to be the bearer of unsettling tidings—perhaps on both counts."

He clapped Hani on the shoulder, and Hani, filled with

emotion, seized his hand and gave it a heartfelt squeeze of solidarity. "I greatly admire you, my lord."

"Save it for someone who is admirable, Hani." Ptahmes turned and made his way through the dark vestibule into the night.

Hani stood there in the salon, staring after his friend's retreating back, trying to make sense of the improbable realities that had descended on him all at once.

CHAPTER 7

Hani managed to avoid Nub-nefer until they were both alone in their bedroom that night. He cringed at the thought of having to explain Neferet's latest original behavior to her mother. Nub-nefer sat at her cosmetics table by the light of a moringa oil lamp, combing out her long hair, which tumbled in a lustrous waterfall over her shoulders.

Hani approached from behind her and kissed the sweet slope of her golden neck. "My dear, I have something to tell you."

She must have picked up on his reluctance, because her smile faded into anxiety. "It's not one of the children, is it? Or the grandchildren?"

Hani fidgeted uncomfortably. "It's Neferet. But there's nothing wrong with her. It's that she's... getting married."

Nub-nefer's face flowered with joy and relief. She rose and faced her husband, holding out her arms. "Why that's wonderful, Hani! I knew she would outgrow that obsession with Bener-ib."

Hani drew her to him. Still, he couldn't muster much enthusiasm. If anything, this calculating match was worse than no husband. "She, er... she wants to marry Lord Ptah-mes."

Nub-nefer started to laugh, then her eyes grew wide. "You're serious? He asked her to marry him?"

"As I understand it, she asked him to marry her."

His wife pondered this uncomprehendingly. "And he agreed? They're going to be married?"

"Ptah-mes asked my blessing. Not because he needs it but because he didn't want it to destroy our friendship if I were opposed."

Hani was taken aback by the excitement that flushed Nub-nefer's face. Her big eyes opened even wider. "But that's an unbelievably exalted match for the girl, my dearest. It's more than any one of us could ever have dreamed of. He's not so old—"

"Older than me."

"But still extremely attractive." She blushed when Hani crooked his mouth. "Not that I would have noticed," she added hastily. "And, dear gods—so rich. So wellborn. I can hardly believe it." She clasped her hands in ecstasy.

So loathed by the king, Hani almost added but held himself back. "It's to be a... a white marriage. He'll be in Azzati, and she'll be in Akhet-aten. With Bener-ib."

Nub-nefer's mouth fell open. "What does that mean?" she managed to stammer. "Don't most diplomats live separately from their families for long periods of time? You certainly did."

"I think it's meant to be a permanent condition. He's still grieving his wife; Neferet's not interested in men."

Hani forced a wry smile and shook his head, tamping down the spark of anger. "She's using him shamelessly."

Nub-nefer turned away and took a few lost steps. "She must have heard our conversation last night." She turned back and put her arms around Hani as if begging for reassurance. "Oh, Hani..." She looked up at him with a spark of hope in her eyes. "Maybe she's really fallen in love with him."

Hani snorted. "Much as I like and admire Ptah-mes, my dove, I find it hard to believe that a girl of Neferet's temperament would fall head over heels in love with him after one meeting. He's a rather chilly character."

"Sometimes young girls don't think about that. They see a handsome face and beautiful manners, and all the rest falls away..."

"That wouldn't be Neferet."

"Perhaps she thinks she can bring him back his joy. You know how she likes to take care of people," Nub-nefer persisted.

Hani shrugged. They both knew what was going on. Neferet wasn't the sort to sacrifice her happiness to restore an older man—her father's friend—to joy. She was using him for cover.

It took Hani a long time to fall asleep that night. He felt Nub-nefer against him, breathing the untroubled breath of the soul wrapped in dreams, while his eyes refused to close and his thoughts raced. First they circled the king's deliberate humiliation of Ptah-mes and his equally inexplicable new fondness for Hani. *Does Nefer-khepru-ra hope to pit us against one another in rivalry—to conquer us by division? Do I dare to refuse an honor at the king's hand?*

It might be taken as a refusal to obey, and much as he seems to love me all at once, that would probably be the end of me.

It would take a lot of courage. Hani thought of all the precious individuals under his protection and wondered how far he dared to jeopardize their safety for his own ideological ends. Wasn't that exactly what he had reproached his brother-in-law for doing—disappearing from sight for four years so he could continue to pour out calls to arms against the king?

Hani rolled over in bed, but the new position proved no more conducive to sleep than the old one. *Neferet—how could she do this? I can't believe she's being so calculating. Ptahmes is undergoing so much, and now to have an adolescent bride who cares nothing for him and will no doubt cuckold him with another woman...* But short of refusing to give the marriage his blessing, he didn't know what to do about it. The two parties were both adults. Hani groaned silently. *What sort of wedding present can I possibly give them?*

After a long time, Hani's thoughts began to slow and blur as sleep claimed him, and he finally slid into welcome oblivion.

The following day, Hani slept rather late. By the time he shuffled into the kitchen, the household had pretty well dispersed to their daily tasks. Nub-nefer had disappeared on her regular mysterious jaunt—no doubt to see her brother—and the house was strangely silent. Hani seated himself in the garden pavilion, braving the chill, to drink his morning milk in solitude. Before long, his father emerged from the house, wigless and unshod like Hani.

Mery-ra came toddling toward him, in his hands a pot-shaped loaf of bread wrapped in a towel. "Morning, son. Baket-iset said you were out here. The servant girl just took this bread out of the oven, and I thought you might like to share it with me while it's hot." He plopped down in the other chair and uncovered the loaf, fanning its fragrant steam toward his son to tempt him.

But Hani needed no encouragement to eat. He broke off a chunk, which was almost too hot to hold, and waved it under his nose, snuffing in voluptuous pleasure. "In the Field of Reeds, I want to eat hot bread all day long." He bit into it with gusto.

"I saw Nub-nefer briefly before she took off for parts unknown," his father said, breaking off a large piece of the bread. "She looked strangely ecstatic and said something cryptic like 'At last something wonderful is happening to this family.'"

Hani snorted. "That's one way of looking at it. You won't believe what I'm going to tell you, Father."

Mery-ra leaned closer, his eyes widening avidly. "Tell. Tell."

Hani lowered his voice. "Neferet is marrying Lord Ptah-mes."

"What?" Mery-ra reared back in astonishment. "Is this a joke?"

"If she'd told me, I might have thought so. But it was Ptah-mes, who certainly isn't the joking sort."

Hani's father continued to gape at him disbelievingly. "And Nub-nefer calls that a wonderful thing?"

"He's a prize catch, Father. Rich and blue-blooded."

"But..." Mery-ra seemed to be unable to come up with

an adequate word. "They'll be miserable together. They're too different."

"That's the way I see it. But she asked him, and he said yes. I suppose if neither has any expectations of the other…"

"Is she finished with that little Bener-ib, then?"

Hani shook his head, feeling the cold weight of gloom descend upon him again. "They'll live together in his house while he's in Azzati."

Mery-ra made a whooshing noise. "I've never heard of such a… a thing."

"Of such a calculating, self-centered thing, you mean? Neither have I. I want to turn the girl over my knee."

Mery-ra stared at the bread in his hand as if he had no idea where it had come from. "Have you talked to her?"

"Not yet," Hani said glumly. "But I'll do it today. I have to get back to Akhet-aten for my audience. I don't think I can stay out the holidays." He thought once more of the decision he was going to have to make and what it could cost his family. "Maybe I'll come back afterward, before I go back to Djahy."

"You think they'll send you back?"

Not if I become the high commissioner of foreign affairs in the north, Hani told himself bitterly. "Someone needs to solve that murder and punish the perpetrator before the Babylonians get any angrier. Burna-buriash would be furious if he knew the investigation had stopped."

Mery-ra heaved himself to his feet and clapped his son on the shoulder. "Better you than me, my boy. And I don't mean the investigation. Tell me how your talk with Neferet goes." He hustled off with suspicious haste, leaving Hani alone again.

Hani stared at the cooling chunk of bread in his hand then stuck it all at once into his mouth and ate it without pleasure. *Great Hidden One,* he prayed. *Give me light, or I could really make a mess of things.*

⸙

Hani returned to the house, his footsteps leaden. He was chilly and went in search of a shirt. In the upstairs corridor, he ran into his youngest daughter, alone for once.

"Papa!" she cried. "Grandfather said you were leaving for the capital. You're not going to dance for Osir with me on the last night of the festival?" She began to weave back and forth and throw her head, her eyes twinkling.

But Hani couldn't manage a smile. "I want to talk to you, my duckling. Let's go down to the garden."

Neferet seemed uneasy at his solemn expression. "Isn't it cold outside?"

"Not if you wear a shawl. I want some privacy."

He headed for the stairs, and she trailed after him, looking scared. Together, they passed through the salon, where Hani picked up his daughter's shawl from a stool and handed it to her without a word. He led the way to the garden pavilion and pulled down the rolled-up mats behind them so that they were enclosed. They seated themselves in the two chairs.

"Well, little duckling," Hani said, trying not to sound as severe as he wanted to be. "Were you ever going to tell us your news, or were we simply going to find out some day that you had left Aha's?"

"What news is that, Papa?" Neferet's eyes shifted aside in unmistakable guilt.

"About your marriage to my friend."

She looked around—anywhere but at her father—and licked her lips. "Oh, that. Of course I was going to tell you and Mama."

Hani beckoned her over to him, and she took her accustomed seat on his knee. "Do you love him, Neferet?"

She looked up at her father reluctantly. "He's very polite. I... I like him well enough. Still, people don't have to love each other to get married. There can be arranged marriages, you know."

Hani stared at her, willing her to open her heart. "You asked the man to marry you, knowing that he was still grieving for his wife so he wouldn't touch you. That's a little dishonest, don't you think, love? What if he decides he wants to get on with his life at some point and wishes his wife were a real wife to him? Would you push him away? You're toying with his heartbreak." It seemed too complicated to explain to her how Ptah-mes already hated himself.

Neferet's lip began to tremble. "I don't mean him any harm, Papa. He seemed happy to do it. He said it would keep the other women off him."

"You're using him. Don't you see that?"

She got that stubborn look Hani knew so well, lip outthrust. "Maybe he's using me."

"You tell me honestly if you believe that's the case, duckling. Everyone is going to think you're after his gold."

Her eyes widened in offended virtue. "But I'm not.

May the Lady Ma'at pull out the hairs under my arm one by one and set *bulti* fish to nibble my feet if I am."

Hani was too dispirited to answer. He heaved a sigh.

Neferet put a hand on his chest. "Papa, you don't think I'm doing something bad, do you? I thought you and Mama would be happy I was getting married."

"And Bener-ib? Is he marrying her too?"

A silence fell. Neferet hung her head. Finally, she replied in a voice of forced cheerfulness, "She'll be my lady companion. And my business partner—we're going to open a practice. Because my husband will be gone most of the time."

"I can see you've thought this through quite thoroughly, little duckling. Except for the moral side of it. 'A youth does not follow the moral instructions although its words are on his tongue.'" He looked at her severely, trying not to give in to the tears suddenly sparkling in her little brown eyes.

Her voice shook when she spoke. "But Papa, it's so perfect for both of us. How can it be wrong?"

Hani let out a long breath of resignation. "You're both adults, and I can't stop you. But I beg you, my dear, be kind to him. He's suffered at lot."

She dropped her eyes, and Hani could see tears rolling down her cheeks. "I don't want to hurt him, Papa. I swear I won't be mean to him. But... but what else can I do?" Neferet looked up at him hopefully. "Mama is happy about it."

Hani heaved a sigh. Nub-nefer was relieved that her daughter's unconventional relationship would be dissembled. She seemed pleased that the girl would take on the luster of high-class connections and maybe even—the thought just occurred to Hani—that Baket-iset would be provided for in luxury no matter what happened. But as for himself, he could only see in it a parody of the sort of relationship he and Nub-nefer had found so sweetly nourishing over the years. A potentially cruel parody.

"It's your life, my girl," he said finally, squeezing her shoulders with an encircling arm. "Do what your conscience tells you."

The next morning, Hani set out for Akhet-aten. Neferet and Bener-ib decided to accompany him—ready, he supposed, to take possession of their new villa, even if it meant foregoing their dance for the Lord Osir. The bridegroom had already left for Azzati, to return the gods knew when. While the girls gossiped and giggled, Hani hung over the gunwales and stared into the green water of the River, which swirled about the bow in curls like the stylized fronds of a palm tree on a Kharuite seal.

His heart was leaden within him. He longed to hear the words "The king has changed his mind, and you won't have to make this choice." But he'd already made it. He just needed to think of a justification that wouldn't look like out-and-out insubordination.

Just before they marched down the gangplank at the embarcadero of the capital, where boats of all sizes gathered like animals at their trough up and down the bank as far as one could see, Neferet slipped up to Hani and threw her arms around him, squeezing him hard. He enfolded her and drew her close to him, kissing the stubbly top of her head. He wanted to tell her he still loved her, but the words were caught in his throat, and he hoped she sensed his love pouring out around her. He felt more than usually helpless and inadequate. The specter of his upcoming ordeal had undermined his confidence.

At last, the girl pulled back and said, with a touch of pleading under her habitual good cheer, "I love you, Papa. I would never do anything to make you not be proud of me. May the seven-headed demons of the underworld gnaw on my liver if I do. May Ammit pull me apart limb from limb and suck out my marrow and—"

"I believe you, little duckling." He smiled tenderly. "Remember the Hidden One present in your heart, and listen to his voice. He'll lead you in the right path." Hani kissed her forehead, and she stretched up to kiss his cheek in return.

He was fighting back his tears by the time the two girls disembarked one after the other. There was no ceremony attached to marriage; it was sufficient that the couple decide to live together—although *couple* was a relative term in this case. He supposed the girls would pick up their things at Aha's and then move on to their new and splendid residence. Finally, in a crowd of other bureaucrats and travelers, he made his way down the gangplank and up the dusty slope to the Horizon of the Aten.

In this month of Mekhir, the city was as dry and raw as it was in the summer, although the cloak knotted around Hani's shoulders felt comfortable in the brisk morning. Finding his nose was running, Hani sniffed hard and girded himself for the audience. He made his way to the Hall of Royal Correspondence to find out when the king would receive him. There, the vizier's secretary told him that he'd secured an appointment that afternoon, wedged in between the other visits of the ruler of the Two Lands with his functionaries.

With half a day to kill, Hani wasn't sure what to do with himself. He could hardly decamp to Ptah-mes's villa, since his daughter was even now establishing her possession over the place. He wanted not to complicate what had to be an uncomfortable situation with the servants. So instead, he headed for his firstborn's residence.

Aha happened to be home. As soon as the gatekeeper introduced Hani, the lad came rushing out to embrace him. "Father! How good to see you! What brings you here? Neferet just left, if you're looking for her." He looked like a thirty-three-year-old version of his father, but more sedentary. Aha's plump square-jowled face was wreathed in smiles, and he wrapped a fond arm around Hani's shoulders.

My, thought Hani in amusement. *I haven't seen this much open affection from the boy since he became an adolescent nearly twenty years ago.*

"Did she tell you about her marriage?"

"Yes, yes." Aha beamed. "Not bad, for the little scamp to marry into one of the oldest, most distinguished families in Waset! That certainly reflects well on our family. Although, after all"—he punched his father jovially in the arm—"we have the Master of the King's Stable."

"Ptah-mes has gone back to Azzati. I guess your sister is establishing herself as mistress of the house as we speak."

"It will do her good to have a household to manage. She needs to grow up. Children will certainly teach her a sense of responsibility."

"No doubt," Hani said evasively.

"The only shadow on all this is that Ptah-mes isn't thought of very highly in the palace. I mean, he's experienced and competent—he certainly has a distinguished résumé—but the king has doubts about him. Your friend tends to be rebellious. I guess that's what can happen if you think yourself so rich that no one can touch you. But the Aten sees all." There was a distasteful smugness about Aha's expression.

"Well, I didn't want to stay there this trip while Neferet is settling into her new role. Could you put me up tonight, son?"

"Of course, Father. Of course," Aha assured him expansively. "The dwarf isn't with you?"

"He's your brother-in-law."

"Yes, well, so is Ptah-mes son of Bak-en-ren-ef." Aha laughed as if he could hardly contain his delight at belonging vicariously to the grandee class. "Let me have the servant girl show you to your old room, Father. You're welcome to stay as long as you like."

"I have an audience with the king this afternoon. I'll probably go back to Waset tomorrow—maybe see the vizier first."

"Splendid, Father. I had no doubt that you would get ahead if you just stopped being so stubborn."

Hani thanked him wryly and gave him a hug. *Nothing like honors to make a fellow rise in Aha's esteem.*

Aha called a servant, who picked up Hani's basket of clean clothes and led the way to his lodging. "We'll be eating lunch shortly, Father. I'll have someone fetch you," Aha called after him.

Lunch was pleasant. Khentet-ka was as delighted as her

husband about the family's new liaison and chattered away, which took some of the pressure off Hani. His stomach was in such knots about the coming audience that he wasn't sure he'd have any appetite, but once the deliciously prepared dishes were borne in, he found he was hungry and ate with a good will. He was especially grateful for the rare chance to spend some time with his three grandchildren, even though he found them rude and imperious little characters.

Hani would have enjoyed a bit of a siesta afterward, but he wasn't sure how early the king would call him in, so as soon as he'd showered, painted his lids, and decked himself in his gold of honor, he headed for the door. Aha met him in the vestibule, his little eyes sparkling with pride. *If he only knew how I felt about this interview.*

"Take my litter, Father. You don't want to be walking down the road all that way in your finery. You'll be sweaty and get your feet dirty." He embraced his father, beaming. "Good luck, eh?"

Hani lumbered down the garden path and climbed into the litter with all the eagerness of a man mounting the executioner's platform. As the bearers lifted him, he sat back and heaved a sigh, wondering if he'd have the courage to do what he had to do. *Great Father of us all, guide me. Djehuty, lord of justice, give your scribe strength.*

⚜

For the first time in two years, Hani found himself at the midtown palace, walking through the magnificent painted pylon and entering a courtyard that reduced him to the magnitude of an ant. He trudged forward with determination across the vast, bleak pavement surrounded with immense statues of the king. He made his way to the second gate, broad and ramped for chariot processions, but he passed through the pedestrian door at the side instead. And now he had one last courtyard to cross, even larger than the last. The few people Hani saw here and there were no more impressive than a midge, reduced to nothing by the scale of their surroundings. Ahead, two obelisks reared to the sky, their golden caps winking and flashing in the midday sun like a pair of malevolent eyes.

His heart hammering within him, Hani mounted the broad staircase to the porch, where he announced himself to the porter. While he waited for the man's return, Hani stared about him at the brilliant colors of the columns and walls—the superb paintings of lions and other predators stalking gazelles through a lush landscape. *I guess this is meant to strike fear into favor seekers. The gods know I feel like a helpless gazelle in the clutches of a lion.* Even if he didn't respect the king as a man, there was no denying that Nefer-khepru-ra Wa-en-ra had almost limitless power.

The porter returned after what seemed like a very long time and haughtily bade Hani enter. This time, they made him take off his sandals at the door. *My clattering footsteps must have disturbed the royal nap last time I was here,* Hani thought with a kind of nervous amusement. Within the great reception hall, an echoing silence reigned, despite the number of servants and functionaries crossing back and forth on bare feet, reflected in the shining gypsum floor. Hani craned his neck to take in the beauty of the place, impressed in spite of himself. Tall columns, like clusters of reed or pole bouquets with water lilies—a magical marsh—towered over him, disappearing into the haze of incense that clouded the ceiling, shot through with mote-spangled rays from the clerestories.

He was just distracting himself with admiration of the lifelike water birds painted on the walls when a majordomo appeared from out of the shadowed corridor and beckoned to Hani to follow. Hani could feel the sweat breaking out on his temples, and a cloud of frightened starlings rose inside him, fluttering wildly to get out. *I must tell him no. I must tell him no*, he repeated to himself, starting to understand the temptation there would be to yield to such power and magnificence and just accept what the king commanded.

Aigrette-bedecked Nubian guardsmen pulled back the tall gilded doors of the audience hall, and Hani was ushered ceremoniously into the king's presence. Someone led him forward and urged him into a full prostration at the foot of the dais where Nefer-khepru-ra sat. As he rose, Hani was dimly aware of gilding and color and incense, of ostrich-plume flabella and the massed white garments of the Fan-Bearers and other courtiers and the watchful gaze of a hunting cheetah on a leash, but he had no more eyes for his surroundings. It was as if his world had shrunken to the line between the king of the Two Lands and himself.

"Hani," said Nefer-khepru-ra in his silky, mesmerizing voice. "We see too little of you."

"I am yours to command, My Sun."

The king smiled, but his green-painted eyes were narrowed and considering. Beneath the blue crown, his pointed face looked gaunt despite the slack overhang of his belly above its jeweled sash.

He does look sick, Hani thought.

"We are inclined to reward those who are faithful to

us. A man like you is valuable on many levels." The king eyed Hani up and down, and Hani dropped his gaze, not so much out of respect as to keep the Lord of the Two Lands from reading his thoughts. "We are pleased to see you in the gold of one who has been useful to his king."

Hani had a sudden memory of Ptah-mes reluctantly putting on the penknife the king had given him because one dared not seem ungrateful for the royal favor. Hani saw that it had been no mistake to wear his *shebyu* collars. "My lord's favor is the breath of life," he murmured.

"We had hoped to reward you with a promotion, a token of our esteem for a faithful servant, but there have been developments that make your presence on our borders yet more urgent."

Hani listened, stunned, hope flickering to life. *No promotion after all?* He felt he had just awakened from a long and terrible nightmare. He could think of nothing to say that wouldn't give him away, so he bowed.

"The king of Sangar has attacked Urusalim."

Hani's eyes flew wide open, and he could hardly keep from gaping. *One shock after another!* "Is he declaring war, My Sun?"

"We think not yet. He is upset by the assassination of his emissary, of course. This seems to be an expression of his displeasure. But we must proceed to find the killer and punish him, or Burna-buriash's anger will become more destructive."

"No doubt," Hani murmured. He was beginning to see where this was leading—he was back on his case.

"This is your task, Hani. Identify the man, and bring

him to justice. If he's a *hapir*, we must strike them a damaging blow in reparation."

"I accept, My Sun God. Consider me en route already."

"That is all." The king sat back languidly in his throne, and despite all the jewels and ceremonial splendor, he looked weary, too weary for a man who was only thirty-two.

Hani dropped into a deep bow, and he felt the majordomo's hand on this elbow, guiding him as he backed from the royal presence. He heard the king say to one of his gathered courtiers, "You see how loyal he is."

As Hani emerged from the palace into the blinding sunlight of a winter day, he slipped on his sandals once more then took off across the broad processional street toward the cluster of long, low mud-brick buildings that housed the Hall of Royal Correspondence. He drew a profound breath of relief, as if he hadn't gotten any air since he'd arrived in the capital. His steps were downright jaunty as he entered the vizier's office. He'd had no opportunity to report the mysterious visit of the Hittite emissary to the king in person, so he realized he needed to tell Ra-nefer. It wouldn't do to be having secret meetings with semihostile powers on the sly.

The tubby little vizier received him promptly. His chair looked to be just a little too high for him so that only his toes touched the footstool and the heels of his sandals dangled a bit. "Here you are, Hani," he said fretfully with something like a belch, which he stifled with a fist at his mouth. "What's going on up there?"

"I'm sure you know about the murder, my lord. I've just been missioned back to continue the investigation."

"Murder?" The vizier looked momentarily confused.

"Ah, yes. The Babylonian. Burna-buriash has attacked one of our towns, you know. Hazurru, I think, or Urusalim."

"I'm aware of that, my lord." *And I even know which city it was*, Hani thought wryly. "But there's something else I need to report to you. While I was in Kumidi, an emissary of the king of Kheta came to see me."

"Kheta? But we have no diplomatic relations with them." Ra-nefer looked ineffectually outraged, widening his little round eyes with their semicircular brows. "Why did he come to you and not to court?"

"I suppose because I was nearby. He wanted precisely to open diplomatic relations with us, to begin trading. Apparently, their king, Shuppiluliuma, is tired of the cost of conquest and wants to settle down to an alliance." Hani watched Ra-nefer closely. He said slyly, "They're allies with Sangar now. If Sangar turns on us, they make two against one."

The vizier's eyes grew even wider in alarm. "What must we do?"

"I'm sure Lord Ptah-mes could give you some advice, my lord. He has long years of experience with foreign relations in the north."

But Ra-nefer made a dismissive *poof*ing noise. "Ptah-mes, whatever his capabilities, is not in good odor at the moment, Hani. What do you suggest?"

"Why, to receive their emissaries. To make a treaty of alliance with them just in case Sangar goes to war against us." *That was a brilliant idea the gods gave me—to tie the treaty to Sangar*, Hani thought modestly.

Ra-nefer continued to look uneasy, his fat little lips pursed. Under his bushy eyebrows, his eyes darted about as if seeking an escape. He clearly didn't relish having to take this advice to the king, nor did Hani much want his own name attached to it. He still wasn't sure whether he was on the good side or the bad of Nefer-khepru-ra.

Hani said blandly, "I'm sure our lord king will value the man who brings him a way to make peace. Maybe dissuade Sangar from escalating their grievance…"

"Very well. No harm in opening a discussion," said Ra-nefer at last. He seemed visibly to be girding himself for the ordeal of advising his master. "Anything else, Hani?"

"Only the things I've told my lord about in my reports," Hani said, wondering if the vizier had even read them.

"Very well, then. You may go."

Hani bowed his way out. As he pulled the door shut behind him, he heard from within the office a prolonged fart. He suppressed his laughter with difficulty. *He's been waiting the whole interview for that. Even the high and mighty.*

Once out of the Hall of Royal Correspondence, Hani set off for Aha's. He was almost giddy with relief, and his steps were light as he sought out his litter waiting in the street. He longed to exchange his impressions with Ptah-mes, but of course, Ptah-mes was no longer in the capital.

Hani hadn't had to make the terrible choice after all, although it might lie somewhere in his future. He'd relieved himself of the burden of the secret meeting. And he'd been sent back to finish the investigation he'd begun. *Not a bad day after all.* He would arrange for sacrifices to the Hidden One and to the patron of scribes as soon as he got back to Waset.

Aha wasn't home when Hani returned to his house.

Hani instructed the steward that he wouldn't be staying the night after all, and as soon as he'd stripped off the gold of honor, he set out for the embarcadero. He would have loved to be able to use Ptah-mes's yacht, with its double crew that rowed all night, but he would be at home soon enough. *And with what joy!* Maya would no doubt be glad to set out once more for adventure too. Hani felt fifteen years younger than he had at the start of the day.

⬩

"Hani, my boy—you're back sooner than we expected. How did your audience go?" Mery-ra came toddling out of the salon as soon as Hani set foot inside the exterior door and drew it shut behind him. The two men embraced.

"Well." Hani grinned. "They're reopening the case of the murder of the Babylonian and putting me back on it."

"You're mighty happy to be on the trail of a ruthless killer," Mery-ra said, raising his eyebrows.

"And the worst of it is," Hani continued cheerfully, "that the king of Sangar has invaded Urusalim."

Mery-ra looked shocked.

"The king thinks it's not intended as an act of war but just as a protest against our dropping the investigation. It saved me from a terrible fate, Father."

The old man cocked his head in curiosity. "A terrible fate?"

"Ptah-mes had told me that the king was planning to make me high commissioner of foreign affairs in the north, but apparently, this came up and took precedence." Hani felt quite fizzy with relief.

"High commissioner? But I thought you said Ptah-mes was still—"

"He was. He's been deposed, and I was to be put in his place. It had to have been a calculated effort to drive us into rivalry with one another." A simmering contempt hardened Hani's voice.

"'Great lakes become dry places; sandbanks turn into depths.' You said it well, son. Presciently, in fact."

Hani looked at his father in surprise. "You've read my aphorisms?"

"I'm having Khawy copy them for practice. I hope you don't mind."

Hani shook his head, chuckling. "Where is Nub-nefer?"

"Gone on her morning jaunt. How long is that brother of hers going to stay hidden away? Someone's been feeding him all this time."

"No doubt some fellow zealot who considers it an honor." Hani handed his basket off to A'a, who was still standing in the outer doorway. "You can take this up for me, my friend." To his father, he said in a low voice, "There's something you can do for me, too, while I'm gone."

"What's that, son? Milk lions? Buy horses? Corner the market on onions? Speak the word, and your old father obeys."

"Do you know a man named Amen-nefer? A Theban. He's in the army."

"I think I do," Mery-ra said, scratching his chin. "A low-level officer of some sort. A ferocious fighter who was awarded the Golden Fly more than once."

"One-eyed?"

"That's him. Why?"

"He's the commissioner at Kumidi now. He seems to have a mysterious past that intertwines with Pa-aten-em-heb's."

"Hmmm. I'll look into him for you, if you want."

"I would be grateful, noble Father." Hani flashed his father a complicit grin.

The two of them made their way into the salon, where Hani knelt to greet his eldest daughter. Ta-miu, curled at Baket's side, looked up with accusing golden eyes, disgruntled at this interruption of her sleep.

"How did your audience go, Papa?" Baket-iset asked.

"Very well, my swan. The king is letting me go back to the investigation that was abandoned in midstream. In short, they could have left me up there and never called me back, and the results would have been the same." He exchanged a knowing look with his father. "But I'm not complaining."

"How long can you stay?"

"I'm afraid I have to leave right away. It was self-indulgence to come back down at all, but I wanted to see my girls." He patted her arm.

Baket-iset stared up eagerly at Hani. "Did Neferet get to her new home all right, Papa?"

"I suppose. She collected her things and had left Aha's by the time I got there." He fell silent, reflecting, then asked quietly, "My love, what do you think of this marriage? It seems doomed to me."

"Oh, I don't know, Papa. If they never see one another..."

"But Ptah-mes gets nothing out of it. Neferet has Bener-ib and every material thing she could want, but what does he have? A stranger occupying his house."

"I can't see that it's any more bizarre than the relationship he had with Lady Apeny. Maybe strangers in his house excite him," said Mery-ra with a suggestive wag of the eyebrows.

Baket-iset was pensive. "He agreed to it, didn't he? He doesn't seem like a rash man to me. He must have thought it had some value to him." After a moment, she added, "He could always get a concubine."

"I defer to your wisdom, my swan. I guess I'm just shortsighted." Hani sighed and squeezed Baket-iset's shoulder. "Papa is always trying to make things right."

"That's what makes you a good diplomat, son," Mery-ra said affectionately.

A sound of footsteps in the vestibule told Hani that Nub-nefer had returned. He rose and called out eagerly, "My dove, I'm back."

❖

The next morning, Hani was in the garden, watching his ducks, while Nub-nefer paid her daily visit to her brother. A crunch of footsteps on the gravel path made him look up, and A'a emerged from behind the bushes. The man cleared his throat. "My lord, a young lady and a young gentleman are here to see you."

Hani rose in surprise. "Who are they?"

"They gave me names, but they said you wouldn't know them. I... I can't remember them any more." A'a's face fell in apology. "They've been here several times before, looking for you, but they didn't want to leave a message. They're in the salon now, my lord."

"All right." Hani shrugged, his eyes widening in

curiosity. "Let's go see who these persistent young people are." He followed A'a to the porch, where the gatekeeper peeled off as Hani made his way into the vestibule. From within, he could hear a low murmur of voices. He moved to the doorway with a hospitable nod. "Welcome, my guests. What brings you here?"

The two visitors exchanged an uneasy glance. The woman was in her early thirties, tall, and extremely attractive in a voluminous wig and rich jewelry. There was a familiar fineness in her face. The man was perhaps ten years younger, and while beautiful in much the same way, he had a tentativeness about him that was a little less than manly. He seemed very much in the woman's shadow.

Indeed, it was she who spoke for them in a frosty low-pitched voice heavy with the drawl of the upper class. "My name is Mut-em-wia. This is my brother Huy."

"Welcome, my lady. My lord." Hani smiled. "What can I do for you?"

"We are children of Lord Ptah-mes."

Hani's smile froze. *Iyah. Trouble's on its way.* He managed to say calmly, "Your father is a man whom I am honored to call a friend, my lady." He made a little bow, as much to hide his face while the horror of the situation passed across it as in respect.

Mut-em-wia advanced on him in a manner that was almost threatening, standing so close that Hani could smell her expensive jasmine-scented perfume. Her tone became hard. "I will mince no words, Hani. We're here to tell you that you must make your daughter divorce our father."

Hani felt a flush of rebellion rising to his cheeks. He spoke gently but couldn't hide the edge in his voice. "My lady, they're both adults. There's nothing I can do to stop them if they want to be married."

"It's a farce," Mut-em-wia barked, tossing her beautifully coiffed head. "The girl is only after his property. You must call her off, I say."

"And *I* say I have no voice in the matter. Am I to tell a magistrate of the Two Lands he can't be married to my daughter? He can marry anyone he chooses."

The youth spoke up at last, his arched black eyebrows, so like his father's, wrinkled in distress. "But it isn't fair. She'll inherit everything, and we'll be cut out."

Yahya, thought Hani, enlightened all at once. He should have foreseen that—as he was almost sure Ptah-mes had. *Of course they're furious, the seven greedy children.* He said in an icy voice, "After treating your father as shabbily as you all have for years, I marvel that you have the nerve to expect an inheritance."

Lady Mut-em-wia swelled with anger, drawing herself up like a cobra ready to strike. Her black-painted eyes sparked. "Isn't it rather out of place for you to admonish us—you whose daughter is a conniving little minx?"

Anger had Hani by the throat now. *Stay calm*, he warned himself, but he could feel a pulse ticking in his temples. "Have you ever even met her, my lady?"

Mut-em-wia's bluster sagged for an instant, but she curled her shapely mouth scornfully. "No, and I never plan to. She's nothing but a concubine. She's far below Father socially. It's a travesty."

"She's taking advantage of the fact that Father's grieving," said Huy. "She's preying on him."

"I think your father is not so easily preyed on, my lord,

my lady. And I think you wouldn't care if he were. You might actually be glad to see him cheated—except for that inheritance."

Her nostrils tense, Mut-em-wia glared at her brother then turned to Hani and, with an unconquerable bravado Hani almost admired, shot back, "How dare you!"

"I have eyes and ears, my lady. It's pretty clear what you two are up to. At least your brother is honest enough to admit to your motives." Hani smiled coldly. "You held Lord Ptah-mes in scorn for collaborating with the regime, but you didn't know why he did it. It was all for you, ingrates that you are. He was afraid that if he resisted, he would be stripped of his property and would be unable to leave you anything. I think if he'd seen the kind of serpents he was harboring in his bosom, he would have been a resister from the start."

Mut-em-wia looked ready to explode with anger. Her mouth had become a thin line, trembling with the effort to come up with a rejoinder. Her brother glanced at her for directions, a half-guilty expression on his handsome face.

At last, the woman said in a quivering voice, "Come, Huy. We don't have to put up with these insults. This baseborn man is trying to steal our property through his daughter—that's clear."

She spun on her heel and stalked to the door, her brother in her wake. Hani watched them go and offered no gesture of courtesy. As their footsteps receded into silence down the garden path, he could finally feel the heat of anger ebbing from his face.

No sooner had the two departed in their seething cloud

of fury than he actually gave a laugh. "I think you mean 'our father's property,' don't you, dear?"

"Whew! What a bunch of little flint chips! Poor Ptah-mes," said Mery-ra as he emerged into the room from the stairwell.

Hani turned on him with a grin. "Were you listening to that whole conversation, you old rascal?"

Mery-ra stared at the door as if to be sure the visitors had well and truly left the property, then he said, "Not on purpose, son. I was coming down the stairs when I heard their voices, and I decided to lie low. Unworthy little scions of their parents, aren't they? Ptah-mes and Apeny were both always so perfect in courtesy."

"Imagine what their family life must have been like. No wonder Ptah-mes always seems down in the mouth."

"I must say," Mery-ra said, lacing his fingers across his belly and tapping his thumbs smugly, "baseborn though we are, at least we always loved one another."

Hani gave a laugh and shook his head. The confrontation had left him with a leaden lump of sorrow in his middle. Something had gone very wrong to produce such voracious greed.

CHAPTER 8

Maya had been reluctant to leave his renewed connubial bliss, especially since Sati would be giving birth in only a few weeks. But the lure of adventure—and the desire to see justice done against the perpetrator of a horrible crime—had been too strong. He and Lord Hani had sailed from Peru-nefer up the coast to Beruta, and now they had entered once more into the commissioner's residence.

"Welcome back, Lord Hani," Amen-nefer said genially. "That didn't take long."

"True," said Hani. "It's not altogether clear why the king needed to see me in person. Any breakthroughs since I left?"

Amen-nefer shook his head. "I haven't pursued anything. You're the one who knows what you're doing. I'm just a simple soldier."

"Well, I'll let you know if I need your troops for anything. Thank you again for your hospitality."

Amen-nefer saluted smartly and strode off about his duties. Hani and Maya exchanged a look.

"What do we do next, my lord?"

"After taking a shower and eating, you mean? I think we need to talk to those slaves again. And maybe a few more. Somewhere out there is a man who is willing to tell tales on his fellow."

"We could always torture them, my lord. I bet they'd talk then," Maya suggested with a savage grin.

Hani eyed him askance.

"I mean threaten to torture them, of course."

"They looked cowed enough. I hate to frighten them even more." Hani sighed.

"But if they're frightened, they'll talk, won't they?"

"Maybe." Lord Hani seemed reluctant. "Unfortunately, we couldn't trust anything they'd say under torture."

The two men fell silent. Hani's thick, straight eyebrows were drawn down in a deeply pondering expression. Maya had no idea what he was thinking.

At last, Hani said, "Let's go get cleaned up for dinner. Afterward, we'll split up again, and you can take the Egyptian-speaking slaves. I'm hoping that the night shift will have come on by then. Those are the people who are likely to have seen or heard something."

But there'd been a change since the last time Maya had tried to interview Zalaya and the others. When people saw Maya from afar, they melted away. When he actually managed to confront one of the servants, the man made the excuse that he was urgently engaged in some important task that couldn't wait.

Maya could feel his annoyance mounting like an icy

tide. *What game do these lowborn bastards think they're playing? Don't they know by now that the demands of the king's emissary take precedence over their class loyalties?* Eventually, he called off his interviews—his intended interviews—and stumped back up to Lord Hani's room in a dudgeon to wait for his return.

And there he found Zalaya stooped over with a bow drill in his hands, trying to light the wood in the brazier. He twirled it back and forth so rapidly that it shook his whole body. His skinny back was to the door, and at first, the slave didn't seem to hear Maya enter.

Maya stood in the doorway, his arms crossed in what he hoped was a menacing posture. "You there," he growled.

Zalaya whipped around in guilty haste, and seeing Maya, he made a low bow. "How may I serve you, my lord?"

"By telling me the truth, Ammit take you. What are you and the others hiding?" Maya swaggered toward the slave. "I guess you know the murder has provoked an international incident. Sangar has invaded one of our cities, all because you won't tell us who killed their emissary."

The slave's round face crumpled, somewhat in shame but mostly in terror. He fell to his knees, his hands clasped. "Oh, master, I swear I don't know anything about it."

"Right." Maya sneered. "A man is bludgeoned to death with a heavy piece of furniture in the quiet of the night, and no one hears a thing. A broken, blood-soaked stool is carried down the stairs and hidden in the storeroom, and nobody sees anything. Whoever did it must have had bloody clothes to dispose of, but the laundrymen have no idea what I'm talking about. Is the whole staff here deaf, blind, and dumb?" His voice had risen till he was almost shouting, the spittle shooting out at the man, who cowered, his head to the ground.

"I... I don't know who did it," Zalaya sniveled, his face on the floor. "Please, my lord. I don't know."

"He does," said Lord Hani from the door, "but he's afraid for his family. Are they here at the palace, son?"

Zalaya crawled toward Hani on his knees and began to kiss Hani's feet, weeping desperately. "Please, please, don't make me talk. They'll kill her. She's not even supposed to be here anyway, but we're trying to make enough to save up and buy our freedom."

"You can go now, Zalaya, but if you ever decide you can tell us anything at all, please come to me. You could prevent a war." Hani spoke kindly, and he lifted the slave to his feet and patted him on the shoulder.

Maya, breathing hard, watched Zalaya go. "He's got to talk," he said fiercely. "How are we going to make any progress unless one of these sons of jackals tells us what he knows? Maybe we should bribe him. If he had enough to free himself and his wife, he wouldn't have to worry anymore."

Hani quirked his mouth thoughtfully to one side. "Not a bad idea. I'll have to clear it with Lord Ptah-mes. Meantime, we'll try to work around them as long as we can. Let's look for a man with a motive. Who would want to stir up enmity between us and Sangar?"

"Could it have been personal? Are there any Babylonians on the staff who might have had a grudge against this Shulum-marduk?"

"We can look. And then there's Shum-addi, the would-be *hapiru* chief, who has a certain vested interest in drawing our attention elsewhere. Maybe we should talk to him." Hani clapped Maya on the back. "Our next few days will be busy, my friend."

Hani had Maya draft up a letter for Ptah-mes, asking permission to offer the witness whatever payment was necessary to make him feel he could get away safely. Then they parted company and set off once more to interview the servants.

✦

"There are no Babylonians. But you know what I notice, Lord Hani?" said Maya when they met again that evening. "There are no women, either, employed at the commissioner's residence."

"No? Apparently Zalaya's wife is."

"Where? I haven't met a single maidservant, a single spinner, a single kitchen girl." Maya tilted his head. "Does that seem odd to you?"

Hani looked thoughtful. "Maybe Amen-nefer considers it an army post. He's a widower; he must have a concubine or something. Or maybe he just uses the local resources." He grinned.

"Well, other than that, nothing to report, my lord. No one will speak to me. They're linking elbows and making a wall of silence against our questions." Maya let out an aggrieved breath through his nose. "Somebody must know something."

Hani nodded. "Indeed. Until we hear from Lord Ptah-mes, let's try to think of another line of inquiry. Maybe Amen-nefer can tell us more about this Shum-addi, the would-be leader of the *hapiru*. Although it's not clear to me how he or his men could have infiltrated the staff. Let's ask the steward if there have been any new hires—or purchases—in the last year or so."

※

Several days had passed before Maya and Hani were able to catch the steward in private and interrogate him. As it turned out, there had been only one new purchase—a twelve-year-old kitchen boy.

"So much for that theory." Lord Hani snorted as he and Maya left the steward's little closet of an office. "A lad that age wouldn't have had the strength to wield a heavy stool so energetically."

Maya, steaming with frustration at yet another dead end, trotted to keep up with Lord Hani's brisk stride. Hani, too, chafed at being stymied, he could see.

"I wish our Babylonians were still here. I'd like to know if there were any connections between the robbery of their caravan and this murder."

"Could we go track them down, my lord?"

But Hani's mouth twitched in a rueful little smile. "I don't think we'd get a very warm welcome in Sangar at the moment."

They'd almost reached the door of Hani's room when a voice behind them called, "My lord! The diplomatic pouch has arrived."

Hani and Maya turned simultaneously to see a soldier approaching them with long strides. He held out toward them the scuffed leather courier's bag that brought their mail.

"Thank you, son," Hani said as he accepted the bag

into his big hands. He turned to Maya. "Well, my friend, let's take a look before we do anything else. Lord Ptah-mes may have given us directives."

They entered the room and sat cross-legged on the floor. Hani emptied out the several tied-up packets of papyrus the bag contained. One by one, he read the address or looked at the seal. "Here's one from Nub-nefer. And one from Sat-hut-haru for you." With a twinkle in his eyes, he held that one out to Maya, who snatched it up eagerly and unfolded it as Hani continued to murmur, "Here's one from my father. And here's Lord Ptah-mes's answer."

Maya looked up. "What does he say, my lord?"

"He says to go ahead and pay Zalaya for his information. The commissioner will give us whatever funds we need. Excellent!"

Maya settled back to his letter, warmed to the very tips of his toes by his wife's loving and newsy report on the children. Sat-hut-haru was due any day, and Lady Nub-nefer had set up the birthing bower at Hani's house, so the mother wouldn't be alone and the other children would have family around for the fourteen days of Sati's seclusion. *Another son. I can feel it!* Maya thought gleefully. *By the time I get back, I'll have three children. The girl is a goddess.*

"Listen to this, Maya. My father has been doing some research on our friend Amen-nefer," Hani said, looking up. His little brown eyes were lit with the eagerness that new information always evoked in him. "He's from a Theban family of low-level gentry—the men are mostly in the cavalry. His father died when Amen-nefer was young, and he was raised by his mother. There was some kind of scandal when his wife died violently eighteen years ago. She was pregnant, and the baby died too. Her family claimed Amen-nefer had killed her, but no one could ever prove anything."

"*Iy*," Maya murmured, horrified by the information and all the more at the thought that something so terrible could happen to his beloved Sat-hut-haru and their child. *Never at my hands.*

"There were a few cases, in his military career, where he was almost kicked out for fighting with his fellow officers, but he was such a valuable soldier that nothing ever came of it except for brief reprimands. He won the Golden Fly four times for bravery in battle."

Maya whistled. "Once a fighter, always a fighter."

"He was garrisoned at Kumidi for the usual six-year hitch but ended up being appointed commissioner, just as he told us."

"Typical—a man like that being rewarded."

"That must have been shortly after our new king came to the throne alone, which has been ten years. So seven or eight years ago. Well, at least he's competent—that puts him in a class apart up here. A lot of people have quick tempers."

"But to kill his wife?" *And slash the face of a would-be sweetheart?*

"Ah, but we have no reason to think he did. The Master of the Hall of Justice found him innocent."

"I'm surprised he didn't change his name to Pa-aten-nefer. That's how you get ahead under Nefer-khepru-ra. Life, prosperity, and health to him," Maya said with a sarcastic sneer. "Did Lord Mery-ra say how the commissioner lost his eye?"

"I don't see any mention of it." Lord Hani dropped his own eyes once more to the letter and then looked up. "Listen to this. Father says the coregent Smenkh-ka-ra is taking as his queen the king's eldest daughter, Meryet-aten. They seem to be knitting the dynasty tight for the fight that's certain to break out when the king dies. For sure, a small child like Prince Tut-ankh-aten would be too young to rule on his own. What is he—seven or eight?"

"Seven, my lord. Born the same day as Tepy," Maya said proudly. "So now we have two kings and two queens? What happened to Lady Nefert-iti as she-king?"

"She's still there, a prominent visual counterpart to the he-king, but not, apparently, eligible to reign on her own. Maybe Nefer-khepru-ra doesn't trust her."

"Or her father."

Hani chuckled, his belly bouncing. "Neither would I." He heaved himself to his feet. "Well, Maya, I leave you to read your letter from your wife in peace, and I'll go out into the garden and read mine." He tucked the folded-up papyrus under his arm and disappeared into the hall.

With a burning heart, Maya resumed devouring his precious missive. He pressed the sheet to his nose and took a deep, voluptuous breath, fancying that a whiff of Sati's perfume clung to it.

⁜

Hani caught Amen-nefer in one of the commissioner's brief interludes in his office. He looked up pleasantly as Hani bowed. "Ah, Lord Hani. What can I do for you? How is the investigation coming?"

"Slowly, my lord. The servants, who show every sign

of having information, refuse to tell us anything. You can help us, though. I have a requisition here for a large sum of copper *deben*s to be paid to potential witnesses to encourage them to talk." Hani extended Ptah-mes's letter.

Amen-nefer glanced at it so briefly that Hani wondered how well he could read—or maybe he took Hani's word for its contents. "Who is it you're wanting to pay?"

"Well, Zalaya, for one. He acts like a man who knows more than he's telling. I suspect that one of the slaves is guilty and the others are covering for him."

"I wouldn't be surprised. They're probably in the pay of the *hapiru*. Gold will make them talk, all right. They would do—and probably have done—anything for gold."

"Theirs is a hard life," Hani said with a compassionate sigh.

But Amen-nefer snorted. "Hard? They hardly ever work, and they get room and board and medical attention for nothing. Plus prestige. And I even pay them a little something for their personal needs. I don't feel very sorry for them."

But they're not free. There's a reason why we don't have slaves in the Black Land.

Hani said, "Do you prefer me to get the *deben*s from you now or to give you an itemized list of the disbursements and let you pay me then?"

"If you aren't afraid to leave that much copper in your room, I can give it to you now. Otherwise, bill me, so to speak."

"Why don't we wait, then? I can't know in advance who's even willing to talk."

Amen-nefer nodded amiably. "As you prefer. Is there anything else I can do for you, my lord?"

"No, no. I thank you for your cooperation, though."

"I should think," the commissioner said with fervor. "This assassination reflects very badly on all of us, especially me. That it should have happened under the very roof of a magistrate of the Two Lands…"

Hani took his leave. He couldn't make up his mind about Amen-nefer. The commissioner seemed to be a curious mix of hardheartedness and uprightness, of prejudice and geniality. *At least he's cooperating in the investigation.*

He joined Maya at lunchtime, but instead of ordering something from the palace kitchen, the two of them set out into the town to forage. The market was still open before the siesta's lull, and they bought flatbreads and little fried balls of something spicy. By the wall of a temple, they found shade where they could sit down in the street and spread their lunch on their knees.

"This is probably a bit lacking in dignity for the king's emissary," Hani said wryly. "Fortunately, nobody knows who we are."

"So Amen-nefer was willing to give you the *deben*s?" Maya asked, his mouth full of bread.

Hani tore off a half ball with his teeth. "He had no choice—it was a direct order from Ptah-mes. Even though our friend is no longer high commissioner of foreign affairs in the north, he still has jurisdiction over Djahy."

The two ate in silence. "What about the defecting soldiers?" Maya finally asked. "Are we ever going to do anything about them, my lord?"

"We need to. If some of ours are in with the *hapiru*, they

might have known about the passage of the Babylonians and reported it to their leader."

"You think it was the *hapiru,* then?"

"I'm assuming so. Or some other bandits. But how many simple bandits would have attacked an armed convoy? Why—are you thinking that's political too?"

Maya shrugged and lifted an eyebrow. "I don't know. But it's hard to believe the two events weren't related somehow."

"I think we need to talk to the emissary from Urusalim who said he saw the renegade soldiers with his own eyes. It's possible that one of them entered the garrison and carried out the murderous orders of Shum-addi."

"But how would Shum-addi know that the Babylonians were even here in the palace?"

Hani nodded slowly. "Unless he was responsible for the robbery of the caravan. Maybe its purpose was to drive the emissaries into Kumidi overnight." He snorted. "And so, of course, the question of how they knew is still open."

Maya pursed his lips. "How are we going to get into Urusalim? Troops from Sangar hold it, don't they?"

"Ah yes." Hani laughed ruefully. "But perhaps if we tell them this is part of the investigation of their countryman's murder, they'll be helpful."

Maya scrambled to his feet, brushing the crumbs off his lap, and hitched up his kilt, looking businesslike and eager. "I'm ready when you are, my lord!"

Hani was tempted to hold out a hand for a pull to his feet, but he was afraid he'd only tug Maya down on top of himself. He rose gracelessly under his own power and dusted himself off. "Since we don't have any idea where

Shum-addi is to be found, I suggest we head for Urusalim first."

Through the quiet streets of siesta hour, they made their way back to the commissioner's residence, where Hani sought out Pa-aten-em-heb. "Will you be able to accompany us with a few men, my friend? Apparently it's not safe for diplomats around here." He exchanged a knowing look with the young officer.

Pa-aten-em-heb said, "Of course, Lord Hani. I myself am scheduled to visit a few of the other local kings about provisions, so I won't be able to join you, but I'll certainly send some men with your party. How many do you need?"

"Oh, five or six should do it. We don't want to look to the Babylonians at Urusalim like a military expedition."

The officer laughed. "I'll see right to it." He bowed respectfully and took his leave.

"I need to go tell the commissioner where we'll be." Hani grinned mischievously. "So they'll know where to look for our bones."

Maya's eyes widened, and then uncertainty puckered his brow. At last, having evidently decided his father-in-law was joking, he laughed. "Shall I go pack our things and tell the others?"

"Tell them we're going, but I don't think we'll need any additional staff. It will just be you and me and the escort."

His secretary looked pleased. Drawing himself up to his full negligible height, he strutted away, while Hani turned his steps toward the administrative offices of the commissariat, hoping their host wouldn't be off with his troops somewhere.

Fortunately, he proved to be in. Amen-nefer was seated

cross-legged on the floor of his office, some maps spread out across his knees. As Hani entered, he looked up pleasantly and rose with rather more grace than Hani had exhibited after his picnic in the town. "What can I do for you, my lord?"

"I wanted to tell you that my secretary and I will be in Urusalim for a few days. I need to talk to the emissary who saw Egyptian soldiers among the *hapiru*. While I suspect someone attached to the palace as the actual murderer, the robbery was almost certainly carried out by *hapiru*, and I'd like to know how they were aware of the Babylonians' presence."

"I wish you good luck, then, Lord Hani. Although it doesn't surprise me at all that the *hapiru* knew they were there. They seem to have scouts all over, or else how would they be able to descend on any caravan?"

"That's a good point," Hani said, musing. "Well, hopefully this trip will elucidate a few things. And when we return, I'll approach Zalaya yet again with an offer of gold to encourage his garrulity."

"Have a safe journey, my lord," Amen-nefer said, nodding respectfully.

By the time Hani returned to his room, Maya had already packed their bags and baskets and was sitting on the bed.

"Ready, Maya? It's a seven-day journey on foot, so I want to start promptly. The soldiers are bringing tents for everyone."

"On foot, my lord?" Maya said dubiously.

Hani laughed. "We'll have a litter—don't worry. But

the soldiers will be on foot, and we can go no faster than they do."

Around midafternoon, the little party set out for Urusalim, some distance south and west. Their first stop was Temesheq, where they spent the night. King Biryawaza wasn't there. *Out sharing a pot of beer with the* hapiru, Hani told himself sarcastically. But the king's staff provided Hani's party with everything they needed. Maya had slipped off into the city to do a little shopping for the next day's journey.

As their assigned slave, having left dinner for them, prepared to bow himself out, Hani asked him in a friendly voice, "Where is your king? I had hoped to talk to him."

"He's in Qidshu, my lord. He had an important meeting with the commissioner of Ullaza."

"Ah, well, bad timing on my part, I guess," Hani said with a shrug. But he thought, *Qidshu? To meet with that despicable Hotep? What's Amen-nefer doing in Qidshu? It's not in his jurisdiction.*

As soon as the slave had left, someone knocked on Hani's door. "Come in," Hani called, and Maya eased into the room with a huge hempen sack of dried dates.

"I bought these for the road, my lord. An old lady was selling them in the plaza just outside the palace wall."

"Well done. Dinner just came, so we might as well eat. We can have some of your dates afterward."

They tucked into the rich and delicious meal with a good will. "Guess where Biryawaza is," Hani said through a mouth full of bread. "In Qidshu."

Maya's eyes bugged. "Qidshu? Why? It's a hotbed of the *hapiru.*"

"To meet with the commissioner of Ullaza." Hani watched with amusement as Maya's eyes grew round and a flush of anger rose up the secretary's cheeks.

"What's Amen-nefer doing up there?"

"Slapping wrists, perhaps. I don't know. It's under the jurisdiction of the commissioner of Ullaza. But as soon as we left, our friend hotfooted it to the north."

Maya pondered this. "Do you think his soldiers are the ones who have gone over to the *hapiru*?"

Hani shrugged. It wouldn't have surprised him. That would make Amen-nefer just one more corrupt commissioner in a long line of them. *The temptation in an unsupervised and remote post must be too much for people.* "Biryawaza, Amen-nefer, and Aitakkama. Quite a team."

❦

It was a surprisingly cold early morning when they finally reached Urusalim, bundled in cloaks and blankets. The rocky golden hillsides were silvered with frost until the sun began to steal over the horizon, raising a pale, pearly mist that only gradually unveiled the ridges and ravines of barren scrub. Hani was unsure if the Babylonian occupiers would even receive them, but a soldier of Sangar summoned him and Maya from the gate and led them to King Abdi-hepa's modest palace.

The Babylonian officer in charge greeted them courteously, if coolly. Hani responded in Akkadian with all the warmth of someone who'd been met with a smile and a hug. "Thank you for your welcome, my lord. My name is Hani son of Mery-ra. I'm the emissary of the Great King of

Kemet, here to investigate the unfortunate murder of your countryman."

"Finally," said the officer. "How can we help you?"

"I would like to talk to anyone who knew Lord Shulum-marduk. And I'd like to see the emissary of the king here who reported nearly a year ago about seeing Egyptian soldiers among the *hapiru*."

The Babylonian's face darkened. "That's a pretty thought," he said caustically. "Are you implying that the attack on our embassy was engineered by your government?"

"By no means. But it's possible that renegades from our army have joined up with the brigands. Or else someone else altogether is masquerading as Egyptian soldiers in order to stir up bad will between our nation and yours." That idea had only just occurred to Hani.

The officer grew thoughtful. "I'll ask if anyone on my scribal staff knew the late Shulum-marduk. Then you might want to talk to King Abdi-hepa. He would know who that emissary you're looking for is." He added, with a thawing of expression, "My name is Esagil-kin-apli. I appreciate your learning our language."

"Ah, but your eminent tongue binds all the civilized kingdoms of the world. Where would international correspondence be without it?" Hani smiled benevolently. *Nothing like a little flattery to soften up hostility. This is more than half of my work as a diplomat.*

Esagil-kin-apli called a servant to show Hani and Maya to their quarters. The palace wasn't large, although it had an impressive gate. Hani and his escort were all housed in a wing of guest rooms facing a court. It was close to the throne room and other public parts of the building and therefore not as quiet as Hani might have hoped. But the suite was pleasant, and on a brazier, some fat wood crackled invitingly.

Maya chafed his hands over the fire. "And to think, it's harvest season back home." He looked up at Hani with an expression of tremulous hope. "I guess Sat-hut-haru has had our son by now, eh, my lord?"

Hani grinned. "I wouldn't be surprised. You may well have a letter by the time we get back to Kumidi."

Maya turned back to the brazier with a beatific smile.

A knock at the door made Hani turn around, and he strode to the panel and opened it. Standing in the doorway was a slight young man of medium height—not much more than thirty—with a thin, delicate face, a smooth crescent nose, and the most mournful eyes Hani had ever seen on a human being. The man was expensively but unostentatiously dressed in a tunic of lapis blue, with no jewelry at all, not even a signet ring.

"How may I help you?" Hani said pleasantly, wondering who this was. He didn't look like a Babylonian.

"I'm Abdi-hepa, the king of this place," the young man said.

Hani drew back, nonplussed, and folded in a reverence. "My lord! Forgive me. I wouldn't have expected you at my door."

"May I come in?" The king's voice was strangely flat.

"By all means. Please take this chair."

Abdi-hepa sank onto the chair with a sigh. He slid down into it, his knees splayed. "We need to talk, Lord Hani. The gods know what sort of story these Babylonians will give you. But Our Sun God needs to have the truth."

"By all means, my lord. This is my secretary"—Hani indicated Maya with a gesture—"and with your permission, he'll take notes."

The king nodded. Maya crossed his legs, took his seat on the floor, and spread out his writing tools.

"Well, you know we were invaded, I assume. But how? That's the question. I sent a horseback courier with a call for help to our high commissioner in Azzati, not far away, but he took no action. I sent a second call, and he said he had never received the first one. By that time, the men of Sangar had overrun us."

"I know Lord Pta... *Maya* well, my lord. And I can tell you that if he said he didn't receive the first message, he didn't."

The king's melancholy face grew longer. "Oh, I believe it. Because the second messenger found the corpse of the first one lying by the road."

Hani's heart sank within him. "The *hapiru*?"

"No doubt. Such a thing would happen only to me." Abdi-hepa looked vacantly into the distance. "I labor under a curse."

"Oh, surely not, my lord king," Hani said kindly.

Abdi-hepa's chest heaved in a discouraged breath. Finally, he resumed. "And then, there's the matter of Egyptian soldiers among our nomadic friends."

"That's precisely why we've come. I wanted to talk to the emissary who told Lord Maya he'd seen soldiers in their ranks some months ago."

"I saw them, too, Lord Hani. And lest you think we're just provincials who might have mistaken the uniform, I was raised at your court. They were Egyptian. They were red skinned, if you'll pardon me saying so, and had on infantry uniforms."

Hani dropped his eyes and twisted his mouth in thought. "Only that once, my lord? Or is it habitual?"

"Frequent. Among their other misdeeds, they attacked my escort once when I was traveling and have made several attempts to enter the city." The king looked at Hani in sorrowful accusation. "Since we're not permitted to fortify our city, defending it is difficult. We have only the casemate formed by our outer ring of houses, no proper wall. No gates we can close."

"I understand, my lord," said Hani in a low voice. The system was an embarrassment as far as he was concerned; only a weak nation would be so nervous about being resisted by its vassals. "What I'd like to know is whose soldiers they are. Has the commissioner at Kumidi done anything to investigate?"

The king's face grew gloomier, his thin hands absentmindedly rubbing the arms of his chair. "No. He seems to have no interest in our safety." He looked Hani in the eye. "I understand that the Great King is planning to lead troops up here to settle the *hapiru* once and for all."

Lead? I'll believe it when I see it, Hani thought. "That's the plan, my lord. Probably in the fall, before sailing season ends."

"We are an inland kingdom, Lord Hani. Sailing season means little to us. We need help now."

"When I return to Kumidi, I'll certainly tell the commissioner." Hani wrestled with the propriety of the question before he asked in a low voice, "How is Lord Amen-nefer viewed by the kingdoms of Djahy, my lord?"

"He holds us in contempt. Unless a great cavalry battle with waving banners and the opportunity for conspicuous heroism offers itself, he won't lift a finger for us." The king's lusterless eyes glittered suddenly with resentment. "But we have to choke down our feelings because he is our only hope of protection. I've written directly to Our Sun God on more than one occasion, but he just refers me to our local dignitaries—Amen-nefer, in short. Or Maya, who is as helpful as he can be, but he, too, depends on the commissioner to carry out his will." Abdi-hepa gazed into space with an air of hopelessness. "I don't know what to do..."

Hani asked quietly, "Do you have any reason to think the commissioner is less than loyal?"

Abdi-hepa shrugged listlessly. "Your king is far away. Amen-nefer is loyal to the idea of Kemet in Djahy, which is him."

Hani pondered this perceptive observation. "He seems to hate the *hapiru* with a more than common level of vitriol."

But the king looked up, surprised. "Hate them? I doubt it. We suspect him of harboring them."

A bolt of amazement skewered Hani to the spot. A moment passed before he could regroup and ask, "How so, my lord? That's a pretty grave accusation."

"Which is why I've never made a formal complaint. Considering how isolated we are, Amen-nefer would be free to wreak his vengeance on us." Abdi-hepa looked up at Hani with a meaningful stare. "And he's a frightfully vengeful man."

Remembering Pa-aten-em-heb's story, Hani said

somberly, "I can well believe it." He fingered his chin. *Is there any way I can get the man replaced? It can't be in our best interests to have as commissioner a person his subjects so despise.* "Let me tell you this—perhaps you're already aware. As soon as I left Kumidi, the commissioner took off for Qidshu in the company of King Biryawaza of Upi."

Abdi-hepa's thin, beaky face grew cynical. He said sarcastically, "No surprise there, my lord. They're all three birds of a feather."

"What do you mean by that?"

"All three are protectors of the *hapiru*."

"But why?" Hani cried. "What can any of them hope to gain by such an action? Aren't their cities endangered as much as anyone else's?"

The king shrugged apathetically. "Are they being paid off? Do they think they can gain some control over the nomads by being cozy with them? I'm sure I don't know." He sat staring into space for a few heartbeats then said in a dull, disillusioned voice, "When I left your court ten years ago, I was full of loyalty and enthusiasm. I felt I was doing a noble work for the Great Kingdom of Kemet by shepherding one of its vassal states. Since then"—he looked up with his melancholy black eyes—"it has become clear to me that your king doesn't respect me or my country. We are only being exploited as a disposable buffer for your eastern border. And no one cares what we are suffering. If we can't even count on your protection, why do we remain loyal?"

A pang of shame skewered Hani. *He sees clearly. We have become a soulless beast that eats up our vassals, sucks their marrow, and spits them out.* He said with feeling, "My lord, I assure you, there are many in the Two Lands who value

217

and respect your people. You may trust Lord Maya to have your best interests at heart. And I'll certainly carry your message to the vizier when I return to the capital."

Abdi-hepa smiled thinly, a smile that left his eyes untouched. He rose and heaved a sigh. "I hope so. We don't complain—not because we don't have needs—but because we know it won't do any good."

Hani bowed deeply, and the king of Urusalim drifted off, trailing a mist of gloom. When Hani had closed the door behind Abdi-hepa, he exchanged a look of shared disgust with Maya. "Our commissioner is sounding more and more like the sort of appointee Our Sun God would make. What do you wager that he and Hotep, the commissioner of Ullaza, are at that meeting exchanging ideas on being ineffective?"

Maya scrambled to his feet and said with ferocity, "I'll bet anything it's Amen-nefer's soldiers who have gone over. And probably he himself, the swine."

"But remember what Abdi-hepa said—maybe this is an effort to infiltrate them. We mustn't rush to judgment." Hani wanted to believe his own words, but he knew they rang hollow. "What would Amen-nefer's motive be otherwise? And I can't help but remember how the very mention of the *hapiru* made him break out in anger. He certainly didn't sound like a man who was hobnobbing with them."

Maya expelled a breath. "That's gotten me confused. Maybe he contemns all foreigners."

"Hmmm." Hani didn't know what to say. While Abdi-hepa's visit had provided some interesting information, it didn't really advance his case. "Why would Amen-nefer's men be involved with the raid on the Babylonians—assuming they were? Was it to herd them into Kumidi? But then what? What earthly motive could he have for killing an emissary? It reflects so badly on his administration that it may even get him recalled."

"The emissary was a foreigner," Maya said with a shrug.

But Hani found none of their conjectures convincing. He stretched. "Let's try to find one of the Babylonians who might have known Shulum-marduk. And if there is no one, then our trip here is ended."

✝

That afternoon, Hani asked the commanding officer if he knew of anyone who might be able to give him information about the deceased emissary. "You might ask our military scribe," Esagil-kin-apli said.

"And where might he be found?" asked Hani pleasantly.

"I'll send him to you. I'm not promising he'll know anything, though." The officer shooed off a subordinate with the instructions "Find Nabu-ahhe-idin and send him here, soldier."

A brief while later, a neatly built little man with a prominent belly that didn't seem to match the rest of him approached. Hani estimated he was in his early forties, his hair beginning to gray around the temples, but still bouncing and youthful in his movements. A long reed stylus was tucked over the ear through his oiled curls. He glanced briefly at Hani and Maya then looked to the officer, eyes wide-open in curiosity, and slapped himself on the chest in a military salute. "How can I be of service, my lord?"

"Do you know the diplomat who was just assassinated?"

The scribe's face fell. "Shulum-marduk? Yes, my lord. We were good friends since scribal school."

"This gentleman is investigating his death and has some questions he'd like to ask you." The officer nodded to Hani as if to say, "He's all yours," and made his way off across the courtyard.

Hani said in Akkadian, "My name is Hani, and as your superior just said, I'm the investigator of the unfortunate death of your friend. Could we go somewhere private?"

"I've been working in the chancery here, and none of the local scribes has come around, so we should be alone." Nabu-ahhe-idin led the way, and Hani and Maya followed. They came to a room that was perfectly familiar to scribes anywhere, with clay tablets and scrolls of papyrus stacked on shelves. A large table with stools around it reigned in the middle of the floor, littered with styluses and brushes and pots of water. Hani breathed in the comforting smell he knew so well and turned to the Babylonian. "Do you mind if I ask you a few questions about Lord Shulum-marduk?"

"If it helps you take vengeance on the despicable assassin, ask away," said Nabu-ahhe-idin fervently.

"With your permission, my secretary will take notes."

The man smiled as if he recognized the assignment. Maya settled himself on the floor and pulled off his writing case while Hani and the scribe seated themselves at the table.

"You say you'd known one another since school."

"Yes. We were both training to be translators. We went to Mizri—Kemet—together in our youth to perfect our accents. We were there perhaps six months then came home. Shulum-marduk drifted into the foreign service. I found a post in the army."

"What sort of man was he?"

"Friendly. Loyal." Nabu-ahhe-idin's lip trembled. "He could be stubborn, but it was because he was so upright."

Hani thought that the deceased was probably just the sort of man who was greatly needed in the present crisis. But the gods had their reasons for permitting tragedy. He said in a gentle voice, "Tell me about your stay in the Two Lands, my friend. Did he cross anyone who might have had it in for him?"

"But that was seventeen years ago, Lord Hani. Who carries a grudge for so long?"

You'd be surprised how long people can harbor grudges. "Anything of any note otherwise?"

The Babylonian pondered for a moment, stroking his beard. "He told me he'd witnessed a terrible accident once. He was coming back from your king's jubilee—I wasn't with him—when a girl fell off the boat and was badly injured."

Hani froze, his heart pounding. *It had to have been Baket-iset!* "Did he... did he have any observations about that accident?" he asked, scarcely daring to breathe. For a long time, he'd been unable to fully forgive himself for not having been there for his daughter—for not having caught her before she tumbled into the water, screaming. He'd jumped into the River after her, but the damage had been done. How many times had he asked himself how a graceful girl like Baket could have lost her footing? But he'd never again met any of the many people who were on the fateful ferry from the Per-hay, the king's jubilee palace, to the east bank who might have relayed to him what had happened.

"Not much. He told me everything he'd observed, but there was a crowd. He said the girl was talking to a man, and then she was overboard. I don't know who that man might have been—perhaps he saw things up close."

Hani had trouble restraining himself from grabbing the scribe by the breast of his tunic and demanding that he summon up some concrete recollection. But of course, Nabu-ahhe-idin knew only what Shulum-marduk had told him. Hani forced himself to ask casually, "Did your friend ever return to Kemet, do you know?"

"Not to my knowledge, my lord. At least not until this year. That's where he was heading when..." Nabu-ahhe-idin lowered his eyes and clasped his hands in a gesture that might have been prayerful or simply humble in the face of the gods' inscrutable will. After a moment, he said uncertainly, "I recall he said the man the girl was talking to had one eye."

A thrill ran up Hani's spine. *Dear gods! Could it be Amen-nefer?* After all these years, could Hani be positioned now to hear from an eyewitness's mouth what had cost his beautiful daughter her future? She seemed to have no recollection of anything before they fished her out of the water... Hani forced himself to still his hammering heart and say casually, "Anything else from that trip or any other time that you think might have earned someone's enmity?"

The scribe shook his head pensively. "I don't think so. If something should come back to me, I'll send for you, my lord. Of course"—he looked Hani in the eye—"I'm not sure how much longer we'll be here. I think our king and yours are trying to work something out, and then we can go home."

Hani had trouble keeping his mind on the Babylonian's assassination. He kept telling himself, *Perhaps I'm about to learn what happened—after all these years!* "Thank you. I appreciate deeply your cooperation. May our two lands enjoy peace and brotherhood for many generations." The men exchanged amicable bows, and Nabu-ahhe-idin made his way out the door and down the corridor with a brisk stride. Hani remained staring into space, his thoughts in a tumult.

"Whew!" Maya exclaimed. "Do you think that could be Baket-iset's accident? And that the witness was Amen-nefer?" He ranged his pen and ink in his writing case and got to his feet. He looked up at Hani with concern on his face. "Are you all right, my lord? You look pale."

Hani forced a laugh. "It could be him. And if so, I may finally get the story." He gathered his diplomatic self-control about him and said matter-of-factly, "I guess we've gotten the information we needed here for our case. Time to migrate north with the birds. Tomorrow, let's head back up to Kumidi."

CHAPTER 9

Maya and Lord Hani reached the administrative city before the end of the week. Maya had fully expected that the brigands would fall upon their party somewhere in the bleak stretches of the desert across the River Yardon, but the journey was quiet. Passing through Temesheq, they found that Biryawaza was still not back in his capital.

By the time they arrived in Kumidi, Maya was drenched with sweat, which the dry air lapped up quickly, leaving an itchy layer of salt on his skin. He was miserable and cross. Nothing but the thought of the little son Sati had to have given him by now kept his mind off the annoyances of the journey.

He and Hani dismounted from their litter in the courtyard of the commissioner's palace with relief. Only then did Maya realize how much hotter it had been—hip to hip in the litter, with no breeze—than it was outside.

"Well, here we are," said Lord Hani, stretching expansively. He fanned himself in the rapidly warming spring air and repositioned his wig, which he'd abandoned during the trip. "Let's see if our commissioner is back from his shady meeting." He shot Maya a knowing grin.

The two men waved goodbye to their escort and headed up to the porch of the official residence, where the majordomo greeted them. "Shall I send a servant for your things, my lord? You can leave them right here, and I'll see to it they're brought to you," he said smoothly, bowing with just the right amount of servility.

"Yes. Zalaya is the person assigned to us." Hani gave him a friendly smile.

But the man's face grew suddenly stiff, and he stammered, "He... uh... he's no longer with us, my lord."

Maya and Hani exchanged a look of surprise. *What's this?* Maya thought, an uneasy feeling making his way up the back of his neck.

"You mean he's been sold? Run away?"

"I mean he is no longer alive, Lord Hani. But I'll send someone else." The majordomo turned in haste, as if he couldn't wait to be away, and set off inside the palace, leaving Hani and Maya staring at each other.

"What's going on? This place seems to be getting dangerous." Maya's forehead grew damp with the realization that something could well and truly happen to him, too, and he might never see his little son.

"Let's go back to the room," Hani said in a low tone, and the two of them set off into their wing, where they attained the room with a sense of relief. Hani closed the door quietly behind him.

Then he turned to Maya, a troubled expression knitting his bushy eyebrows. "I'd like to know more about this. It seems very suspicious—just before we had a chance to interrogate him with an incentive to talk."

"Was this the same murderer who assassinated Shulum-marduk, do you think?"

"It's very likely. But who is that? The one thing that's clear is that it's someone on the palace staff."

"Leave it to that Amen-nefer to surround himself with thugs," said Maya in disgust.

Just then, a knock sounded at the door. Maya jumped, his instincts of survival suddenly all alert. Hani moved quickly to the door and stood there a moment as if listening, then he pulled it open with an abrupt gesture. It was only the slave with their baggage.

"Where do you want me to put these, my lord?" the man asked meekly. He was a sturdy-looking fellow in his thirties, with a mashed nose and the same crushed air that all the other slaves seemed to carry with them.

"Right here is fine," said Hani with a smile. The slave deposited the baskets and leather pouches in a heap on the floor and made to withdraw, but Hani stopped him with a friendly hand on the shoulder. "I understand Zalaya has died."

The slave's eyes grew round, and he froze. "Yes, my lord," he said in a faint voice.

"Was he ill?"

"No, he… he was killed."

Yahya! thought Maya. *Just as I suspected. Zalaya did know something, and somebody in this residence didn't want to take chances.*

"How? Do you know?" Hani persisted.

"I... I think he was strangled." The slave had grown pale, as if he were on the verge of fainting with fear.

Hani clapped him kindly on the shoulder. "What's your name, son?" It would be a frightened man, indeed, who wouldn't be reassured by that gesture.

"Bin-addi, my lord."

"Why are you all so scared, Bin-addi?" Hani asked in a gentle, encouraging voice. "A fine, strapping young man like you—I'll bet you're plenty brave."

"It's... it's that strange things are happening here. Zalaya's dead, and his wife..." The man hung his head with a grimace.

"You know, I'm the king's investigator. I'm here to figure out what those 'strange things' are. But someone who knows something needs to give me information, or I'll never solve the case. I've been authorized to pay. I could even buy your freedom and take you back with me if your information is helpful."

The slave looked at Hani with hope in his eyes. "You would do that? Take me away?"

"I swear on my mother's *ka*."

I do believe he's going to crack, Maya thought, a spark of excitement alight within.

"Who killed Zalaya?" Hani asked again. "And what happened to his wife?"

"His wife... she wasn't supposed to be here. The commissioner doesn't want women around. He says it's bad for discipline. But she was in the kitchen working. The others covered for her. The children worked there too—doing the tasks little children can do. Turning the spit or carrying things."

"How do people who are married usually manage around here?" Maya asked.

"They keep a little place in the city somewhere. It's a lot safer anyway." Bin-addi swallowed. "She was found out and... and raped and beaten, my lord, right in front of the children. And on top of that, she lost her husband."

Maya suppressed a wave of nausea and disgust. He could see on Hani's expressive face the same emotions.

"Who did this terrible thing?" Hani asked in a strangled voice.

Bin-addi had opened his mouth to speak when a knock sounded at the door. He froze, his face twisted with terror.

"Lord Hani?" It was the brassy voice of Amen-nefer. "I've found out something for you. Can we talk?"

Maya caught his breath in fear, and Bin-addi looked absolutely petrified, staring around him, wild-eyed, as if he would like to bolt out the window.

Hani called, "I just took a bath, my lord. I haven't dressed yet. Can you give me just a moment?"

"Of course, of course," the commissioner said through the door.

"You, into the clothes press," Hani hissed at the slave.

Bin-addi jumped into the chest and compacted his muscular body into a remarkably small space.

Hani lowered the lid on him quietly. Then Hani poured water from his drinking gourd over his head and grabbed up a towel. "Come in."

Amen-nefer entered to find Lord Hani toweling his wet hair. "Forgive me, my lord commissioner. I don't usually receive in this condition, but we just got back." He smiled amiably and threw the towel over a shoulder.

Amen-nefer said, "I hope I'm not intruding. I thought I heard voices."

Hani laughed. "That was my secretary Maya here. He's a master of impersonation. Maya, do Lord Maya for the commissioner."

Maya caught his father-in-law's eye in horror. His face burning, he drew himself up and lifted an eyebrow. Looking haughtily down his nose, he said in an upper-class drawl, "I wish you wouldn't let just anyone in, Hani, my friend." He had to swallow precipitously and hoped his audience wouldn't hear the evidence of his nervousness.

Amen-nefer threw back his handsome head and laughed. "Amazing! He's damned skillful."

"Yes," said Hani with a conspiratorial sidelong glance at Maya. "He's a man of many parts." He smiled his broad, gap-toothed grin at the commissioner, to all appearances completely at ease.

With a breath of relief, Maya thought, *What a master of concealment. I'm practically shaking, and he looks cool as can be.*

Amen-nefer seated himself on the bed. "I wanted to tell you that I sniffed around in Qidshu when I was up there recently, and I learned a few things. The garrison at Temesheq has a handful of men missing. We may have found our renegades."

Maya heard the words in amazement.

Hani said, "That's a good lead, indeed, my lord. We wondered why you had gone to Qidshu, since it's not in your jurisdiction."

"I wanted to meet with my fellow commissioner and hear the explanation of our two vassals, Temesheq and

Qidshu, both accused of disloyalty. They were quite open, although naturally they blamed it on others."

"What did they confess to?"

"To fraternizing with the *hapiru*. They said they had to keep them pacified, that their protection was a sort of payoff so the nomads wouldn't attack their cities and convoys." Amen-nefer snorted. "They said that if we were protecting them as we ought, they wouldn't need to be so opportunistic."

Hani nodded with an understanding smile. "So it's our fault, eh? They should be happy that our lord king is planning an expedition up here."

"Perhaps. Although I rather think they enjoy their status as fence-sitters."

"Are they tempted to go over to Kheta?"

"They didn't admit to it. I made it clear to them that the yoke of Kheta is considerably more burdensome than ours." The commissioner grinned.

"Any leads about the murder of our Babylonian?"

Amen-nefer knit his brows. "Not in so many words. But I suspect the *hapiru* more and more. They've clearly been emboldened by the lack of resistance shown by our mayors. No doubt, they would love to see our position weakened still further on the eastern border by a conflict with Sangar—perhaps even an invasion."

Hani nodded. "This has been very helpful, Lord Amen-nefer. Thank you for sharing your observations." He paused and then said in a casual tone, "It seems our servant Zalaya has died."

"So it seems. I was gone at the time, but the other slaves have told me that. Well, they're cheap. We won't lack for domestic help. Did someone bring up your bags?" Amen-nefer's eye rested on the baggage stacked on the floor and then seemed to flicker toward the clothes press. Maya prayed Bin-addi wouldn't sneeze or otherwise give his presence away.

"He did. Thank you for your attention to our comfort."

The commissioner got to his feet and tipped his head graciously. "You're the representative of Our Sun God, Lord Hani." With an amiable word of goodbye, he exited the room and pulled the door shut behind him.

Maya and Hani stood staring at one another for a long space while Amen-nefer's footsteps clopped off into the distance, then Maya burst out, "The lying dog. I'll bet anything that he was the chief of the conspirators. And that pig Hotep. These are the men guarding our borders?"

Hani raised an eyebrow and looked pensive. Finally, he opened the lid of the clothes press, and Bin-addi emerged, shaken and red-faced. Hani helped him out and urged him to seat himself where the commissioner had just been. The slave sat there stiffly, but he was no longer meek—a light of resolve flashed in his eyes.

"Did you hear that?" asked Hani.

"I did, my lord, but I can't judge such matters. What I need to tell you is that the commissioner was lying when he said he was out of town. He's the one who killed Zalaya and raped his wife."

A stunned silence fell over the room, although Maya had to admit that he wasn't altogether surprised. It seemed to fit the commissioner's record of violence.

Lord Hani finally asked, "Did you see this happen?"

Bin-addi shook his head, but he said in a firmer voice, "Zalaya's children saw it. They told me."

Maya let out a whistle. Children would have had no reason to lie. The horrible deed must have been imprinted on their young memories forever.

Hani's jovial face had grown pale and set. "Did the wife survive?"

"Yes, my lord, but she's not in good shape."

"And why do you think this happened, Bin-addi?"

Bin-addi's voice dropped, and he cast his eyes around nervously. "The Lord Commissioner wanted to shut Zalaya up, my lord. He knew something, but I don't know what."

"Isn't Amen-nefer worried that the wife saw him do it? She'll be in more danger now," Maya said.

"But, my lord, Zalaya was only a slave. No one cares if his master killed him."

Maya cringed. *Thank the gods no such barbarous custom exists in the Two Lands.*

Hani said quietly, "Do you happen to know anything about the murder of the Babylonian?"

"No, my lord. It wasn't me assigned to be his valet."

"Who was, do you know?"

Bin-addi shook his head, looking apologetic. He said, as if embarrassed, "Will you help me get away, my lord? And my wife and children?"

"I told you I would, son, and I keep my word," said Hani earnestly. "I'll take you all to Azzati and free you. But I beg you, keep your ears open until then. Some one of the servants knows more than he's revealing. Perhaps you could find out the man who served Lord Shulum-marduk."

The slave dropped to his knees and threw himself on

Hani's feet. "May the gods of both our lands bless you, my lord."

※

Before he and Maya and their staff departed for Azzati, Hani wanted to speak to Amen-nefer about the perception of the vassals that he was perhaps closer than he ought to be to the *hapiru*. But there was another topic even more urgent than that.

"Well, my lord, we'll be off to the south tomorrow," he said to Amen-nefer when the latter received him in his office. "I would like to buy a slave from you to serve me on the way, if you don't mind."

"Don't think of it, Hani. Anyone you want is yours— no need to pay me. Let's just call it the cost of your bribery that wasn't needed," the commissioner said, his curvaceous lips drawn upward in a smile.

Hani acknowledged the gift courteously. He wasn't sure how to launch into the conversation that was trying to force its way out of him. Breathing was singularly hard. "On a completely different matter, my lord, something of personal interest came up in my discussion with one of the friends of the deceased. It turns out that Shulum-marduk was in Kemet seventeen years ago and witnessed a terrible boat accident in which a young girl fell overboard and was injured."

Amen-nefer listened politely. When Hani stopped for a painful swallow, the commissioner said, "And?"

"That girl was almost certainly my daughter. The Babylonian said she was last seen talking to a man of your description. I wondered if you had any recollections of what happened that day? Her mother and I have long wanted to know how it befell her. We—"

"I think it must have been someone else, Lord Hani. I certainly never witnessed such an event," Amen-nefer interrupted with every evidence of compassion. "I'm very sorry. I know how much it would mean to her family to have those recollections, but I can't supply them." He smiled wryly. "I'm not the only one-eyed man in the Two Lands, you know."

"Of course not," Hani said, so disappointed he felt tears burning in his nose. *To have come so close...* He got a grip on himself and decided to feel out Amen-nefer with something a bit safer. "That's more or less all, my lord commissioner. I did feel I should transmit to you, friend to friend, something I've heard repeatedly from the locals, however."

"What's that, Hani?" Amen-nefer asked with a smile that was a little chillier than it had been a moment before.

"King Abdi-hepa, for one, seems to think you aren't as hostile to the *hapiru* as you might be, my lord."

The commissioner's face grew dark with anger, and although he maintained his white smile, it had become sharklike with contempt. "That hound-eyed little pansy? If anyone sneezes, he fancies himself threatened."

"It's not the first time I've heard questions about you from vassals. Let's just say that it's to your advantage to appear as loyal as you no doubt are in your heart." Hani smiled amiably, suspecting that Amen-nefer was probably quite close to striking him.

The man's face grew redder and redder, a vein bulging in his temple. When he spoke, his voice had turned into a snarl. "I told you why I was dealing with them in Qidshu. You don't believe me? It's my word against that perverted scum Abdi-hepa. I'm not a liar." He approached Hani, his head low between his shoulders, his fists clenching and unclenching. "Is this how you repay my hospitality, Lord Hani? By concocting accusations?"

The commissioner's reaction was so disproportionate to the provocation that Hani felt he'd fallen into a scene from the *Book of Going Forth by Day*. Amen-nefer had about him something of the incendiary wrath of a demon with a head of flame. "I'm accusing you of nothing, my friend. Just reporting what others have said. Since I know that you want to be a loyal magistrate of the two lands, I tell you this in private. Your actions, of course, speak louder to Our Sun God—life, prosperity, and health to him—than the reports of others." Hani managed to sound calm and friendly, but he felt the cold sweat on his forehead. He bowed and withdrew toward the door. "I leave you, Lord Amen-nefer. Thank you for everything. May the lord of the horizon bless you."

He closed the door carefully behind him, his heart pounding, and had gone no more than a few paces when he heard something violently strike the inside of the panel and shatter. Then another. And another.

"I hope he has copies of those tablets," he said to himself, amused, but the hair rose on the back of his neck nonetheless. This display was a revelation of an aspect of the commissioner's character that his previous behavior had only hinted at.

As Hani walked across the courtyard and into the wing he and his staff inhabited, he formulated revised plans. He didn't want to spend another night under Amen-nefer's roof; he didn't trust the man's volatile temper. *I'm the king's representative, here for no other reason than to set things right. Why should I have to mince my words?* He wanted to get away before Amen-nefer threw *him* at the door.

As soon as he regained the corridor where his party was lodged, he began knocking on doors and telling everyone, "Get ready to leave. We're going this afternoon."

Maya stuck his head out of his room. "What's that, Lord Hani? Leaving so abruptly?"

"I don't want to delay our departure. I'll explain later. Go round up our new slave, Bin-addi, and I'll alert Pa-aten-em-heb," Hani said under his breath.

He had to go looking in the barracks for the officer and his men. Pa-aten-em-heb reacted with surprise to Hani's sudden orders, but he asked no questions and said simply, "I'll see to it the men are ready."

By the middle of the afternoon, the party was out the gate and on its way south. Bin-addi and his wife and three small children trudged along with the troops, casting fearful looks behind them until they'd entered the mountains and Kumidi was well out of sight.

❦

When they made camp that night, Hani felt at last that he could speak to Maya and Pa-aten-em-heb about the reason for their precipitous departure. They sat on the ground, elbow to elbow, around the campfire the soldiers had built. The night was chill, even this late in the season, and the age-old trees about them cast a darker blackness that swallowed up the sky, lit with its friendly stars. Crickets pulsed rhythmically, and now and again, a cry in the woods reminded Hani of why they kept a fire burning all night. He heard the shriek of a barn owl on the hunt.

Hani began quietly so that none of the soldiers or his own staff could catch his words. "The commissioner and I had an interview this morning, and everything was cordial. Then I brought up some of the disenchantment of the vassals with his so-called protection, how he seems to be a little soft on the *hapiru*. I said all this nicely, of course, not confrontationally. In fact, I said it in private so he could explain himself, or better still, quietly make an effort to improve. But the man fell into a rage. I got out as fast as I could, only to hear him throwing things at the door in my wake." Hani managed a smile, but he spoke seriously. "I honestly expected him to attack me, and I wanted us to get away from him before he lashed out at one of the secretaries or something. Slaughtered our pack donkeys."

Maya looked shocked, his jaw hanging open. "But you were only doing your duty, my lord."

Pa-aten-em-heb seemed less surprised. "That seems in character, frankly," he said with a bitter sneer. "Anyone who would attack a woman wouldn't scruple to attack the king's emissary."

All at once, something shifted in Hani's mind. He murmured, the words finding themselves as he spoke them, "Could it have been he who murdered the Babylonian?" Then he answered his question with a shake of the head. "He had no motivation, though. It will only bring shame down on his administration, as it already has to an extent."

"He had no motivation to attack you, either, my lord," Maya said. "He just lost his temper."

"Although I had confronted him at least. That was more provocation than some foreigner passing through would have given."

"But why else would Amen-nefer have killed Zalaya unless he was afraid of what the slave would say?" Pa-aten-em-heb fixed Hani with a piercing stare of his black eyes.

Hani said pensively, "I told him that I planned to interview Zalaya—because I had to ask for the *deben*s, you remember. And after that, the slave turned up dead." He wanted this not to be the way it looked. Apprehending a magistrate of the Two Lands for murder was more than he wanted to take on. *But if the man is guilty, someone must restore* ma'at...

The other two men stared at Hani, and he could almost see the thoughts battering the walls inside their heads, trying to take shape—as his own were. "I need to ask Lord Ptah-mes how to proceed with this. We have to find some proof. I can't get Amen-nefer convicted with no direct evidence."

"Convict him of rape and battery on my sister, then," said Pa-aten-em-heb, barely suppressing a snarl. "We know he's guilty of that."

"But didn't the Master of the Hall of Justice find him innocent?" Maya's face was stretched with incomprehension.

"True." Hani fell silent. *Maybe Ptah-mes can at least get him removed from office on the grounds that he has alienated the vassals under his charge.* He earnestly hoped so. The black marks were piling up against the commissioner, even if he hadn't murdered Shulum-marduk. Hani stood up and stretched. "It's getting chilly, gentlemen, and we have another long day of travel ahead of us tomorrow. I think I'll head to bed."

He bent to light a brand and made his way toward his tent. The night closed in around him as he moved farther from the fire, the brave little flame of his burning branch a feeble protector against the black. A jackal yelped from afar. Hani entered his tent, bone weary. Yet as the hours of night passed, he found he couldn't fall asleep. If it were proved that Amen-nefer, an official of Kemet, had murdered a foreign dignitary, Sangar would view it as an act of war. It would *be* an act of war. *Who could ever be sure the deed wasn't on orders from the Great King himself? How far do I pursue this?* Hani asked himself. *Is* ma'at *best served by punishing the villain or by letting him go and preventing open hostilities between our kingdoms?*

And of course, he had no real proof that the commissioner was the perpetrator of the murder. To be sure, he was a violent, volatile man, but that didn't make him guilty of that particular crime. "I need a witness," Hani murmured. "I need a motive."

CHAPTER 10

THE LITTLE CARAVAN WAS DUE to reach Siduna on the coast the next evening. From there, they would take a ship to Azzati, a journey of three or four days, depending on the winds. So far, the weather had held. It was pleasantly cool crossing the hill country and even cold at night. But as they descended the coastal side of the range, the heat began to close in on them once again. The humidity was rising; Hani could see it hanging like a pale scrim that blurred the horizon, where the deep blue-green of the sea met the washed blue of the sky. They were following a road that looped and looped back on itself, and the forest had fallen away behind them, the rolling foothills stretching on all sides. The view of the coastal plain, spread out below, was heart-stoppingly beautiful—the well-watered green fields and silvery olive orchards, the reed-thin black cypresses, the scattered pale cubes of farms. In the middle distance, clustered along the water's edge, the salt scatter of Siduna rubbed into the carpet of green and gold and gray.

With a lump in his throat, Hani murmured to himself, "This must be how the gods see us."

They stopped for lunch right there in the middle of the road. Their scout had gone ahead a ways to check the condition of the road because it would be hard enough for their carts to descend the slope safely even if the cherty surface of the passage were clear. And sure enough, as Hani spread out their basket of small breads and olives and cucumbers in green grape juice, the scout came jogging back into the camp. Hani got to his feet and followed him to where Pa-aten-em-heb sat eating with his men.

"My lord," the panting scout said to his commander, "there are several dead trees across the road not far from here, all in a row."

"That doesn't sound natural," the officer said grimly. "It must be a deliberate roadblock." He rose to his feet and shouted, "Men, form up, and be prepared for an attack. You, you, and you"—he pointed at several soldiers—"go get those trees cleared in case we need to make a run for it."

The soldiers abandoned their food and dived for their weapons. Hani asked quietly at Pa-aten-em-heb's elbow, "*Hapiru*, I wonder?"

"Almost certainly, Lord Hani. Who else would fall upon a traveling party under such heavy escort?"

But Hani thought uneasily, *Even if we have trained soldiers, a dozen men doesn't seem very heavy to me.* He made his way back to where Maya still sat, looking up in confusion.

The secretary sprang to his feet and dusted himself off. "Are we being attacked, my lord?" His eyes were round but not with fear. A look of fierce anticipation sparkled in them.

Hani envied him his innocence. He himself knew better what the cost of a battle would be. "It looks like it. You and I had better find some weapons, but don't be too quick to get out into the fray to use them, my friend." He thought he'd do well to find something to arm Bin-addi and the rest of his staff with as well, just in case. They couldn't throw reed pens and ink blocks at a gang of desperadoes.

Apart from the brief clang and clatter of arming, a curious deadly silence lay over the camp so that the twittering of birds in the bushes became almost loud. No one spoke. All eyes were fixed on the boulders and scrubby trees and gorse that surrounded the road. It was late afternoon, and the declining sun hit them full on from the west. Below, some *iterus* away, where the ground leveled out, the sea glittered, too bright to look at. Hani, weighing a heavy war club in his hand, looked at the soldiers around him. They were defended only by their quilted aprons and thick scarves, their chests completely bare, yet they seemed unafraid as they prepared methodically for a conflict that would no doubt become deadly for some of them.

Lord Montu, protect us, he prayed.

He saw archers mounting a few of the rocks around them and crouching there, ready to spring up and loose their arrows into the melee. Yet how vulnerable they were to an attack from higher up the hillside. The road wasn't wide enough to form the defenders into a circle—they were all strung out, the carts turned sideways and the animals unhitched, while Bin-addi's wife and children had crawled under the vehicles, hoping to stay unnoticed. Hani's heart was pounding in expectation, but he didn't yet feel fear.

They waited in silence for what seemed like an endless afternoon until Hani had a sense that perhaps they had overestimated the urgency of their situation. The sun was sinking into the sea, at its feet a dazzling path of light that seemed to lead right into the incandescent golden heart of itself. The great Amen-Ra would be the witness to their defense. *Lord Ra, look mercifully on us.* He could see the men around him getting restless from standing alert for so long. No doubt, they had to pee, and they needed water. They wanted to close their eyes for a minute. Then, just as the sun slid into its own golden juices, the birds stopped singing abruptly, and the *hapiru* attacked.

They came pouring out of the woods and rocks and bushes, places where no man should have been able to hide. They shrieked and uttered spine-chilling ululations, waving their axes and clubs, a few of them with swords. The archers on the boulders rose and took aim, but one of them quickly toppled into the crowd, pierced through by someone else's arrow.

Now the fear hit Hani. His stomach fluttered, and his anus clenched. He and his staff were in the middle so that the soldiers would be the first line of defense, but it was worse to watch the battle than to take part, so strong was the delusion of being able to save oneself.

Pa-aten-em-heb's men flailed away with ax and sword, but the *hapiru* kept pouring out of the brush and rocks to either side. *How can there be so many?* Hani saw clearly that he would have to join the active fray at any minute. A sword cut whistled alongside his ear, and he loosed a mighty swing of his club. Blood sprayed over him, his own or someone else's. He was in the thick of the fight, slashing, smashing, the breath sawing in his nose. Fear had turned into the mindless desperation of battle. A man arched and fell beside him, pierced by an arrow from above that sprouted, swaying, from the middle of his back. Others grunted with effort—or screamed as they received a bone-shattering blow. A soldier fell against Hani and almost pulled him down, but the man rose and pressed off into the melee once more. Hani was conscious of nothing outside his little circle of vision. As soon as anyone approached, he laid on him with his club until he was gasping and panting for breath. Then all at once, as if someone had opened a stopcock, the *hapiru* drained away, melting into the brush or hightailing it back uphill by the road.

Hani dropped his club and stood, swaying, trying to catch his breath. He didn't seem to be bleeding, although his arm felt as if it had been wrenched from its socket. Exhaustion crushed him; sweat ran into his eyes. But he wasn't dead. He wasn't even injured.

"I'm too old for this." He gasped, staring around. He needed to account for his staff, none of whom he could see, and above all for Maya. The fear was back, pushing his heart into his throat. "Maya," he called, his throat so dry he could hardly yell. "Where are you, son?"

From somewhere lower down the road, In-her-khau came staggering up, to all appearances unhurt, but his dark face was downright pallid with horror. "Tuy is dead, Lord Hani," he stammered, then he began to cry.

Hani put a weary arm of comfort around his shoulders.

"Help me find the others. We need to know who's alive and who else is dead. Have you seen Maya, my friend?"

"Yes, but that was early on. He was swinging his bronze rod at people's knees, taking them down."

Early on. Hani was left with a flutter of trepidation in his middle. "Round up as many of ours as you can find uphill, and I'll look downhill." If In-her-khau had seen him, Maya must have ended up lower on the road. But darkness was falling fast. Hani trudged down the slope, edging around the wagons, shouting, "Maya! Maya, where are you?"

Pa-aten-em-heb intercepted him after a few cubits. He was sweaty and red-faced, and his arm was bound up in a bloody scarf. "Hani, we're going to have to get out of here soon—we can't navigate the road in the dark, and we certainly can't stay here."

"What about the wounded?"

"The men are carrying them to the wagons. We'll leave the dead until we can come back to bury them." No doubt seeing Hani's wild face, the officer said more gently, "We have no choice, my lord."

"Have you seen Maya?" Hani hardly dared to ask even so much. What he wanted to say was "Dead or alive?" but the words wouldn't come.

"No, I haven't. But your slave and his family are alive."

The twilight was deep now; night was closing in, and all efforts to identify the fallen would soon end perforce. Instead, the soldiers pulled the bodies off the road to permit the passage of the carts. Of the twenty or so unmoving forms stretched out on the sloping ground around him, most appeared to be *hapiru* or other locals. A stunned-looking soldier was sitting up, holding his ear, the blood trickling through his fingers.

"Have you seen a dwarf anywhere?"

The man just stared at him, glassy-eyed with pain.

Anxiety was a ticking pulse in Hani's throat. *How can I ever face Sat-hut-haru if anything has happened to Maya?* He overturned corpse after corpse, knowing full well not one of them was his son-in-law. And now it was night in good earnest. Torches sprang to life here and there. The men had hitched the donkeys back to the carts and loaded the pack animals. Pa-aten-em-heb was shouting orders, and anyone who could still walk was forming up. *I can't leave him.* But Hani knew that there would be no finding anyone in the dark. With a lump of lead for a heart, he rose and joined the halting procession.

They moved slowly by the light of their torches down the narrow road twisting its way into the tunnel of darkness ahead of them. In a slight breeze, the leaves rustled with a dry, ghostly sound. The not-quite-full moon—the injured eye of Haru, the one his brother, the god of chaos, had wounded—rose, blotting out the friendly stars, shedding a cold, unreal light that made bright patches and shadows on the road. Hani was stunned with hopelessness. He hadn't found Maya among the dead, but neither did he seem to be among the living. What could have happened? To his shame, Hani realized that he was more distraught about his son-in-law's disappearance than he was about the death of his translator, Tuy. *I should never have encouraged him to arm—any of them. They're scribes, not soldiers.*

Pa-aten-em-heb drew alongside Hani and said quietly, "I didn't want to spend the night up there in case our friends planned to come back, but we can't go far at this pace. It's too dangerous along this stretch of the road. One of the carts is likely to miss a turn. And the men are tired, and many have lost blood."

"Anytime you want to make camp, I'm ready." Hani tried to force a smile, but he hadn't the heart for it.

The two of them walked elbow to elbow for a while—through the leaves of the trees, the moonlight white blotches on their shoulders as if the darkness were peeling off like the bark of a plane tree. Eventually, the officer asked under his breath, "Did you ever find Maya, my lord?"

Hani shook his head, his throat constricting.

"He'll turn up," Pa-aten-em-heb said with feeling. He strode ahead. "We'll make camp here, men!"

＊

Maya was in the midst of the melee, swinging his bronze rod at the legs of the men around him, darting in and out like a terrier, maddening and distracting his prey. At some point, he dodged under a sword swipe and was retreating to attack elsewhere when, in the gathering darkness, he tripped backward over a prone body. His heart in his mouth, he fell heavily on his bottom and dropped his rod.

Immediately, two men were on him, crushing him to the ground. He cried out, "Lord Hani! Help me!" but he had no idea where Hani was—or even *if* he was any longer. Maya fought desperately, kicking and biting, but the men were too much for him. One of them twisted his arms behind him and pinned him tight. Maya glimpsed a battle-ax raised over his head and felt, in a split second, the terror of imminent death. Then, before he could so much as murmur Sat-hut-haru's name, everything went black.

When Maya awoke, it was daybreak. He found himself lying on the ground, bound and gagged. His shirt had been torn off rudely, its tattered neck still around him like a collar. His arms and chest were scratched and laced with fine, stinging lines of dried blood. His head hurt murderously. Maya remembered the ax lifted over him and thought in a panic that his skull must be split, but surely, he would have been dead under such a blow. He decided that the man must have struck him with the flat of his blade. *Where am I? Did they drag me here?*

He sat up and, once the wave of pain and nausea had ebbed, stared around. He was somewhere in the forest. An encampment was spread around him—white linen tents and brown leather ones and shelters made of old blankets—taking advantage of the natural clearing beneath the huge oaks and plane trees. It was impossible to tell how many people it might harbor. A few men were stirring in the early dawn's half-light, talking occasionally in quiet voices. They seemed to be speaking the language of Djahy. *The* hapiru *have me*, Maya thought. It made sense that it should be they. What didn't make sense was that they had taken him captive rather than killed him. *Will they try to extort ransom from Lord Hani?*

The morning wore on, and Maya's stomach began to gripe with hunger. After a while, a man in a threadbare woolen tunic, an ax and a knife tucked into his sash, approached. Maya made furious noises from under his gag but could shape no words. The man squatted at his side, grinning through scattered black stumps of teeth.

"Mornin', little man. You hungry?" His hands and arms were as hairy as a monkey's.

Maya nodded vigorously. *Thanks be to all the gods I've managed to learn the language of this place.* With luck, he might overhear something that could be useful. The man took the short knife from its scabbard at his waist and sliced the rag that was tied around Maya's mouth.

Maya blurted, "Why have you taken me captive?"

The man chuckled. "Because you're cute. You'll make a good slave. You c'n dance and prance around, and people will pay to own you."

Maya's face grew hot with indignation. "I most assuredly will not! I'm a royal scribe."

"You *was*, little man. Now you're a slave. An' be glad we didn't jes' kill you, like we done a bunch o' the others."

Maya hoped with all his soul that Lord Hani wasn't among that number. They'd been split up in the fray, and he hadn't seen his father-in-law again after things heated up. Maya said nothing, his outrage giving way to gnawing anxiety. Sat-hut-haru would never forgive him if he let anything happen to her father. But then, Maya might well be dead himself in short order...

His captor got to his feet and headed off, hopefully for the promised food. Maya tried to make himself more comfortable, but his ankles were shackled as well as his wrists, and he couldn't even cross his legs. He craned around at the encampment. There was no way he could hop his way to safety. He grew less hopeful by the moment.

The swine. Buying and selling human beings. He remembered how the cowed slaves of the commissioner had been trained by brutality that they were worthless wretches.

He resolved that he would never submit to *dancing and prancing*. Better to die with dignity, his pen case proudly over his shoulder.

After what seemed like an inordinately long time, during which Maya observed more and more of the *hapiru* rising and setting about their tasks, Maya's monkey-armed captor returned with a bowl of something that steamed in the chill of morning. He set it down just outside of Maya's reach and said, "I'm gonna free your hands now, but don't you be gettin' no ideas." True to his word, he drew out his knife once more and severed the rope that bound Maya's wrists. They'd been chafed raw in places, and Maya rubbed them in an agony of relief as the blood came rushing back.

Monkey Arms turned to go, and Maya cried, "Aren't you going to give me the food?"

The *hapir* chuckled. "Figure out how to get it, little man." He headed away into the increasingly busy encampment.

Steaming with anger that helped to drive away his fear, Maya rolled over onto his stomach and thence rose to his knees, but he couldn't even crawl because of the tightness of his hobble. He pulled himself forward laboriously with his short arms until he could reach the bowl of porridge. By that time, he was exhausted as well as hungry, but he scooped up the cooling mass feverishly with his fingers and stuffed it into his mouth.

Sated but still thirsty, he observed the activity around him. The only people he saw were men, so despite its size, this was probably a raiding party, not a home encampment. *Did they intend to rob us and were thwarted by the military presence, or was it a deliberate attack on an emissary? Did they kill Lord Hani, or is he, too, a prisoner somewhere in the camp?*

How easily Maya himself might have been lying dead in the road. *Lord Bes, thank you for your protection.* Maya reached for the gold amulet around his neck... but it wasn't there. His heart sank. *What a terrible omen.* It had saved his life once. *Where has it gone?* he asked himself, distraught. From the condition of his shirt and the scratches all over him, he seemed to have been dragged through the brush at some point—perhaps it had fallen off then.

He hung his head. Suddenly, all the discouragement that he'd been holding at bay toppled in upon him, and the realization sank in that he might well find himself the slave of some brigand chief, reduced to cutting capers in the stereotypical role of the dwarf jester. After all his efforts to get an education, to rise through the ranks of the royal chancery, to become someone with a fine future... this.

And Lord Hani. His father-in-law wouldn't know where to look for him. That Hani himself might be dead or captured was somehow beyond his ability to accept. Hani was a rock of solidity, the bulwark of those around him, strong and comforting and fatherly. Tears were burning in Maya's nose. His life was as good as over. Perhaps he would have been better off killed outright. But to die here in a foreign land, with no hope of a proper burial, so that his soul would wander through a painful eternity—and leave Sat-hut-haru and the children orphaned...

No. It mustn't be. I have to get out of here. The thought made him grit his teeth with resolve, chasing away self-pity.

The morning wore on. Maya got to his feet occasionally just to relieve his buttocks. And as for relieving other things, Monkey Arms let him hop a brief way into the woods, knowing he wasn't able to run off. Maya couldn't guess how long he'd lain unconscious, so he didn't know how much time had passed since his capture. He wondered where his fellow travelers were by now—if they'd made it to Azzati and would be coming to his rescue with a company of the high commissioner's soldiers. He tried to evaluate the best way to sever his bonds and sneak away, but he was in plain sight all the time. After a listless morning, during which no one seemed to be doing much but resting up after the battle, a bowl of the same disgusting porridge marked the arrival of midday.

Almost as soon as one of the brigands had taken away Maya's empty bowl, an alarm seemed to run through the encampment. People dropped their tasks and began to rush around, seeking their weapons. Shouts sounded here and there, urging the men to assume their positions, although Maya noticed that quite a few of them took to their heels and melted into the forest. He sprang to his feet, hope fluttering inside, with its wild, fragile wings, for the first time since his capture. *It must be Hani and the soldiers!*

But before he could even hop toward the edges of the clearing, a band of men came bursting into camp, and to Maya's confusion, they were dressed not in the white uniforms of Kemet's soldiers but in a motley assortment of colored civilian tunics, like the men of Djahy. Whooping and yelling, they descended upon the *hapiru*, who hardly had time to find their weapons before they were clubbed into submission or fled into the forest. It was hardly a battle. The invaders seemed rather jolly, laughing at their captives and mocking them, enjoying slapping them around.

Maya fell to his stomach and tried to drag himself into the trees before the newcomers could see him, but a voice called out, "One's about to get away."

A hand grabbed Maya by the waist of his kilt, picked him up off the ground, and set him upright. His heart pounding, he faced the man defiantly.

"Look what we have here, boys," said the man, grinning. He was about Maya's age, a thickset, muscular specimen with powerful shoulders, a small head, and a very wide neck that gave him the air of a bull-made-man or some inanimate rock formation. "There was thirty-one and a half of 'em, eh?"

"I'm not one of 'them.' I'm their captive," Maya said haughtily. "I'm a royal scribe and secretary to the Master of the King's Stable, Lord Hani."

The man's red grin widened in the midst of his dark beard. "So, they took 'emselves a captive did they? I guess you was easy enough to carry."

Maya tried not to let his desperation show. "If you take me back to the high commissioner in Azzati, they'll give you a reward."

"Tempted, but I'm not sure the high commissioner would give us a very warm welcome. You might say we're brigands. Or at least, that's the way he'll see it."

Maya was confused. Had one group of *hapiru* attacked another, or were these simply highwaymen? "I'm sure Lord Hani would give you a very large reward," he cajoled, trying not to think of what might become of him if they didn't take him back.

"What's your name, little man?"

"Amen-mes known as Maya son of... Turo." To his

horror, he found himself struggling to remember his own father's name.

"And I'm Shum-addi—son of a jackal." Shum-addi gave Maya a jolly wink. "Welcome to the army of our little kingdom in the makin'." The *hapir* gestured around at the camp with a meaty hand. Shum-addi had very red lips that cleft his face in a grin like a wound. His eyes, which were uneven in size, were evaluating as he looked Maya up and down. "Your master's a emissary of the king of the Two Lands, ain't he?"

"He's my father-in-law, but yes. And he's up here in part to talk to you."

"That so? Didn't know I were so famous." Shum-addi bellowed with laughter.

"Who were these other people that captured me if you're the leader of the *hapiru*? Surely, you weren't attacking your own men."

"They likes to call themselves *hapiru*, but them's sons o' dogs. Why, half of 'em is your folks. Renegade soldiers. Ya know, ain't none of us much more than runaway slaves, failed farmers, and escaped deportees, but I ain't got much respect for soldiers who go over to the enemy." His brows drew down in a scowl of contempt, then he added more cheerfully, "Even if the enemy's me."

Iy! Maya crowed silently. *Here's the man who can give us answers!* "Whose soldiers are they, do you know?"

"Some from here, some from there. Some from Temesheq, some from Kumidi." Shum-addi squatted next to Maya. "Say, you're full o' questions, little man."

Maya swallowed his satisfaction and said, unashamed

to flatter, "I told you, Lord Hani came up here to talk to you. He knew you'd know things nobody else would."

Shum-addi laughed, the sort of laugh a bull or a rock might give, and squatted next to Maya. He called out to one of his men, who was passing, "*Oy*, bring us some beer for me an' the little man."

Maya bristled within, but he made himself stay pleasant, even a bit fawning. He accepted the pot and straw with gratitude, only then realizing how very thirsty he was, and drew a long, satisfying pull of the beer. "What about our commissioners? Are they in with these sons of dogs?"

Shum-addi slurped his with not much more manners than the jackal he claimed for a father. "Well, I wouldn't say no, but neither would I say yes. They ain't as hostile as they oughter be—let's leave it at that. May well be it were one o' them who paid those whelps to attack you. And o' course, that Amanappa, why, he's one of us for real."

He must mean Amen-nefer. But Maya found his curiosity piqued. "What do you mean, 'one of us'? He favors your cause?"

"Ba'al's balls, no. I mean his mother was one of us. And a demon she was, from what I hear. I dunno personally, 'cause I'm younger 'n His Excellency, y'understand."

Maya's jaw dropped in astonishment. "His mother was a *hapir*? I thought Amen-nefer was born in Waset."

"Prob'ly was. His father was a soldier. Did a little fraternizin' with the enemy, if you takes my meanin', an' carted her off to the Two Lands. We was glad to see the end of 'er, from what the oldsters say."

Maya took a pull of beer to hide the confusion that washed over him. *Wait till Lord Hani hears that!* "I guess that explains why he's been harboring your people, if the rumors are true."

"Couldn't say. He's done some pretty brutal things to my folks, on and off." Shum-addi heaved himself to his feet. "Hard to know what he thinks." He stretched his massive arms and looked down at Maya. "Guess I'll take you back, little man. Yer no captive o' mine. We don't much like the idea of enslavin' folks, as you c'n imagine."

"Oh, bless you! Lord Hani will reward you, I know," Maya cried gratefully. He supposed he ought to kiss the *hapir*'s feet, but it seemed a little distasteful, considering their condition.

Shum-addi turned back and whipped out his dagger. Maya recoiled in fear, but the man was only setting out to cut Maya's hobble. "You won't get far if yer run, so I don't advise it. Better you wait till I takes yer back." He made as if to go.

"Wait, my, er, lord. One more thing, if I may. Do you know who attacked the Babylonian diplomats' caravan a few months ago?"

"Not us. Maybe them. Prob'ly." He gestured around him at the camp. "We had other things to do round about that time. I don't keep up with these bastards, 'cept when their doings get me and mine inter trouble. One o' these days, though, they'll be bowin' down to me as their king—you watch."

"I'll certainly put in a good word for you."

"I'll have someone take yer to Azzati, little man. You tell the high commissioner what it was Shum-addi that set yer free, got it? Maybe he'll wanna give me some kind o' recognition, eh?" He ruffled Maya's hair in a friendly fashion and strode away.

"May all the gods bless you!" Maya cried, wondering if it were treason to ask a blessing on an enemy, although it struck him that maybe Shum-addi's men were not the enemy everyone assumed.

⸙

From Siduna, Pa-aten-em-heb's men sent a contingent back to the foothills to collect their dead. Hani, gnawed with anxiety for Maya, accompanied them. Even after one night, it was clear that animals had been at the corpses; the vultures and crows were still there, flapping and strutting, confused by the superfluity of choices.

Hani prowled among the dead and saw that most of them were *hapiru*—but he saw no sign of Maya anywhere. "At least he's probably alive," he told himself, marginally encouraged. But *where* was he?

And then his eye was caught by a flash of black. A crow settled on one of the branches a little ways from the road. It bobbed up and down as if shaken by laughter and watched him with a beady, intelligent eye, but—abnormally for a crow—it never said a thing.

"You smug fellow. What's so funny?" Hani called up to it. His love of birds was such that he forgot the tragedy of his predicament, if only for a moment. He could see by a glint of sunlight on the object that the crow had something shiny dangling from a cord in its beak. Something gold. "What have you got there to beautify your nest? Let go of that, you thieving bird." Fearing lest the crow had stolen some personal object from one of the corpses, Hani picked up a pebble and chucked it at the branch.

The crow rose indignantly and flew to another perch, its treasure still in its beak. Then a second crow came swooping in over the road and settled on the branch beside the first. The newcomer cawed accusingly and tried to grab the gold object. The first bird opened its beak to shout out some imprecation, and the gold thing fell from its grasp into the dry grass and brush. Hani waded over to it quickly through the rough underbrush—oblivious to the gorse and brambles that tore at his legs—before the crow could descend to reclaim it. He snatched it up, catching a handful of dry leaves as well, and opened his palm to see it. It was a small solid-gold amulet of the dwarf god, Bes, with a broken leather thong attached.

"It's Maya's!" There was no mistaking the beautifully crafted little figure. *What does this mean? Great Amen-Ra, who sees all, what can this mean? Has Maya been captured and left this as a clue?* Hani stared at the amulet as if he expected it to speak. Had the *hapiru* dragged the secretary off with them, and if so, in which direction? The crow could have flown *iterus* with the Bes in its beak. Or perhaps the bird had robbed it from a corpse...

I must try to get Pa-aten-em-heb to look for him. And I'll head back for Azzati and tell Lord Ptah-mes. He'll know what to do.

Eventually, Hani reconciled himself to leaving Siduna and its neighboring hills and took ship for Azzati, where he would have the sad duty of reporting his son-in-law's disappearance. Perhaps Lord Ptah-mes could mobilize his forces to find him. Otherwise, Hani feared he could never face his daughter again. And probably not himself either.

CHAPTER 11

"THE HIGH COMMISSIONER WILL SEE you now, my lord," said the secretary on duty.

With dragging steps and lead in his stomach, Hani pushed Ptah-mes's door open and entered then closed it carefully behind him. When he turned, prepared to greet Lord Ptah-mes, who should be standing at the side of the high commissioner's chair but Maya, arms outstretched. Hani's heart leaped into his throat with the surge of joy.

"Maya, my boy!" he cried, rushing forward to embrace him so exuberantly that he picked the little man up off the floor. He drew back and pressed the gold amulet into his son-in-law's hand.

"Oh, bless you, my lord. I was afraid my patron had abandoned me!" Maya kissed the little figure. Because the cord was broken, he had to tie it into a smaller loop and then hang it around his wrist.

Ptah-mes sat in discreet silence, smiling.

"Where have you been? We'd given up hope of finding

you," Hani said with a grin as he set his son-in-law down on his feet.

Maya said excitedly, "I was captured by the *hapiru*, Lord Hani. They were going to sell me into slavery, but then along came a different group of *hapiru* and chased them away."

Hani turned to his superior in contrition. "Forgive me, my lord. I was so glad to see Maya that I forgot my manners." He bowed, but there was no hiding the big smile on his face. He felt as if his cheeks were lit up as by a lamp.

Ptah-mes said with more than the usual warmth in his voice, "Quite understandable, Hani. Young Maya has recounted his adventures to me, and they've been very revealing. Tell your... our father-in-law what you found out, Maya." He and Hani locked eyes in a knowing look.

Maya launched in with no further prodding, explaining how the first group of the *hapiru*—those who'd attacked their caravan—had destined him for the slave market, while the second group, led by Shum-addi, seemed to be their rivals. "Shum-addi told me that there were a lot of our renegade soldiers in the other group. He said they come from Temesheq and Kumidi, and Shum-addi's group doesn't respect them. He thinks someone paid them to attack us."

"*Yahya!* As we suspected! Amen-nefer is in league with the brigands," Hani crowed.

"Well, I don't know, my lord. Shum-addi said the commissioner did terrible things to them now and then."

"Imagine. He actually did his duty at least now and then," Ptah-mes said dryly.

"But listen to this, Lord Hani!" Maya's eyes were wide in excitement. "Shum-addi told me that Amen-nefer himself is half *hapir*. His mother was one of them, and his father, a soldier, brought her back to Waset."

Hani's mouth fell open in surprise. He looked up at Ptah-mes. "Were you aware of this, my lord?"

"After Maya mentioned it, I seemed to recollect something. I was only a child at the time, of course, but there was some gossip about the wild woman from Djahy who had married into a decent Theban family. It was the first of many scandals, I fear."

"So how do we explain Amen-nefer's hatred for the *hapiru*? You should have heard how ferocious he grew when they came up in our conversation."

Ptah-mes shrugged. "I can't explain it, unless he was shamed by his association with that bunch of outcasts and criminals."

Hani nodded thoughtfully. "I have another Amen-nefer story to add, my lord. The afternoon of our departure, I transmitted to the commissioner the complaints of various vassal kings, including Urusalim, where I had just been. I wanted to tell him privately so he could respond without a public rebuke. But he grew incensed—way out of proportion to the offense. I got out as fast as I could, fearing, frankly, for my skin. And as soon as I'd closed the door, I heard him throwing things at it."

Ptah-mes lowered his eyes, pensive. "He has a violent temper. It's almost gotten him expelled from the army. There was a case a few years back when he was accused of slashing a girl's face because she repulsed him."

"I know, my lord. Because that girl happened to be the sister of the commander of our upcoming expedition, Lord Pa-aten-em-heb."

Ptah-mes stared at Hani, his black eyes penetrating. "Do you think Amen-nefer might be our murderer?"

"We've wondered. I can't imagine many other people would be vicious enough to treat a perfect stranger the way this person did. But what is his motive?"

"Perhaps he had no motive. Perhaps it was simply a case of rage overtaking him."

Hani gazed into space, pondering. After a moment, he said, "You may well be right, my lord. But we have no proof. We can't take him to the Hall of Justice just because we could *imagine* him committing murder."

"Perhaps I can convince Ra-nefer to remove him from office at least. Even apart from murder, he's curdled our relationship with our vassals by his behavior for seven years." Ptah-mes heaved a sigh. "Once I could have done this myself, but now I'll have to be canny about it—make our esteemed vizier think it's his idea." He smiled thinly. "Find evidence, Hani. I'd like to finish this carbuncle off."

But Hani was a little unnerved by Ptah-mes's cold determination to do Amen-nefer in. "What if there is no evidence? What if, in fact, he's innocent? He was acquitted of attacking Pa-aten-em-heb's sister."

"He has connections, that's all. He was guilty. Bring me proof."

"Very well, my lord." Hani tipped his head in submission. "Oh, Lord Ptah-mes, there's something I've been wanting to tell you ever since my last visit to Waset. It's… it's personal." He glanced at Maya.

"I'll withdraw to the reception hall, my lord," Maya said, rising, and at a nod from Ptah-mes, he bowed his way out the door, pulling it shut behind him.

Hani cleared his throat. "Just before I left for the north, two of your children came to see me."

Ptah-mes's arched eyebrows rose. "Which ones?"

"Mut-em-wia and Huy. Huy looked a little apologetic. I suspect his sister had made him come."

"No doubt." Ptah-mes's mouth twitched in a bitter smile. "Huy is easy to lead, and she is only too happy to do it. Were they welcoming you into the family?" he asked sarcastically.

Hani chuckled, feeling more and more discomfort. "Not exactly. They demanded that I make you and Neferet dissolve your marriage."

Ptah-mes snorted. "What gives them the right to make such a demand? And what would give you the right to carry it out?"

"That's what I told them, my lord. It... it became apparent in the course of the conversation that they felt they would lose their inheritance if you left everything to your new wife."

"And they're absolutely right." Ptah-mes's handsome face had grown flint hard. "I certainly won't be able to count on them to take care of my tomb. Why should I leave them anything?"

Hani remembered how a bereaved Ptah-mes had once admitted that his collusion with the regime had been in the effort to preserve his property for his seven children. Things had apparently changed. Hani could suddenly see another reason for Ptah-mes's unexpected acceptance of Neferet's offer of marriage. She was an excuse for him to disinherit his cruel, judgmental offspring. *I guess he is using her as well as she's using him*, Hani thought sadly. The loveless marriage of convenience between two people dear to him was a ball of lead in his heart. Still, they didn't seem to mind.

"You know, my lord," Hani said in a lower voice, "you don't have to make Neferet your heir. Don't feel we would be offended."

"But I want to, Hani," said Ptah-mes, his smile warming. "I've been able to do nothing for your career, but I can at least relieve you of worry for your daughter's future. I'll tell the servants not to let the children in. I don't want them harassing her."

This is a complicated affair. And speaking of motives, Ptah-mes has a whole list of them. Hani had thought he'd begun to know his superior, but now he wondered. *He's so disillusioned that he can find no good in anyone.* Still, Hani had to admit that he himself had at one point disinherited his firstborn, Aha. Some things really were unpardonable—unless they were followed by repentance.

"Was there anything else, my friend?" Ptah-mes said, rising. He brushed automatically at his caftan, although its pleats were still perfect.

"I think not, my lord. What is my assignment?"

"Take some time to see your family, Hani. Then return to Djahy and find proof enough to arrest Amen-nefer."

❖

"I guess I'll have a two-month-old son when I reach home, eh, my lord?" Maya was in a jaunty mood, breaking into a hum every so often.

Hani, observing with a smile, expected his secretary to start dancing at any moment on the deck of the boat that was bearing them back to Waset. "And I'll have a two-month-old grandson… or granddaughter."

Maya leaned against the wicker gunwales, peering through the withies with a beatific expression on his face. Hani, from a higher vantage point, watched the banks of the Great River sliding past, green with rich farmlands or fringed with marshes. Here and there, the scatter of white and dun cubes that marked a village caught the eye, fringed with palms and plane trees, tossing in the breeze. Hani drew a deep, peaceful breath. He knew each of these communities as a familiar landmark on his route home. *How often have I made this trip!* And still the beauty of the Black Land brought tears to his eyes. The Lord Amen-Ra had made his portion, his Kemet, a magnificent temple to his splendor, which he guarded night and day and guided through the seasons.

And the present season was that of awaiting the life-giving Inundation. Down at Hani's farm, the wheat would have been harvested and stored in the granary. Thanks to the irrigation canals Hani's father had had dug when Hani and his brother, Pipi, were children, the vegetable gardens would be yielding a second crop. A small flock of colorfully feathered ducks rose up in a cloud from the bank opposite, their stubby orange legs trailing. They circled and headed south with the wind.

"It's tranquil, isn't it?" Hani said in a dreamy voice. "There's no sound but the water and the wind in the sails." He fanned himself with his wig. "It will be good to get home, away from murder and hatred and plague. Home to our little island, eh?"

"It will be good," Maya agreed, his mouth spread in a wide grin of satisfaction.

In due time, they could see ahead of them the white walls of the Ipet-isut, shimmering in the summer heat above the low jumble of the City of the Scepter. The city grew nearer, with its blank-fronted houses—their high windows like little dark eyes squinted in laughter—and the walled villas of the more prosperous homes screened with trees. In the distance, the red mountains shimmered in the late-summer heat.

Maybe I'm getting old, but I never want to leave this place. Hani had lived in Men-nefer, when the vizier of the Lower Kingdom had been headquartered there, and he'd spent the better part of many years abroad, but his happiest moments had always been witnessed by this, the city of his birth.

Now the boat was drawing out of the current. Its steersman leaning on his great oars, it glided diagonally toward the quays, and Hani could make out people walking about—sailors and longshoremen and the crowds of passengers who were always headed up- or downriver in a ferry. It was midmorning, and the city was in full motion. Big yachts—all painted and gilded, their sterns like papyrus stems—flat commercial vessels, and humble little boats that could only hold a man or two swarmed the quays, docking and pushing off constantly like birds on a pond. From where Hani stood, it was hard to tell that the city had been virtually emptied out with the construction of a new capital and the suppression of the temples of Amen-Ra and his family.

The boat scraped along the pier, and the sailors rushed to throw out the stone anchors and heave their painters for their counterparts ashore to tie up. At last, the gangplank slid out, its end fell with a crash to the ground, and the passengers began to disembark. Maya was singing under his breath at Hani's side. Hani considered joining him, but he was notoriously tone deaf—his family was always quick to throttle him if he started warbling a tune. He laughed at himself, in the best of moods.

Hani had left his staff at Akhet-aten, so he and Maya and the newly freed slaves set out alone toward their respective homes, carrying their baggage. As they walked along together before their paths parted, Hani asked Maya, "What are you going to name the baby?"

"We thought Mai-her-pri, Lion on the Battlefield."

"Excellent choice," Hani said, remembering that Mai had become Sati's nickname for her husband. They parted company at the street where Maya and Sat-hut-haru lived, and Hani continued, with Bin-addi's family trailing behind. Now he permitted himself to sing. "The one, the sister without peer, the handsomest of all. She looks like the morning star. Hey ho, ho, ho. What are the rest of the words?"

A man passing in the other direction looked at him askance, and Hani realized he had been singing rather more loudly than he'd intended. He reduced his song to a hum as he swung along the road. The neighborhood was quiet now that so many bureaucrats had moved to Akhet-aten. His footsteps on the dry road sent up little puffs of dust. A wren was making its sweet, abrupt call from a tree in a neighbor's walled garden, and the honeyed scent of figs was in the air. Hani heard a woodpecker from somewhere.

He approached his own house, with its high wall and

N. L. HOLMES

gateway painted red and the branches of the broad sycomore fig hanging over in a peninsula of welcome shade, and drew a big sigh of contentment. He set down his baggage and knocked.

A'a appeared immediately. His usually cheerful face was drawn. "Oh, my lord! Thank all the gods you're back! They're inside."

Fear raced up the back of Hani's neck like the red wave of the Inundation. "What is it, A'a? Is there trouble?"

"Better the mistress of the house tells you, my lord." The old man stepped back and hung his head, avoiding Hani's eyes.

"A'a, take these people to the servants' quarters and make them comfortable," he said distractedly, gesturing to Bin-addi and his family, and he set off toward the house.

Hani was stiff with anxiety by the time he'd crossed the garden and mounted his porch. Nub-nefer met him at the door and threw herself into his arms. He could feel her rocking with sobs. Alarm flared up in his stomach, a burst of bright flame.

He said breathlessly, "What is it, my dove? One of the children?"

"Oh, Hani, it's Baket-iset. Day before yesterday she started feeling bad, with a headache and a fever. Then she threw up. Now she's getting those horrible lumps everywhere. It's plague."

It had found them on their little island of innocence. Horror washed over Hani, leaving him speechless. They clung to one another like two shipwrecked boatmen, hanging onto a spar for dear life.

Then she drew back. "I sent one of the servants to the

268

capital, hoping to intercept you, but I didn't know when you'd pass through. Neferet's in Waset, and Aha is visiting her, so they're on their way. Come to Baket, my love. She may not know you, though. She's deep into a delirium." Nub-nefer brushed at her eye with the back of her hand, her mouth twisting with the effort to keep herself together.

Hani's heart was banging in his chest. "How did this happen? She never leaves the house."

"I think it was one of the girls who helps me take care of her. She didn't show up for work for several days, and when I inquired, her mother told me she had died."

Hani lurched after his wife to the downstairs bedroom where Baket-iset lay in semidarkness. Sat-hut-haru sat at her sister's side, bathing her face with a wet towel. Had she had the use of her limbs, Baket would have been flailing, but she just tossed her head wildly, crying out unintelligible words.

Grief and fear shot through Hani like a barbed arrow. *Lady Sekhmet, spare her. This is so unfair; she's never had any joy in her life, and now this…* He crouched beside her couch and laid a hand on her withered arm. "Baket, my swan. Papa's here."

She was as hot to the touch as a brazier. Behind him, Nub-nefer began to cry, and Sat-hut-haru's face buckled. He realized they felt that, now that he'd arrived, the girl was going to die, and his nose burned with incipient tears.

"Pa-kiki comes every evening after work. Mut-nodjmet is taking care of the children. I told her not to let them come." Nub-nefer looked up, her face stricken.

"Where is Father?" Hani asked.

Sat-hut-haru said in a shaking voice, "I made

Grandfather leave, Papa. He's old. I was afraid he might catch it."

Hani nodded, although when a rustle in the doorway made him turn, he was not surprised to see Mery-ra standing there sorrowfully. Mery-ra said, "I've begged Lady Sekhmet to take an old man and spare this young girl."

But I don't want to lose you either, Father, Hani thought helplessly. *I don't want tragedy to strike anyone I love.*

Baket-iset was throwing her head back and forth frantically. "No! No!" she cried. "Take your hands off me."

Hani and Nub-nefer exchanged a look of confusion.

"I'm going to tell my father!" Baket said.

"Is she delirious?" Hani asked in a quiet voice. The hair was standing up on his arms at a terrible suspicion that had just awakened within him.

Nub-nefer shrugged her ignorance, unable to speak. Tears and mucus ran unheeded down her chin as she stroked Baket-iset's arm.

Baket gave a scream that pierced Hani's heart. "I'm falling!" she shrieked. "Help! Oh, help me, someone!"

Hani froze and stared up at Nub-nefer. "She's not hallucinating—she's remembering." He grasped his daughter's thin, lifeless fingers in his bigger hand. "Papa's here, my love. Nothing's going to happen to you."

"He pushed me!" Baket-iset cried in the high-pitched voice of terror. "I'm falling!"

Nub-nefer's eyes grew wide with dismay. She bent over her daughter and pushed back her sweaty hair tenderly. "Who pushed you, my dearest?"

Hani held his breath. *Can this really be a true memory come back to haunt the girl after seventeen years?* He could see them all on the boat together late in the evening, just docked after sailing home from Neb-ma'at-ra's jubilee—he and Nub-nefer at the waterside gunwales, casting one last look out over the sunset-gilded River, the younger children playing somewhere on the deck among the crowd. Baket-iset—where had she been? He hadn't seen her for a while, his graceful little swan. And then suddenly, people were shouting. He'd flown to the shoreside edge of the vessel in time to see her falling head over heels through the opening where they would all disembark. He'd thrown himself after her, even as his daughter slid screaming down the ribbed boards of the gangplank, onto the stone quay, and into the water.

"Yes," he murmured, afraid to hear an answer. "Who pushed you, my swan?"

She probably didn't even perceive his question but was simply living out the whole horrible event in her feverish mind. Sweat dripped from her scarlet face, and she tossed her head in anguish. She screamed again. "He pushed me! Papa! Help me! It's the man with one eye!"

Hani's breath stopped. The room around him seemed to go silent and distant, and he heard others speaking as if through a wall. He was in an empty, echoing place, alone with his worst suspicion—one that he'd never even admitted to himself, it was so unlikely. Someone had done this to her. He whispered between clenched teeth, "Amen-nefer."

No one seemed to hear him; they were both focused on soothing Baket-iset. Hani jumped to his feet and staggered to the door, not knowing what to do with himself.

Mery-ra, camped in the doorway with tears running

down his cheeks, asked as Hani passed, "What is it, son? What's wrong?"

Hani, nearly blinded, had no idea where he was going. *I have to think somewhere quiet.* His heart was hammering, pumping up rage from some well he didn't even know existed in him. "She was pushed, Father," he whispered, forging past the older man.

Mery-ra gaped at him. "What? How do you know?"

"She remembers. It was so horrible she must have put it out of her mind for all these years. But it's come back to her." Hani turned on Mery-ra, his breath sawing in his nose. "And I know who did it."

The servants had told Maya the lady of the house was at her parents' place. After a joyful greeting with little Henut-sen and his adorable new son, whom he left with their nurse, he took seven-year-old Tepy, and together, they set out toward Gammother and Gamfather's. There was a strange solemnity about the gatekeeper and Hani's other servants that made Maya uneasy. He grasped Tepy by the hand, and the two of them mounted the porch side by side.

"My lord?" he called, but no one answered. Yet as soon as he had entered the salon, he saw Lord Hani and Lord Mery-ra standing face to face, their expressions grim as death.

"What is it, my lord? Is something wrong? Is Sat-hut-haru all right? Isn't she here?" A cold hand of fear gripped Maya's heart.

At his mother's name, Tepy cried out happily, "Mama! Is she here?"

Lord Hani steered Maya away from the inside of the house. Maya could see from up close that Hani's usually cheerful face was ravaged with grief and something that resembled rage. "She's here, taking care of her sister. Baket has been stricken with the plague." It seemed Hani could barely get the words out. At his side, Mery-ra gulped wetly.

Maya's jaw dropped in horror. He could feel the blood draining from his face as if he'd pulled a plug. "Sekhmet help us!"

"Get little Tepy out of here, son," said Hani urgently. He laid a hand on Maya's shoulder and pushed him toward the door.

Maya's blood ran cold. *Plague! And Sat-hut-haru is inside there with it. Bes, protect her,* he prayed in a babble of silent plea. *Protect her. Protect her.* "Should I go, then, my lord?" he stammered, although Hani had already answered that question.

"I think that would be safer. Sati may be here for... a while."

Maya took his firstborn by the little hand, and the two of them made hastily for the door, Tepy dragging his feet and stumbling in his reluctance. "Bye, Gamfather. I wanted to show you my tooth. It wiggles," he called over his shoulder.

All you gods—Maya wiped the cold sweat from his forehead with his free hand—*it's among us. It has struck our little island. Sickness and death have breathed even on us. It's not just a story people are telling. Oh, Sekhmet, keep little Mai-her-pri safe. Because this horror is real.*

⚜

Neferet and Bener-ib came storming in later in the afternoon, as did Aha, looking crumpled. Baket-iset was quiet at last and unaware of all around her. Aha, in his wilted splendor, fell to his knees beside his sister's bed and wept. The two girls began their ablutions and prayers with frantic efficiency. Neferet folded down the patient's sheet and began to feel under her arm and in her groin.

After a moment, she looked up at Bener-ib then turned to her father, her eyelids starting to shrivel with tears. Yet there was a pathetic note of hope in her voice. "She's got it, all right. But this isn't the worst kind, Papa. If it doesn't go into their lungs, some people survive."

Strong, healthy people, no doubt. Hani kept his pessimism to himself.

Nub-nefer and Sat-hut-haru sat clinging to one another on the floor beside Baket-iset's bed. At her daughter's words, Nub-nefer looked up at Hani with desperation in her kohl-streaked eyes. "She's young. Maybe…"

But Hani murmured, determined not to take a fool's refuge in false optimism, "Do not say, 'I am young to be taken.' You do not know your death." How had he ever dared to write words of wisdom to instruct others, when he was so far from perfect resignation himself? *Take me instead of her*, he pleaded again, in the parent's most desperate prayer. *I've at least had a chance to live.*

Mery-ra, who was standing at Hani's side, asked in a hushed and tender voice, "How long does she have, Neferet, my girl?"

Neferet exchanged a look with Bener-ib, who said, in her shy, brutal way, "If she's going to die, not long. It's been at least three days already. Today. Tomorrow."

Nub-nefer emitted a loud wail and fell to her face upon the patient's mattress, Sat-hut-haru folding on top of her, and Aha howled with undisguised grief. Hani would have longed for such a release, but he felt frozen—in denial, perhaps, a refusal to permit such an obscenity. Mery-ra clutched at his arm. Hopelessly, Hani drew the amulet of Serqet from around his neck and laid it on his daughter's body.

And that was how Pa-kiki found them when he burst into the room. "Mama! Papa! Is she...?"

Hani shook his head and laid an arm around the boy's shoulders. "Today or tomorrow, the doctors say."

Pa-kiki began to sniff hard, and he sank to his knees at his sister's side, his face in his hands.

After a moment of anguished silence, Hani asked his father under his breath, "Where is Khawy?"

"I sent him away, son. It seemed no place for an outsider, no matter how beloved. I told him to go to a beer house."

Hani nodded and heaved a weary sigh that seemed to empty his very soul from his chest. Grief had turned him into a leaden creature, unable to feel, speak, or move coherently. Perhaps he'd already descended into the Duat, and only his shadow remained.

Behind him in the bedroom, a loud wail went up. Fear chilled him, raising the hairs on his neck. The women were keening and tearing at their clothes, their hair, their faces. Nub-nefer let out a howl like a wounded animal.

Mery-ra clutched his arm. "Has she passed into the West?"

The two men lurched back to Baket-iset's bedside to the blood-freezing sound of mourning women. Hani sank to his knees with his sons and seized Nub-nefer's hand. "Is she... has she crossed to the West?"

His wife could only nod, tears streaming down her face, which was twisted with grief.

Hani felt the tears begin to burn in his eyes and start their descent down his cheeks. *My daughter, my beautiful swan. I will never see you again on this earth.*

But suddenly, Neferet straightened up from where she lay upon her sister's chest. "Wait, everybody—she's not dead! She's still breathing!"

The wails ceased as if they had been turned off, and everyone huddled over the patient's still body, hoping to hear a breath. Her bosom was indeed rising and falling—the most beautiful sight Hani had ever seen.

Neferet sponged her sister's face and wrists with cool water. "If we can just get her fever down... I'll stay with her for the rest of the night. Mama, why don't you and the others try to get some rest? You've been here alone for a long time."

No one had much heart for leaving, but Aha and Sati lay down on the floor, and Pa-kiki fell asleep leaning against the wall. As for Nub-nefer, she sat steadfastly at her daughter's bedside. After some time had passed, her head lolled until she was asleep, too, her forehead on the edge of the couch. Hani and Mery-ra sat shoulder to shoulder on the floor, while the two young doctors kept wringing out towels in cold water and applying them to Baket-iset's face and neck. Every so often, Neferet would moisten the girl's lips with a slurry that smelled of moldy bread.

The night passed with excruciating slowness. Nub-nefer awoke with a start and reached out for Hani's hand. "Is she...?"

"Still with us, Mama, and I think her fever is coming down." Neferet was swaying with exhaustion, but she managed an optimistic smile. Mery-ra was slumped over, snoring into his lap. The other three children lay, dead to the world, on the floor.

Hani settled shoulder to shoulder with his wife, strengthless and resigned, hardly daring to hope. Once more, the hours crawled by in a slow, funereal procession. The little lamp beside the bed was flickering, low on oil. Finally, it went out.

"I'll refill it," Hani said quietly to Nub-nefer.

He rose and, holding the empty lamp, made his stumbling way to the kitchen, felt around for the big jar of moringa oil, and ladled a little into the clay bowl of the lamp then lit the wick with a coal from the oven. A small orange flame leaped up between his hands, like a soul reclaimed from death. Hani stared out at the kitchen court, where a moonless night stretched overhead. It might have been his imagination, but he had a faint sense of the darkness beginning to lighten above the silhouette of the second story.

Holding up the newly relit lamp, he made his way back to Baket's bedroom, where he strained his eyes at the black shapes of his family around him, faithful in vigil, and he prayed, *Save them all, Lady of Healing. Please don't let any of them die.* It was selfish, he knew—the beautiful life of an *akh* awaited them. But how could he endure to be parted from them—never to see them again, to smell them, to touch them? It was worse than death. He thought of Ptah-mes and how he seemed to have been changed forever by his wife's murder, and Hani understood. He set the lamp back on its tall stand.

Neferet had stayed valiantly awake, despite her blinking red eyes, with Bener-ib at her side. The two young doctors continued to offer the patient tiny sips of willow tea and their moldy-smelling potion and to apply the cold towels, although they were almost too tired to wring them out. Their movements had a drunken awkwardness about them that elicited Hani's pity and gratitude. On the floor, Mery-ra stirred and sat up, rubbing his eyes.

Dawn was beginning to bring into view the world outside the circle of the lamp. Baket-iset lay asleep or unconscious. Neferet laid a hand on her sister's forehead and gave a shriek of excitement. "The fever's broken, Mama, Papa!" She felt under Baket-iset's jaw then turned with a triumphant look at Bener-ib and began to bounce up and down on her buttocks. "She's passed the crisis—I think she's going to live. She's going to live!"

Nub-nefer broke into loud sobs of joy. She cradled Baket-iset's face in her hands and kissed her again and again as if hungry for her sweet living flesh. Hani put his arms around his wife and squeezed her with all his tender strength, fighting back the tears that at last sprang forth. Aha, Pa-kiki, and Sat-hut-haru sprang upright, awakened by the cries, and soon, they were all clustered around their sister, weeping and praying aloud to Sekhmet in thanksgiving.

In a delirium of relief, Hani gazed down at his eldest daughter, his eyes blurred with tears. At his back, Mery-ra whispered, "It was your amulet, Hani. Serqet has saved another life."

CHAPTER 12

A WEEK HAD SLOWLY PASSED AS Baket-iset convalesced with Ta-miu curled at her side—the rest of the family feeling a heightened gratitude for all the blessings they were to one another. Within Hani had throbbed the desire for vengeance as well. He hardly knew himself. He kept muttering savagely, "The floodwaters will carry him away; the north wind descends to end his hour…"

He and Maya and Mery-ra were enjoying the evening breeze in the garden pavilion. Aha and Pa-kiki had gone back to their homes, their wives, and their children. In fact, Mut-nodjmet, spending time with her cousins, was at Baket-iset's bedside with Sat-hut-haru as the men chatted outside.

Hani took a deep suck at his straw and stretched out his legs. "I guess I should get myself back up north. We have things to do." He raised a significant eyebrow at Maya. He hated to pull the boy away from his new baby son, but they had a mission.

"Have you any leads in your murder case?" asked Mery-ra, his arms folded over his head to cool his armpits.

"He almost has to be the same man who pushed Baket overboard all those years ago, Father. Not just anyone could muster that kind of rage against a stranger. You'd have to have something terrible against a person to do something like that to him, unless you were Amen-nefer."

"You wouldn't believe how quickly he can fly from all pleasant to insane with anger, Lord Mery-ra," said Maya. "All his slaves are black and blue."

"We need to find out everything we can about him before we go back up to Kumidi. We want an airtight case against him. And maybe"—Hani looked up as a sudden idea crossed his mind—"Bin-addi can give us more information now that he's not in fear for his life."

"I'll bet Meryet-amen will know all the gossip. I'll ask her. And maybe your evil friend has relatives still alive, if they would be willing to talk to us."

"That's a good idea. Why don't you and Maya undertake that investigation, and I'll talk to our newest servant."

Mery-ra and Maya exchanged an eager look. Hani's father loved to get involved with Hani's cases now that he was retired from his career as a military scribe, and Maya was always happiest when he could grill someone, or "rough them up a little verbally" as he put it. *He's the one who should have been named Mai-her-pri*, Hani thought with paternal affection.

"Tomorrow morning, then, we can head off to our respective assignments and meet at lunchtime to debrief." He rose to his feet. "I think I'll go on to bed, my friends. I want to talk a little with Baket on my way."

"I'll start quizzing Meryet-amen tonight." Mery-ra, too, rose.

"It's probably best not to be out on the street too late, both of you. Things have been quieter this year, but one never knows when some firebrand will incite people to riot," Hani said. *Some firebrand like my brother-in-law.*

Maya popped up in turn. "Let me check if Sat-hut-haru is ready to go."

He saw the two men and Sat-hut-haru off at the gate and then made his way inside, where Baket-iset lay in the company of her mother. "How are my favorite girls?" Hani asked with a smile, seating himself on the edge of his daughter's bed and patting her arm fondly.

"Better, Papa. Every day, I'm getting better," she replied, weak but happy.

Hani reached over and squeezed Nub-nefer's hand—a gesture of thankful solidarity.

He said softly, "Baket, my swan, do you remember what you were saying in your delirium last week?"

A cloud drifted across the young woman's face, a look that wanted to be brave but staggered a little. She said in a small voice, "I can remember everything, Papa."

Hani's heartbeat stepped up its pace. "My dear, would it be too painful to tell me what you remember—"

"Oh, Hani, no!" Nub-nefer cried.

"We're trying to prosecute the man I think did it. We know he's guilty of some other crimes but maybe murder as well." *Maybe several murders, if slaves are human beings— and the gods know they are.* He said to Baket, even while looking at Nub-nefer, "I swear to you, my swan, that I'll make him pay for what he's done to you."

Nub-nefer seemed to understand. She stared him in the eye, fierce. "Do it, Hani. No girl is safe with such a monster around."

"But we need evidence of all his misdeeds. What do you remember about that day?"

Baket-iset's face grew paler than its already drained color. She licked her fever-chapped lips and took a deep breath. "We were coming back to the east bank from the Per-hay after the old king's jubilee. The children were all scattered, playing on the deck. I don't know where you and Mama were. There was a man who kept trying to make me talk to him, to stand with him, and hold his hand. I'd move and he'd follow. He was worse than annoying, Papa. It started becoming scary. He reached out to touch me, even, but I kept dodging away, looking around for you and Mama. I was standing at the gunwales, watching them tie up the boat and put down the gangplank, when he reached out for me again. This time, he tried to grab me and make me kiss him, and I slapped his hand away and said I was going to call my father." She closed her eyes for a moment as if gathering her strength. "He became furiously angry, maniacal. He yelled, 'You're all alike!' And then he shoved me backward through the opening and down the gangplank. Perhaps he didn't mean to." Tears had started to leak from her kohl-painted eyes, and her mouth trembled.

Nub-nefer bent over her, stroking her face. "It's past, my love. The man can't hurt you anymore."

Rage was mounting inside Hani, but he managed to say in a calm, quiet voice, "And what did that man look like?"

"Handsome enough. A young soldier. He had a cleft chin and one eye all burned out. A strange, metallic voice."

It could be no one else but Amen-nefer. Hani felt his mouth transforming itself into a snarl of hatred in spite of himself. "That's him."

Nub-nefer's beautiful face had hardened into flint. She fixed Hani with a red-hot stare. There was no question about what she wanted him to do. And for once, the calm, easygoing man who was Hani was perfectly ready to do the worst.

He rose, his breath steaming from his nose, and stalked out onto the porch, where he stood in the sweet air of a summer evening, incapable of clear thought. *Surely* ma'at *demands the bastard who did this to my daughter should pay a heavy price. Or does putting a price on her blighted life cheapen it? Perhaps killing him is too good for him—a quick death is too merciful.* Hani realized with horror that what he really wanted to do was to bash Amen-nefer to pieces as someone had done to Shulum-marduk.

He shook himself, as if to cast off the shadow Hani who'd shown his hideous face, and headed through the garden to the service yard, where Bin-addi and his family were quartered in the small apartment adjoining the goat pen.

The ex-slave was sitting in front of the little house, legs crossed, leaning back against the whitewashed wall. He wasn't visible as much more than a dark silhouette against the pale limewash. Bin-addi rose at Hani's approach and bowed, with a trace of his old subservience. "My lord. I was just taking in the evening in your beautiful garden."

A dim orange light was shining from the high window of the house, and a woman's voice was singing nursery songs. It had to be the children's bedtime. Hani clapped

Bin-addi on the shoulder. "Listen, my friend. If you want to work for me as a free man, you're welcome. I'll pay you a normal wage for domestics. And no doubt, Nub-nefer could find something for your wife to do."

The former slave fell to his knees and stooped to kiss Hani's toes, murmuring, "You're too good, my lord!"

Hani drew him to his feet and said in a friendly tone, "You'll earn your wages. It's no kindness on my part." He pondered for a moment. "In fact, you can do *me* a kindness now that you're safe and free."

Bin-addi's face was barely visible in the gloaming, but the sudden stiffness of his body told Hani that he knew what was coming. "I—"

"Who killed the Babylonian?"

Bin-addi backed up slightly as if ready to make a break for it. "I can't say, my lord."

"You mean you don't know, or you don't want to say?"

"I've sworn an oath."

He knows, Ammit take him. "You told me before that Amen-nefer killed Zalaya because he knew something," Hani persisted. "Did Amen-nefer kill the Babylonian?"

"I... I don't know, my lord."

Hani forced himself to keep his tone gentle. "Bin-addi, you're going to find life hard in a foreign country without a patron. You need my good will. Tell me. The commissioner can't touch you here."

But the man repeated obdurately, "I've sworn on my father's soul, my lord."

Hani bit back his frustration. *It has to be Amen-nefer, but I've got to have evidence. And the damned slaves know but won't tell.*

"Who else knows, Bin-addi?" Hani said. "Is there anyone else who will tell me?" A sudden idea flashed through his mind. "What about Zalaya's wife?"

Bin-addi hung his head for a moment. Then he said, "No, my lord."

"You're lying, my friend. After all that I've done for you."

The former slave was squirming. "Forgive me, Lord Hani, but I just can't…"

"All right, my friend. Have it your way. Amen-nefer will go free to rape and murder other people in his rages."

Bin-addi stood cowed, head drooping, and Hani walked away in disappointment so massive he thought it might weigh him to the ground. He directed his bare footsteps into the garden, where the crickets pulsed rhythmically in the darkness, and took a seat in the pavilion. There were mosquitoes, but he barely noticed them. He watched the half-moon rising in the east, among the branches of the sycamore, shedding patches of silver light on the gravel, and it reminded him of the battle against the *hapiru*.

How do they come into this affair? Maya said there were two factions. The men who attacked us seem to be renegades, rather than the 'official' troops of Shum-addi. Did someone really put them up to attacking our caravan specifically? And could it have been the renegades who attacked the Babylonians? And if so, what relationship do they have with Amen-nefer, who is apparently half of their blood? He let out a sigh of frustration. "Maybe the others will find out something."

If only I knew our friend's father's name, I might be able

to find someone who knows where his family live, Maya thought. *Curious neighbors would certainly be full of gossip.* He decided that he would pay a visit to the former Hall of Royal Correspondence in the hopes that a public figure like a commissioner would have some kind of dossier predating the present regime.

They knew Maya well in the Hall. One of the nicer scribes was on duty in the reception room that day, and Maya said in a friendly, if slightly officious, tone, "May the lord of the horizon bless you, my good man. I'm the secretary of Lord Hani, the Master of the King's Stables."

The man nodded, unimpressed and perhaps a little amused. "I know you, Maya."

"He's conducting an investigation and would like to know the full name of the commissioner of Kumidi. I trust that's hardly a secret. Could you tell me? It's Amen-nefer son of...?"

"The records are probably in Akhet-aten. Oh, wait one moment. I think I know where it might be, if he held any kind of position, military or civilian, more than ten years ago." He disappeared into an archive room, and Maya could see through the open door that the man was scanning the labels on the papyrus scrolls shelved inside. At last, he drew one out, ran his eyes quickly down the columns, and rolled the scroll up again. He returned to the reception hall and said to Maya, "It's Amen-nefer son of Ah-hotep-ra."

"Thank you. You've been very helpful to the royal investigator."

Pleased with the first step in his day's work, Maya exited the cool shade of the building. The outside court was baking and afire with glare, even in this early hour of the morning. He put a sheltering hand over his eyes to improve his vision. *Where to now?* He decided that the army would have some sort of records on Amen-nefer and maybe even know the whereabouts of his family home.

Maya trudged south toward the garrison, which was still the major one along with the one at Men-nefer. As a Theban, Amen-nefer should have left some sort of enrollment record there. The secretary approached the walled compound with an optimistic spring in his step. An inquiry at the gate brought him an officer who was willing to give Maya some time.

The man, a square, broad-shouldered block of a soldier in his early forties, greeted Maya with his fists on his hips. "My name is Isesi-ankh, standard-bearer of the Pride of Montu company. What can I do for you?"

"The vizier has commanded an investigation of the commissioner Amen-nefer, my lord. Can you give me any information? Perhaps the location of his family home?"

Isesi-ankh gave a short bark of laughter. "Why? Has he killed someone?"

"Why would you say that?" Maya could feel a ripple of excitement climbing its way up his neck.

"Because he's the most vicious attack dog of a man I've ever met. An asset on the field of battle but a man I would avoid at any cost in real life."

"In fact," Maya confided, "he is being investigated for a possible murder."

Isesi-ankh gave a snort. "No surprise."

"Anyone here in Waset who might know something about his actions? Relatives?"

"He has a sister, still living in their father's home, poor

woman. Never been able to marry. Word has it that your friend Amen-nefer used to abuse her terribly as a youth—you know what I mean. She probably wished he would die in battle every time he went on campaign. And I should know," the officer said bitterly. "I courted her in our youth. She was already broken irreparably. Her brother was still in the cavalry at that point."

Maya sucked in his breath in horror.

"He hated women. With his good looks and charm, he could attract them easily enough. But he meant them nothing but harm. I always felt really sorry for the poor fool who married him. And sure enough, she didn't last long."

Iy, Maya thought, chilled. *What a monster.* "Do you think there's any point in trying to see his sister? Would she know anything that might be useful—his friends or his political alignments?"

"Word had it—I don't know this to be true, mind you—that he was a creature of Lord Ay. That that's the way he got out of the trouble he stirred up in the cavalry and got slid over to us."

He was in the cavalry? How odd. I wonder why the God's Father protected such a person. "Do you think there's any point in interviewing his sister? Would she even talk to me?"

The officer's brows knotted in hatred. "I doubt it. There's not much left of her. You have my blessing on any charge of misdeeds you find on the bastard. He's a disgrace to the army."

"Did he... did he have anything against foreigners? Against Babylonians, let's say?"

"I don't have any idea, but he was a man filled with hatred. It's a fair guess he hated foreigners as well."

Maya thanked Isesi-ankh and headed in the direction of Lord Hani's house. The morning was late. He couldn't wait to tell his father-in-law what he'd learned.

⸙

After lunch, Hani, Maya, and Mery-ra retreated to the garden pavilion to review what they had learned. Hani could see that his father was about to burst with something juicy. "Father, did your lady friend have any insights?"

"Oh yes, indeed." Mery-ra's little eyes twinkled. "It turns out our boy was in the cavalry, and Meryet-amen's late husband was his commanding officer for a while."

"Cavalry?" Hani cried in surprise. "But he seems to be in the infantry now—at least he has command of infantrymen."

Mery-ra grinned. "He was expelled from the cavalry for fighting with his fellows, and somehow, he wangled his way into the infantry as a sort of fresh start. His record would more or less be wiped clean, and no one would know his past."

"I heard the same thing," said Maya eagerly. "And that it was Lord Ay's influence that got him transferred and not kicked out."

"Lord Ay is head of the cavalry. I suspect anything he wanted to happen would." If Amen-nefer had some sort of relationship with the Great Queen's father, that would explain how a man with such a spotty career might be appointed commissioner of Kumidi. Not for the first time,

Hani was overwhelmed with disgust at the corruption in his own government. He looked up. "Anything else?"

"Meryet-amen remembered clearly a scandal attached to Amen-nefer's family. Of course, a man from the lower aristocracy marrying some bandit from Djahy was bad enough, but then the father died and left the two children in the care of his widow. She drank, Hani, and would fly into terrible drunken rages. She beat the children and the slaves mercilessly. It was common knowledge."

"Like mother, like son," Maya said, his lip curled.

"And apparently, she was the reason he lost his eye. She hit him so hard it ruptured the eyeball, and the doctors had to take it out. They cauterized the socket."

Hani cringed. What a terrible thing to happen to a boy—maimed at the hand of his own mother. In spite of himself, he felt a twinge of pity for the child who had become a monster in turn. "How old was he?"

"This was five or six years after the father's death, so he must have been nine or ten." Mery-ra settled himself in his chair. "Meryet-amen said the next scandal was the mysterious death of Amen-nefer's wife—some years later, obviously. Her family suspected he'd murdered her."

"And killed their unborn child with her, from what I understand," Hani said. "How did our friend get away with this one?"

"Unknown, son. After his trial got off to an aggressive start, the judge dismissed the case, but what made him change his mind... who knows?"

"I'll bet Lord Ay intervened," said Maya fiercely.

Hani nodded, torn between sorrow for his land and icy disgust.

"Well, I found out some things, too, Lord Hani," Maya said. "Although it may not add any new information—we're already getting a pretty clear picture of the sort of man the commissioner is. I found where his sister lives—at the old family home. Unmarried."

"How strange. Did you talk to her?"

"The officer I spoke with said there was no point. She's apparently gone a little…" He tapped the side of his head. "Not only did the poor woman have to deal with a drunken, abusive mother, but her brother abused her too. I think sexually. And I'll bet not gently."

Mery-ra made grimaced, and Hani let out a breath. "What a specimen. Just the sort you'd promote to represent us abroad, isn't he?"

"Isesi-ankh—that's the man I talked to—said Amen-nefer hates women. Well, not too surprising, I guess, if he thought they were all like his mother."

"Maybe that's why he wanted all the *hapiru* to be sent to the gold mines too."

"No doubt," said Mery-ra.

The three men were silent. Hani felt contaminated even by the thought of such malice, yet he could picture a frightened child beaten by his mother until he lost an eye, and he felt his own thirst for vengeance losing its fangs. He said dully, "May the gods protect us from ourselves. Plague is a terrible scourge, but it's nothing compared to what we inflict upon one another."

"Speak for yourself." Mery-ra—as usual, trying to lighten the moment—smiled at his son, but the sparkle of genuine levity was missing.

Hani heaved a sigh. "I think it's time you and I went

back north, Maya. We've found lots of evidence that our suspect *might* have murdered Shulum-marduk, but no actual proof that he did."

"You mean go back to Kumidi? Knowing the commissioner has it in for you? I'll bet it was he who sent the *hapiru* to kill us." Maya's eyes were wide.

"Well, at least to Azzati. I'm hoping that Lord Ptah-mes may have some ideas about how to proceed."

Mery-ra said avidly, "If there is anything else you want investigated in your absence, my son, your old father is ready."

Hani grinned affectionately. "My *reverend* old father, you mean?"

No doubt seeing Hani in a better humor, Mery-ra chuckled. "I'll accept *noble* or *august* in a pinch."

Hani rose. "Well, gentlemen, let's relax this afternoon, because you and I, Maya, have a long trip ahead of us."

◆

That afternoon, as Hani was sitting cross-legged on the floor of the salon, trying to add a few maxims to his collection, he heard from the vestibule a loud, cheerful female voice that could only belong to Neferet. Sure enough, she burst into the room and flew to her father, but since he was seated, she could not throw her arms around him. Instead she squatted in front of him. "Papa! I'm so happy!"

"Why, my duckling?" he asked, thinking this was the setup for a joke.

"Because Baket-iset is alive, of course." She plopped down on the floor at Hani's side and hugged his arm.

He stroked his daughter's shaven head and gave her a

kiss on the ear. "Thanks to you, my love. We're forever grateful to you and Bener-ib."

"There wasn't much we could do for her, Papa—just try to get the fever down. It was Sekhmet who cured her."

"How is it you're here? Don't tell me today is another feast day."

She grinned, a look somewhere between pleased with herself and guilty. "I'm on a mission for the queen."

Hani froze. He didn't want to have anything more to do with the queen and her machinations, and he certainly didn't want his nineteen-year-old daughter to get sucked into court politics. He said warily, "Oh?"

"Yes." Neferet snuggled up to him, and Hani had the feeling she was softening him up to ask something of him. "She wants to talk to you."

May the Hidden One protect me, Hani thought, alarmed. *Is my investigation cutting too close for the comfort of the queen's father, Lord Ay?*

"When does she want to see me, my duckling? It will take me half a week to get to Akhet-aten."

"Oh, she's here in Waset, Papa. I mean Queen Meryet-aten."

Hani stared at his daughter in surprise. Meryet-aten was Nefer-khepru-ra's eldest daughter and the newly crowned great royal wife of Ankh-khepru-ra Smenkh-ka-ra, the coregent. "How does she even know I exist?"

Neferet grinned proudly. "I told her you could help her."

Hani buried his face in his hands. "Oh, Neferet. I'm trying to avoid getting tangled in the affairs of the royal women." He thought of how close to disaster his involvement in the rivalry between Queen Nefert-iti and the Greatly Beloved Wife, Kiya, had swept him. "I'm involved in a case in Djahy."

"But, Papa, how long can it take just to talk to her? She's only seventeen. She needs somebody's advice."

He put an arm around his daughter and heaved a reluctant sigh. The damage was done. Once the queen had summoned him, he was obliged to go. *But I need to get back to Kumidi to prosecute my case against Amen-nefer before the commissioner kills off all the slaves who witnessed his crime. Before the king of Sangar declares war...* "When, then, duckling?"

"She said you should come with me tomorrow when I come to the palace with Lord Pentju."

"Lord Pentju? He'll see me going to talk to the queen? Oh, Neferet, this sounds like a very bad idea, my love." Hani could feel sweat starting to break out on his forehead. Pentju, a priest of the Aten as well as a physician, was close to the king.

But Neferet waved her hand dismissively. "No, no, Papa. He and I go separately. I just meet him there. He takes care of the men, and I take care of the women."

"What happened to Lady Djefat-nebty? I thought she was the royal *sunet*."

"She is, but she's in Akhet-aten. Now that there are two courts, somebody has to take care of the younger queen and her ladies. And that's me and Bener-ib!"

Hani was proud in spite of himself. He squeezed Neferet to him. "She trusts you like a colleague, eh, duckling? You're getting to be a real professional."

"Of course," she said matter-of-factly. "I've been studying for six years."

Dear gods, has it been that long? The years were passing so quickly that Hani felt they must be picking up speed as they rolled along. *Father is nearly seventy*, he thought with a twinge of fear. Mery-ra certainly seemed strong and hale, but for how much longer? Hani wanted that no one he loved should ever grow old and die.

He asked in a gentle voice tinged with amusement, "Neferet, my dear, why did you even mention my name to the queen? You've listened in on enough grown-up conversations over the years that you should realize I'm trying to stay below the notice of the royal family."

Neferet faced him earnestly. "But, Papa, she's just a young girl. And she doesn't trust her family to tell her the truth. And I know how wise and comforting you are." She leaned up and kissed his cheek, her little brown eyes melting.

The irresistible puppy look again. "Truth about what? What under the sun do I know about any royal affairs?"

Neferet shrugged extravagantly so that Hani suspected she knew but wasn't going to tell him. He let out a heavy breath. *Ammit take it. Trapped again.* "Very well. I'll be ready whenever you want to set out."

Victorious, the girl scrambled to her feet and chirruped gaily, "I'll see you tomorrow morning." She bounced out through the front door and away, leaving Hani both disgruntled and curious.

❧

Neferet—Bener-ib in tow—came for her father the next

morning with a pair of Lord Ptah-mes's litters. *She seems to be adapting quickly to the role of very rich mistress of the house,* Hani observed in amusement, although the thought of her manipulative marriage still annoyed him. They mounted the two vehicles, girls in one and Hani in the other, and set off in luxury, swaying and bobbing, for the new southern palace near the Ipet-isut and the Ipet of the South. *Not far from Ptah-mes's mansion. That makes it easier for her to go to work.* Hani wondered if she took a litter or walked every day. Certainly, Neferet wasn't lacking in energy, and he couldn't imagine her being concerned with what people would think of the wife of a grandee afoot.

The new palace, *Teni-menu*—"exalted are the monuments of the Sun Disk forever"—was set in among the disturbing temples to the Aten that Nefer-khepru-ra had built while he was still coregent, and indeed, it had a templelike look to it, with its majestic pylon and high whitewashed wall. In the weak, hot breeze, the banners hung limp from their flagpoles, indicating the presence of King Ankh-khepru-ra. With Hani letting her lead the way, Neferet strode up to the guard and hailed him familiarly. He obviously recognized her and Bener-ib, but he cast a dubious eye at Hani.

"This is my father. He has an audience with the King's Great Wife," Neferet said confidently.

The man bowed and stepped aside for the three of them. Within, a majordomo appeared from nowhere and led the way respectfully toward the apartments of the queen and her ladies.

Hani was curious to see the differences between this Theban palace and the old Per-hay across the river. It was smaller, simpler in layout—a home rather than a state residence—but with comparable beauty and luxury. They hastened through richly painted corridors splashed with sunlight from a courtyard garden he could glimpse only obscurely. Scenes of the late king's first *heb-sed* festival decorated the walls.

Our Sun God had a taste for jubilees even then, Hani thought wryly. According to Amen-em-hut, that was when the Osir Neb-ma'at-ra had turned into the Aten and all their present woes had begun.

At a magnificent pair of gilded doors, the majordomo stopped Hani and the girls. "I'll announce your presence." When he returned, he bowed them through without a word.

Two handmaids stood within, silhouetted against the sunlight filtering in through gauzy curtains. One led the young doctors away with her, and the other approached Hani. "If my lord would follow me..."

She turned and, Hani at her heels, made her way through the airy room to a porch, where the curtains billowed inward with the faint breeze from a garden beyond. She led Hani down the steps between painted columns and across the garden to a small kiosk that overlooked a long pool. Reed blinds were drawn along the sunny side to create some shade, but he could see a flash of white clothing from within.

The handmaid melted away, leaving Hani at the step of the pavilion. He looked up to see the Great Queen of Ankh-khepru-ra standing before him. Meryet-aten was a slim, beautiful young woman—very young, in fact. Neferet had told him she was seventeen, and Hani would have said that she looked both older and younger than that, her body still slender and undeveloped but her face, beneath her round wig with a jeweled sidelock, poised and serious and every inch the queen. She had her mother's broad, juicy cheekbones and her father's pointed chin and lush lips. *What a little beauty*, Hani thought then chastised himself.

The queen said, "Lord Hani." There was something of Nefert-iti's smokiness in her voice.

"My lady." Hani made a deep court obeisance, hands on his knees.

"Your daughter and I have become friends, Lord Hani. She is honest and innocent, unlike everyone else in this place."

Hani smiled, pleased that her royal mistress appreciated Neferet's qualities. "My lady is too kind. I thank you on behalf of my daughter."

Meryet-aten seated herself gracefully on an inlaid chair and motioned Hani to the stool that stood before it. "She said you might be able to help me." The young queen stared at Hani, and he could see that, despite her regal poise, there was uncertainty there inside. Her voice dropped. "Who is Prince Tut-ankh-aten?"

Hani sat back, on alert. He dared not let her know that Neferet had revealed there was any doubt about the prince's identity. "The Haru in the nest? Why, he's my lady's brother."

A skeptical smile hardened her face. "Is he?" The queen rose as if too full of nerves to remain still, and Hani followed suit. Meryet-aten began to pace. "The day my mother gave birth seven years ago, I was present at her lying-in. I was only ten or eleven, but I remember it all very clearly. Neferet was there, too, a young apprentice to

Lady Djefat-nebty, not much older than I was. As soon as my mother had borne her child, even before she'd seen the baby, Djefat-nebty whispered to Neferet, and she took the child and disappeared with it. A few minutes later, she returned with another baby, and the *sunet* laid that baby next to my mother. It was a boy. Everybody was all happy that the queen had borne an heir at last, and they went off to tell my father the good news."

Hani's heart was hammering. Neferet had been involved in this—she'd told him long ago—but it made him uneasy to think that her role in the deception was so clearly remembered. "What makes you think it was another baby, my lady?" he asked mildly.

She stopped walking and faced Hani, her eyes burning. "Because the first baby was dead."

He stood there for a long space, unease rising in him like a tide. *Does she hold this deception against Neferet?* Finally, he said, "I don't see how I come into this, my lady."

The young queen drew a deep breath as if to calm herself. "I asked Neferet about it recently. Asked her who the baby really belonged to. She told me that Sit-pa-aten, the sister of the king, my father, had given birth elsewhere in the palace, and that they wanted to give my mother the joy of a boy child. But, Hani," she said grimly, fixing him with a burning stare, "my aunt was never pregnant."

Hani was caught short. The situation was even more complex than it had appeared to be. He said nothing—dared to say nothing.

"Neferet honestly believed that she was the mother. Someone had obviously told her that, and why would she question it? She had never seen Sit-pa-aten. But she didn't know what I knew. And so I ask you—whose child is he who will wear the double crown, Hani?" The queen took a step toward him.

Hani swallowed hard, suspecting where this was going. "I'm sure I have no idea, my lady. Are you telling me to investigate this?"

"Yes. And find out who is behind it. Although I'm almost sure it was my grandfather. He would do anything to keep my mother in favor, even making sure by trickery that she bore an heir."

"Does Our Sun your father know about this?"

"No, I think not—although I could be mistaken." She dropped her gaze and bit her lip, but it was not a gesture of hesitancy. Her eyes were aflame when she looked up. "If the crown prince is not of royal blood, he must not come to the throne, Hani."

Hani felt beads of sweat beginning to spring forth on his temples. *Of all the things I didn't want to be involved in.* He said, "Perhaps he never will, my lady. Your royal husband is coregent—"

"But not heir," she cut in, a bitter expression on her face. "And with good reason. My father just wants to put Waset under his thumb, and so my uncle is a useful figurehead."

"But surely, Ankh-khepru-ra Smenkh-ka-ra will serve as the crown prince's coregent. If you and he have a son, perhaps that son would follow rather than a child of Tut-ankh-aten."

But she hung her head as if reluctant to show Hani her expression. "He won't have a son by me."

Hani was curious, but the story behind that statement was none of his business. "My lady, you should be aware that

I have no contacts in the palace or in royal circles generally. I'm not sure how I'm expected to proceed here..."

"Of course you have a contact, Hani." The queen smiled, triumphant, her deliciously appled cheeks blazing. "Neferet."

No. No. I won't get my daughter—my dangerously indiscreet daughter—involved in court politics with such high stakes. Ay would kill her in a moment if he thought she was onto his secret. If it was Ay. Hani stood silent, wondering if he dared to refuse this imperious girl who was both the daughter of a king and the wife of a king.

Meryet-aten's smile fell. "She told me you could help me," she said in a pouty voice. Suddenly, Hani realized how young she was, despite her cool adult ways.

"So you just want me to find out whose child the crown prince is? Who the woman who gave birth in the other room was?"

She lifted her chin, her eyes regaining their avid spark. "I command you to do it. And I'll make it worth your while."

Hani's heart sank like lead. "If my queen commands, I have no choice." He bowed deeply, hoping she couldn't see his expression of distaste.

"No. You haven't," she said with a satisfied smile.

A few minutes later, Hani was escorted alone from the palace, the two young doctors having remained for their day's work. It was still early outside out there in the normal world—the world untouched by deadly royal luxury, sophistication, and lies. Hani wondered if Nefer-khepru-ra would be informed of Hani's visit.

Why did Lady Meryet-aten get me involved? If she knew I

would use Neferet as a source, why didn't she make use of her herself?

He crossed the external court and made his way out the pylon, deeply preoccupied. To his surprise, in the street, Maya popped up from the sliver of shade cast by the wall. "Maya, my friend. What are you doing here? Nothing wrong at home, I hope?" Hani remembered anxiously another occasion when Maya had been sent as a bringer of bad news.

Maya beamed. "None at all, my lord. Lady Nub-nefer told me where you were, and I thought I'd come down to see the palace myself. I thought you might have need of a secretary."

Hani clapped him on the back affectionately, and the two men fell into stride, although not the same stride. "Maya, I had a very troubling interview with the younger great royal wife," Hani said in a low voice. "Apparently, Neferet told her I could help her."

"You're getting quite a reputation among the king's women," said Maya with a naughty grin.

But Hani let out a snort. "This is a rather scary assignment." He proceeded to describe the meeting to his son-in-law, who would inevitably get drawn into the investigation.

Maya gave a low whistle. "Court intrigue at its worst."

"Yes, and now I'm expected to get my young daughter involved in it—spying for me, you might say. Gods help us both if she lets slip any of this."

They walked in silence for a moment, then Maya asked hotly, "But what about the murder of the Babylonian?

You're closing in on Amen-nefer. Can we just drop that? It was the king himself who gave you that order."

"Clearly, that takes priority." Hani didn't know how to sort all this out, although it certainly wasn't the first time he'd been given conflicting orders.

"So are we going back up to Djahy?"

"I think we'll have to. But on the way, I want to make a little stop in Hut-nen-nesut. I'm still wondering what Amen-nefer was doing there seven years ago when he had his run-in with Pa-aten-em-heb's sister. This must have been immediately before his elevation to commissioner."

Maya nodded. He said with a smirk, "And you can see the flamingos."

Hani grinned. "You're too smart for me, son."

CHAPTER 13

Lord Hani broke the seals and unfolded the papyrus that a messenger had laid in his hand just as they marched aboard the northbound ferry. "It's a letter from Pa-kiki." His straight, tufted eyebrows rose. "He's on his way back."

He and Maya were standing side by side at the gunwales of the ferryboat bearing them downriver. "They're finished with their reconnaissance, my lord?" asked Maya in surprise.

"Apparently so. Pa-kiki says they're going to stop off in Hut-nen-nesut to visit Pa-aten-em-heb's family, then come down to Waset." Hani looked up, his little brown eyes shining. "What a divine coincidence! If we can intercept them, it will make our work there a lot easier."

"How so?"

"Our officer is from Hut-nen-nesut, remember? He must know of people who know people. Maybe his own family can give us some insights."

"But how are we ever going to coordinate our arrivals? We don't even know when they left Djahy."

"Well, this letter was sent by military courier, so it probably took a rather short time to reach us. They'll be marching to the coast with all their supplies, then it's at least ten days back to Men-nefer, then a few more to Hut-nen-nesut. I think we'll get there before they do."

Maya made a dubious noise.

"My gut tells me this is a valuable opportunity to gather information, Maya. There'll be a breakthrough. You watch." Hani was suddenly quite buoyant. He shaded his eyes with a hand and gazed around over the water then audibly drew in a deep, luxurious breath and expelled it, his wide mouth settling into a smile.

As for Maya, he was rather less optimistic. They'd decided to start their inquiries at the local barracks, thinking Amen-nefer's fellow officers would surely know something about his posting—if any of them were still around after so many years. Hani was convinced there would be records at least, but Maya wasn't so sure. Seven years was a long time.

They stood in silence, watching the swirl of the water and listening to the rhythmic splash of the paddles as they raced ahead of the current. From the far bank, afternoon shadows had begun to stretch over a River the deep, earthy green of bloodstone. It was almost too hard to look in that direction. Maya turned his back to the gunwales and gazed up into the dry blue sky, but Lord Hani continued to squint pensively into the west. After a while, a low rumbling began to emerge from him, which Maya realized was off-key humming. Maya suppressed a snicker. For all his many and considerable talents, Hani certainly couldn't carry a tune.

✦

In midmorning, they disembarked at Hut-nen-nesut, sacred to the Lord Haru, and clattered down the gangplank, followed by the scribal staff and a few servants. Hani had offered to take Bin-addi to see his people, but he'd begged not to go back. Clearly, he feared that nothing good awaited him in Djahy.

The City of the Sun was a beautiful place—a veritable garden, located as it was on the west bank, at the juncture of the River and the great canal that fed Lake Pa-yom. The finest fruits and vegetables were grown there in the rich soil, irrigated year round by the teeming marshland, so unlike rocky, arid Waset.

"I've arranged to stay with the mayor. We can unpack our things, then you and I will make a little trip to the garrison to see if Pa-aten-em-heb is here yet."

The gods' protection was definitely still upon them, because Pa-aten-em-heb and his company had only just arrived. Hani and Maya waited in the garrison reception hall while a messenger went to fetch him. Hani gazed around him in satisfaction. Everything was going well, which permitted him to scrub from his mind the disturbing mandate laid upon him by the young queen. But a shadow fell over his good humor as he remembered the look on Nefert-iti's face at the ceremony of his gold of honor. *Could she possibly know what her daughter is up to? And if she knows, does her father, Ay?* Meryet-aten had indicated that her mother was ignorant of the switch of babies, but perhaps she'd been in connivance with the plan. *Better walk wary, my boy*, he warned himself.

Not long after, Pa-aten-em-heb strode into the office with Pa-kiki at his heels.

"Father!" Hani's son threw himself into his father's arms for a long, affectionate hug. His superior watched their greeting with a benevolent smile. "It was good of you to sail to meet us here. But we were coming back to Waset."

"I confess, my noble soldiers, that Maya and I have come to Hut-nen-nesut on business." He shot a significant glance at Pa-aten-em-heb out of the corner of his eye. "We're hoping our good commander here can be of some help, since he's a native of the city."

Pa-aten-em-heb seemed to understand and said to Pa-kiki, "Why don't you go and unpack all the documents, my friend."

Pa-kiki looked surprised and disappointed, but Hani was pleased to see him acquiesce without demur. He obediently took off across the courtyard, a big, lumbering, muscular boy. *The last one you'd ever suspect of being a scribe.* Hani smiled fondly after him.

"How can I help you, my lord? Is this about the commissioner?" asked Pa-aten-em-heb in a low tone.

Hani nodded in a gesture full of meaning. "I've been wondering what brought him to Hut-nen-nesut seven years ago. According to him, he was still on duty in Kumidi at that point. I think this must have been just before he was named to his present office."

"I suspect we can find that out right here in the garrison, my lord. What if I talk to the archivist? I don't know how far back the records go." Pa-aten-em-heb's face had grown hard. He, more than anyone, had an interest in understanding just why his sister's attacker had been in the city.

"Shall we wait here for you, then, or meet this evening?"

"Wait for me. It shouldn't take long to see if we even have a hope for information." He fisted his chest in a conspiratorial salute and took off with a brisk stride into the dark corridors that led away from the reception hall.

As soon as he'd disappeared into the shadows, Hani and Maya exchanged a long look. "He'll find something," Hani said confidently. "I just hope it will be something useful." In fact, he wasn't quite as optimistic as he managed to sound. It would be interesting to know why Amen-nefer had been in Hut-nen-nesut, but the knowledge might shed no light on his guilt in Shulum-marduk's murder.

Pa-aten-em-heb was gone a long time. By the time he finally returned, with an older man in civilian dress in tow, Hani and Maya were sitting cross-legged on the floor, leaning against the wall—much to the puzzlement of the officers who passed in and out around them. The scribes scrambled up at the approach of the two men.

"This is Lord Hani, the king's investigator," said Pa-aten-em-heb to his companion. "Lord Hani, this is Wah-ib-ra, the garrison archivist. I'm sorry it took us so long to return, but I needed to get the commandant's permission to bring Wah-ib-ra along."

The archivist bowed to Hani. He was an elderly, dried-up-looking man with a long, drooping nose—taller than Hani, but Hani thought he probably could have picked Wah-ib-ra up and heaved him across the room, had the need arisen.

"My lord, I have combed the archives for any postings

of this Amen-nefer son of Ah-hotep-ra," said the scribe in a reedy voice. He pulled out a stack of potsherds upon which he had written notes. "Shall I read them to you here?"

"Let's go to my office," said Pa-aten-em-heb. He led the way to a small, faceless cubicle resembling the one in Waset where Hani had met with him before. There the four men stood, almost filling the room.

"Maya, my friend, take notes for us, will you?" Hani asked.

The secretary seated himself and prepared to write.

Wah-ib-ra said, "These are only abbreviated copies of the main records, which are in Men-nefer. But here is what I found, my lord. How far back do you want me to go?"

"About twenty years," said Hani, suddenly thinking of Baket-iset.

"That's about the time he was transferred from the cavalry to the infantry." Wah-ib-ra dragged his finger down the potsherd, skimming it.

"Is that normal?" Maya asked.

"Normal? It certainly isn't common. Normal?" Wah-ib-ra shrugged. "It was by the command of the head of the cavalry, Lord Ay, and our Generalissimo Ra-mes, so I suppose they had their reasons."

"Where was he seventeen years ago?"

"Let's see… in Waset, my lord. He was assigned to duty for the jubilee of our lamented Osir Neb-ma'at-ra. He was there for the year. Then he was sent to… Kush, where he helped put down the insurrection. He received the Golden Fly there. It was his second, I believe."

The mark of conspicuous bravery. He must be a savage

on the battlefield, where polite custom isn't holding him back from violence.

"From there, he was sent to Ullaza for two years, then back to Waset, under Lord Ay's orders. Let's see... to Djahy, where he won another Golden Fly when his troops were ambushed. Back to Waset for a month, and then Djahy again. Then, about seven years ago, he was posted here briefly, with the assignment to escort a woman from the House of Royal Ornaments back to the capital. That would be the new capital, my lord." The scribe looked up with his dark-ringed eyes as if to be sure Hani understood the geography involved.

But *capital* wasn't the word that had caught Hani's ear. "To escort a woman, you say? What woman? One of the Royal Ornaments?"

"A servant, my lord. It just says a servant woman."

Hani and Maya exchanged a puzzled glance. That sounded like a bad combination—Amen-nefer and a lower-class woman who would be at his mercy, together on a boat for weeks.

Pa-aten-em-heb said skeptically, "I'm not sure why a servant needs an escort. And Amen-nefer is an officer. Were they carrying some sort of secret cargo?"

"It says 'request of the God's Father,' my lord. I can't tell you anything else."

But you just told us something very interesting. "What's next, my good man?"

"Then shortly after... he was sent back to Djahy, where he earned another Golden Fly. And then he was appointed commissioner of Kumidi."

At whose instigation, I wonder? "Any record of censures?

I had heard he was reprimanded for fighting a time or two," Hani said.

"Yes, my lord. But you didn't say you wanted those records." Wah-ib-ra looked back and forth apologetically between Hani and Pa-aten-em-heb.

Hani answered for them both. "Not for now. I think we have the general picture. Thank you for your cooperation." He smiled genially, although within him, anger was starting to build up like steam in a closed pot.

The archivist bowed, pleased. "Anything for the royal investigator." He bowed again, a gesture that included Pa-aten-em-heb, and padded away on his bare feet.

Hani and the officer were left staring at each other.

"Why does Ay keep recurring in his dossier? The God's Father got him transferred to the infantry." Pa-aten-em-heb looked thoughtful.

"And he wasn't even God's Father twenty years ago," Maya said, getting to his feet.

"No, just a cavalry officer. And then he calls him back from overseas to escort a servant woman to the capital. What's that all about?" Hani stroked his chin, pondering. "One gets the feeling that Ay was using him as a sort of personal agent, beginning with Amen-nefer's years in the cavalry. I guess that's not too unusual, but that he got him switched to the infantry and still continued to give him orders..."

"Well, Ay was the late king's brother-in-law and cousin as well. I suppose he had more clout than the average cavalry officer, even then," said Pa-aten-em-heb with a sneer. "He certainly picked a fine specimen to be his personal agent. A soldier who was repeatedly censured for brawling."

"Perhaps that's what attracted him to Amen-nefer—his propensity for violence. If the tasks Ay had him carry out were, let's say, assassinations or roughing people up..." Hani had a suspicion that was true, but it would be hard to prove. And if it were true, then obtaining any kind of justice for Amen-nefer had just grown immensely more unlikely.

"Surely all the things we know he *did* do will weigh against him, my lord," said Maya as if he'd read Hani's thoughts.

"I think we need to go back up to Djahy. I want to talk to Lord Ptah-mes about all this, see if there's any other information on our criminal from his record of overseas postings. It was Ptah-mes who first told me he was a despicable person. He must have been getting that from somewhere."

Pa-aten-em-heb said, "I'm sorry I won't be able to accompany you, Lord Hani, but I'll send some men as an escort."

Hani grinned and clapped the officer on both arms. "Thank you, my friend. You've been more than helpful. Will you visit your family while you're here?"

"I will indeed. And I offer to take you to see the marshes in the lake, if you have time."

Longing overwhelmed Hani as if it were teasing his heart out of his chest, drawing it toward the placid waters of the lake and the birds that lived there. *A trip without goal on the water, with the spectacle of the flamingos and the beauty of the summer morning...* It seemed like a million years since he'd floated quietly on his little reed boat among the peaceful reeds, where no crimes disturbed his tranquility. "I'm afraid we need to get back up north," he said reluctantly. "But I'll hold you to that promise."

The men parted company, and Hani and Maya left the shadowy confines of the garrison offices.

They made their way, silent except for the clopping of their sandals, across the spacious court and out the gate, where two pairs of soldiers kept guard. No one spoke until they'd gone some distance down the street toward the mayor's residence.

"What do you think, Lord Hani? Sounds like our man is in thick with the God's Father." Maya's eyes were bright with the fierce light of discovery.

"It does. But I can't see that that has any connection with the murder of a Babylonian diplomat."

"What motive might Lord Ay have for provoking an international incident, do you think?"

"None that I can see. Unless he is, in fact, angling for the throne and wants to embarrass Nefer-khepru-ra." Hani added sarcastically, "Life, prosperity, and health to him, of course."

They walked on in pensive silence once more. After a while, Maya said, "Maybe that's exactly it."

Hani rolled that over in his thoughts. *Is it conceivable that Ay directed Amen-nefer to do away with a member of the embassy from Sangar, hoping to stir up trouble between Sangar and the Two Lands?* As close to the king as he was, the God's Father would no doubt have been aware of the mission of the Babylonians, and he might well have told Amen-nefer to be on the watch for them. Hani gave a bark of bitter laughter.

"What would we do without Lord Ay to blame for

everything? It's just as likely that the commissioner lost his temper with Shulum-marduk and flew into a murderous rage." The affair left a sour taste in his mouth. Amen-nefer's whole record marked him as a dangerous man, yet no one had ever—successfully—called him to account. Instead, he'd been promoted.

Is ma'at *never served in this kingdom? If someone had actually stopped him early in his career, he wouldn't have pushed Baket-iset from the boat. He wouldn't have defiled Pa-aten-em-heb's sister.*

Hani marched in disgusted silence for a while, and then he said with a sigh, "We'll leave tomorrow for Azzati."

⸎

Hut-nen-nesut wasn't far from the coast of the Great Green, so barely two weeks had passed by the time Hani and Maya set foot in the administrative capital of the northern vassal states. Ptah-mes welcomed them with evident pleasure. "How goes it, Hani? Neferet told me your daughter had been ill."

"She was, my lord. But thanks to Neferet and her friend, she pulled through. It was almost miraculous," Hani said, thinking of the Serqet amulet. "My daughter has been writing you?"

"Regularly," Ptah-mes said, smiling dryly. He seated himself in his chair with a graceful sweeping aside of his skirts. "It's very nice of her to do it, actually. I certainly don't expect it."

The whole issue of Neferet's marriage left Hani with a curious sense of unreality. "I'm glad she's being... nice."

"How have your investigations gone?"

Hani told him what Mery-ra and Maya had found out in Waset. "It seems his mother was a *hapiru*. She was a drinker and used to fly into terrible rages and beat the children, once so badly that Amen-nefer lost an eye. He seemed to get his revenge by violently molesting his own sister."

"An early start to his career as a blackguard, eh." The edges of Ptah-nefer's nostrils grew stiff with disgust.

"And then, my lord, in her fever, my daughter began to recall the details of her accident—or what we had thought was an accident." Hani's voice hardened, and rage chilled him inside, so much so that he had to pause to gather himself. "It turns out that she was pushed overboard by a man with one eye, for rejecting his advances."

Ptah-mes stared at Hani, his black eyes growing brilliant with a terrible light. "You must want to see him ruined, Hani. I would."

Hani remembered how Ptah-mes had put to death his wife's murderer, who was in his custody. Hani said, trying to rein in the ferocity that had control of him, "I do, my lord. I cannot lie. But unless we find some kind of proof that he's the murderer, I don't know what I can do. Pa-aten-em-heb's sister's case was judged, and Amen-nefer was acquitted. It's been a long time since he pushed Baket-iset. It would be easy enough to say the girl has misremembered. Or—as he told me—it was some other one-eyed man."

Ptah-mes nodded, his eyes lowered. When he looked up, he said, "You certainly can't go back to Kumidi with Amen-nefer around. But here's an idea. I've recently created a new commissariat very nearby"—he smiled the cold smile of a shark—"cutting Amen-nefer's authority in half. Alas, it was all I could manage without the permission of the vizier."

"A new commissariat?"

"One of the local kings just built himself a fortress in the desert at a place called Mankhate. I appropriated it for a second commissioner who has yet to be appointed but who will share responsibilities for the area to the south of Temesheq. I'm sure the commandant of the garrison will be happy to put you up if I write you a letter."

"Excellent, my lord," Hani said with a grin not quite untainted by the desire for vengeance. "But what can I actually accomplish there? All the people who are likely to know anything are in Kumidi."

"There must be times when Amen-nefer is away. Those times are fairly frequent, from what I understand. I can give you a soldier to spy for you."

Hani nodded, starting to formulate his plans. Then it occurred to him he hadn't completely informed his superior of what he and his son-in-law had learned in Hut-nen-nesut.

"Oh, Lord Ptah-mes, we examined Amen-nefer's army records and learned something interesting. He seems to have been under the patronage of the God's Father Ay from early in his career. It was Ay who got him transferred to the infantry, presumably to cover for some infraction that might have threatened his advancement. And then there were other times when he was recalled from a distant front to fulfill a mysterious assignment for his patron. Seven years ago, he was sent by Ay to Hut-nen-nesut to accompany a servant woman to the capital."

"A servant woman, you say? How strange…" Ptah-mes knit his brows in thought. "That was about the time the

Haru in the nest was born. Perhaps she was some sort of special midwife from the House of Royal Ornaments."

"Altogether possible, my lord," Hani said, but something began sounding a clapper of alarm in his mind. He wondered if he dared to tell Ptah-mes about his interview with Queen Meryet-aten, but as implicitly as he trusted his superior, something held him back. It wasn't his story to share. "I'd like to talk to her, but I suppose there's no way to find out who she was."

"I suppose not." Ptah-mes rose, his impeccable white clothing hanging in perfect pleats. "Keep me informed, Hani."

Hani bowed. "Thank you, my lord. We'll take off tomorrow morning for Mankhate." He took his leave of Ptah-mes and regained the reception hall to find Maya seated on the floor, writing busily. "Maya, my friend, let's go prepare ourselves for the rest of our journey. We'll leave tomorrow morning. But before we take off, I want to dictate a letter for Neferet. She's being a very attentive wife, and I'd like to commend her."

Maya climbed to his feet. His eyebrow was cocked skeptically. "We're still going to Kumidi, Lord Hani? Is it safe?"

"I doubt it, but we're not going there. Lord Ptah-mes has established a new administrative capital for upper Djahy, and that's where we're going." He turned to the door, and Maya hustled after him. Together, they emerged into the dry yellow courtyard of Ptah-mes's chancery.

"But what difference does the city make, if we're going to run into Amen-nefer?"

"Ah, but we won't. This is an additional capital,

with its own administrator. Carved out of Amen-nefer's jurisdiction." Hani couldn't restrain a smile of satisfaction.

Maya goggled at him for a moment. Then a slow grin of comprehension spread across his face. "We might have known Lord Ptah-mes would find something he could do to that abominable man."

"Moreover, he's promised to send a spy to Kumidi, who will warn us when the commissioner is out of town. *That's* when we go back."

Maya hooted. "This should be interesting. Who exactly are we going to question this time, my lord?"

Hani turned toward him with an innocent smile. "I have absolutely no idea."

✦

It was a surprising distance to Mankhate from Azzati. The little fortress, bleak and sharp edged, rose from the arid hills inland of Kumidi, its stone still blinding and unsoftened by time. But a secure crenellated wall of mud brick surrounded its diminutive footprint.

"I thought the vassals weren't permitted to wall their cities," said Maya, hanging out through the curtains of the litter to observe. The autumn air had grown a little chillier.

"That's probably why Lord Ptah-mes appropriated this one. Plus, it's not far from Temesheq. Not a bad idea to keep an eye on Biryawaza."

Maya remembered the groveling king of Upi with his hard, sarcastic eyes. "You know what I find about this trip, Lord Hani? All the locals we've met seem so… gray."

Hani laughed. "Do you mean middle-aged? No unkind comments about middle-aged men!"

"No, no. Some have been young like Abdi-hepa. But they all seem like colorless people. They're putting on a bland mask, and you have no sense at all of what they really are inside. What I wouldn't give for one honest eccentric like Rib-addi." Rib-addi had been the king of Kebni, a loyal vassal who had been abandoned to his enemies.

"He was pretty unforgettable, wasn't he?"

Yes, and he made a perfect character in a Tale, with Neferet acting out the part. These people... it's going to take some imagination.

The two men fell silent, and Maya sank back against the rear of the litter. His allotted space seemed to be growing smaller as Hani gained in corpulence over the years. Maya shot his father-in-law an affectionate and worshipful glance. There could never be too much Hani. His little eyes were fixed on the view out the crack of the curtains, but he seemed to feel Maya watching him and turned to his secretary and winked, a big grin crinkling his cheeks.

They came to the city gate, and Hani flashed his diplomatic papers at the guard. It occurred to Maya that such papers had not been sufficient to save Shulum-marduk.

"Well, here we are. We just need to wait for our spy to give us the word that Amen-nefer has left Kumidi." Lord Hani swung his legs out of the litter, and Maya scooted to the edge and slid down after him.

A martial-looking man approached across the plaza that surrounded the gate. "You must be Lord Hani. Our high commissioner sent a message to say that we should expect you." He bowed. "I am Ah-mes-ankh, the commandant of the garrison and interim authority in this city. We are to serve you in any way needed." He was a frank, open-faced man about Baket-iset's age—a little coarse featured, with a shapeless, pockmarked ball of a nose—but friendly and respectful.

Of course, that reprobate of an Amen-nefer was friendly and polite enough too—at first. Maya faced him with a hand on the hip so as to make it clear he, Maya son of Turo, was no servant.

"Before I show you to your rooms, my lord, I want to tell you that a courier arrived this morning from Kumidi." Ah-mes-ankh's voice dropped. "He says it's a message for your ears only."

"Thank you, my man. Send him on up as soon as you're ready." Hani gave the officer a conspiratorial smile.

Ah-mes-ankh called one of his soldiers, who led the way into the commissioner's residence. It was rather meager in comparison to Kumidi, built in the style of Djahy, with exposed beams between unwhitewashed mud-brick stories and the round beam ends showing as a decorative element below the flat roof. Hani and Maya followed, while another soldier trailed them with their baggage. The afternoon was still fresh—autumn, with its rains, would be coming soon in the north. Maya could almost smell it in the air, although the sky was blue with only benevolent white puffs of cloud, like roves of carded wool ready to be spun.

Hani and his secretary had been quartered together once more, which suited Maya just fine. Their room was as modest as the rest of the place and none too bright—its single window faced north. But there were a pair of stools, a small table, and two comfortable-looking Egyptian-style beds made up with high, fresh bags of straw and spotless linen. A little brazier sat, unlit, in a corner.

"You may actually need that tonight, my lord," said the soldier who accompanied them. "It's already chilling off after dark."

"Thank you, my good man. Whenever you like, we're ready to see the courier."

"Yes, my lord."

"Oh," Lord Hani said as if it had just occurred to him. "How far is it from here to Kumidi?"

"Perhaps ten *iteru*s, my lord. About three hours on foot. The road is good."

Hani's face split in his winsome gap-toothed grin. "Then that will be all. Thank you."

The soldier slapped a fist to his chest in salute and left, drawing the door shut behind him.

Hani turned to Maya. "That's good. We can go early in the morning and get back by nightfall. But to take the best advantage of the day, we need to plan exactly whom we're going to try to see and where we'll go."

Maya made a dubious moue. "Is there any point in quizzing the slaves again?"

"Probably not, unless some new lead comes up. They all seemed to be sealed like mussels."

Further reflection was interrupted by the arrival of the courier from Kumidi. Red-faced and sweaty, he greeted Lord Hani.

"What news, son?"

"The commissioner left the city this morning, my lord, by the north gate. I trailed them a ways just to see which fork in the road they took. And I spied his party meet up with a bunch of men who looked like *hapiru* to me. Then they all headed northeast together."

Hani and Maya exchanged a significant look. "Interesting. Anything else you noticed? Did you see the bandits' chief, that Shum-addi?"

"No, my lord," said the courier. "In fact—and I'm not sure about this, because I was a long way off—they didn't look like that bunch at all. Far wilder. They were commanded by a hairy fellow with an overgrown beard, surely not Shum-addi, whom I've seen before. And there's a certain discipline about his men that these lacked completely."

"It's Monkey Arms, I'll bet anything!" Maya cried.

"You're sure the *hapiru* weren't attacking the commissioner?"

"No, my lord. They all went away together with no sign of hostility."

Hani thanked the man, and he departed. Maya could see that his father-in-law was deep in thought, his straight, bushy eyebrows contracting. "If they were heading northeast, it wasn't to Temesheq."

"What's to the northeast?"

Hani looked up, a flicker of avid flame in his eye. "Qidshu."

❖

They arrived in Kumidi in early midmorning, having set out as soon as it was light. The cicadas chanted half-heartedly—they seemed to know their summer was drawing to a close. Hani and Maya had brought no baggage since they didn't intend to remain longer than a few hours.

"Although we may have to go on to Qidshu after all. It looks like we may be back on our first mission in spite of all the distractions," Hani said. Amen-nefer's recent meeting in Qidshu with Hotep, the commissioner of Ullaza, looked less and less like an innocent confabulation. "I just hope our friends in Sangar are willing to be patient."

Maya shook his head and raised his eyebrows. "Time is passing, and no arrest. They'd better be patient. But at least we have an almost sure suspect."

"I think, just for the sake of thoroughness, that we'll talk to the majordomo at Amen-nefer's residence. He would know who had been assigned to Shulum-marduk's service."

They entered the residence, and the majordomo approached them almost immediately. He said, bowing, "Welcome, Lord Hani. The commissioner is not here at the moment, but if I can serve you in any way..." He was an Egyptian, thin faced and dressed as the steward of any prosperous estate in Kemet would be. *No lack of discipline in this household.*

"I do have a question for you, my man. Do you remember who was assigned to the Babylonian diplomats who were here some months ago as their body servant?"

"I do, my lord. It was a man named Bayadi. He is, unfortunately, sick at the moment."

"Not the plague, I hope?" asked Hani, thinking it was more likely a case of having been beaten.

"No, no," the majordomo assured him. "He's an elderly man, and he's been getting sicker for a long while. He used to be the best valet in the palace."

"Is there any chance we could talk to him? I would like to get some different perspectives on the murder of the diplomat."

The official twisted his long mouth, considering.

"I think I can do that, my lord. Since this is a royal investigation."

Good man! Hani thought gleefully. The majordomo led them inside the residence, through the audience hall, and into the dark corridors behind the staircase that Hani remembered only too well. He passed the door to the furniture depot that had given them their best clue and turned finally into a narrow hall that was none too clean and stank of unwashed bodies. At the second door, he knocked and ushered Hani in. Maya waited in the corridor.

A man lay on the floor on a flattened straw mattress, with a woman in attendance at his side. He looked to be a hundred years old, but that couldn't be since he'd been serving until only recently. Gaunt and wasted, his face an ocher yellow and his eyes bloodshot, he was a pitiful specimen. Clearly, his days were numbered, and Hani regretted the necessity of bothering him. But it had to be done.

"This man is a royal investigator," the majordomo announced. "He has some questions he wants to ask you, Bayadi."

"Should I go, my lord?" the woman asked faintly. She might have been the slave's daughter. *She must have come to tend him, because she certainly doesn't work at the commissioner's residence.* They all looked to Hani.

He said kindly, "I don't see why. As long as he'll answer honestly in your presence." Hani squatted at the man's bedside. Bayadi followed Hani with his bloody-looking eyes, his mouth hanging open. "I don't want to tire you, Bayadi. But I'm trying to find out who killed the Babylonian. Anything you could tell me would help. Were there any arguments the night before he was killed? Was he on friendly terms with his fellows?"

The sick man's voice came out like a creak of unoiled hinge poles, and Hani had to strain his ears to hear. "Friendly, my lord. No fights. Lord Amen-nefer put 'em all down the hall together, even though he had to move out of his own room to do it. I heard 'em coming, a little drunk, after dinner, all of 'em together, and I helped get 'em ready for bed, then I left. Didn't hear nothing after that—I was down here asleep."

But Hani's ears had pricked up. "Lord Amen-nefer moved out of his room, you say? Which one was it?"

"The one across the hall from the others." Bayadi's breath was growing labored.

The woman's glance darted back and forth between his and Hani's face with a look of desperation. No doubt, she longed to cry, "That's enough. Leave him alone."

The hair rose on the back of Hani's neck. He asked gently, "Would anyone be able to get into that room, Bayadi? Let's say the door was locked from the inside. Could someone get in?"

The slave's voice was growing fainter and more agitated, as if he had to force himself against the will of his failing body to speak. "Yes. There was a corridor that come around to the bedchamber from behind, a parallel corridor, what few knew existed. To serve the commissioner quietly—or to bring up girls for 'im." His eyes sagged shut, and Hani realized with a pang that was probably all he was going to get out of the man. He stared at the poor old slave, and hesitantly, he slipped the Serqet amulet from around his neck and gave it to the woman. "This has healed others. If you prefer, just sell it, but it's yours."

She looked up with tear-glistening eyes and whispered, "Thank you, my lord."

Hani rose with a creak of his joints and sorrow in his heart. "Thank *you*." He let himself out of the room, so overcome with compassion he'd forgotten about the news the man had imparted. He was still pensive, trying not to picture his own beloved father old and dying like that, when Maya popped up at his side from where he sat in the corridor.

"Did you find out anything, my lord?"

"I'll tell you later, when we're alone," Hani said under his breath. In a louder tone, he addressed the majordomo. "Could we see the commissioner's former room?"

"Of course, my lord. But it… it's the scene of that murder and is still…" He trailed off, looking queasy.

"It's all right. We've seen it once. I'm really more interested in a service passage that leads to it."

"Of course. But I assure you that no one knew about it, if you're thinking that's how the murderer got in."

No one except the commissioner, Bayadi, and you, Hani thought grimly. They followed the majordomo up the stairs and into the hall of bedchambers where Hani had been housed before. But instead of stopping at the door of the murder scene, the man led them around the bend in the hall to a low, narrow panel that had the look of a cupboard.

"It's through here, my lord. I'm sorry, it's dark, but I can bring you a lamp if you want."

"That might not be a bad idea, if you would. We'll wait here."

As soon as the majordomo had clopped off down the hall, Hani said to Maya in barely more than a whisper, "This secret corridor serves the murder room, which used to be Amen-nefer's. I was told nobody knows about it, but clearly, the commissioner himself does."

"One more piece of evidence against him." Maya grinned, a look of savage satisfaction.

The official returned with a lit lamp in his hands, and Hani and Maya opened the little door, Hani stooping to enter the shadows. "This doesn't lock from the outside, does it?" he called back out.

"No, my lord. Just be sure it's pulled to when you come back out. I have some duties to see to, if you don't mind."

"Go on. We'll be fine. And thank you."

Hani entered the suffocating little corridor, holding the lamp out in front of him. It smelled stale, but there were no cobwebs, so it was maintained, perhaps regularly used. *To sneak the battered girls out unseen*, he thought bitterly. So inadequate was their little light they almost stumbled into the door at the other end, which had a high sill. Hani fumbled it open with one hand only to find more darkness waiting, but a twilit darkness this time, with a bright crack a hand's span up from the floor. He gave the obstruction of the door a push and discovered it was a curtain or hanging, which clung about his hand like a heavy cloak.

"Here, Maya, take the lamp for a moment." He passed the little clay vessel back to his secretary and pushed with both hands, drawing the curtain to the side.

They stepped over the raised sill and found themselves once more in the room where Shulum-marduk had died, with its scrubbed brown-stained walls and floor and its ruined bedframe. The shutters at the window were closed, but they, too, had been splattered. They must have been drawn when this happened; it had been night. Hani let the curtain drop behind him. It was a handsome tapestry, with palm trees and hunting animals, such as might grace any luxurious bedchamber in Djahy, but splattered and defiled by droplets of blood. Hani only dimly remembered seeing the hanging, so riveted had his eyes been on the marks of violence.

"Well, then," said Maya, looking around. "So that's how the murderer got in without unlocking the door."

"That passage must be cut into the thickness of the outer wall. The majordomo said it was used for discreet services, like getting girls in and out."

"What shape were they in when they left, I wonder?" Maya said, wrinkling his nose in distaste.

"I'm sure Shulum-marduk had no idea his room was wide-open despite the locked door. The others said they'd all been spooked after the robbery of their caravan. Perhaps that's why Amen-nefer vacated this particular room rather than giving his visitor another." Hani stared around, hoping some new detail would leap out at him from the shadows.

"So you think the commissioner had it in for our Babylonian even before he arrived?"

"That's the part I can't figure out. What could his motive have been?" Hani stroked his chin, his thoughts in confusion. "Although if he had something nefarious in mind, that might have been the explanation behind the attack on the caravan. He probably would have known the Babylonians were crossing his territory; that's his duty, after all."

Maya gave a snort. "So is defending them."

"Well," said Hani, "let's get out of Kumidi before our friend comes back and catches us interrogating his slaves."

They made their way out of the residence and across the broad court to where their escort and litter bearers awaited them. The wind had freshened, kicking up little curly cyclones of dust in the footsteps of passersby.

"I hope the rains aren't coming. That might mean we'd have to travel home by land."

Maya looked stricken. "Oh no. That would take so much longer."

"And someone has a new baby to play with," said Hani with a smile.

◆

When the two scribes arrived back in Azzati, they found the diplomatic pouch had arrived. Hani unrolled the first papyrus eagerly and sniffed it. It was from Nub-nefer—still redolent of her perfume of lilies and bergamot. In the bold script of Mery-ra, she brought him up to date on news of the family. Baket-iset was continuing to recover. She felt a little sad sometimes, her thoughts drawn back and back to the freshly recalled memories of her accident. But true to her nature, she was brave and managed to be cheerful most of the time. Mai-her-pri had become a sturdy little fellow.

"In-hapy says he's going to be a dwarf," Mery-ra wrote. "I hope Maya doesn't mind. Sat-hut-haru certainly doesn't seem to." And Tepy was losing his second tooth. At the end, Mery-ra conveyed his usual greetings and added a bit of news. "The king hasn't been seen at recent ceremonies, only Ankh-khepru-ra, or whatever Smenkh-ka-ra is calling himself, and the two queens. The beautiful Nefert-iti is getting quite plump. Love, your esteemed father."

His heart filling with tenderness for his family so far away, Hani folded the papyrus bundle. He saw Maya beaming as he read his missive from Sat-hut-haru. Then he saw another folded letter with Lord Ptah-mes's seal, although Hani didn't recognize the script, which was a little rickety and not very expert.

When he opened it, he found it was Neferet's reply to his own communication. She must have had one of her husband's mounted couriers bring it to Azzati. "Dear Papa," she wrote. "You asked me to sniff around and see if anyone in the capital remembered anything about a strange woman being hustled up here when the crown prince was born. Of course, I'm not in Akhet-aten much at the moment, but I made a point of going. I saw the old midwife who was on duty that day—why, she must be your age."

As old as all that? Hani thought with a fond smile.

"Here's what she said: there were no additional midwives or anyone brought in from the House of Royal Ornaments. Then she sort of stumbled and said, 'Of course, there was *her*...' I tried to pump her, but she said it was worth her nose and ears to say. What do you suppose she meant? I hope you've found out something for Queen Meryet-amen. I've sworn to help her. May Ma'at bite my nipples and the seven-headed demons carry off my favorite kitten if I don't. So you can see this is serious business, Papa. Love, Neferet. Qenyt said to greet you."

Hani chuckled at his irrepressible daughter, but a little shiver of excitement raised the hair on his arms as well. *Was this mysterious "her" the woman Amen-nefer accompanied from Hut-nen-nesut, at Ay's behest? Who could she have been?*

CHAPTER 14

B EFORE HANI DEPARTED THE FOLLOWING day, Lord Ptah-mes called him into his office. "A soldier dragged in last night, Hani. He'd been making his way across the desert on foot for some days, a survivor of another caravan raided by the *hapiru*."

"Which group of *hapiru*, my lord?"

"You'll have to ask him, my friend." Ptah-mes called his secretary to bring the man in.

The soldier was a thin, sunburned, ill-shaven youth with his hair cut in the shape of a round wig. The man saluted the high commissioner.

"Tell Lord Hani what you have to report, soldier," Ptah-mes said.

The young man looked back and forth between Hani and Ptah-mes, not sure exactly whom he should be addressing. "I'm stationed at Kumidi, my lords, and have been these four years. I was part of the escort of a trading caravan heading for the coast. After all that's happened, someone seemed to think we couldn't be too careful."

"That was me," Ptah-mes inserted. He caught Hani's eye with a knowing glint.

"Well, we weren't far away from Kumidi. The traders had come from Temesheq and were heading to Siduna, you see. I was a scout, so I went ahead of the group, and that's what saved me. We were following the pass through the mountains where the Abara flows—if you've never seen it, it's all high mountains, full of rocks and dry forests—when suddenly, out of the mountains, a group of ragged men, whooping and making odd noises with their tongues like mourning women, came pouring. It was an indefensible spot we were in, and they outnumbered us. I could see all this from higher up the mountainside, where I'd gone to scout."

He swallowed with difficulty, and Ptah-mes poured him a cup of water from his beautiful bronze ewer. After downing it gratefully, the soldier continued. "They were surely *hapiru*, my lords, but not like the other *hapiru* I've faced. These were a wild, undisciplined group. Everyone seemed to be fighting for himself, if you follow me. Some of them got to ransacking the wagons, and they completely forgot there was a battle going on—they just filled their arms and ran. But I saw an Egyptian or two among them who seemed to know what they were doing. I've heard... I've heard that some of our own men have gone over to the brigands."

The scout looked back and forth between Hani and Ptah-mes as if he didn't expect them to believe him. "But I swear I saw them. And then..." He swallowed again. "I looked up the hillside, and I thought I saw the commissioner, Lord Amen-nefer, standing with a group of men, watching.

I crouched in a bush so they couldn't see me in return. There was another fellow there whom I've seen before, but I couldn't place him. A powerful-looking man in his middle years—curly graying hair, balding on the crown. I couldn't see his face very well. He seemed to be in charge."

"Biryawaza, I would wager," Ptah-mes said with that pinched white nose that said he was angry.

"Merchants and troops were pretty well wiped out, my lords. I went down after the battle to try to help any wounded. But all I could do was put them on one of the carts and hope they could get back somewhere safe. I couldn't go back to Kumidi, seeing what I'd seen."

Ptah-mes let his breath out heavily.

"Did you happen to notice a man with unusually hairy arms, son?" asked Hani, his heart pounding.

"Could be, my lord. But I wasn't very close, so it would be hard to say for sure."

Hani turned to Ptah-mes, who was staring into space with a stony expression on his face. "Surely we can convict him now, my lord. For treason, if nothing else," he said, the too-familiar gush of icy rage pouring through his body, weighing down his breath.

"I think we can do that, yes." Ptah-mes's face was like a blade of flint, and Hani saw a muscle jumping in his cheek. "Thank you, soldier. You're dismissed."

The scout saluted and left. Hani and Lord Ptah-mes stared at one another. Hani could feel his face growing so cold that it burned as the rage made its way to the top. "How do we proceed?"

"Legally, I should notify the vizier and ask his permission to make an arrest." The high commissioner shot

Hani a glance, his eyes glittering. "But he'll say no, because Ay won't let that happen to his henchman."

"He mustn't get off," Hani cried through gritted teeth.

"So," Ptah-mes continued, his voice expressionless, "we will stay calm, my friend."

"But—" Hani protested.

"And we will resist." Ptah-mes looked up at Hani, and an icy smile spread over his fine features. "We'll arrest him anyway."

By the time Hani had regained his apartment, the frightening, ugly inundation of wrath had ebbed. *We're going to be operating illegally*, he reminded himself. The two men had done that once before, when Ptah-mes's wife's murderer had seemed likely to escape punishment. It had ended with Ptah-mes broken in rank and sent to the ends of the earth. *If only I could find a witness to the assassination of Shulum-marduk. That would remake an act of insubordination into a heroic solution to an international crime and avert the threat of war.*

"You know," said Hani to Maya as they sat down to lunch in their room, "I would feel a lot safer if we could find a little more evidence of this murder."

"But you said Amen-nefer was caught in the very act of treason, my lord." Maya stared at Hani incredulously. "Surely, that's enough."

"That's enough to get him put to death, but it won't satisfy the Babylonians unless they're convinced he was really the murderer of their man. Our case isn't quite closed." Hani tore off a chunk of flatbread and swiped it through the creamy white sauce they'd been served.

"What do we do now, then?"

"We wait once more for the all clear and head to Kumidi. I want to talk to Zalaya's wife."

They fell to, their appetites sharpened by danger—because they *were* in danger if Amen-nefer got wind of their snooping around his residence in his absence. The two scribes had no sooner licked from their fingers the last of their lunch when a knock sounded at the door. Maya popped up and went to open it.

A servant of Lord Ptah-mes stood in the opening, with another man in the shadows behind him. He called out over Maya's head, "Lord Hani, there's a soldier here to see you. Lord Maya thought you would want to talk to him."

Hani exchanged a surprised look with Maya, who stepped aside to let the soldier enter. He couldn't have been much more than Aha's age. He looked around him uncomfortably then fisted his chest in a salute. "Lord Hani, my name is Neb-amen. I'm assigned to this garrison. Lord Maya said to tell you that he looked at the dossier of the man you're interested in and found out something of interest. I... I was a witness to it, and so he asked me to speak to you."

A thrill of excitement lifted the hair on Hani's arms. *At last—a new lead!* "Come in, Neb-amen. Have a seat. Maya, perhaps you'd be so good as to record this conversation." Hani and the soldier settled themselves on the stools while Maya folded his legs and unrolled a sheet of papyrus across his knees.

The soldier swallowed hard and sat up erect on his

stool, as if he were making a formal report. "Lord Maya saw my name on the register of assignments and thought you'd want to hear what I have to say. Seven years ago, I was part of Lord Amen-nefer's mission to take a woman from Hut-nen-nesut to Akhet-aten. He was just an officer at that time. Lord Amen-nefer and I were both posted up here at Kumidi, so I don't know why they didn't just use some troops from Hut-nen-nesut. But we went down there anyway. We collected the pregnant woman from the House of the Royal Ornaments. She was dressed like a servant—for sure not one of the king's Ornaments, although she was pretty enough. And we escorted her up to the capital and turned her over to the God's Father at the palace."

Hani was tingling all over. "You say a pregnant woman?"

"That's right, my lord. Ready to give birth, seems to me."

"What happened to her afterward? Did you escort her back?"

"No, my lord. I never saw her again. She must have had her baby, though. Lord Amen-nefer was promoted to commissioner soon afterward." The soldier rubbed his knees nervously.

"Were you told anything about this mission—why the woman was wanted?" Hani pressed.

"No, my lord. Nothing. Not to me, at least. Maybe Lord Amen-nefer knew."

"And this was seven years ago, you say. Do you remember the season?" Hani knew he was throwing too many questions at the poor man, but his pulse had quickened with eagerness.

"I'm afraid not, my lord. One mission runs into another after a while."

"Anything you can add to that, my friend? Any other recollections at all?"

Neb-amen chewed his lip in an effort to recall. "I think I heard Lord Ay say to Amen-nefer, 'The queen must remain upon the throne.' Or something of that sort." He looked up at Hani apologetically. "I'm sorry; it's been a long time. And they told us not to say anything to anyone. But what could I have said? I knew nothing."

Hani stood up. It sounded as if one of the cases he was investigating had just been solved. "You've been very helpful, Neb-amen. I'll certainly put in a good word for you with the high commissioner."

The soldier rose and saluted. "Thank you, my lord."

Hani let him out with a smile and turned to Maya, beaming.

"What's that all about?" his secretary asked, climbing to his feet.

"Ah, I've never told you about my other case, eh. Doing a little investigation for Queen Meryet-amen."

Maya goggled at him, and Hani proceeded to tell his son-in-law about the mission Neferet had brought him. "So you think that this woman was brought in because her birthing day corresponded to the queen's?" Maya said. "And that her baby boy was the one switched out for the queen's dead child?" His eyes wide, he shook his head. "How could they have foreseen that Nefert-iti's baby would be born dead? Or that that woman's child would be a boy? This strikes me as very dangerous knowledge to hold, my lord."

"Too true. It might have been worth it to Ay to take no

chances. The queen's baby might well have been another girl, even if it had been born alive. We know how ruthless he is. But the queen and the king himself have just as much invested in not letting this become public. Prince Tut-ankh-aten is the heir to the throne, after all." This was not a secret Hani was happy to guard. He couldn't help but wonder what had become of the hapless mother.

Maya considered the situation. "Do you think Lady Meryet-amen will contest the throne with him? After Ankh-khepru-ra Smenkh-ka-ra, she's closest to the king by blood, and she certainly seems to be unwilling to accept a spurious prince."

Hani sighed, his euphoria cooling. "Probably." The specter of civil war again floated before his eyes. He gathered himself and said more cheerfully, "Well, off to Kumidi as soon as we get the word."

⚜

The word came the next morning. The courier must have traveled by dark, Hani thought, marveling. He and Maya precipitously loaded into their donkey-borne litter and, the small escort surrounding them, headed for nearby Kumidi. They arrived late the same morning, and Hani presented himself before the majordomo again. He had no idea how to find Zalaya's widow—he wanted to hear anything she might recall of her husband's death—but it seemed safe to assume that one of the slaves would know.

The official said, "You may ask any of them you find, my lord. Some of them should be cleaning while Lord Amen-nefer is absent; others will be at work outside. Do you want someone to accompany you?"

"No, no. I know the place fairly well by now," Hani said with a genial smile. He wondered if the man had reported his last visit to the commissioner. *Almost certainly.* Hani hoped Amen-nefer didn't decide to make a surprise return.

Hani and Maya looked around and saw a trio of men beating the laundry at the cistern in the center of the courtyard. "The skinny one with the big nose is the one I talked to at the beginning," Maya said under his breath.

Hani strolled up the men, who were engrossed in their work, bare-chested, glistening with sweat, and splashed with wash water. The sodden linen was heavy, and the cords of their muscles stood out as they raised and lowered the clothing violently, smacking it upon the stone rim of the cistern. They were so intent upon their work that they didn't even notice Hani until he stood directly behind them. Over the whacking and splattering, he yelled to make himself heard. "*Oy*, my friends. Can one of you help me?"

The men stopped, uneasiness taking over their faces as they recognized him and Maya. One of them wiped the water from his eyes. "We don't know nothing, my lord."

"Including my question!" Hani said with a friendly laugh. "I only want to pay my condolences to Zalaya's widow. Anyone know where she can be found?"

The big-nosed slave looked suspicious, but he said, "From the north gate, second street over on your right and down to the end, my lord. There's a big house, and she has a room there."

"Thank you, my friend. And what's her name, if I may ask?"

"Amaya."

"That information is worth something." Hani produced

from the waistband of his kilt a pair of copper bangles. "Buy yourself and your colleagues a pot of beer."

They thanked him profusely and bobbed many a bow, and Hani and Maya headed toward the city gate to count streets on their right.

"What do you hope to find out from her?" Maya asked as they walked the baked, dusty lane toward its end.

"Anything at all. Maybe she knows why Amen-nefer killed her husband. It apparently happened before her eyes." Hani tried not to think of the horror of such a spectacle. *How can she or the children ever get over it?*

The shade came and went as they passed taller or shorter houses, but as noon approached, even that little was withdrawn. Down in the canyon between walls, Hani was slippery with sweat by the time they reached what was a conspicuously larger house than the others.

With some trepidation, he knocked on the door. No one responded for a long time, but finally, an old woman with a dark veil over her head unbarred and opened it. She stared at them suspiciously. "What is it?"

"Is the master or mistress of the house at home?" he asked politely, putting on an amiable smile.

"I'm the mistress of the house. What do you want?" She was a squat, spindle-shanked old personage with a nose and chin that met over her toothless mouth.

Hani was completely uncertain about her class, but she didn't seem very prosperous, despite the large house. He would have thought she was the doorkeeper. "I'm looking for a woman named Amaya. She recently lost her husband. Is this where she lives?"

The old woman eyed him with mistrust. "Who are you? Why do you want to see her?"

Hani could barely understand her garbled speech. He put on his best disarming smile. "My name is Hani son of Mery-ra. I'm the king's investigator. My mission is to bring to justice the murderer of her husband."

The old woman stared at him for a moment more then opened the door and drew back for them to enter. "The room in back, next to the kitchen."

"Is she your servant?"

"No. She pays me for a room for her and her brats. She works for a weaver."

"Did her husband come here often?"

The woman shrugged. "Sometimes. He was a slave at the commissioner's residence, from what I hear. Brings down the tone of the place, you know—having slaves live here. But grain is grain. She pays."

Hani thought that the tone of the place was none too elevated even without slaves renting rooms. The packed-earth floors didn't seem to have been swept clean of their detritus for a long time. Grimy handprints marked the walls and dirty scuffs the risers of the plastered stairs. He sniffed a suggestive odor of rotting garbage. *Perhaps the dimness of the light is a mercy.* Hani nodded pleasantly to the mistress of the house, and he and Maya set off through the dark room toward the shaft of sunlight that proclaimed an exterior court. Open to the court was a primitive lean-to kitchen, and adjacent to it was a door that Hani took at first for a cupboard. But from within, he could hear the cries and shouts of children squabbling.

"I guess this is it," he said to Maya with a rise of the eyebrows. He knocked.

The voices of the children stopped abruptly. After a moment, a small, thin woman peeped from the doorway. Her face was purpled and disfigured with swelling so that her normal appearance was impossible to imagine, and her movements were painful looking. Behind her, set up against the wall, was a loom, the colored wool warped but not yet woven.

"Who are you?" she asked in a faint, scratchy voice. Her veil was tied back over her hair as if she'd been working.

"Are you Amaya?" Hani asked kindly, conscious of the horrors the woman had undergone in recent months.

She nodded vaguely, her eyes apathetic as if she were still in shock. He'd expected her to be fearful of visitors who for all she knew might have been sent by Amen-nefer, but she didn't seem to care. Perhaps the idea of losing her life was attractive to her.

"My name is Hani. I'm investigating the misdeeds of the commissioner. I understand he has dealt your family a cruel double blow. Would it be too painful to tell me everything you remember about that terrible day? It may help us arrest him."

She opened the door wider and stepped back in silence. Hani entered, ducking under the low lintel, and Maya squeezed in behind him. Except for a space under the ceiling beams where a slit of sunlight came in, the room was tiny, dark—almost surely intended to be a closet. Two children stood staring at them, round-eyed and fearful.

"Is he gonna hurt you, Mama?" the smaller one, who must have been around six, asked in a trembling little voice.

Amaya shooed them toward the door. "Go play in the courtyard, you two."

The children scampered off, giving the men a wide berth.

She turned her suffering face to Hani. "What do you want to know?" As if remembering her manners, she gestured for the two scribes to have a seat on the floor and stiffly lowered herself to the ground as well, leaning back against the wall.

"Did the commissioner say why he'd come after Zalaya?" Hani asked in a gentle voice, as if speaking to a frightened animal.

"He was mad at him for not setting up somebody's room right. This was in the kitchen, with other slaves looking on. At first he just threw words at him, and Zalaya didn't answer back except to say, 'Yes, my lord' and 'No, my lord.' But Lord Amen-nefer got madder and madder. I think he wanted Zalaya to fight him back, but he dared not." She was overcome with a need to swallow, which she did several times and then continued in a fainter voice that had risen in pitch. Hani saw her thin hands twisting in her skirts. "The commissioner got all red in the face and was spitting saliva all over as he yelled, and his eye was like a demon's. He picked up Zalaya by the front of his tunic and slapped him around and knocked him on the wall a few times and then grabbed him by the throat. I was screaming and tried to pull away his hands, but he just threw me against the wall too. He kept calling me a bitch. And then"—she put her face in her hands—"Zalaya was hanging limp in his hands, and the commissioner let him fall to the floor like an old rag." She was openly crying by then. "Then he came for me."

Hani cringed. He deeply regretted having reawakened those terrible memories, but the woman had told him something interesting. "The others never intervened?"

She shook her head, dashing at her eyes. "They were afraid, my lord. No one dared to raise a hand against his master."

"Amen-nefer never said anything like 'You know too much'?"

She shook her head, wiping her nose on her sleeve. "No, my lord. Just that he hadn't done his job right. For that, my husband had to die. What are we going to do now? We can't live on the little I make. It barely pays for the room."

His heart heavy, Hani pulled off his faience ring and passed it to the woman, folding her fingers around it. "This should feed you for a few days at least," he said quietly.

She seemed dazed. "Th-Thank you, my lord."

"Had the commissioner ever roughed up your husband before that?"

The woman gave a bitter snort. "His slaves were always bruised and bloody, and some of them even crippled. They lived in dread of their master. I'm surprised nobody's ever killed him."

We'll do our best, Hani resolved silently. "Tell your husband's friends that if they have any information, we'll be in Mankhate for a few days."

They took their leave and made their way sadly back into the bright street. Hani stood for a moment until his eyes had readjusted. "I don't think I've ever met a truly evil human being before," he said, wondering. "He may be possessed by a demon."

Maya mopped his face and blew out a breath. "I just don't want to be here when he comes back from wherever he is, Lord Hani. What else do we need to do in Kumidi?"

They set off back down the little street, heading toward the gate. The sun had declined just enough to cast a permanent shadow over them, and Hani shuddered. "I was surprised at the motivation for Zalaya's murder, if you can call such an overreaction a motive. I would have expected Amen-nefer to say something about knowing too much. That's what the other slaves suggested, remember? If Amen-nefer was afraid Zalaya knew he was the murderer, that would explain why he killed him."

"This whole business is depressing," said Maya with a sigh. "*Somebody* has to know something. But no one is willing to talk."

"You can understand why they're terrorized." The two scribes were drawing into the courtyard of the commissioner's residence. Hani hailed their escort, and they set off as soon as the donkeys could be hitched up. Hani guessed that it was early afternoon, which his stomach confirmed with a growl. "We've missed lunch. But I don't want to dawdle. We can get some food in Mankhate."

They rode in silence. Not a bird passed in the sky, which was white and still with the distant threat of rain. Their trip in the litter seemed more than usually quiet, in fact, as if the great cloak of silence that had held them off from any testimonies from the commissioner's slaves had folded itself around their very faces and was clogging their noses, thickening in their throats. Hani felt as if his thoughts were being weighed down by the silence, as if he couldn't latch onto something that was right before him. It was early evening by the time they reached Mankhate and could breathe freely once more.

✦

"And so that's all we could find out in Kumidi, my lord," Hani said, concluding his report.

Ptah-mes looked into space, his face set. "That doesn't particularly help us. But I may have something that will. A courier arrived yesterday from Sangar with a letter addressed to you. It's from a man named Nabu-ahhe-idin. Do you know him?"

Hani ransacked his memory and then cried, "Why, yes, I do. He was the military scribe of the invasion force at Urusalim—longtime friend of the murder victim. It was he who told me about Amen-nefer's involvement with my daughter's death. Have you looked at the message, my lord?"

Ptah-mes shook his head. "I didn't know if it was a personal letter or not." He reached under his chair and held out to Hani a clay envelope, such as the Babylonians used to conceal the contents of a tablet from prying eyes.

Hani took it carefully, a bulging packet about the size of his hand. "Do you want me to open it now, my lord?"

"As you like, Hani. If it's personal, you certainly don't have to let me see it."

Hani cracked open the envelope and laid the pieces in a careful pile on the floor, then he drew out the letter. "Lord Hani," he read aloud, translating as he went, although he was fairly sure Lord Ptah-mes would understand the

Akkadian. There followed a florid greeting. Hani skimmed a few sentences and continued reading. "Mindful of your questions when we saw one another in Urusalim some time back, I've done a little inquiring of our late friend Shulum-marduk's widow. I asked if she could remember any details of the tragic boat accident in Waset seventeen years ago or if her husband had ever spoken of it at all. She said she remembered it well because it was so horrible and she'd been a little frightened every time she got into or out of a boat ever since. Shulum-marduk had told her that he saw the one-eyed man arguing with the girl in an increasingly furious tone and trying to force himself on her. Shulum-marduk himself had just resolved to step in to protect her when the man pushed the girl through the open gunwales. He turned and gave our friend a wild-eyed look of hatred and melted back into the crowd that had gathered. She said that Shulum-marduk was sure the man had fixed his face in his memory forever, just as he himself would never forget the one-eyed man. The rest you know. I hope this was useful. Your colleague from afar, Nabu-ahhe-idin."

Hani lowered the tablet and looked up at his superior. Rage was starting to build within him again like the River rising in its banks at Flood season, blinding him, taking away his breath, and he fought to subdue it and remain rational. "Here is our motive, my lord. Shulum-marduk had seen him commit what might well have become a murder. He must have recognized the Babylonian when he and his colleagues entered the palace that night, seeking protection."

Ptah-mes spread his lips in a grim, predatory smile. "I'm sending troops. Do you want to go along when they arrest him?"

CHAPTER 15

THAT EVENING, AS HANI AND Maya finished their supper, Lord Hani said, "I'm going back up to Kumidi to be present at the arrest of Amen-nefer, son."

"What?" cried Maya, horrified. He could think of no place in which it would be less safe to be. Amen-nefer probably wouldn't go down without a fight. "Oh, Lord Hani. Are you sure that's a good idea? He'll surely hold this against you."

"Since he'll be dead and unburied, there won't be much he can do to me, will there?" Hani smiled, remarkably calm. "You don't have to come if you don't want to, Maya. I certainly won't think any the worse of you. This is just something I need to do for Baket's sake."

Maya sat for a moment's silence, considering. He was torn between his need to be with Lord Hani—especially in a dangerous situation—and the need to think about the safety of his family if anything should happen to him. "I'm coming, of course, my lord. It will make an exciting Tale." He smiled a little wanly. *And Sati would want me to help avenge her sister.*

"Don't worry. We'll be surrounded with troops. And Lord Ptah-mes is coming, too, as the representative of the king. It's an official act of state." Hani winked at him because they both knew very well that it was *not* official. It was clandestine. It was outside the law, and Lord Hani and Lord Ptah-mes were in a very dangerous position if word of it should get back to the vizier. Maya hoped fervently that the solution to the Babylonian murder would make a sufficiently positive impression that it might erase the shame of this insubordination, were it to become known. He let out a big breath. Lord Ptah-mes, who used to be such a force for temperance, had become quite the reckless one. Maya had the impression that the high commissioner downright enjoyed thumbing his nose at his superiors—even at the king.

They pushed back from their little tables, and Maya rose, brushing the crumbs off his kilt. "I'll leave you to your sleep, my lord. When do you foresee us taking off for Kumidi?"

"When Ptah-mes's spy tells him the commissioner is in residence. And I hope that will be soon." Hani pushed to his feet and stretched his arms wide with a huge yawn. *Surely, nothing can overturn such a man*, Maya thought worshipfully. *Look how broad and thick and immovable he is.*

Maya took his leave and went back his own room. He was tired, too, and gave a big stretch and a yawn, with a roar like Lord Hani's. *Satisfying.*

Maya awoke sometime in the night, hearing footsteps in the hall. He opened the shutters of the window to look at the stars, hoping to judge the time, only to find that the sky was beginning to lighten. He pulled on a shirt and wrapped his kilt around him then tied the belt in a nice half hitch—he wanted to be ready to go when the word came. He'd just hung his writing case over his shoulder and splashed a little water in his face when a knock sounded at the door.

He opened, and Hani stood there, dressed, his toiletries basket under his arm. "The courier came back early this morning," he said under his breath. "Lord Ptah-mes said we're going to move up to Mankhate to be ready to pounce. We'll send the scout back to be sure Amen-nefer hasn't left again before we arrive." Hani thrust a flatbread into Maya's hand. "Here's some breakfast so we don't hold anyone up while we eat." He looked calm and cheerful, but Maya knew he must be salivating inside, ready to tear apart the monster who'd stolen his daughter's life.

"Thanks, my lord." Maya joined Hani in the hall, already tucking into the bread.

The two men made their way through the corridors, carrying their sandals so as not to awaken the sleeping household. But in the audience hall, it became clear that not everyone was sleeping. Torches were lit all about. In the flickering orange light, Lord Ptah-mes stood, one hand on his hip, talking to his commandant. The high commissioner appeared quite martial himself, erect as a soldier in a short kilt and plain shirt, with a bag-like wig cover over his long wig.

He looked up when Hani and Maya entered. "Well, my friends, the hunt is up. I've changed my strategy. We'll wait till Amen-nefer leaves Kumidi, then we'll enter and take possession. We'll intercept him when he returns. That way, we'll have the element of surprise."

"Whatever you think is most likely to succeed, my lord." Hani had a dangerous slit of a smile on his face now. Clearly he, like Maya, could feel the tension mounting as their desperate adventure grew closer.

Ptah-mes, Hani, and the officer strode out together, while Maya paraded after them with a bit of truculence to his steps. No litter this time. They mounted light, fast courier's chariots, Ptah-mes and Hani together, Maya accompanied by the commandant. Maya tried to look blasé, as if he rode in chariots all the time, but his heart was beating fast and not out of fear—this was a working-class boy's dream, notwithstanding the peril into which they were headed.

Yet to his disappointment, they didn't take off with a thunder of hoofs and dust billowing behind them. Mankhate was a long way, and their pace was sedate, to match that of the soldiers who marched at their side. It occurred to Maya that they might have to stand up in their vehicles for days.

You wanted adventure, my boy. I rather think you've got it, he told himself with a carnivorous smile.

By the time the party reached the new administrative capital, they'd crossed mountains and something very like the desert. Maya was sunburned, and his back and legs ached. Since he could barely see over the rail of the car, he'd rested his face against it to steady himself and, at one point, had almost gotten his teeth knocked out. He was not in the best of moods.

He climbed down stiffly and staggered after Lord Hani

into the residence, at the heels of Ptah-mes and the officer. As they made their way to their accustomed room, Hani said under his breath, "Ptah-mes told me that there have been raids reported on a number of cities up toward Qeden and Qidshu. And they've corresponded with absences of Amen-nefer."

"He's guilty as can be, the traitor. Impaling is too good for him," Maya said fiercely. Hani would usually have tried to temper his secretary's vengeful spirit, but now he just looked grim and said nothing, letting Maya continue. "But I don't understand how he could be so hostile to the *hapiru* on one hand and in league with them on the other. Which is real?"

Hani sighed. "I can't answer that. But we know there are two factions of *hapiru*. And so far, all the evidence suggests that Amen-nefer is working with Monkey Arms's boys." They walked along for a few more strides, and Hani asked, "Wasn't it Shum-addi who told you about the wild woman from their group who was married to the Egyptian officer? If that's where Amen-nefer's mother came from, maybe that's why he particularly hates this faction, and why he's in league with their rivals to overthrow them."

"Phew." Maya considered his own sweet, indulgent mother, who didn't have a mean bone in her small body, and tried to imagine hating her whole family—his doting aunts, his worshipful little cousins. "This is ugly business."

They made their way to their accustomed rooms and changed into clean clothes. Not too much time later, a servant announced that lunch was served in the audience hall. Below, they found Ptah-mes and some of the officers, the former sitting by himself at a small table, preparing to eat.

When Hani and Maya entered, he waved them over with a pleasant smile. "It shouldn't be long now, Hani. You'll have your revenge, and the Babylonians will have their satisfaction."

They ate in silence for a while, until Hani finally said, "Should we recognize Shum-addi as king and help him defeat the rival faction? I'm not sure he's quite the enemy we've been assuming."

Ptah-mes turned to Maya. "Here's the only one of us who has met him. What sort of man is he, Maya?"

Maya, flustered and more than a little proud to be consulted by the grandee, said, "He's not Aziru, my lord. He's as uncouth as Aziru is slick and urbane. It was hard to tell how smart he was, frankly, but I had the feeling there was a bloodthirsty streak under the affability somewhere. Still, certainly a more humane specimen than that Monkey Arms."

Ptah-mes nodded thoughtfully. "We need to consider that. From what I see, Shum-addi is motivated less by any desire to go over the Hittites than to propel himself to a position of power. Granting him what he wants might be worth it. That might secure his loyalty." He picked up a chunk of bread and mopped his dish, his eyes fixed on the maneuver. His voice dropped. "What do you think about the Hittites, Hani?"

Hani leaned across the table and said quietly, "I'd rather have them for a friend than an enemy, my lord. If we have a treaty with them, they won't be poaching our vassals. And two of us together could solve the problem of the *hapiru*, who wouldn't have a place to run to if they antagonized one of us."

"My feelings exactly."

Soon after, Hani and Maya headed back to their room, leaving Lord Ptah-mes and his officers to confer. Hani said with a grin, "I don't see any reason not to have a wee nap, Maya. Very soon, things are going to get busy."

❦

The following day, their scout rode in at top speed and threw himself from his horse before it had even stopped. "Lord Maya!" he cried. "He's on his way back!"

Hani and Ptah-mes were standing together on the porch, discussing the best way to break to the vizier the news that a magistrate of the Two Lands had killed a foreign ambassador and participated in the *hapiru* raids on his own territory and that they'd had him summarily executed without a trial. But upon the arrival of their scout, Ptah-mes ran down the steps of the porch and demanded, "Which gate?"

"The north, my lord. Our spies have been following him unseen. He's been in Qidshu."

Lord Ptah-mes's lip curled. "How surprising. How many men in his escort?"

"It's a small party, my lord."

"He must not be afraid of the *hapiru* attacking him," Hani said dryly.

Ptah-mes and he exchanged a significant look. To the soldiers clustered around the scout's sweating horse, the high commissioner called, "To your posts. North gate."

They dispersed at a run, and Hani could hear shouted

orders and pipes calling the men to muster. There were to be no company standards or fine maneuvers; this was just a policing action. But their number was sufficient to overwhelm Amen-nefer's troops if it came to a fight.

"It's almost done," Hani murmured to himself, strangely exalted by the thought of a confrontation. *Soon this abomination will never hurt anyone again. And at the weighing of his heart, it will sink like lead. Ammit will feast on his black soul.*

As if he'd heard Hani's thoughts, Ptah-mes shot him a look from the corner of his eye and smiled. The commissioner turned and strode off across the court, while Hani and Maya stood watching him as he disappeared into the crowd of soldiers. Excitement was tingling along the hair of Hani's arms.

At last he said, "I guess we need to take a position at the gate, too, my friend."

The two of them headed off briskly after the departing troops. An occasional servant stopped to stare, but for the most part, it was too early for the inhabitants of the town to be abroad. There were still no shadows but only a pale, diffuse light. Their dull footsteps pounding on the earthen streets were the sole sound. It was too late for cicadas, and not a bird trilled. Kumidi was encircled by a wall, a kind of fortress breached by two gates—one to the south and Azzati, one to the north and Temesheq and Qidshu. *I guess we'll need to confront Biryawaza, too, at some point.*

Within him, eagerness was sharpening into an expectancy not without fear. He and Maya wouldn't be directly involved with the fighting, but so many things could go wrong. Amen-nefer might suddenly become suspicious and turn away. He might have attracted a larger escort than foreseen. The fulfillment of Hani's desire for vengeance was drawing closer, and he could hardly bear to be bilked of his prey so close to the end.

We'll get him, he reassured himself. *If Ma'at still reigns in the world, his own vileness will bring him down.* "He who does evil, the shore rejects him, its floodwaters carry him away. The north wind descends to end his hour."

Hani and Maya clumped their way up to the parapet over the gate, where they sat against the north wall, not wanting to be visible to anyone coming up the road. The usual sentry paced up and down at intervals; Amen-nefer wouldn't find that strange. The wall had just begun to cast an oblique shadow stretching out—bottomless and purple as a bruise—across the courts and outbuildings of the compound when a distant rumble of wheels and clopping of hooves made its way into Hani's consciousness.

Maya started to stand up, but Hani pulled him back down. "We don't want to be seen," he whispered. But the apprehension in his middle tightened every orifice of his body and made his jaw clench. The tension had become almost unbearable, like the buildup to a sexual climax. *Does hatred have as much power as love?* he wondered.

It was agony not being able to rise and watch as the wheels and hoofs and softer shuffle of men's feet drew nearer. Now he could hear the jingle of harness and Amen-nefer's brassy voice barking out to the guards at the gate, "Look sharp there, soldiers." Hani heard the cavalcade pass beneath his feet, the noises echoing briefly as they navigated the brick tunnel made by the parapet overhead. And then they were within the compound.

Hani rose cautiously and peeked over the inside crenellations. He could see the commissioner's erect back in his chariot and the rest of the escort starting to move across the plaza. *Now! Now, by all the gods! Before they get in among the buildings*, Hani willed Ptah-mes.

All at once, directly below his feet, he saw soldiers running to shut and bar the gate. At the sound of slamming panels and the *wham* of the descending bar, Amen-nefer looked around, surprised, as troops closed in on him from all sides, their spears leveled, their bows drawn. "What is this insurrection?" he sputtered in fury. His escorts stood staring about them, disbelieving, not daring to reach for their weapons.

Ptah-mes stepped forward in full court dress, with his gold of honor about his neck. He said calmly but with a voice like flint, "This is no insurrection. Amen-nefer son of Ah-hotep-ra, I, a magistrate of the Two Lands and your superior, do accuse you of murder, high treason, and too many attempted murders to number. You have cast your vile shadow upon the earth too long. I sentence you to death by impalement."

Amen-nefer blustered, "What murder? Where is my trial? I—"

But at a gesture from Ptah-mes, the ring of men drew closer until their spear tips were almost touching the commissioner's guard. "Anyone who fights on his behalf will be sentenced with him as an accomplice," Ptah-mes said, and one by one, the seven or eight soldiers who had accompanied their commandant unbuckled their sword belts or threw down their axes and raised their hands.

Amen-nefer stood alone in the box of his chariot, his eye goggling with disbelief.

"They probably all hate Amen-nefer anyway, if he treats his troops the way he treats his servants," Maya whispered at Hani's side.

It appeared that the arrest was going to occur without resistance, but all at once, Amen-nefer cracked his long whip over the backs of his horses with a cry, and they bolted forward, whinnying with fear, knocking soldiers out of their way in a storm of hoofs and tossing heads. The chariot streaked for the narrow streets of the town, Amen-nefer no doubt hoping to lose the men among the buildings and get out through the south gate, but Ptah-mes had thought to station other troops at every exit from the plaza. Spears down, they formed a human chain across the street mouth that even the panic-stricken horses feared to breach, and as soon as the chariot slowed, another wave of men threw themselves upon it. Braving Amen-nefer's whip, they pulled him from the box and wrestled him to the ground none too gently.

Hani's pulse was hammering with eager ferocity. *Our bird is caught!* He beckoned to Maya, and they clattered down the steps to the inside of the wall. The loyal troops were binding their fellows' arms and collecting their weapons. Someone had led away the horses to unhitch them, and Amen-nefer lay on the ground, his wrists tied to his ankles behind his back, like a common criminal. He'd lost his wig, and his thick wavy hair flopped into his eye.

Ptah-mes approached and stood over him, tall and composed. He said in a voice like that of the Lord of Souls on judgment day, "I hope you are prepared to die, Amen-nefer." He turned as Hani and Maya approached and smiled coldly. "How does it feel, my friend, to see this abominable specimen lying at your feet?"

Amen-nefer craned his neck and threw his hair out of his eye. When he saw Hani, his face contorted with rage. "You're in on this, too, eh, you meddling bastard? You two renegades are going to regret it when the God's Father hears about this affront. We'll see who's putting people to death."

"You, alas for you, won't be around to enjoy it," said Ptah-mes, and he spun on his heel and walked away, Hani and Maya behind him.

They made their way in silence back to the residence, leaving the soldiers to deal with the former commissioner and his men, many of whom had probably been quite innocent of anything worse than following orders. As they mounted the steps of the porch, Hani saw standing in the street at the foot of the wall a stocky, youngish man, plainly dressed, his eyes wide, his mouth gaping. *One of the servants*, Hani thought. *I'll bet they're all stunned—and happy.*

"My lord," Maya said, plucking at Hani's sleeve. "That man over there is one of the slaves I interviewed on our very first trip up here. He was Amen-nefer's valet. I bet he has no idea what to do now."

"Well, for one thing, he can stand up straight. Whoever replaces Amen-nefer, I'm sure he won't be as cruel and unpredictable as his predecessor." Hani followed Ptah-mes through the empty audience hall, thinking, *Perhaps I should buy him and set him free, like Bin-addi.* But he couldn't buy every slave in the palace. And more would only replace them. He felt less celebratory than he'd anticipated. In the attainment, vengeance was proving a little stale. Nothing would ever undo the harm to Baket-iset. He heaved a sigh.

His kohl-painted eyes as black and sharp as obsidian and a flush on his cheeks, Ptah-mes said, "Well, that's over. I suppose you can go back to Kemet now and tell the Babylonians that their murderer has been found and punished. I'll deal with the vizier. He'll be a hero, of course."

Hani grinned. "Of course, my lord." He saw from the corner of his eye that the slave had returned to his task, which seemed to be wringing out rags.

Ptah-mes caught the shift of Hani's gaze. "Are you interested in that man? You can have him if you like. The next commissioner will probably bring his own staff."

"Why, thanks, my lord. I think I'll do that. And... and thank you for everything." He took Ptah-mes's hand and bent over it in a grateful kiss.

Ptah-mes laid a hand on his shoulder. "No. I thank *you*."

⸸

Hani and Maya left the next day. Lord Ptah-mes was staying to "try" and execute Amen-nefer, so they made their affectionate goodbyes and mounted their litter for the long trip home. For a long while, neither of them seemed inclined to speak.

Finally, Maya said in a voice that was both fearful and disapproving, "What are you going to do with that slave? Will he be your body servant, my lord?"

"No, no. I don't need that sort of artificial enhancement to my beauty." Hani grinned at Maya, detecting his jealousy. "I may just leave him at Azzati rather than take him home—although he does speak Egyptian. He looks like a strong young fellow. Perhaps he would be useful at the farm."

Maya, reassured, asked more lightly, "What's his name? I never even asked when I talked to him."

How typical, Hani thought. *Slaves are invisible. They're just pieces of furniture, not men.* It made him sad. "His name is Kalbaya. He's a mild fellow, even with the terrible yoke of a cruel master lifted from him. One of those big, gentle sorts, like a mellow old mastiff carrying a tiny chick in its mouth. I rather like him." Hani saw with amusement the scowl that settled on Maya's brow.

Silence fell again, accompanied only by the trudging footsteps of their entourage and the creak of harness. Within the litter, body next to body, the heat had begun to mount, and Hani pushed back the curtains only to find that the glare made it even hotter. He began to think about his family, as he so often did when on assignment. With all the terrible things people did to one another, he could only lay his dear ones in the hands of the gods and hope for the best. *It seems Baket-iset has borne more than her share of hardships. My poor little swan.* But at least, a certain kind of divine justice had come down upon the perpetrator. Hani wished he could enjoy it more.

Although it wasn't far, it was a good week to the port of Surru, because much of the journey was spent crossing the high mountains that stiffened the spine of the coastal plain. Hani got out of the litter and walked from time to time, eager to observe the local birds that twittered and cried from the branches of the forest canopy. He enjoyed walking as an action—the rhythmic movement of his legs, the drawing of deep, satisfying breaths. Maya had joined him for a while, but trudging *iteru* after *iteru* up and down the steep roads on his short legs was a bit more than he could relish, so for the most part, Hani was alone with his thoughts.

Occasionally, he would fall back and walk with Kalbaya, who kept trying to serve as his valet. Hani laughed it off. "You're a free man now, my friend. You'll see your old fellow Bin-addi when we get home. Unless you prefer to stay at Azzati."

"I'll follow you, my lord," Kalbaya said in his excellent Egyptian. He turned doglike eyes of gratitude upon Hani. "You've saved me. How can I ever repay you?"

"Saved you from servitude or saved you from a terrible master? I'm sure the next one wouldn't have been so bad. Not all Egyptians are like Amen-nefer."

"He was a demon," the former said between his teeth. His deep voice was so full of emotion that it trembled. Hani, a little shocked, cast a glance at his amiable face contorted with hatred. "I would gladly have killed him if I could. All of us would."

Hani said grimly but no longer with much anger, "I think I understand that. I would have too. He did something terrible to my daughter."

Kalbaya stared at him with a sudden surge of hope in his eyes. But then a look of pain crumpled his bushy eyebrows. "One of these days, I have something to tell you, my lord. But not till I'm out of Djahy."

Hani turned a compassionate face toward him. "Whenever you feel ready, son."

Kalbaya dropped back, and Hani continued his march,

pensive. *Another sad story of Amen-nefer's crimes, no doubt. How could such a man ever have been given a position of power?*

From Surru, they sailed not to Azzati as planned but directly for home. There was no longer any reason to visit the administrative capital—Ptah-mes was at Kumidi. It occurred to Hani that there might have been letters for him and Maya there, but it would be even better to be home and get the news in person. And at last, the Great Green, with its heaving waves and smell of fish, was behind them, and they glided through the marshes of the Lower Kingdom in a river ferry. Hani felt he could draw a pure breath of air for the first time in a long while.

At Akhet-aten, his military escort left him. Hani wrote his wife a letter and sent it ahead by mounted courier, pushing his diplomatic privilege. At some point, he would need to report to the vizier, but he knew Lord Ptah-mes had informed him of events, so he followed his heart up to Waset. Maybe, in the depths of him, he wasn't keen on returning to the Hall of Royal Correspondence and the censure that could be waiting for him at Ra-nefer's hands.

He and Maya stood leaning on the gunwales as the City of the Scepter slid into sight, reflected in the brilliant faience blue of the water. Hazy in the steamy air, he saw at a distance the towering pylons of the Ipet-isut, the greatest temple in the world. *May your reign be restored, oh Hidden One*, he prayed. *And perhaps that may be sooner rather than later.*

They drew nearer and nearer. Their ferry was angling

toward the quay, where hundreds of other boats swarmed like bees, some coming and some going, sails spread or rowers plying the paddles, the legs of aquatic insects. Hani took a deep breath. The smell of the land was perfume to him. Rich earth. Green fields—yes, green had a smell, he realized—and the deep, corporeal, intimate if slightly musky tang of the Great River itself. It had always reminded him of the smell of what lay between a woman's legs, and it was just as much the source of life. Maya, gazing out through the wickerwork, was silent as well, dreaming, no doubt, of his wife and children and the baby he'd barely seen before he had left.

Behind them, Kalbaya expressionlessly watched the shore as they approached the city. Hani wondered what was in his thoughts. He'd apparently left no family behind him in Kumidi. *Is he sorry or exhilarated to find himself in a strange land?*

The hull scraped the landing, the stone anchors were dropped, and the sailors threw out their painters to be tied to the rings ashore. One by one, the passenger gathered their baggage and made their way down the gangplank.

"Home again," said Maya, a broad grin on his face.

"Seems like a long time, doesn't it?" Hani said.

Kalbaya meekly carried their baskets; he was a strong young man with thick arms and a deep chest—a far cry from some of the poor starvelings in Amen-nefer's employ. Hani set off for home with a light step, for once relieved of his bags.

Maya split off and left for his own home—the redone goldsmith's studio his mother had given him and Sat-hut-haru. Hani turned into his own lane with its many empty houses and villas falling into decay during the ten years since the capital had withdrawn and the temples had been closed.

A'a joyfully opened the gate at his knock. "Lord Hani!" he cried. "The mistress of the house will be so happy to see you! She just got your letter this morning."

That courier didn't ride very fast, Hani thought, amused. But he was placid. Now that he was home, nothing could ruffle his calm. "All is well, I hope."

"Yes indeed, my lord. Yes indeed." A'a took the bags from Kalbaya and led him into the stable yard, where he could see his old colleague, while Hani headed through the garden toward the porch of his home. A gray shadow in the bushes told him Qenyt was on the hunt. He chuckled benevolently.

As Hani mounted the porch, Nub-nefer appeared in the doorway, where the reed mat had been rolled up. Her eyes alight, she threw herself into Hani's embrace. "Oh, Hani my love! It seems like it's been forever!"

He surrounded her with his arms and clutched her to him, his pure gold, the most precious possession of all, savoring her warmth and drinking in the faint sweetness of lilies and bergamot that seemed to float about her. When at last he could speak, he said quietly into the top of her head, "It does, my dove. I guess we've been spoiled by those years I was able to spend at home."

"Your father is inside, waiting eagerly to hear all the gossip from abroad." She beamed up at him, her almond-shaped black eyes full of love. "And Baket-iset too. Oh, you'll be so happy to see how well she's doing. I've taken offerings down to the temple gates every day and left them in thanksgiving."

"Are the children and grandchildren well? Have you seen Amen-em-hut?"

"They're all in good health," she said, smiling as she drew him into the vestibule. "Tepy has a huge gap where he used to have front teeth. And my brother is well and cheerful." Her eyes flickered downward. "I told him what Neferet said she'd overheard at the palace."

"I suppose it can't do any harm, as long as it doesn't become public." Hani chuckled, incapable of any anxious or angry thought. "No doubt that made him happy."

"Hani, my boy!" cried Mery-ra from the salon. He rose from his chair, beaming, and toddled toward his son. He embraced him in a gruff, affectionate hug and punched him lightly on the arm. "All is well? You haven't told us much in your letters."

"I'll fill you in on everything, Father. There's some good news."

"Ooh, tell. Tell." The men made their way to the two good chairs, and Hani sank gratefully into one. Mery-ra scooted his forward eagerly, while Nub-nefer disappeared into the kitchen.

"Where is Baket-iset?"

"She's taking a nap. The girls were all here this morning, and I think so much feminine chatter must have tired her a bit." His broad, cheerful face looked sly, and there was an avid gleam in his little brown eyes. "So, what did you find?"

At that moment, Nub-nefer and a servant girl emerged with two beer pots on their stands and set them down beside the traveler and his father. "Do you want anything to eat, my love? It's a while until dinner."

"A little cheese or some dates, please?" He looked up with unashamed pleading, and his wife slipped away once more. "We caught the man who pushed Baket-iset, Father. He was also guilty of the murder of the Babylonian emissary. And he was witnessed by several people in a treasonable action—probably only one of many—in the company of Biryawaza of Upi. There seems to be a suspicious correlation between Amen-nefer's absences from Kumidi and *hapiru* attacks on the neighboring towns."

"I thought you said he hated them."

"It seems there are two factions. There's Shum-addi's 'official' group, and there's the ragtag bunch headed by Monkey Arms. You might be interested to know that our noble commissioner suffered at the hands of a *hapiru* mother, so his animosity is understandable."

Mery-ra gave a low whistle and said fiercely, "The bastard. I hope you punished him harshly."

"He's to be impaled, if it hasn't already happened. Lord Ptah-mes is trying him rather summarily right there in Kumidi."

Mery-ra sat for a moment, digesting this news, then he said, "I guess the Babylonians will be happy now, son. They've apparently been making quite a stink. Meryet-amen said her nephew told her the news was all over the palace—their ambassador was demanding huge reparations and even threatening war."

"I don't doubt it, although it's rather shameful that the culprit should be a magistrate of the Two Lands."

Mery-ra snorted in disgust. "How did such a man

become a commissioner—unless the king just wanted to get him away from here?"

Hani fixed his father with a wry look. "In a word, Father: Ay. This blackguard was his henchman for more than twenty years."

"What a surprise." Mery-ra rolled his eyes. "I hope you won't fall afoul of the God's Father because of this, my son."

Nub-nefer appeared with a plate of dates and fresh cheese. She pulled up a little table and set it down then caressed her husband's face with a smooth hennaed hand. "You must be famished, dear one. How long have you been traveling?"

"Years." Hani laughed. "Or at least, it seems like it."

His wife settled herself on a stool next to him. "Who mustn't you fall afoul of?"

"Lord Ay."

Her eyes widened. "Is he involved in the murder of the ambassador?"

Hani shrugged. "Maybe and maybe not. But it came out through a Babylonian colleague that Shulum-marduk happened to witness our Baket-iset's 'accident.' Amen-nefer must have recognized him and feared discovery. I think that's more likely than a political motive, frankly. Everyone agreed he was a vengeful man." He stopped to pop a date into his mouth.

Nub-nefer's face hardened to ice. "Nothing they do to him can be bad enough." She clutched Hani's arm.

"He should be dead and standing before the Judge of Souls by now, my dove."

※

The next morning, Hani awoke late to find his father already in the kitchen, poking about for something to eat.

"Where is Nub-nefer?"

"Gone on her daily errand, son." Mery-ra waggled his eyebrows significantly. "Oh, a courier from the high commissioner came by this morning. He had a letter for you."

"And did you use it to light the oven? Where is it, you rascal?" Hani shook his father by the arm in affectionate menace.

"In the salon, lying in your chair." Mery-ra poured a cup of milk for himself and one for Hani. "This is yesterday's bread. It'll be all right if you dunk it."

Balancing his cup and the bread in one hand, Hani made off into the salon and picked the folded-up papyrus from the seat of his chair. *This must be the news that Amen-nefer is dead,* he thought, rather more gleefully than he wanted to admit. He set his breakfast on the floor and pulled off the sealing string then unfolded the letter. But as he skimmed it, his jaw sagged.

"Here's some bad news, Hani," he read aloud with growing horror. "Our prisoner managed to escape. Apparently, he had a few loyal soldiers left in the garrison. He was seen heading for the *hapiru* camp near Qidshu. I'm sure they'll smuggle him north and beyond our borders." He threw the letter to the ground and let out an anguished howl. "No! I don't believe it! All that work, and the turd is going to get away?"

Mery-ra growled a curse. "There is no justice."

Hani beat a fist helplessly on his knee then stared at the

floor. "Don't tell Nub-nefer. She'll be furious. She thought we finally had vengeance for Baket."

"And don't tell the Babylonians, or they'll be cutting their own vengeance out of our hide." Mery-ra let a discouraged breath escape through his nose.

"I wonder if Ptah-mes dares keep this quiet. If not, our insubordination will be revealed for what it was, now that war with Sangar won't be averted after all."

Mery-ra raised his eyebrows, dubious. "Will he lie outright?"

"To thumb his nose at the vizier? Perhaps." Hani looked up hopefully. "Or maybe he's already reported the execution, in which case he'll only have to say nothing." But the whole affair was so monumentally unfortunate that he could hardly muster an ember of optimism. He sighed and got dismally to his feet, breakfast forgotten. "I'm going outside."

"I'd join you, son, but I promised my company to Meryet-amen."

"Go, Father. I need to think about things."

Hani drifted idly through the garden, so preoccupied that he scarcely noticed the things that usually gave him such deep pleasure. His steps took him into the stable yard in back, setting the geese cackling in flight from under his feet. There he saw Bin-addi and Kalbaya, heads together, whispering. At the sight of him, they straightened up, looking uneasy, and the bent-nosed Bin-addi nudged his fellow forward a little.

"Good morning, my friends. Is there something you wanted to talk to me about?" Hani asked with a curious smile.

Kalbaya glanced back at Bin-addi nervously and stammered, "There's something I need to tell you, my lord. You've been so kind to us and all, I... I just feel I have to say it. But nobody must know, I beg you." He clasped his hands nervously at his waist, his knuckles white.

Hani could feel a crackle of eagerness up the back of his neck. Maybe he was finally about to learn something conclusive. *Did Kalbaya witness the murder after all?*

"Come with me, unless you don't mind Bin-addi hearing you," Hani said, drawing him toward the granaries. The man's arm, for all that it was so powerful, was trembling.

"He knows already, my lord." They stopped, and he licked his lips. "You'll have power of life or death over me," he said faintly.

Hani's gaze softened. "I'll protect your secret. Have no fear. Amen-nefer is marked for execution anyhow."

Kalbaya took a deep breath and said, "I killed the Babylonian emissary."

Hani's jaw fell. He certainly hadn't expected this. He goggled at the man. "But why?"

"I didn't mean to, my lord." Tears were starting to wet Kalbaya's lashes. "I was trying to kill the commissioner."

Dumbfounded, Hani stared, half expecting the former slave to laugh and say it was a joke. But he looked terrified and deadly serious. Behind him, Bin-addi had much the same expression. "Tell me about it, my friend."

Kalbaya covered his face with his hands, as if to wipe away his fear, then he straightened up and said bravely, "We all hated him—more than hated him. He made our lives more horrible than the Lake of Fire. We wanted to kill him or else more of us would die. So when the king of Upi offered us gold to murder him, we were happy enough to accept the offer."

"Wait. Biryawaza of Upi paid you to assassinate Amennefer?" Hani thought he must have heard wrong.

But from behind his friend's back, Bin-addi affirmed, "That's right, my lord."

I thought they were allies, Hani thought in confusion.

Kalbaya continued, "Since I was the commissioner's valet, we all decided that I could most easily do the job. I knew about a secret passage that opened into the commissioner's bedchamber that couldn't be locked. It was to serve him at night, usually to bring him girls."

He stopped to swallow and cast another almost pleading look at Bin-addi. "One night we decided to do it. I would… I would use the stool right there in the room. I knew just where the bed was and where in the bed he slept. I waited until he was likely to be asleep, and then I made my way, without a light, through the passage. I knew it all well. There was a sliver of starlight through the shutters, and I could see the stool and the body on the bed. I picked up the stool quietly by one leg and crept over to the bedside, and I smashed it down on him."

Kalbaya ran a hand over his face, which had grown terribly pale. The hand was unsteady. "And once I had hit him, I couldn't stop, my lord. It was as if some demonic force had hold of me. I grew more and more enraged, thinking of all the things he'd done to us and our wives and our children. Things I wouldn't even say aloud. And I hit and hit until the stool started to break apart, and then I hit some more. He never awakened. I sent him straight into the underworld without the chance to so much as say a prayer. By then, I was exhausted, and the madness was cooling off. I took the stool and left it in the passage until I had the energy to hide it somewhere. I went down to the kitchen, where everyone who wasn't on duty had gathered, waiting to hear. The laundrymen took my clothes and hid them in with the butcher's aprons and cleaning rags, and I washed myself off. All the ferocity had gone out of me. I was shaking like a frightened baby. Everyone swore they would never tell what had happened. Except…"

"Except?" Hani prompted gently, thinking he knew where this was going.

"Except nobody had told me that Lord Amen-nefer had moved out of his room that afternoon and that one of the Babylonians was sleeping there." He stared at Hani with tear-filled, pleading eyes. "I killed an innocent man, my lord." Kalbaya fell to the ground and began to clutch at Hani's feet, weeping. "Save me, I beg of you."

In a daze, Hani stooped and lifted the ex-slave to his feet. His thoughts were in a turmoil. *What am I supposed to do with this terrible information?* He could understand only too well the white-hot madness that slavered for revenge, for justice—as if all the violence in the world couldn't make good the wounds the past had inflicted. Yet once it became known that Amen-nefer had escaped, the Babylonians would think that the killer of their emissary had gone unpunished. It might well mean war. *Should I point out the real culprit?*

He said, just above a whisper, "I think you need to disappear, Kalbaya. You speak good Egyptian. You're a skilled body servant. I'll give you something to live on for now, and you'll find a job easily. Be gone by nightfall, my friend. Even if someone should find out what you did, no one will be able to find you."

"Thank you, my lord," Kalbaya whispered. He kissed Hani's hand, hanging onto it with desperate gratitude.

"Wait here," Hani said, disengaging himself. "I'll be right back." He set off back through the garden, hardly looking at his duck pond. But instead of going to the strong box where gold jewelry like his *shebyu* collars and *deben*s of gold and bronze and other valuables were kept, he headed into the kitchen. *If Kalbaya tries to barter with a piece of fancy jewelry, everyone will think he stole it.*

The cook was just taking bread for the day out of the oven, and Mery-ra was standing over her, sniffing hungrily. They both looked up as Hani swept in and starting shoving the still-steaming round loaves into a bag, as many as would fit.

"That's quite a snack you're preparing, my son," his father said with a twinkle in his eye.

But Hani had no time for badinage. "I'll tell you later what I'm doing."

He looked around the room, grabbed a bag of chickpeas and a few strips of dried meat, and swept out in a whirlwind. The two ex-slaves were standing where he'd left them. Bin-addi had his arm around Kalbaya, who sagged on his feet, all the emotion drained from him. They looked up as Hani approached.

"Here you are, my friend. Now, go. If anyone sees you with all this bread, they'll just think you're delivering for a bakery."

Kalbaya murmured, "How can I thank you?" He turned

and started as if to run, but Hani stopped him with an outstretched hand.

"Wait. I just had a thought. Go to the villa of Lord Ptah-mes. His wife will give you a job. It's near the huge temple south of the city. Anyone can point it out to you."

Kalbaya nodded gratefully and shot off through the service gate and into the street, the sack of food over his shoulder. Hani listened to his footsteps disappearing down the hard earth lane. He was left staring at Bin-addi. "So that's what everyone was hiding, eh."

"We didn't know what had happened until Lord Amen-nefer showed up alive and well the next morning, Lord Hani. And then everybody started talking about how the Babylonian had been murdered." Bin-addi hung his head. "No one meant any harm to that stranger."

"No." Poor Shulum-marduk's confused *ba* must have wondered what had happened when it awoke suddenly in the underworld.

As if compelled to explain, Bin-addi said, "The commissioner had raped and killed Kalbaya's wife, my lord. They weren't born slaves—they were captives, and Lord Amen-nefer took what he wanted from the captive women and enslaved their menfolk. You can't blame Kalbaya for wanting to kill him."

"I don't. I would have done the same, I'm afraid." Heavyhearted, Hani started to go back to the house, but he was aware of Bin-addi still standing there staring at him. He turned and asked with a kindly smile, "Is there anything else?"

"Do you want us to go, too, my lord?"

"Not unless you want to. Why would I want you to go?"

"We all knew..."

"You'd sworn on your father's soul, Bin-addi."

✦

When Maya arrived later in the morning, ready for dictation, Hani told him about Kalbaya's confession. The secretary's eyes popped. "You mean it wasn't Amen-nefer obliterating a witness to his crime after all?"

"Apparently not. Although you might say that the plot those desperate slaves concocted was a testimony to other crimes Amen-nefer had perpetrated." Hani forced out a sigh of disgust.

Maya blew out a breath. He said, scratching his head, "What I still don't understand is why Biryawaza wanted to kill him. They both seemed to be in league with the *hapiru*. That scout saw them together at the attack on the troops, remember?"

"I'm confused about that too. But regarding Kalbaya, I'm not sure whether to say anything or not. If Ptah-mes has told the vizier about Amen-nefer's escape, then the Babylonians are still expecting us to find the murderer. But I can hardly think of poor Kalbaya as a criminal."

"And if not?"

"They think we found him and executed him. But Ptah-mes and I could be in bad trouble, depending on the vizier's mood—or on his digestion perhaps." Hani's face split in a cynical smile. "So maybe we need to write the high commissioner a letter and find out where we stand. I guess he's back in Azzati by now."

Maya took his pen case off his shoulder, sat down on the floor, and spread his implements around him. He'd just unrolled a piece of papyrus when A'a appeared in the doorway from the vestibule. The outer door was closed because of the morning chill, so he was almost reduced to a voice in the darkness. "My lord, Lord Ptah-mes is here to see you."

"Here?" Hani exchanged a glance of astonishment with Maya. *It's as if I conjured him up.*

"Yes, my lord. He said he'd wait in the garden. Lady Neferet is with him."

"Neferet? She's with him?" *Too many improbabilities at once.* Hani couldn't take all this in. "Invite them into the salon, A'a. It's too cold to stand in the garden."

A'a turned, but Hani had rushed after him, still barefoot. Sure enough, they were standing side by side on the porch—Ptah-mes tall, slim, and elegantly attired and Neferet short, blocky, and clad in a rumpled working-class-looking shift. She rushed forward and threw herself on her father in her usual exuberant way.

He managed to extricate himself enough to say, "Lord Ptah-mes! My duckling! What brings you both here? I thought you were still in Djahy, my lord."

"I was summoned back to make a report to the king in the presence of the Babylonian ambassador." Ptah-mes's lips twitched in one of his bone-dry smiles.

Hani's heart leaped into his throat. "Did you tell him about Amen-nefer's escape?"

Ptah-mes gave a crafty smile. "No. As it happened, it wasn't necessary."

Hani remembered his manners suddenly, and despite the

burn of curiosity that ignited within him, he said, "Please come in and have a seat, my lord. Neferet, dearest, perhaps you could go see your mother while we talk business..."

"I have something to say, too, Papa," she protested.

Hani shot a questioning look over her head at Ptah-mes. The high commissioner smiled noncommittally, with a twitch of his eyebrows. "Very well, my duckling. But you must never repeat any of what you hear, please. This is very important." Hani suspected Ptah-mes had no idea of how indiscreet Neferet could be.

"I swear I won't. May Meret-seger the Lover of Silence bite—"

"All right, my dear. I believe you."

The two men took the good chairs. Maya had risen to his feet and bowed to the high commissioner, who nodded acknowledgment. Ptah-mes seemed to be in a jaunty mood.

Maya asked, "Should I go, my lord?"

"No, no," Ptah-mes said. "You know most of this."

Hani saw Maya staring in surprise at Neferet, an unlikely presence at a diplomatic confab, and he almost laughed. *You're no more astonished than I, my boy.*

Ptah-mes began, "There were quite a few developments right after you left, Hani. As you know, Amen-nefer took off to join the *hapiru*, presumably the renegade bunch. But not long after, Biryawaza sent a letter reporting that the commissioner and some of his men had been seen among the nomads, raiding our cities. It seems that the renegades are the ones giving us the problem. Shum-addi has been working with Biryawaza to decimate the rivals. He wants to be made a king, of course—which the opposition leader apparently refused to let happen—and so he's playing the good boy."

"Hah!" Hani snorted. "As if Biryawaza could talk. Remember what that scout told us?"

"I don't think it's that simple, though. Biryawaza chronicled a whole long list of contacts and joint raids the commissioner and various vassal kings had made with the *hapiru*, including the one our scout survived. It went back at least two years. He said he'd pretended to be one of their collaborators in order to get names, and he did just that. A most valuable document. He had more interest than anyone in seeing the *hapiru* controlled since, as Qidshu's neighbor, his cities suffered more than anyone's."

"That part, at least, is certainly true. I could never figure out why he would be attacking his own territories. As for the rest..." Hani remembered the exaggerated servility of the king at Temesheq, how he'd declined to receive Hani when he went there to meet Aziru, how his groveling exterior could barely close its lips over his angry pride. "That would explain why he tried to have Amen-nefer killed perhaps."

Ptah-mes's eyes widened in question.

"I'll tell you about that in a moment, my lord. Please continue."

"What Biryawaza particularly wanted to say was that he'd seen Amen-nefer murdered by his fellow renegades. And sure enough—we found the corpse."

Hani suspected that Biryawaza himself might have had a hand in Amen-nefer's demise, but he still felt a thrill of satisfaction. The monster who'd maimed his daughter was dead, facing the Judge of Souls.

"Fortunately," said Ptah-mes with a cool smile that

bordered on smug, "I had not yet informed the vizier of our apprehension and intended summary execution of Amen-nefer. So I was able to report that he'd been killed by some of his treasonable confederates before we could accuse him of the Babylonian's murder. When I spoke yesterday to the king, he was very pleased. And the ambassador of Sangar was even more pleased—with you, in particular, who had discovered the identity of the murderer."

Hani was washed with relief. The worst had, yet again, been averted, and he wouldn't have to make the decision he dreaded. He felt he could tell Ptah-mes in confidence about the eventual unmasking. "My lord, it seems Amen-nefer wasn't the Babylonian's murderer after all, even though he had a good motive."

"No?" Ptah-mes lifted an elegant arched eyebrow.

"In fact, just this morning I heard a confession by the real perpetrator, one of the commissioner's slaves. It seems our friend Biryawaza paid Amen-nefer's slaves to assassinate him, and since they all loathed their master, they were happy enough to agree. His valet got into the room through a service passage and beat the occupant of Amen-nefer's bed to a pulp, as only a man with long and terrible grievances could. But then they learned that it had not been the commissioner sleeping in his room."

"It was Shulum-marduk?"

Hani nodded. "Amen-nefer told me he had vacated his usual chamber so the three emissaries could be near to each other. But it seems no one told his valet."

"Is that who that man who came to our door looking for work was, Papa? He said you sent him," Neferet said excitedly.

Ptah-mes looked thoughtful. After a moment, he said, "I see no reason why any of this has to be known, Hani. The murderer has already been found. And you and I have no innocent blood on our hands."

"Thanks be to all the gods. Much as I hated him and wanted vengeance, he wasn't guilty of that particular crime. I don't know if it's according to *ma'at* to kill someone simply because they're bad in general."

Ptah-mes rose and heaved a sigh of satisfaction. "So your case is solved, Hani. Well done." He gave Hani a complicit look. Then he said, as if it had just come into his mind, "Oh, you might be interested to know that Mankhate's territory has been folded back into the commissariat at Kumidi and a new commissioner has been appointed—your friend Pa-aten-em-heb."

"But that's wonderful!" Hani exclaimed happily. "He's upright and competent and well deserves the promotion. Did the vizier name him spontaneously?"

"I named him. But the vizier is probably not yet aware of that. He thinks it was his idea." The two men exchanged a look of complicity. "He intends to go back to his own name, Har-em-heb."

"There's something about the air up there in the north! Everyone seems to change their name!" Hani laughed.

Ptah-mes smiled and turned as if to go, and Hani started after him to show him to the door.

But Neferet, who'd risen out of respect, looked at her father with barely contained eagerness. "Wait, Papa. I have some news too."

"Should Lord Ptah-mes stay?" Hani asked, exchanging an uncertain glance with his superior.

"Unless I must, I have a few things to see to. Training my new valet among them." Ptah-mes smiled, real humor in his face, and he clasped Hani's hand. Then he turned and left, the clopping of his fashionable upturned sandals fading gradually into the vestibule.

As soon as Hani heard the outer door close behind him, his daughter asked breathlessly, "What have you found for Lady Meryet-aten, Papa?"

Hani debated whether he wanted his daughter to be party to the disturbing information he'd uncovered, but as if she could read his mind, she said smugly, "She told me to ask you."

"Well, my duck, it turns out that the awful man who pushed your sister from the boat was the same one who brought a pregnant servant girl to the palace seven years ago—on the orders of the God's Father."

Neferet let out a very unladylike whistle. "A servant girl? The Haru in the nest is the son of a servant girl? Oh, the young queen will be so happy."

"Why, Neferet? Is she intending to push him out of the succession?"

"Well, of course. Why should they let a commoner on the throne when there's a real live princess around?"

"What about Ankh-khepru-ra? He's a genuine brother of the present king, isn't he? Nefer-khepru-ra made him his coregent after all. How old is he? Surely he'll live to succeed the Great King."

She shrugged and said sententiously, "My medical opinion is that no-o-obody knows when someone's going to die."

Hani received her medical opinion in silence. *Is she*

aware of something? He would find out, no doubt. For the moment, his case was concluded, and he could rejoice in the company of the family until his next assignment came along. He escorted Neferet to the door, only to find, as they stepped out onto the porch, that there was a chilly north wind blowing.

Did you enjoy this book? Here is a sample of
Lake of Flowers, the next volume in
the Lord Hani Mysteries:

HANI WOULD FOREVER REMEMBER WHAT he was doing the day he learned of the coregent's death.

He and his father, Mery-ra, were strolling in the garden before dinner, on their leisurely way to the garden pavilion where they would eat on a midsummer evening. As if they were synchronized everywhere on earth, the cicadas roared in rhythmic waves, and the late afternoon sun was a golden liquid, spattering the gravel of the path where it sifted through the leaves of the big sycomore. Hani breathed deeply of the shady air. Despite all the troubles in the world around him, he couldn't help believe that life was good. Jasmine and lilies were in bloom, and earthy aromatics and white daisies; the air was syrupy with their perfume, as if scent had mass. Could a man ask for more?

"Look, Father," Hani said with a smile. He pointed to where Qenyt, his pet heron, stood as frozen as a statue on one leg in the shallows of the pool, her gray color making her almost invisible among the reeds that swayed there—a whisper of feathers, a deadly shadow of bird. All at once, her long neck unfurled and her dagger-sharp beak plunged into the water. A moment later, she stood with a twisting silver fish in her bill, which almost immediately disappeared down her throat. "She's ruthless."

Mery-ra chuckled, his belly bouncing. "I've found that to be true of females generally, son. Haven't you ever noticed, with all the devious ladies you've had to serve over the years?"

Hani joined his laughter. "You have a point. Certainly the royal women are a cutthroat bunch." But he added with a twinkle in his eye, "Of course, *our* women are very different."

"I should think," said Nub-nefer from behind him. She emerged from among the bushes, a tray in her hands upon which were arranged a variety of cheeses and pickled vegetables and bread cut into chunks. "However, our *men* tend to get hungry before a meal." Hani's wife set the tray down on a little table in the pavilion. I'll bring you some beer. The kitchen girls have had it cooling in the well. Dinner will be a while yet."

"Thank you, my dove," Hani said fondly. He stroked her coppery arm. As Nub-nefer's name proclaimed, she was his pure gold, his golden treasure. Even after thirty-six years of marriage, he felt he had yet to plumb her perfections.

The two men settled into their chairs on the porch of the pavilion and stretched out their legs. Mery-ra expelled a big breath with a whoosh. "Hot." He folded his arms over his head to cool his armpits.

"That shouldn't surprise you, Father. It's almost time for the Inundation."

Without lowering his arms, Mery-ra scrubbed his

close-cropped gray hair. "I'm not surprised, but it's hot nonetheless. These are the *Heriu-renpet*, the intercalary days. The old year is fast coming to an end. What will the new one bring, do you suppose?"

Nub-nefer and one of the serving girls approached with the beer pot and its stand. "Here you are, my hungry men," Hani's wife called from the porch of the pavilion, her voice rich with affection.

Suddenly Hani heard a wild noise of footsteps pounding down the gravel path from the gate, and Neferet burst into the open, red-faced and panting. "Mama! Papa! Grandfather! Ankh-khepru-ra Smenkh-ka-ra is dead!"

Hani and Nub-nefer exchanged a stunned look. Hani struggled to swallow, wondering if he had heard his daughter correctly. The coregent, only in his twenties, had died?

Mery-ra was the first to regroup. "When, my girl? How?"

"The plague, Grandfather. It only just took him off like that." She snapped her fingers. "It hasn't even been made public yet." Neferet, who was a physician of the ladies attached to Ankh-kheperu's court in Waset, would have been one of the first to know.

"That's what happens when the king doesn't perform the Appeasement of Sekhmet ritual," Mery-ra said in a dire tone. "She gets mad."

"Today's the birthday of Sutesh," Hani murmured. "A day of ill omen."

They all got to their knees and scraped up dust to strew on their heads in a gesture of mourning. Hani climbed heavily to his feet, sweat beginning to spring on his forehead. He thought, *This is the first brick falling out of the edifice King Nefer-khepru-ra has built. Ankh-khepru-ra was supposed to outlive his brother and serve as a regent for the Haru in the nest. Now what will happen?*

Nub-nefer's face had lit up with hope. She fastened huge glowing eyes on her husband, and Hani knew she was thinking the same thing: *the building is starting to crumble.*

Hani stared around him, the tableau of his family fixing itself in his memory. This was not just an occasion to tie on the white headband of mourning and participate in the lavish funeral rites of a king. Something significant had shifted—far more significant than the young deceased himself, who had been none too bright and was undoubtedly under the sway of others, probably his brother—or his wife. The likelihood of civil war breaking out when the present king died had just grown immeasurably greater.

Everyone stood there, frozen, until Neferet, unable to remain silent any longer, said, "Can I stay for dinner?"

Hani finally returned to the world around him. He laid a paternal hand on the girl's shoulder. "Of course, my duckling. Where is Bener-ib?" Her fellow *sunet* and friend was always to be found trailing after Neferet.

ACKNOWLEDGMENTS

THE AUTHOR GRATEFULLY ACKNOWLEDGES ALL those who have helped her in the production of this book. To the wonderful women of my writers' group, for their critique and encouragement, my thanks. To Lynn McNamee and her editorial team at Red Adept—Jessica, Sarah and Irene—profound gratitude (and Lynn, for so many other forms of help). To the flexible and talented gang at Streetlight Graphics for the cover and map. To my cousin and her husband, my technology guru: thanks, guys. To Enid, who urged me forward by her support, I can't thank you sufficiently. And most of all to my husband, Ippokratis, who put up with the months of fixation it takes to write a novel, many, many thanks.

ABOUT THE AUTHOR

 N.L. Holmes is the pen name of a professional archaeologist who received her doctorate from Bryn Mawr College. She has excavated in Greece and in Israel, and taught ancient history and humanities at the university level for many years. She has always had a passion for books, and in childhood, she and her cousin (also a writer today) used to write stories for fun.

Today, since their son is grown, she lives with her husband and three cats. They split their time between Florida and northern France, where she gardens, weaves, plays the violin, dances, and occasionally drives a jog-cart. And reads, of course.